P9-BZV-402

by Francine du Plessix Gray

Lovers and Tyrants
Hawaii: The Sugar-Coated Fortress
Divine Disobedience

Lovers and Tyrants

Francine du Plessix Gray

SIMON AND SCHUSTER

NEW YORK

LIBRARY OF CONGRESS CATALOGING IN PUBLICATION DATA
GRAY, FRANCINE DU PLESSIX.
LOVERS AND TYRANTS.

I.   TITLE.
PZ4.G7783LO   [PS3557.R294]   813'.5'4   76–17614
ISBN 0-671-22338-0

To my parents
Tatiana and Alex
In love and friendship

Et par le pouvoir d'un mot
Je recommence ma vie
Je suis né pour te connaître
Pour te nommer

Liberté.

And by the power of one word
I begin my life again
I was born to know you
To speak your name

Liberty.

—PAUL ELUARD

The Governess

1 9 3 5

I

My childhood lies behind me muted, opaque and drab, the color of gruel and of woolen gaiters, its noises muted and monotonous as a sleeper's pulse. My childhood memories are smothered in sterile, unjoyful smells, in odors of eucalyptus and of mustard plasters, of ether and of belladonna, of camphor and of musty textbooks. I never ran, or sang, or mothered dolls, or wrestled with other children, or preened before a mirror. I spoke in a hushed, stuttering voice, I cried, I confessed, I communed, I read voraciously, I loved secretly and outrageously. My temperature was taken twice a day, my head was perpetually wrapped in some woolen muffler or gauze veiling, I was scrubbed, spruced, buffed, combed, polished, year round, like a first communicant. In one of the few family photographs left to me, taken on a rare outing near Paris, a stooping child with melancholy eyes awkwardly and fearfully clutches a small mongrel dog. In another photograph, my father bends solicitously over my bashful body, and I remember him saying cynically to relatives standing by as that picture was taken, "Stéphanie is the result, dear friends, of a modern education."

I shall never cease to marvel at the way we beg for love and tyranny. The first offerer of these charities came into my life when I was four years old. From the moment she stood at the entrance of my nursery, sunken-chested and mackintoshed, her rodentlike eyes distorted grotesquely by voluminous horn-rimmed glasses, her mouth pinched into a sour, pitying smile, she assumed a power over me that was particular to her vocation. She was a governess—one of that race of women who choose rejection and obsolescence as their fate. And who, in the unlovely span of their career, elect one child to be the recipient of their life's love, the prime mover of their unhappiness, and the instrument of their self-pity.

It was not only the difficult pronunciation of her name—Lydia Romanovna Mishanskaya—but also her furtive, burrowing manner and the anxious blinking of her small eyes that led me the same day to nickname her Mishka, "Little Mouse." She had a dry and ageless body, an ageless face swathed in an aureole of apricot-tinted hair. Both her past and her age were to remain as mysterious to my family as they did to me. We knew only that she came from a family of professional Army officers, had been briefly and unhappily married, had been thrust out of Russia by the Revolution, had taken a degree at the Sorbonne, had once danced, at a ball, with the King of Rumania. And her entrance into my life, notwithstanding its subsequent drabness, must have seemed to me as festive as that dance. In one of those simpering, self-lauding letters of hers, which I have only recently begun to open, I read: "Do you remember that your previous baby nurse, before I came, was still pushing you in a baby carriage at the age of four? Imagine the joy I offered you in allowing you to walk down a street for the first time, to press your nose against the shop windows, imagine your joy!"

Governesses' recollections are too filled with self-pity to

allow any room for guilt; they are more accurate than those of parents, whose guilts about the past are constantly molding and recasting that malleable, pragmatic substance called memory. My governess' words resound, like a tuning fork, to a tone in my recollections. I remember—a monstrous doll of four already cognizant of the alphabet—being spoon-fed some meal of watery gruel by that first nurse, and then being wheeled in a baby carriage, figuring out words in a worn red-and-gilt edition of *Alice in Wonderland* as I voluptuously soiled my pants, watching the nanny's white bandanna flapping against the pink balloons and the green bandstands of a Paris park as I slouched, sucking on a worn rubber nipple, into my afternoon nap. The baby nurse cried when she left my room to return to her distant village, and I wailed, and clutched at her as desperately as I clung to Mishka the next day. Children of estranged parents are quick to devour tenderness; especially if the parents live, as mine did, under the same roof.

Mishka's first action, as she settled into my room for a six-year stay, was to unpack her oilskin bag and organize her medicine closet. As with many governesses, hypochondria was her most powerful weapon, the sweetest luxury of her unhappiness. She suffered from migraine, constipation, chronic bronchitis, piles, fallen arches, ingrown toenails, eye infections, slipped discs. Her instant and excessive love for me, as well as her hatred for the outdoors, made her share as many of these diseases with me as my strength could support. The closet of my room was turned, overnight, into an apothecary shop filled with phials of ointments, unguents, salves, emetics, and vermifuges; with clysters, enema bags, poultices, icebags, and hot-water bottles; with paper bags, labeled in her fine slanting hand, containing unbleached wheat germ, fresh yoghurt culture, linden, mint, camomile, dried verbena. Finding imaginary ailments, confining me to bed whenever possible, was her manner of owning me, of protecting me from my father's erratic devotion, and of avoiding the detestable outdoors. Was I the first child lonely enough to passionately return her love, to so docilely submit to her fantasies?

Our day goes thus. She cautiously opens the creaking, louvered metal shutters of my room, offering the view of a gray, unlovely inner courtyard of the Sixteenth Arrondissement. "How are you this morning?" She tiptoes to my bedside, blinks anxiously. "Oh, what a bad night you had! How you coughed!" I kiss her soft dry cheek, admire the brilliant tangerine hue of her hair (a tint fabricated secretively, every few weeks, during my sleeping hours), and I look forward agreeably to the daily ritual of the rectal thermometer. Holding it in place, thick and vaselined, between my thumb and index, I half hope for that minuscule rise in centigrade reading which will force me to stay in my room. It is a blue, cramped, and narrow room, adjacent and parallel to my tutor's, in which I treasure the boyish toys neatly stored on the shelves—tin soldiers, building sets, and trains—and the only dolls I own, two ancient taffeta-robed waxen beauties permanently sheltered from my touch by their great domes of glass. But the fascination of this room lies in the bookshelf above my bed. I am an only child, and my sole friends are the beloved first cousins whom I visit briefly every summer in my father's distant ancestral home. On my bookshelf live the only companions of my childhood winters, the roguish boy heroes of Jules Verne, with whom I sport during the two or three days a week I spend confined to my room with some imaginary chill or gastric disorder. Longing for such a day of companionship, I hold the vaselined glass bulb as long as possible, and, as I withdraw it, Mishka's eyes and mine meet to register disappointment over the reading of 37.1. We sigh. I rise, lifting my camphor-scented nightgown to pull on my long flannel underdrawers. I am muffled in a cashmere shawl to protect me from drafts as she bends myopically over me to lace the boned and rigid little corset that will correct my stooping posture. I am shirted, sweatered, shod, and we go on to breakfast.

My family is not prosperous. The governess is often housekeeper, laundress, cleaning woman, cook—a plenitude of duties that are the subject of her frequent crises of self-pity. As I finish spooning bread out of my cocoa in the dim and lonely kitchen I begin to hear the splashing of my father's shower in his corner of the apartment. His stirring becomes clearer as I march toward the discipline of the w.c. My pulse quickens at the prospect of his morning visit. I sit in the minuscule privy in the hall facing my room, strain, push, rehearse my catechism, strain, push—will this day's result please her? "You did very well today, Mademoiselle Stéphanie, very well!" The governess' genteel laugh fills the tiny dank closet. I wipe. "Front to back," she warns. "Girls always front to back, or else . . ." Aware of some catastrophic danger in reversing the motion, I pull up my underdrawers and rush to embrace my father as he walks up the hall for his morning visit.

He is beautiful and unhappy, and wears shirts embroidered with a viscountal crest. Every summer we travel together to the little family castle in Brittany where he was born. Throughout the years I shall remember the rare gaiety of those trips, my cousins and me swarming over him as if he were a large oak tree, the nights we slept as tenderly enlaced as lovers in the room which he had had as a child. My memory having long ago shed the flatteries of mourning, I now see his mouth as selfish and sensual, his amber eyes as unctuous, his jowls as too replete. That is my view today. He was, that morning, perfect. We nuzzle and embrace. How is his rabbit, his beloved pigeon? He enters my bedroom to examine the day's program of lessons. A scholarship boy from a noble and impoverished provincial family, he puts obsessive stress on education. I am denied the joys or hardships of public or private schools, but follow correspondence courses with a tutoring organization where I go one morning a week to be tested on the previous week's work, standing inevitably second to a pale, flaxen child whom I am never allowed to meet because of Mishka's suspicion that she carries a strain of tuberculosis. His face twisted with dislike for the governess, my father hovers over the maps, the copybooks, the grammars, trying to find fault with some detail in her program. But he is helplessly bound to tolerate her. Her impeccable spelling in three languages, her painstaking accuracy in mathematics, her distaste for art, and a respect for history that allows her to be hypnotized by his family's lineage make her, in his eyes, a faultless educator. Does he also consider, at this moment, her agreeably low wages, her convenient lack of vacations or evenings off, her motherly and total devotion? Sighing, approving, protesting about the lack of air in the room, about her imposition of ailments on his sturdy but cowardly child, he leaves the worktable. "Not bad, Lydia Romanovna, but we need more exercise!" he remonstrates from the door. "Less medicine! Long walks! More fresh air!" The door closes, and I am left to my analysis of sentence parts.

Some indiscreet aunt had told me, when I was five, that for three days after I was born my father refused to look at me, because I was not a boy. During my lessons, at a desk facing the dismal gray courtyard, my fantasies center around masculine feats of athletic prowess and physical stamina. I drift from conjunctions and adverbs into a recurring fantasy of naval heroism: having masqueraded as a deckhand on a large passenger boat, I save countless lives by extinguishing a fire in the engine room, earning the respect and admiration of my cousin Daniel, the first mate. I whip off my transvestite costume, my curls cascade out of my sailor's cap, Daniel's esteem turns into passion. He carries me to the deck, where we sit tenderly enlaced, watching the dolphins dart from the water, planning our future together as the boat carries us to Madagascar. . . . "We're lost in the stars, young lady!" Mishka's metal ruler raps on my knuckles; her rodent eyes are glacial as I return to the substantive and the partitive, to the sickroom smell of eucalyptus and mustard plaster. The noon siren is my deliverer. I am stuffed into sweaters, smothered with scarves. For twenty minutes before lunch, we take a stately, dirgelike walk around

the Trocadéro, our principal airing of the day. "Dignity before speed!" she orders. "Running is bad for the lungs! Calm
before agility! It is bad taste to skip and hop in public."

Through that selective, pragmatic sieve that is a memory,
my mother has not yet filtered into the day's recollections. For
purposes of biography, of convenience, let us go back and say
that I had slipped into her bathroom during an intermission in
my lessons. She does not belong to the sequence of this particular day, but if I do not intrude this blond and aloof abstraction
into some hour of the morning she will never appear, for my
afternoons, my evenings are totally bereft of her. Let us say I
slipped into her bathroom between an account of Henri IV's
wars and a three-digit division, and saw her lying in her bath,
her white breasts floating lightly on the water. She registers
neither pleasure nor anger at my intrusion; she filters wordless,
odorless and indifferent through the mesh of my memory, an
industrious, aloof stranger who supports the family throughout
my father's bouts of unsuccessful business ventures, a much
courted beauty whose migraines hush and mute the little
childish din I dare to make. The constancy of her indifference
to me breaks only once, at the single memory I have of lunching with both my parents. There is an instant in this recollec-
tion in which I bite an apple with unusual lustiness and suddenly this unique event occurs: my parents' eyes meet,
somewhere over my head, to record their mutual happiness in
my existence, their common joy in my well-being.

This is a unique, abstract event in a concrete, habitual day.
Usually I enter the living room, rescrubbed, recombed, re-
spruced, to lunch alone with my father. Our apartment is of
sober elegance, reflecting my father's traditionalism and my
mother's fashionableness: white walls in the new style of the
nineteen-thirties, inherited Louis XIV chairs upholstered in
taupe velvet, a few Chinese antiquities in a glass cabinet. We
are joined, at times, by an angular, impoverished cousin from
Tours; by my gentle Aunt Colette, my father's sister, who lives

19

in Nantes. "Second in her class at the Cours Hattemer," my father praises me to his relatives. "The stiffest tutoring institution in Paris." From my jumper dangles a cross on a white taffeta ribbon; blue is for first place in the class, white is for second; the decoration (there is something crested and titular about it that makes us both like it) will go into the shoe that I place yearly under the Christmas tree. My father says, "Next year Stéphanie will be first, with a blue ribbon." His eyes grow severe. "And then she will be even better rewarded than last Christmas." I stutter some alexandrines impeccably, tell Aunt Colette the capitals of seventeen French prefectures, and multiply forty-seven by thirty-three before being sent to my nap.

I spend the afternoons accompanying Lydia Romanovna on her interminable errands. She looms above me in the slow, creaking glass-cage elevator of our apartment house, dressed in her invariable mackintosh, her slouching felt hat. "No, mademoiselle, we're not going to the park today, we're going to the social-security office. . . . We're not going to the merry-go-round, we're going to the pensions office . . . to the eye clinic . . . to the orthopedist. . . . We're not going to the zoo, but to the Immigration Bureau. The Im-mi-gra-tion Bu-reau," she repeats with a sigh, a short and bitter laugh expressing the rootlessness, the insecure status of her emigré's life. And then begins our daily subway ride. My childhood afternoons, if I had total recall, would be an excruciatingly tedious list of Paris subway stops. We spend our afternoons riding from Chaillot to Denfert-Rochereau to buy some miraculous new kind of yoghurt sold by a fellow emigré, from Trocadéro to Clichy to attend to her health-insurance plan, from Alma-Marceau to Javel to buy a particularly salubrious form of unbleached wheat germ from another Russian health-food store. My afternoons wind through a serpentine white tile corridor marked, in large cobalt type, KREMLIN-BICÊTRE, PORTE DE VINCENNES, PÉREIRE, BATIGNOLLES, LA VILLETTE, WAGRAM, where we shall also emerge on Sunday mornings to attend a ten o'clock Orthodox service for the sake of her soul, before riding to Etoile to follow a Roman Mass for the sake of mine.

Her small nervous cough echoes daily beside me as she grips my hand to emerge from the green entrances of these stations, shielding her mouth against the hated air. I do not passionately yearn for those rare sunny afternoons of the month when we go to the park. For it is only to huddle together on a lonely bench, our pale faces turned with convalescent dutifulness toward the sun. The unknown children wrestling and shouting in the sand piles, climbing on the metal gyms, riding wooden horses, suspect for microbes and ill manners, are as poisonous and forbidden as the candies and ices sold at the green stands of the public parks. And until I leave Europe they will remain as distant and heroic as my summer playmates and the beloved boy heroes of the bookshelf over my bed.

I return to eat another meal in the dim and lonely kitchen, then enter my father's room as he is preparing to go out to dinner. We look at family albums, memorize from a book of heraldry the blazons pertaining to various dukes, marquises, viscounts, and barons. He asks me about the meeting of the Jeannettes, the French Brownie Girl Scouts, the previous day—an activity he has imposed, over my tears and Mishka's protests, "to toughen her up a bit." He receives the sad news that at the yearly award of prizes for running, jumping, most cooperative, most courageous, etc., I received the prize for the scout with the cleanest nails. He consoles himself by rehearsing with me the theme song of the Jeannettes:

> *Ne pleure pas, Jeannette, tra-la-*
> *lalalalalalalalalala-la-la,*
> *Ne pleure pas, Jeannette, on te*
> *mariera, on te mariera,*
> *Avec le fils d'un prince, tra-lalala-*
> *lalalalalalala-la-la,*

*Ou celui d'un baron, ou celui d'un
baron. . . .*

He paces the length of his study, his hands behind his back.
I absorb with passion the burden of his unhappiness, of his
failures, of his desperate refuge in caste, in the sequence of
his familiar aphorisms. "You must be a good Catholic, even if
it is not quite true, because it improves one's intelligent understanding of history." "Your mother is an intelligent but misled
woman, who does not love us." "All her friends are Jews or
artists." "Jews are intelligent but detestable." "All artists are
pests." "Never forget that we were knighted in the First, not
the Second, Crusade." "Your Great-Aunt Lara is a saint but an
idiot." "The Spanish republicans are threatening the world
through lack of intelligence on Europe's part." "Paul Reynaud
is wrecking France through lack of intelligence. . . ."

I love him more than anyone else in the world (along with
Mishka) and walk beside him like a docile pony as he paces
the length of his study. "Lydia Romanovna is fairly intelligent
but a maniac, ruining your perfectly good health with her
imaginary diseases. I must get you a new governess, who will
teach you to run, play tennis, be a normal child." I stop in my
tracks, explode into tears, and he stops pacing. "A young and
pretty one?" he pleads, with a gleam of longing in his eyes.
"A young, pretty, English governess who will go horseback
riding with you?"

I run back to my nursery and cling fervently to my aging,
myopic love. Her eyes blink reproachfully at him as he comes
to kiss me good night, they hold a quick diplomatic reconciliation, the two poles of my love are once more in harmony. He
closes the door; I am in bed, belonging to Mishka again. We
take my temperature to better gauge the next morning's program. I drink cough syrup and cod-liver oil, my chest is mas-
saged with salve and wrapped in flannel, we say our prayers,
the inhalator is filled with tincture of benzoin, I kiss her beloved

2 2

sunken cheek. Her scurrying, her mysterious burrowing in the next room, her anxious attention to my every sigh keep me awake for hours.

I go to sleep wishing desperately for a small animal to have near me, to share my loneliness and my wakedness, and my father's words answer me in the dark: "An animal, my poor child! Don't you think life is made difficult enough by people?" I realize already how much of an intrusion I must be into my parents' separate lives, how much of a drag upon their pleasures. My obsession for something smaller than me to alternately love and torture grows to a crescendo and fixes upon the following fantasy: I am the owner of two small monkeys, which I imprison nightly in a small tight shoebox. They cry stridently until they are on the verge of suffocation, at which point I release them, rescue them from death, and bring them into my bed to pet them, feed them, and enjoy their gratitude. The cognizance of their suffering, my total power over them, the strident whining of their suffocating voices bring me a sensation of delight and power, which I rehearse, almost nightly, between my sixth and ninth year.

I I

My maternal great-grandmother, my Baboushka, was the third person I loved. How clear my memory is of her verbena smell, of her firm, square, stubborn chin, of every cameo pinned to her lace ruffles! Baboushka is a soft flutter of watery silks at my side, an aureole of thick silver hair; her dove-gray eyes still follow me with adoration. Once or twice a month, during my governess' rare outings, I spent the night with my great-grandmother in the neat three-room flat she shared with her daughter Lara. I listened to the story of her icons, her ivories, her Fabergé boxes, and examined all the treasures of her exile from Russia.

Released from Mishka's hygienic discipline, I ate Turkish delight by the pound, built puppet theaters, made Baboushka play card games by the hour, traced my name on my *kissel* with sickeningly heavy condensed milk. We walked to the Bois, and she introduced me to some small boy whose offer of a sand pail brought vibrant fantasies of love. As I lay down to sleep on Baboushka's living-room sofa, she bent over me to give me her fragrant triple benediction, the most treasured gesture of my childhood.

Her apartment smelled of verbena and rose water, of old laces and of steaming kasha, of dried apricots and of a thin sweet wafer that she kept stored in her larder for the ritual of our teas together. My Great-Aunt Lara, a melancholy-eyed opera singer in her late forties, exhaled the odor of an abrasive raspberry-pink dentifrice whose tube was decorated with the face of a mirthful, cape-swathed toreador. Symbolized by the bullfighter's impeccable denture, this product claimed to impart maximum brilliance to the teeth of opera stars and an irresistible fruity pinkness to their gums. (Sopranos swarmed about me. My mother's sister, Olga, was a climbing, unsuccessful, constantly warbling coloratura very envious of her Aunt Lara's career.) But a flashing smile was the only brilliance of Lara's submissive, resigned personality. Baboushka, with all her gentleness, was an authoritarian who had early assumed a patriarchal role in a family of sybaritic men. She had been one of the first women in Russia to receive a university degree, and for twenty years had managed her family's foundry business in St. Petersburg with a firm hand. Most romances of Lara's life had been ruined by her mother's possessiveness. "On all my concert tours! Even from Peru!" Lara often said, to illustrate her high standard of filial conduct. "Even from Peru I write Maman every day that I am not with her."

My great-grandmother, Lara, my governess, and I spent a few weeks of the summer together in a low-ceilinged wooden cottage in a flat, monotonous plain near Bordeaux. The cottage belonged to Baboushka's brother, my Great-Granduncle Panov. It lay on the outskirts of a toylike village offering single, arche-typal objects: *the* castle, a small manor set on a hill across from our house, from which two heavily veiled spinsters emerged once a day for Mass; *the* Communist, a portly personage in a red flannel shirt who sat on his porch every Sunday, playing the "Internationale" from sunrise to sunset on a crank-up Vic-trola by his elbow; *the* grocer on the one street of the village, who vainly attempted to keep out flies by a clanging curtain of wooden beads at the entrance of his store; *the* village pump one hundred yards (my first assessment of distance) from our house; *the* old Russian, Monsieur Panov, who had fled from St. Petersburg with that baroque sequence of events that only Russians seem to bestow upon an exodus: he had married a circus acrobat in Germany, had spent his savings on buying her a riding academy of her own, she had fled with a trapezist. Uncle Panov, during his last years, was a benign, doddering old man with a senile habit, which I particularly detested, of letting his tongue protrude from his thin, perpetually smiling mouth.

My great-grandmother, in her authoritarian way, treated all generations as subservient to hers. "Good day, children!" she addressed, every morning, my aunt, my governess, even my great-granduncle, as she sallied from her room. Crisp and erect, she distributed her benediction, her fragrant kiss. "How are the children today? Off to the beach!" she commanded, bran-dishing the long-legged bloomers which she had worn decades ago when she had been one of the first women in Russia to swim in public. We packed into one of the swaying buses that rumbled slowly to the seashore. Uncle Panov's tongue darted delightedly through his pink mouth. Lara, her teeth blazing with Dentifrice Toreador, had wrapped herself in a tasseled robe acquired on a South American concert tour; Lydia Roma-novna, her mouth pinched with distaste for the inevitable outings of summer, carried an oilskin bag bursting with anti-mosquito lotions, unguents and gauze veilings for my supposedly fragile skin. Once arrived at the beach, where long tides receded over miles of dark-gray sand, Baboushka changed briskly into her suffragette bloomers and a flounced rubber cap and swam a leisurely, elegant sidestroke parallel to the beach. Never allowed into the water because of the chronic bronchial condition my governess required of me, I searched for dead starfish on the tide-littered beach.

At night in the summers, we sat around a table under a green glass lamp, Uncle Panov absorbed in solitaire, my great-grandmother martyrized by one of my card games, while Lara played operatic recordings on a crank-up Victrola. One night, as Flagstad sang in *Parsifal*, she ventured to follow the aria in a voluminous and cracking mezzo. Toward the end of the aria her doelike eyes filled with tears, her increasingly cracking voice dissolved into a medley of sobs punctured by single, heroic tremolo notes. Uncle Panov stopped his solitaire, his tongue darting nervously from his mouth. My great-grandmother rushed to Lara's chair and rocked her large sobbing daughter in her arms. "My soul, my little pigeon, you have had a fine career, a wonderful life, why these tears?"

Lydia Romanovna blinked by the lamplight, repairing an undergarment. "But, Larissa Alexeevna, you still sing so well!" Her genteel, hypocritical laugh extinguished my aunt's sniffling and the embarrassed tapping of Uncle Panov's cane. "You still sing so well, I don't understand. . . . It is this early change of life," she continued. "Wellborn women of our country all have it early."

Keeping my eyes averted from my weeping aunt, I concentrated on the lamplight gleaming with particular brilliance on Uncle Panov's pink, wet tongue. I was suddenly enraged by the ugliness and helplessness of that tongue, by a vague smell of urine on his clothes, by a spot of soup on his shirt. Did the childishness of the senile adult repel me—these infantile traits so repugnant to children because they are the very habits they are trying to emancipate themselves from? Was I abruptly exploding, in that narrow room filled with icons and the smell of steaming kasha, against the suffocation of my sheltering, adoring guardians? My small fist began to punch at Uncle Panov's helpless mouth. "Can't you keep your tongue in?" I shouted. "Can't you ever keep it in?" The meek, submissive child had turned into a braying urchin. "Keep your tongue in!" I screamed. "Keep it in!" My feet slammed at the floor as I shouted, as Lydia Romanovna ran to the bedroom for a calming potion of belladonna, as Baboushka, her ancient silks and mended laces fluttering like the feathers of a frightened dove, ran from Lara's side to shuttle me to my bedroom, while Uncle Panov, his now motionless tongue protruding farther than ever, sat astounded and sad-eyed at his solitaire.

I recalled with guilt, later that winter, this incident which had made my beloved Baboushka stare at me with such reproachful, questioning eyes. Her angel had momentarily vanished, and perhaps she was never to recover her total faith in that treasured child whose picture she carried in a locket near her heart. Several months later, in my eighth year, my great-grandmother died as I was spending one of my precious afternoons with her. Reaching for a picture book on a high shelf, she had closed her eyes and fallen to the floor with a soft rustle of silks. In the impact of her fall a light aluminum lamp had tipped over, and its hood settled as snugly as a chloroform mask over her peaceful face. Wresting from her face this metal mask, which I assumed to be the cause of her spell, I saw her eyes closed as in sleep, heard her breath rasping with a mechanical, motorized sound. . . . I do not know how long I cradled in my arms my silver-haired companion, shaking and pleading, how many hours passed before Lara returned to the apartment and stood at the door of the living room, her face twisted in terror and resignation. I mourned, then, the death of a precious third of my world, its only undemanding love, and its only escape from Mishka's possessiveness.

2 7

Uncle Panov died shortly after his sister. Since my parents went their separate ways during most of the summer, a new place had to be found for me for that part of the vacation I did not spend with my father. It was then that Lydia Roma-novna realized the greatest ambition of a Russian immigrant's life: she spent two vacations in French watering towns. She had been pleading for years with my father for such a trip. "The child is so fragile, so weak in the lungs, a perpetual cold all winter. Perhaps a few weeks at La Bourboule, La Baule, Évian . . ." He kept her at peace and gave her the money to take me to a resort. Of these establishments I remember particularly well La Bourboule, where we stayed at a dim, rusty boardinghouse named Joie de Vivre. Waking in our stark room overlooking the mountainous, rainy Auvergne landscape, I daily admired in the bed across from mine the two spots of rouge, like a Pierrot's awkward makeup, coloring Mishka's pointed cheekbones, the carrot-hued hair that lay frizzled on the pillow like the wig of a discarded doll. We rose, swallowed our cough syrup and unbleached wheat germ, and walked from our room to a small wooden pavilion standing, over the springs, in the center of the watering town. At the counter of the pavilion, attached on chains, hung shoddy, bent tin cups—such rickety cups as blind beggars hold out for char-ity—from which we dutifully drank, three times a day, a sul-furic, asphyxiatingly pungent water that was supposed to clear the liver, purify the kidneys, and vacuum the bronchi.

We spent our weeks in those watering towns reading in our room and walking, three times a day, to drink the waters. We walked slowly and rhythmically, our hands perpetually clutched in each other's, and painstakingly avoided talking to strangers. She had set herself, at La Bourboule, to correct my stutter. Every afternoon we walked cautiously to the top of a hill in the surrounding countryside. There, my mouth filled with pebbles collected on our walks, which she had carefully rinsed in our hotel room, I had to recite her favorite lines from

Lamartine. "Like Demosthenes," she proudly said, "who stuttered, too!" The lines that I tearfully stammered from my make-believe podium were peculiarly suited to the uprooted fates of Russian governesses:

> *Ainsi, toujours poussés vers de*
> *nouveaux rivages,*
> *Dans la nuit éternelle emportés*
> *sans retour,*
> *Ne pourrons-nous jamais sur*
> *l'océan des âges*
> *Jeter l'ancre un seul jour? . . .*

Lydia Romanovna shortened the number of her private outings in our last two years together, and grew more sullen. I had been dimly aware, throughout the years, that, just as my parents had lovers whom I never met, so also in her life there hovered a companion, and that he seemed to torture her increasingly. Her mouth was grimly set when, every six or eight weeks, she dropped me off at Aunt Lara's on a Thursday at noon, her hair freshly tinted. My great-aunt and I spent a tender but nostalgic afternoon in the apartment she had kept after her mother's death, playing Baboushka's favorite game of cards, nibbling on the same thin raspberry wafers she had stored as a treat for my afternoons. Lydia Romanovna reappeared at six, sullen and red-eyed, to pick me up. I cringed with fear of the oncoming crisis as we returned, muffled and silent, to the abandoned apartment.

She referred to her tormentor as "they." I imagine him now as a testy, dyspeptic Russian holding an underpaid post in some obscure philanthropic organization formed to aid Russian emigrés. He must have come, like his victim, from a family of professional Army people. He must have been too educated to drive a taxi, not accredited enough to teach, not wellborn enough to enjoy a melancholy dignity in exile. I see them meeting in small tearooms of the Seventeenth Arrondissement, near the subway stop Péreire. I imagine that they spent their hours commiserating on the indignities of their exile, on their unfair treatment at the hands of the hostile French. And as a chief instrument of his self-esteem the tormentor, this dyspeptic clerk, must have emphasized her maternal and unrecompensed devotion, her low wages, my family's selfishness, the hypnosis of their indisputable charm upon her, her eventual annihilation at our hands. In other words, he must have spoken the truth.

She returned tearful and abject from her outings. As we entered our room she threw her mackintosh over the bed with a desultory gesture, her pinched mouth twitching nervously. "Each time it gets worse, my poor child!" She wrung her hands, paced the room, slammed a window, sat down at our study table, laid her head on her folded arms. "Each time they say how much older, how tired I look, how I must be over-working myself for you and for your family, out of sheer love, with such devotion. A degree from the Sorbonne, and I am reduced to scrubbing for you. Each time they say how much older, how more tired I look!"

She would burst into tears, her arms cradling her head, as I cowered at the edge of my bed, staring at my aloof, glassed-in dolls, strangled by the weight of her suffering, by the full burden of my guilt in her misery. I crouched beneath the bookshelf that held my beloved editions of Jules Verne adventure stories. *"Five Weeks in a Balloon, Mysterious Island, Journey to the Center of the Earth,"* I repeated to myself through the beginning of my tears. Avoiding the sight of her shrunken, shaking body, I stared at the closet where the instruments of her devotion, the mustard plasters, inhalators, and infusions, lay stored, where the small animals of my fantasies nightly screamed in their narrow boxes. The long minutes of our single, strangled crying at opposite ends of the room ended in a lovers' reconciliation. We fell into each other's arms, sobbing pledges of eternal fidelity, of unending love and companionship, apologizing for our faults, promising perfect behavior. I was her only one, her squirrel, her mouse, her beloved child. Did I realize fully enough that she was giving up her life for me? Was her beloved mouse aware of her sacrifice? I cried, clung to her, embraced her, assuring her that I found her as beautiful as ever. She was my only continuity, my only rootedness, my only safety! A few calm weeks followed before her next outing.

The monotony, the drab rigor of my early childhood was ended by the Second World War.

III

Three days before the Germans entered Paris in June of 1940 I left my Mishka, with that brutal severing of tenderness that only a war can bring, and began a friendship with my mother. With a curiosity that verged on exhilaration, I puzzled what novelties a trip with this tall blond stranger would bring as her long pale hands packed my clothes on that June day. I had traveled with my father; I had listened by the hour to his homilies against Jews and my mother's unlovingness. But my father was at the front. As I leaned out of the living-room window to look at my mother's burgundy-colored Citroën, which had seldom taken me farther than the Rue de la Paix, I wondered what the first trip alone with her would be like.

Our bags were packed. Aunt Lara and Lydia Romanovna stood at the doorway of the apartment to say goodbye. My governess blinked confusedly through her thick lenses with that critical, molelike gaze with which she had first looked at me five years before, when I lay screaming for tenderness in a narrow crib. From under the armature of her spectacles she wiped a rhetorical tear. It was assumed we would all be reunited in a few weeks, when the Germans were thrown back behind the Maginot Line, beyond the Siegfried Line, all dangers past. Oh, fickleness, mendicancy, of childhood! I left her as docilely as I had loved her. And the political boundaries of the world, for the next five years, stopped any further communication between us.

Under the smoke screen of the evacuation of Paris, my mother and I drove at medieval speed in the procession of carts, trucks, cyclists, and pedestrians making their way out of the capital. We found temporary shelter in a hostel for refugees, where I caught lice playing with children from the north. Nightly I laid my head on my mother's lap, and her white hands traveled tenderly through my hair, her long lacquered nails making the fat noise of the insects' death echo exquisitely through my head. Our companionship was as new and as suspect as a freshly minted coin, but I was constantly surprised by her generosity and tenderness. Had my father's resentments, my governess' possessive love drawn a curtain around my mother all those past years?

After the fall of Paris, my father joined the Free French in North Africa and my mother and I eventually made our way to America. I entered a school for the first time, ran, argued, shouted, scraped my knees, whispered confidences. I conquered my stutter by joining debating teams, my shyness by running for class president. I compensated for my hopelessness in athletics by being first in English. I was an obsessed, compulsive sort. My adolescence was driven by the desire to meticulously destroy the image of that wan, cringing child in the photograph.

My love for Mishka had already paled in the first months of our separation. Over the years of the Occupation it waned, disappeared, and turned into increasing resentment. "Give me a child before seven," both the Jesuits and the psychiatrists say. She had deprived of joy my most precious and malleable years. The selfish tyranny of her love had held me back, had arrested some process of growth that I could never recapture. She had instilled in me for life a sense of isolation from others, the guilt of her misery, and the addictive need for protection and for tenderness that drags upon any courage I have. The damages wrought by her seemed irreparable and odious.

Her letters, when they began to trickle through the mails at the war's end, were filled with sentimental pledges of our past intimacy, with plaintive appeals for news of me, with accounts of her miserable Occupation years. She had stayed in our apartment for a few weeks to guard it from the Germans' loot-ing, had spent the rest of the Occupation taking any part-time work she could find with children, barely wresting a living from this and from her carefully nurtured social-security, old-age, and retirement insurance. She had built upon me, during these years of loneliness, a fantasy of love even more mon-strously distorted than it had been before. I opened the first two or three of these letters, filled with the embarrassing ap-pellations of our old tenderness, and methodically threw the succeeding ones away, unopened.

The first summers I returned to France, I was obsessed by the necessity of avoiding a reunion with Lydia Romanovna. I stayed with Aunt Lara, who was living in the same three-room flat she had shared with her mother. Still handsome and doe-eyed, her once jet-black hair turned to a bright chrome yel-low, she had survived frugally throughout the war by giving singing lessons. She had found it impossible not to receive Lydia Romanovna during those years—how could Lara forgo this one family link she had left? And she described these visits with a weariness mixed with pleasure: "Your governess comes here, but instead of sitting quietly in a chair she shuffles around the apartment saying, 'Let me take a better look at you, Larissa Alexeevna, let me take a better look!' and she creeps up to within an inch of me to stare at me through those thick spec-tacles of hers. I say to her, 'For heaven's sake, Lydia Roma-novna, what is there to look at? An aging singer!'" Lara laughed sadly, the raspberry odor of Dentifrice Toreador still emanating from her splendid mouth. This one family duty had allayed the monotony of her war years. She finally persuaded me, in a gentle manner that conquered me because it so resembled that of her mother, that I must see Lydia Romanovna; she would bother us too much if I did not. A short visit would keep her quiet for six months. I did not realize the annoyance that she, Lara, underwent from being constantly telephoned by her. I lived far away, in that wonderful large country. Could I not bother myself with this small family duty?

The reunion took place in Lara's living room, by the window where, many years earlier, I had tried to rock back to life the limp body of my grandmother. Lydia Romanovna sat on a chair by the window, the artifice of tint gone from her steel-gray hair—a timid, peevish, genteel old woman in a faded mackintosh. I remember little of our conversation. I sat frozen in my chair, stiffly offering information about the courses I had taken during my first year at Radcliffe. Throughout that painful half hour, her blinking eyes strained to devour me through her spectacles; her wrinkled hand clutched shyly at her faded tweed skirt. And when she rose to leave she said, with a brave, sad smile, "I hope we shall see you again, Stéphanie." Her simpering laugh echoed through the frugal rooms. I felt the awesome duty of a farewell kiss. As I approached her dry cheek, amid the wealth of odors, still intact in those rooms, that radiated the sparse gaiety of my childhood —the verbena and rose water, the raspberry biscuits stored in the larder for my teatime—as I approached that sunken cheek I breathed with horror those feared medicinal smells of bandage, camphor and belladonna that had filled the air of my nursery. And to her who had nursed me through so many real and imaginary illnesses, bestowed upon me so much misguided tenderness, offered the maternal love of my early years, I could not return more than my disgust.

I came in and out of Paris a few more times, lived there once for two years, and meticulously avoided ever seeing her again.

I returned to America, married, and had children. Did Lydia Romanovna's letters, which came persistently two or three times a year, plead for my reply, for the briefest news of my activities? I never opened them. They were tossed into fireplaces or wastebaskets, token upon token of a callous youth.

And yet through solitude, the brutality of love, the oppressions of marriage, the epiphanies of time, there comes a year, a sudden break in life when one stops feeding exclusively on the enjoyment of the present. At some point in my growing understanding of loneliness and pain, I found myself worrying about the health of aging aunts, wondering about the fates of former lovers, sending Christmas greetings to friends whom I had abandoned, years ago, because they had made the mistake of needing me more than I needed them. This solicitude for the past, this concern for the causality of suffering, may be the end of a youth, the beginning of middle years.

Out of a combination of guilt and this new hunger for continuity, one blustery New Year's Eve as I was sorting my mail, I looked at the envelope of Mishka's New Year's letter before discarding it. With a curiosity that still refused to be tinged with pity, I noticed that the letter was sent from an old people's home on the outskirts of Paris. I opened the envelope. On a greeting card ornamented with tinseled birds and simpering angels the handwriting was spindly and barely legible, slanted at different askew angles. The frequent interruptions in its composition were made evident by the varying colors of ink and by its varying degrees of legibility.

As you can see, it has taken me many weeks to write you this single little message, to wish a happy new year to you and your family. As you know, my eyes were never good, I have been suffering from cataracts for some time. I have had three eye operations in the past year and the success of the last one is still very doubtful. . . . This may be the last letter, my darling child, which I can write to you. You remember how much I loved to read, how I instilled in you that love of books which made you excel in your schoolwork. . . . Even the pleasure of reading is now denied to me. I sit, hands folded, ending my life in this sad retreat for the aged. Goodbye, my adored child, light of my life. . . .

I stared around me, at my prosperous house stocked with the furnishings of a placid happiness, and shook with a dual and confused rage. How dare I be so heartless as to discard one who had, without recompense, given me so much of her love? How dare she thrust her misery into my peace after I had so patiently constructed a womanhood from the cringing and lonely child she had fashioned?

As I wept on that cold, bleak winter evening, filled with a sense of futility, of guilt, and of disgust, my husband tried to console me. "Why don't you write her?" he suggested, "it might make you feel better. But always remember: these women have chosen to suffer; suffering is their vocation, and one of the ingredients of their self-pity is to make some child in their past bear the guilt of their suffering."

Ever since that day when I dutifully began to read Lydia Romanovna's missives (Easter, my birthday, New Year's), I have persevered through the painful creation of a return letter to her. The approach of this letter-writing fills me with growing desperation and embarrassment, reminding me of those childhood mornings when, stoked with wheat germ and cod-liver oil, I sat in the narrow closet, straining for hours with no result, her demanding rodent's gaze fixed on me, encouraging me to communication, to success. The conquest of my procrastination, the final resolution of the letter, fills me with a quiet and heroic joy. I strike a note of semi-affectionate detachment that, devoid as it is of any sentiment, infuses some cheer into her dark, still life. I write about my children: "Tommy is three, already interested in the alphabet. Jeff is two, sings on perfect pitch. . . ." "Tommy is four, does not wet at night anymore. Jeff is three, a splendid eater. . . ." "Tommy is five, the image of my father. . . ." And with this bland, non-committal news, I enclose a ten-dollar bill. She never mentions it. There would be plaintive, sentimental remonstrances if the gesture embarrassed her. The trick would be, I reflect each time, to be rich enough to send her a few thousand dollars a year, to drown her suffering and my guilt in some situation of impeccable comfort, of luxury even—a little villa in a watering town. But I am not rich. The bill is a cheap symbolic gesture that buys out my guilt, while burdening my conscience with a small, new culpability: how to treat memory like a whore! And yet it cuts out, as if it were a wart, the sentimentality of our situation.

The methodology of discarding parents is natural and guilt-less. It is the equitable due for the egotistic animal joy that they receive from our existence. But what moral or biological rationale can one construct to discard guiltlessly these lonely women who give us part of their life without ever enjoying a parent's biological pride? An added brutality hovers over the fate of governesses: one forgives parents as naturally as one emancipates oneself from them—usually shortly afterward. My mother looked at me with admiration on my twenty-sixth birthday and said with disarming candor, "I simply was not interested in you until you were ten years old. Thank God the war threw us together." I had forgiven her years before, as completely as I had forgiven my unhappy father. Indeed, she would bring to the rest of my childhood much of the light and happiness that I had missed in my first nine years. I forgave both my parents even that they had allowed a stranger to misshape my early years: their chief mistake, after all, had been to not love each other enough. But forgiving governesses is a more difficult matter.

Some months ago, I had a curious dream about Lydia Romanovna. She was coming to visit us, in this dream, for a holiday. She arrived in a wheelchair, waited upon by a cringing teen-age girl who served her silently and fearfully. Her physiognomy in this dream was red, swollen, monstrously deformed—not by old age but by some generic mutation that had transformed her face into the eyeless head of a small water animal, a newt or a slug. Yet it was not so much the hissing of that monstrous face that filled me with horror as her right hand, a red stump both viscous and granular to the touch, like the barnacle-grown trunk of a coral reef. However, what another, joyous transformation the dream offered! She was no more her simpering, plaintive, cloyingly sentimental self; she was imperious, demanding, aloof, peevishly disturbed by the noise of my children's voices, rejecting the advances of their affections and uninterested in mine.

I had, then, by some mechanism of compassion or of growth, destroyed the burden of my guilt! *She* had been the tormentor, the tyrant, the guilty one. She had elected one child, because of some incapacity of love for men, to torment with her self-pity, to feel guilty for the loneliness of her fate. She had practiced a form of despotism characteristic of governesses, that almost vanished race which was, until lately, a distinctive feature of European educations.

The Cycle
of the Year

1940

I

My cousin Cécile lay as always in a chaise longue of faded blue velvet, in that tower room where she had slept since her child-hood. It was a Sunday morning in May 1940.

Wispy, smoke-colored hair surrounded her wan face like a saint's aureole. Cécile liked saints. She wished to be one. At the age of nineteen she spent her days huddled in shawls, praying a great deal and reading Vatican-approved literature. She had a chronic cough. Fires were kept lit throughout the year in her room to counteract the dampness of the old stone walls.

It was said that she had been in love with a first cousin, that a variety of ailments had plagued her since this romance had been thwarted by the proprieties of kinship. But then, cousins, cousins! Whom did my father's relatives ever see but their hundreds of cousins! They were all hell-bent on procreation, unless they were nuns and priests. And many were.

Occasionally a doctor drove through the iron gate that en-circled Saint-Seran, her father's estate on the southernmost border of Brittany, which had belonged to our family since the year 1560. The doctor stood in Cécile's room taking her pulse and exclaimed, "Altitudes! She should have altitudes!" But Cécile's parents seldom traveled, except to visit still more cousins, uncles, aunts in some nearby province as flat and damp as their own.

Cécile welcomed me that Sunday with the startled little laugh which fluttered out of her whenever anyone interrupted her isolation. She rose, clenching both fists on the edge of her seat to support her body. She stared for a moment out her window. Wheat and barley fields fired by the crimson of new poppies, the monotony of the flat plain. I followed her with familiar anticipation as she walked, shawled and stooped, to the bathroom adjoining her room. Cécile took out a flask of pale-blue glass from a shelf adjoining the window. She walked back to her bedroom, faster this time and less bent, the bottle clasped furtively to her chest. She lay down on the chaise longue. Her eyes were languidly closed, her face was now devoid of anxiety or surprise. She unstopped the flask and put it to her face, the smell of ether filled the room, and I clasped my hands over my ears as if to avoid some dreaded memory of my own, but the ecstatic smile on her lips, the sudden peace of her face as she reached her desired stupor gradually gave me the courage to remove my hands, to hear only the light rasping of her breath rising rhythmically with the purring of doves under the eaves. I gave rein to one of the most exquisite rituals of my childhood: I lay on the cool tiled floor at my cousin's feet, I stared at her limp body and partook of her euphoria, I shared with her a territory of forgetting, refuge, withdrawal, escape.

Many images come to mind, from that same Sunday morning of the war:

Exit from Mass in the village chapel. Smell of young grass and sour milk pails, of incense and freshly baked bread. My father is on weekend leave from the Air Force, wearing a blue-gray uniform. He walks alongside his brother and sister-in-law, Uncle Jean and Aunt Charlotte. Their children follow. Cécile, nineteen, is the oldest. She is stooped and bent, her pale eyes have a secretive, vaporous look.

Gentle swaying of all those rosaries. Aunt Charlotte's beads of deep-blue crystal, Cécile's of mother-of-pearl translucent as teardrops, the men's rosaries of black jet, the younger children's of small amber beads. Voices buzzing to my father, on this yearly visit, about the past months' events: Last spring was so warm the first hay was cut at Pentecost. . . . The local priest died the week of Whitsuntide. . . . At Assumption time we went to Brest to see Cousin Marie. . . . Daniel will have his First Communion on Trinity Sunday. . . . Time measured here, ever since I can remember, by the wheeling of the Church year, by the rhythm of the saints. The Joyous Rosary. The Sorrowful Rosary. The Glorious Rosary. All those rosaries swaying as we walk in the tiny rain, delicately stepping over the amber pools of dung that glisten between the straw-crusted cobblestones.

Straight ahead as we walk back the half mile from church, the little family castle reached through an alley of flowering chestnuts. For the rest of my life I shall dream about the pale, exquisitely symmetrical structure where my father was brought up, the silvery slopes of mansarded roofs sliding down gently to the long, narrow windows framed by clumps of pale-blue hydrangeas. All is pale, evanescent, bathed in a haze of fragile Sleeping Beauty light.

"Fabulous grouse-shooting ever since Good Friday this year! The quail is even better!" As he walks back from Mass talking to my father, Uncle Jean tightens and retightens the fit of his pigskin gloves, which makes a little *squeak-squeak* sound. He puts on a bowler hat and gloves the minute he exits from his house, even on the hottest days.

I skip on the cobblestones with my cousins—Louise, Daniel, Pierre, Catherine. Here I am free of Mishka, I am free and brave. *Am stram, gram!* Don't always be so scared, Stéphanie! Hop, jump, skip two stones, three stones, four! I am in love with Daniel. We are both nine. Perhaps I shall tell him; if I do not become a nun like Cécile, we can elope someday to Madagascar. The cobblestones end as we enter the chestnut alley. We start singing, in canon: "Oh, we shall hang our linen on the Siegfried Line . . ." (It had blared over the radios that first spring of the war, along with Chevalier, the last of Mistinguett.) "Oh, we shall hang the dirty Kra-auts with their pa-ants down . . ."

"Oh, stop that, my rabbits, for heaven's sake," my father cries out. "Be realistic! The Maginot Line is obsolete! The Germans are already threatening the Belgian front!"

"*Pah, pah*, as I was telling you, our entire lunch right here, in this copse of the wood," Uncle Jean says, his arm stuck out in the shape of a gun. "Pah, pah, these succulent quails about to be served for lunch were all shot down right here, in this very copse."

Uncle Jean is fifteen years older than my father, over draft age. He has been to Paris once in his life, for my father's marriage to "that foreigner."

"Marvelous quail this season, surpassing even the partridge or the grouse. Have I told you that our apples yielded fifty gallons of cider last fall? And the pears, forty quarts of the finest Poire ever! The beets were low, but the artichokes were the finest of the decade. . . ."

"Daladier at Munich," my father says. "That was the beginning of the end. An infamous capitulation." He raises me up to straddle his shoulders. I am almost too large for the ride. He brushes his stubbly cheek against my leg. "It's going to be a disaster, my beloved pigeon," he continues. "What are we going to do?" That's the way he has been talking to me in the last few months, whenever he comes home on leave, as if I were completely grown up. "Weygand and Reynaud are idiots, dragging us down to disaster." "Someday after the war we'll live all alone in a country house, you and I, we'll cultivate prize-winning roses."

"This little Stéphanie is so sweet, I can't get enough of her," Uncle Jean croons, reaching up to my perch to pinch my cheek. Uncle Jean and Aunt Charlotte love children. My father adores children. If he'd had his way he would have had five of us, his relatives always say, but my mother barely wanted one.

Aunt Charlotte smoothes a lock of hair off my forehead. "Oh, you treasure. Always so pale and frail like poor Cécile, what are we going to do with you?" Smell of a minted unguent on her hands with which she treats her children's colds, smell of sweet cooking leeks, of fermenting cider rising from a nearby shed.

Uncle Jean removes his hat and gloves, goes into his wine cellar. Sound of his cane vigorously tapping his wine barrels to check the condition of his last vintage. Sound of Cécile's thin cough, of the faltering rustle of her steps as she leads me with the younger children into the dining room.

"You stuck-up Parisian devil," Uncle Jean says to my father, "we'll show you how one can still eat and drink in this country! Then maybe you'll deign to visit us more than once a year!"

Three vintages of Uncle Jean's wine appear at the table, are sniffed, coddled, sampled, discussed. The excellence of home-bottled wine for the liver, the digestion, for general fortitude, is praised. Like everything grown on one's own land it is replete with potassium, forestalls arthritis, cures rheumatism.

Aunt Charlotte gives my father a final accounting of family activities: "Would you believe that our cousin Paul has had to close his farm in Algeria? . . . Did you know that your nephew Roger, your brother Pierre's oldest child, has just received first prize at the Nantes school of engineering? . . . And I forgot to tell you that your niece Alice has just entered the convent in Tours. . . ."

That's what I remember best of all from that day, Cécile's pale face twitching at the mention of that convent, my happy premonition that she will launch into my favorite story, into the tale that so obsesses both of us. Ah, yes, yes, there she goes, she intones it in her high thin voice, her pale hand cradles her cheek, her eyes focus wearily upon some area of the faded wallpaper behind my head.

"No one is ever allowed to look at the outside world again upon entering the Carmelite order. The gates around the convents are very high, the only air in the nuns' cells comes from a slit in the wall right close to the ceiling. . . . As you know, our Great-Aunt Jeanne entered a Carmelite convent in Clermont-Ferrand in 1883. Those were still the horse-and-carriage days, no railroad existed yet in the center of France. Well, imagine, twenty years later a railroad line began to be built just a hundred yards from her convent's walls, the first to connect Paris to the South. For a few years Aunt Jeanne heard the workmen hammering down the rails outside her cell, and then for several decades she heard the Paris train rumbling in and out of the station twice a day, in and out, without ever being allowed to see it. Finally, as she was about to celebrate her fiftieth year in the Carmelite order, she asked her superiors if she might be allowed to break one small rule, if she might be allowed to stand upon a ladder and look through that aperture at the top of her cell. She wanted to see what this monster whose rumbling she had heard all those decades looked like! Permission was finally granted, for her service had been of exemplary holiness. But when the letter of dispensation arrived, Aunt Jeanne renounced her wish, she chose the way of self-mortification, she died quietly a few months later without ever having seen that train which rumbled by her cell. . . ."

"Admirable," Uncle Jean says.

"Deeply affecting," my father murmurs.

The ritual of Sunday coffee commences in the Saint-Seran living room. The water heats in a bulbous, rounded vessel over a small kerosene flame. The water darkens ever so slowly, first to a pale muddy yellow, then to amber.

In each room at Saint-Seran a crucifix hangs over the door,

ornamented with dried palm and bay and surmounted by a receptacle for holy water. Frayed, weathered Louis XV furniture, splendor of moldings not painted since the war of 1870, family portraits and heraldic blazons hanging on the delicately flowered wallpaper long spotted with dampness. History, loyalty, continuity, ancestors, ancestors . . . A few times Uncle Jean has given me the name of every ancestor who has lived in this house.

Aunt Charlotte calls the pigeons to the window ledge. "Courrrou . . . courrrrrou . . . courrrrou," she purrs, shaking handfuls of fat, buttery yellow corn seeds onto the ledge. Sitting at my father's feet, my head against his knee, I fall asleep as the coffee turns the color of chocolate. My aunt is clicking the fragile green-and-gold cups emblazoned with the family crest. The birds are gathered at the window, purring, pecking. The violent iridescence of their feathers. And outside: the goldfish pond into which I started wading at the age of three, the oak tree I climbed at the age of five, the sheep dog I had been small enough to ride the previous summer.

My father bends over me in his blue-gray Air Force uniform, stroking my hair. "Time to go, little one, the end of the day, the end of our freedom."

Speaking his love for me, exhorting me to patriotism, mapping our future happiness together, talking ceaselessly, he drives us back to Paris in the last days of our brief life together.

On the other hand, my mother:

My mother frequented and courted, with equal passion, musical-comedy stars, Spanish grandees, Swiss alpinists, eminent nobles, gifted physicians, champion jockeys, medaled academicians, fashionable dressmakers, racing-car winners, champion bridge players, Italian poets, American tycoons.

Her favorite precepts: "Geniuses are permitted everything." "One does not argue with winners." "Snobs are always right."

She had gone to Saint-Seran once ten years ago, and never

returned. "They have not accomplished anything for *centuries*."

Her milieu in Paris was brilliant, her acquaintances international. Her reputation: "An ebullient, magnanimous woman, one of our great beauties, a force of nature!"

Squatting in a corner of her bathroom some mornings of my childhood, I had stared at her like a serf staring at the suzeraine, like a believer staring at an idol. She would blow me a kiss, out of her bath, the way politicians offer a wave of the hand from passing carriages. She was that beautiful, that radiant, that cool. Until we left Paris together, few words had been exchanged between us. I had learned to worship her as silently as a rat, always fearing to be brutalized by some gesture of dismissal. It took me some twenty more years to jot down the following epiphany:

"With her contemporaries she was joyous, loquacious, effusively affectionate. With children she was remote, glacially silent. A little child is a mere possibility, the very negation of success. So what a gamble I must have seemed to this idol of mine, what a waste of her precious time! Her silence, her indifference to me were caused by her overwhelming adulation of human accomplishment. What else did this atheist have to worship, needing gods, and being unable to believe in her own greatness?"

So she did not know the language of children, she fondled me with the silent tenderness with which one tousles a young pet; when we were finally thrown together by the war she could only state her affection for me by material gestures, by hugging, kissing, waving, feeding, offering candy, buying stuffed bears, never by explanation, never by words.

I had never shared a room with my mother until Paris fell, and we found shelter in a castle of the Loire Valley which had been turned into a refugee hostel.

At night as we lie by each other's side the sound of her

breathing fills me with anxiety. I am uncomfortable at the thought of having emerged from her belly, of having suckled at her breast. Her body is too novel, unfamiliar, I do not know her enough, she has the darkness of silence, its brutality, its terror.

I want to put my head to hers and say, Talk, can't you talk so I can lie here at peace, can't you transmit something clear about who you are, who your mother was, whether you had a father, what was your childhood like, who your friends are, I think I know you love me but it is not enough, I want more, or something vastly different, I want your history, your words, your admiration.

I lie in the dark on a June night fantasizing about my father's military prowesses, staring suspiciously at the outline of my nipples. My mother has large breasts. Would mine ever get large? Breasts do not belong to the boy my father wished for. They identify me with my mother, whom he taught me not to trust; who until now has never asked for my trust.

A moan pierces the silence of our room. My mother is crying out in her sleep. It is a desperate, raucous scream, subhuman and lugubrious. It could be the yell of a woman in the agony of childbirth, the moan of a prisoner witnessing atrocities. I sit up in terror, waiting for the voice to desist. The nightmare subsides. She lies quietly again. Her cries will wake me again and again throughout my childhood.

Every day from the end of that June, my mother wears a black serge skirt and a black crepe blouse that contrast poignantly with the paleness of her face and hair. Many mornings, shortly before eight, we lean together at the window to watch the company of Nazi soldiers quartered in the nearby village. They goosestep along the narrow country road directly beneath our window, chins thrust forward by the thick straps of their helmets, impassive faces gleaming under knobs of flaxen hair, eyes of ice narrowed in the summer sunshine. The thrum of their footsteps clangs heavily upon the gentle landscape. And every morning I thrill to the animal smell of their polished boots, to the radiance of their stern faces, with an enjoyment which I sense is infamous. Delectation of evil! The child's deadly love of power! I love all virile odors, virile stances, virile sounds. With that razor's edge of patriotism which could have led him as easily to fascism as to the Resistance, my father taught me to delight in the muscular din of parades and national anthems, the gleam of insignias, medals and blazons, the waving of flags and banners. And my crass little soul holds great respect for the pomp of liveries and uniforms, the appurtenances of all rank and might. The sight of these soldiers fills me with the same perverse excitement with which, huddling against my mother in air-raid shelters that summer, I measure the deadly interval between the whistling of the bombs and the explosion that follows.

A swan screams in the moat. A flock of refugee children, their hair greased slickly for the extermination of lice, chase each other through the alleys of the castle's park. At all hours of the day, I carry in my pocket the one letter I have received from my father since we left Paris. He has mailed it in mid-June, on his way to North Africa. The letter stresses the power, the loneliness of our love, it begs me to retain trust in him notwithstanding the long silence that might follow.

In the month of July, when I know every word of the missive by heart, I spend my afternoons crouched inside the boxwood labyrinth of the castle's park, mapping elaborate itineraries of his secret missions. I have a talismanic need to keep my fantasies as clandestine as the routes of his journeys. Every day I hide in the labyrinth with a map of the Mediterranean, tracing, erasing, retracing alternate voyages. He travels through North Africa in a variety of disguises. He masquerades, for instance, in the souks of Damascus and Beirut, he lives incognito among black-marketeers in Tangiers, he hides on an islet off the coast of Zanzibar. In between two imagined adventures I sit on in the labyrinth for hours, my head buried in my hands, praying for his safety. Then, amidst the dusty, pulsating smell of my boxwood hideaway, I conjure again my naïve landscapes of his travels—camels, palm trees, deserts, Arabs in burnooses, treacherous souks. I accept the rightness, the valor of his silence; he is following a patriotic calling whose nature must remain confidential! He is under an oath of the most absolute secrecy!

Nine. That age when I can still drag myself on my knees through the Stations of the Cross, when I still believe in miracles, in the sheer cannibalism of Communion, in men dying and rising again. I pray to my father at night, staring at a photograph of him I have placed by my bedside next to a crucifix which had hung by his own childhood bed. From that soft, seductive face, the gaze of the immense chestnut-colored eyes seems to answer me, to plead for my increased patience. The Sorrowful Rosary: kneeling beside those stark symbols of a Catholic childhood—the crucifix's drooping head, the thorn-ripped flesh, the twisted bleeding feet—I continue to spin an elaborate tale of his adventures. As if sworn to a secrecy as rigorous as his, I mention him to no one, least of all to my mother.

Increasingly often in the past weeks she has been spending her days lying in our darkened bedroom, blowing me kisses every few hours, pleading a throat infection, addressing me less than ever.

August: I remember it as a *bang! crash!* and the blood spurting out of my forehead, onto my hands, my neck, onto my mother's black clothes. Driving through Tours, the Mercedes-Benz of a highly placed German officer crashed into our tiny Citroen car at a street intersection.

My mother stands regal and disdainful in an office of the bomb-torn city hall. Her sore throat miraculously gone, talking volubly again, she offers the Kommandant of Tours a glorious, outrageous account of our family tree. This afternoon, the Kommandant's glossy eyes upon her, I am annoyed that her black blouse is too tight.

She says, "On her father's side, my daughter is descended from Cardinal de Richelieu, directly from his oldest bastard, and also from two governors of Brittany and from the great courtesan Camille. . . . Don't tell me you don't know who that is! La Dame aux Camélias! As for *my* family, we are related to Tolstoy, Stanislavsky, Genghis Khan. Ah, yes, I forgot, through my Turkish grandmother we are also related to Sultan Ahmed IV's favorite concubine . . ."

"All of history could be obliterated by her quest for notoriety," I later wrote. "And her perpetual striving for brilliant status may have saved our lives." The Kommandant was also a snob, the Kommandant was most impressed. He complimented my mother on my Aryan looks. I shall never forget the graze of his moustache on my wrist as he kissed my hand, my desire to kill him. He offered us a visa into unoccupied France for which we had been waiting for two months.

We wound our way a few weeks later into the South of France, where we spent the rest of the year. As we were about to sail to America from Lisbon in 1941, my mother announced that she had a father in the United States—Baboushka's son, Lara's brother. It was the first time I knew that she had a parent, that she did not come out of an orphanage, that she was not an immaculate conception.

I still have in my possession the only photograph my maternal grandfather brought to the United States. Taken at the turn of the century in his mother's apartment in St. Petersburg, it shows him in the full regalia of his Imperial Cadets uniform, indolently slumped in a tasseled velvet chair. He is all slender limbs, with the sleek beauty of a racehorse. His lean greyhound's face encases my mother's high cheekbones and her slanting almond eyes. A silver cigarette holder is poised in his right hand, a white kid glove held languidly in the other. His extraordinarily long and slender legs, encased in high knee boots shined to a metallic gleam, stretch over an intricately patterned Turkish carpet. The photograph well conjures up his life: gambling rooms in early-morning hours, capricious duels, erotic intrigues at masked balls, the hedonism of a Russian caste about to be doomed.

Ivan Alexeivich's odyssey to America began on a winter night in 1918, when, exiting from a casino, penniless after one of his constant bouts of gambling, he was approached by an elegant veiled woman who asked him what he wanted most in the world. His answer was that he wished to leave for the United States. At the end of their night together she took him home in her carriage, handed him a purse, and drove off. It contained the equivalent of several thousand dollars. Leaving behind his two daughters and his wife, whom he later divorced, gambling his way across Siberia and China, he traveled to San Francisco. He had been destitute in this country for only a few weeks when another enamored women—a Russian exile, like himself—offered him her hard-won savings of five years. He promised to stop gambling, and married her. From that year on, he had to make his own way. Luck had carried him on her shoulders like some infatuated goddess, and then had dumped him where I later found him: on a bleak street in Hershey, Pennsylvania, where he lived the listless, narrow life which his great indifference to achievement and to love made him quite suited for.

A few hours after we have disembarked in New York, my mother decides that I should live with her newly discovered father until she finds work and is settled enough to take care of me. We sit across from each other on a night train to Pennsylvania. I am awake throughout the night, furious that I have had to leave my mother, furious that I have to accompany this dozing stranger to some obscure town known solely for the excellence of its chocolate. A sudden swerve of the train wakes the tall moustached man. He shakes his head and looks at me with startlement. He had abandoned my mother in Russia some twenty years ago, when she was the same age as the child now placed in his charge. He leans forward to pat me timidly on the knee. I stare back at him with distrust.

It is a rarity for a Russian gentile to change his name. Sikorsky, Obolensky, Seversky are still with us. But it is in my grandfather's character to have chosen the most inconspicuous Yankee name he could find, and live accordingly. John Johnson lives in a five-room frame house, one of several hundred identical habitations, a few blocks away from the factory where he works as an electrical technician. His second wife, Tanya, is a tiny, timid woman easily given to tears. During the months I live with them I find her tears romantic and beautiful, a superb respite, the only respite, from the monotony of the Johnsons' existence. They have one son, Victor, a thick-limbed sixteen-year-old with a savage laugh who excels at taking radios apart and putting them together again. Also living with them is Tanya's mother, a dour, kerchiefed old Russian woman who cries punctually, every Monday morning, over the week's wash. It is my favorite day of the week.

"Reduced to this," she wails in Russian as she stands in the kitchen, feeding sheets into the creaking mangle. "Reduced to manual labor. If you knew how well we lived in the old country, my little soul! Servants bringing us tea every hour, such pastures, such orchards!"

She points silently at the narrow back yard, identical in size and shape to some three hundred in the street, where the muddy ground lies like mangled flesh under the dirty bandage of the melting snow. Several hundred sheets, shirts and underdrawers flap desolately in the icy wind as far as the eye can see.

Tanya sobs in punctual response, tears falling abundantly on her husband's overalls. "Yes, we thought we'd come to a land of freedom, of happiness! What freedom in this drudgery, my little dove, what freedom?"

The two weep on, sitting across from each other in the

kitchen, their heads swaying, their hands rising rhythmically in this weekly ritual of lamentation. I join them to gain their affection. "Mother Russia," I sob, adding any phrase I can think of in our native language: "The sight of the Neva! The beauty of St. Petersburg!" And I join copiously in their weeping as I feed sheets into the relentless mangle which creaks in rhythm with the cadence of our tears.

At times my grandfather comes home a trifle early from his factory and catches us still crying. He towers above us at the doorsill, his haughty body incongruously elegant under the folds of his faded overalls. He shouts his most violent Russian word: "*Irunda!* What nonsense! *Irunda!* Siberia for this women's folly! My slippers!"

He retires to the living room and slumps into his Grand Rapids chair with the evening edition of *The Hershey Banner*. Tanya patters into the room, bends down to unlace his shoes and put on his slippers. The living room is furnished with a folding couch which serves as my bed, an electric imitation coal grate, a bookshelf holding collections of *National Geographic, Understanding Your Radio, The Radio Fan's News*. John Johnson has never had need of friends. And the only social event of our life that winter is to drive to Victor's high school to admire an exhibition of seventy-five radios pulled apart and put together again by the junior class.

The apogee of John Johnson's week: Saturdays, 8:30 P.M., *The Major Bowes Amateur Hour*. He paces the living room nervously for half an hour before the program. At eight-thirty sharp he shouts with the announcer, with a wild and reckless gesture of his arm, "Lady Luck, there she goes! Where she stops nobody knows!" It is the only moment of the week when his languid body shows animation, when his voice is raised above its habitually gruff, hollow timbre, when there is some passion in his cold, indifferent eyes.

Like an alcoholic gone berserk on one drop of sherry, he wildly cheers on Lady Luck. He cheers for the several hundred amateurs sitting in a New York radio station with numbered tickets in their hands. Their chance to astound the nation is determined by an enormous wheel of chance which shuffles their numbers. Each time the wheel has chosen a contestant, the old gambler sits back in his chair, his Oriental eyes slit with contentment like those of a purring cat. He listens reverently to trained dogs playing the harp, quadruplets from Ontario singing arias from *Pagliacci*, ventriloquists and imitators of parrots, drum majorettes performing "Jingle Bells" on the xylophone. "Fantahsteec!" he exclaims after each number, in that gruff voice still sonorously tinged with the Russian accent. "Put eet there, Major Bowes! Fantahsteec what Lady Luck can do!"

In this house where I cry every night about my father's silence and the sheer horror of the passage of time, I crave tenderness and vainly try to gain my grandfather's love. I allow myself to be infected by his passion for the radio. I begin to learn English by spending my entire afternoons glued to the set, daily rehearsing for improved diction and enlarged vocabulary the parting lines from *Our Gal Sunday, Life Can Be Beautiful, When a Girl Marries, Right to Happiness, Orphans of Divorce, Young Dr. Malone.* "What will Nancy do? Will she tell Dr. Malone about her suspicions?" To discuss these programs, to report on the development of their plots, is the only contact I have with John Johnson.

There is little else.

There is his occasional use of the French language, learned at the knees of governesses, old-fashioned and subtly Voltairian, dusty and suave as a kid glove preserved for decades in a drawer.

He occasionally asks about my father.

Briefly, cautiously, I delineate the possible nature of his secret missions. John Johnson clucks his tongue. "*Voilà de l'héroisme, ma Stéphanie! Mais quel héro!*"

But I know that the valor of the tale seems as much of an

irunda to him—a nonsense—as any other human striving. That, radically unlike my mother, he is smugly nestled in the comfort of his defection from all ambition, all endeavor of the will.

I am labeled and registered like a piece of luggage or a small dog. A tag is pinned to my lapel with my age, name, and nationality. I am traveling from Pennsylvania to New York via the Travelers' Aid Society, returning to my mother at last.

I decide to practice my nascent English on the train with an affable neighbor who has studied French at Vassar. I admire, in turn, a station platform, the size of the clouds, the color of the sky. "Thank you, thank you," she repeats each time. Oh, what delicacy, after the Johnsons' Hershey.

The train approaches New York. We see bonfires burning in the New Jersey flatlands. I point to the flames, requesting the word. "Fire, fire," my neighbor teaches.

"Fayou, fayou," I murmur. As we pull into Grand Central Station I am still struggling to master those syllables in the new language which I shall embrace like a lover for all consolation.

My mother stands at the gate, frantically waving a stuffed panda as a sign of welcome.

Wherever we lived, from then on, all would be painted white, white like a scream, white like forgetting the past, white like the shroud to wrap yesterday with. She had not felt settled in our two-room apartment until it was blindingly, totally white. In these gay, hollow rooms of hers every ashtray, every lamp, every plate had to be white, it was her fetish and her obsession, it was like the disinfectant paint swabbed on Mediterranean villages after a plague. During the following year the color came to mean something terrifying to me. It came to mean that we had left Europe without a hue of memory, that reality and history were the plagues that threatened her, that fact had to be constantly rewritten for her convenience, history redecorated for effect, all memories wiped out, out, out.

And so what a perfect land for her to come to. Destroy all memory, New World immigrant, be free again from the pain of history.

One of my first breakfasts there in the white room: I hold my spoon poised over my grapefruit, staring out the window at the electric ribbon of world news that flows relentlessly around the top of the General Motors Building at Columbus Circle, a few blocks from our apartment: "Germans invade Crete . . . Roosevelt orders 24-hour shifts in war production. . . . King Carol and Magda Lupescu flee to Cuba . . ." Suddenly the dam that holds my fears breaks down, the salt well erupts. My tears flow in fast, thick rivulets into the grapefruit. My mother rushes to my side. "My dove, my angel, is something wrong?" Our hands meet over the cool white furniture. She tousles my hair like a mother cat licking her young. My cowardice is as great as hers.

We live on.

She is working as a hat designer in a fashionable New York store. One of her many new American friends has arranged a scholarship for me at an exclusive New York school. She holds a dinner party scarcely two weeks after I have returned from Hershey. "Do come, do come," her voice trills, "we are having a musical evening . . ." She instructs me loquaciously on points of diplomatic etiquette as we set our Woolworth flatware on a rickety white garden table: "When seating guests, Stéphanie darling, one must always remember that a papal nuncio takes precedence over any ambassador, and that a grandee of Spain, even if not of royal lineage, takes precedence over any other title. However, if there is a title of *royal* lineage, a Bourbon or a Hapsburg, say, *and* a papal nuncio at the same table, the royalty goes to the hostess's right, the nuncio to the left . . ."

The musical soirees proliferate. Every Saturday night a wheezing Russian prince pounds out Prokofiev's "The Love for Three Oranges" and the coronation scene from *Boris Godunov* on our rented upright. My grandfather comes to visit us on a spring weekend and sits through the evening craggy-faced, regretting Major Bowes, snoring through the Bach. With what outrage my mother stares at him! Some years later I analyzed why: He had abandoned her to the anarchy of the Russian Revolution and to a selfish, cold-hearted mother whom she detested. How carefully she had striven to rebuild a hierarchy of caste! All her labor was now brutally rethreatened by the vacant, passive gaze of her father's eyes.

What a treat and a suffering this is: Every few weeks after school I meet her at the department store where she works late into the evening, to purchase some garment she has decided I need to keep up appearances. I find her in a small hot workroom, pressing felts and velvets onto wooden forms with a heavy iron, or working the steam machine. Her delicate hands are often bleeding from the prick of pins, their whiteness all the starker against those perpetual black clothes. Or else she stands in the showroom selling a hat to a jeweled French-speaking New Yorker she has charmed the previous week at some dinner party. She thrusts me toward her client with pride. "My daughter, doing remarkably well at the best American school!" When the client ventures a genealogical query my mother has her field day: "*Of course* she is descended from the famous Cardinal de Richelieu. . . . Certainly he had bastards, all cardinals did in those days. She is also descended from the great courtesan Camille, La Dame aux Camélias. As for our Russian side, we are descended from Tolstoy and from Genghis Khan . . ."

The delighted customer promises to bring more clients. My mother grows remote again and appraises me—that mere possibility of success—with distrust. We rush down the employees' staircase to the children's department. She shops like a whirlwind, terrified that she might miss a customer during her absence from the millinery floor. I have begun to yearn for femininities: ruffles, organdies, the color pink. "Vulgar!" she exclaims at all my choices. "Not distinguished! How much time you take up in these things!" She settles hurriedly on a stern plaid woolen, a muted brown velvet, and we gallop back to her office. I sit again in the showroom, peering over my books. I stare at my idol as she drapes jerseys and moirés on the heads of more bejeweled New Yorkers, pinning aigrettes and feathers to felts and velvets, elaborating outlandish genealogies of sultans, harems, and victorious generals.

She sleeps in the small living room, one wall away from me. She sleeps in a large white daybed magically inherited, as was much of our furniture, from a wealthy American friend. At dawn I sometimes wake to that sound which I first heard when we shared a room under the Occupation, that sepulchral wail of her nightmares which is her only way of expressing her anguish. I rush into her room. She lies at the drugged edge of her sleep. "It is about my childhood in the Revolution," she whispers, "only about my childhood . . ." During such nights scraps of her life are occasionally revealed, in lean, disconnected fragments. A broken home, the great famines that swept Russia in the early nineteen-twenties. After her father had left them, she had lived with her mother and her sister, two grasping women who loathed her, in a room twelve feet by twenty. They had been racked by diseases—scarlet fever, diphtheria. From the age of fourteen she had helped to keep her family alive by reciting poetry at street corners to Red soldiers, in exchange for hunks of stony bread. She knew by heart Pushkin, Esenin, Lermontov, Blok, all of the great Russian poets. There had been so much suffering, hatred to forget that she would not write her mother again for over thirty years. Upon the birth of my second child, she sent her a picture of the babies, accompanied by a brief note. Some weeks later, a distant relative wrote back. The letter had arrived the day after her mother had died.

(For years I shall follow mothers and daughters on subways, down the street, in department stores, with the same obsessive curiosity with which a woman traumatized by barrenness follows beautiful children. Eavesdropping on their intimacies,

wondering how mothers and daughters spend afternoons together, what they talk about, how much they disclose to each
other. As for my mother, she will be enormously spoiled by
her second husband, a brilliant, staggeringly successful and
accomplished man. Her beauty of the nineteen-forties barely
altered save for the raucous joy of her eyes, she will spend the
mornings of her middle age wandering through her town house
in floral robes, roaring good-naturedly at her servants, gossiping
on the phone about the dinner party of the previous night,
devoting hours to the sumptuousness of her green plants.
Shortly before one she will put on her newest Saint-Laurent,
make her entrance into New York's most fashionable restaurant, roar her salute to a dozen acquaintances of note, float in
that pale indolence she loves—white walls, white damask, diamonds flashing on cream skins, waiters selling their cream
sauces. In a few hours she will sally forth in another dazzling
gown for her evening out, to pronounce those outlandish
aphorisms with which she continues to entertain her dinner
audiences: Albanians invented baseball, women's brains are
smaller than men's, Eugenia Sheppard is the greatest living
American writer . . . She will exit with a shrewdly devised
coughing fit from every gathering that bores her, continue to
receive poets, ambassadors, and successful playwrights, dance
late into the night at charity balls, refuse to deal with buses,
elevators, subways, plumbers just as she pleaded, in earlier
years, her helplessness in bringing up a child. Ah, let her be,
let her be! She is happier than ever before, her illusions more
protected than ever. After all, is truth a drug? Is truth a rem-
edy? Does it exist? Who's right? Who's wrong? Do we not
need lies as much as we need the truth? More than the truth?
Isn't reality so harsh that we are each entitled to find our own
panaceas—in war, ether, prayer, the playing of cards, the
adulation of success? The arrogance of those moderns who
teach us that we do not need myths to survive! That we do not
need dream, fantasy, ritual, escape to face the harshness of the
little death and the big sleep.)

And this is the way reality is often brought to us: by insects, by jesters who need to manufacture some importance in the little factories of our lives, by humans of such ordinariness that they are not worth more than a few pages of our memory.

Returning from school one day, I see my mother bending over a stranger in the bathroom tub, saying, "Look, Inge's only eighteen, and already a heroine! The heroine arrived today!"

An adolescent girl with short blond hair and wide hips lies in water scented with perfumed oil. She laughs as I come in, a wide studied laugh, and says, "Isn't it too bad I'm not married when I smell so good?" She looks at me shrewdly to see how much I know. She laughs again, sponging herself with a heart-shaped cake of pink soap. My mother is talking volubly at her, cheerfully praising and advising as she scrubs her back. How wonderful to be an adult! How miraculous to be able to talk to my mother!

Inge is a Dutch girl who fled Europe in dramatic circumstances after six months of Resistance work, and my mother pretends to admire her. Inge eats with us, spends weekends with us. My mother plays bridge most nights and weekends. She says that is where she meets her customers. Inge becomes indispensable.

Inge wears an engagement ring given her by a Free French officer she met the preceding spring. And yet she still cannot go to sleep without a rag doll—a fetish of her childhood—placed on her pillow.

Inge and I spend our weekend afternoons at the ballet, the opera. How she scrutinizes me as I slip out of my mother's embraces! As we sit over hot chocolate at Rumpelmayer's her eyes narrow to a greedy, searching gaze. "Why are you so withdrawn? Why do you reject your mother so—might you sense that she is hiding something from you?" I retreat sullenly from her forays. "What a clam you are, what a clam!"

Inge and I come home to play Monopoly. She tries to regain my trust by treating me like her contemporary. "Raise your skirt above your knee when a man looks at you, and he will know you desire him," she instructs me, fingering the skirt over her plump adolescent legs. "No, not like that, slower." Behind her, the electric ribbon winds relentlessly about the top of the General Motors Building, spelling: "British fleet engages *Bismarck* . . . Yugoslavs want neutrality . . ."

Inge raises her skirt still farther. Lascivious Susanna at her bath. Laughing always as if she were being watched by a crowd of yearning men. "Scratch the palm of his hand and he will know that you are willing, scratch the palm of his hands with two fingers."

"Cabinet crisis in Belgrade . . . Nazi troops occupy Sofia . . . Anti-Vichy riots in Syria . . ." Syria, Syria could be on the path of my father's secret mission. I cup my face in my hands and withdraw again into my obsession. I stare at my brown skirt, my drab brown sweater. How curious that she always dresses us in these fecal colors, as if we should be going to a funeral, while all around us the walls are white as forgetting, white as surgery. I start shivering violently, the way I remember shivering in the glacial seconds before surgical sleep, when the green-hatted doctors smile sweetly at me to allay the shock of the liquid finally flowing into my vein. That's it! Amnesia! Amnesia of this whiteness! Amnesia of her history! My own amnesia! "What's wrong with you?" Inge is shouting. "Why do you retreat so from everyone! What's been taken away from you?" I recoil violently from her touch, her voice, as from that of all others about me.

In that month of May 1941, almost a year after we'd left Paris, my obsessions with my father's silence lull me into periods of great withdrawal. I spend much of my free time in churches, or else walking the streets in search of men who resemble him.

My father's mission might last through the whole span of the war; his duty toward the Allied cause is mightier than his duty toward me.

He might be in hiding four, five years, he might not come back for a decade!

Or else he might come back sometime soon, any hour now, for just one day.

The phone will ring some evening as I sit alone in our apartment staring out at the electric headlines of the General Motors Building. I shall be beckoned to a secret meeting place: near the large meteorite at the Hayden Planetarium, in front of the Bronzino at the Frick. His Air Force uniform will have been temporarily changed for the incognito of a worn tweed suit. His hair will be grayed, he will be thinned and jaundiced by malaria.

I shall embrace him as I reassure him of the fervor of my faith in him. I shall search his eyes for that look of approbation which it is still the aim of my life to glean. We shall talk thus for an hour, our hands clasped, discussing our future together, the end of the war, the improvement of our fortunes, the purchase of a country house.

I am satisfied with such a brief meeting. I am resigned to the idea that after a last kiss, a benediction, he will fly back to his underground missions the very same day.

At Mass, when the tinkling of the bell announces the moment of total devotion, I stretch my tongue out and let the Host lie upon it, meditating on those irreverent questions I shall have to confess before I take Communion again: what kind of flour, what kind of water is it made of, how long is it baked, what makes it so flat, how would it taste if I chewed it, what would happen to my soul if I chewed twenty in a row? And just before I bow my head to acknowledge the wafer's touch, I remember how my father's adoring eyes used to laud me as his only happiness, his only immortality as I returned to our pew from the Communions of my childhood.

When I am not in church I simply spend the weekends pacing the streets, seeking a sign from him. When my mother goes out to her card games, I try to avoid Inge's outings, pleading headaches and indigestions, lying. On each of my walks the color of a uniform, another man's gait, make me follow a stranger with crazed energy. I follow him for many blocks at a time, delaying the sight of his face in order to delay the recurring, bitter disappointment.

We are walking down Fifth Avenue on a sunny June afternoon on which I have not been able to shake off Inge. I see a man walking a few yards away from us—my father's height and willowy build—vigorously stretch out his arm as if to relieve it of a cramp and then replace it in his jacket pocket. This simple gesture recalls precisely a habit of my father's. Inge is laughing next to me, swinging her wide hips, pointing at a barking dog. I step ahead of her, my schoolbag dragging limply behind me, and the din of the traffic grows like the roar of an oncoming train as I start following the stranger. Inge observes me as I follow him at a quickened pace. I pass him and look up at his face: a blond moustache, two glacial blue eyes. I stand still, head bowed. Inge picks my schoolbag off the pavement.

We lie in bed that night. Blazes of war news flood my room rhythmically with spurts of blue and orange radiance. In a flash of neon I see Inge's ring sparkle against the worn gingham of her rag doll. "Are you so strange because you do not know" —her pudgy child-woman's hand caresses the toy—"because you do not know enough about your father's death?" Her words fill the room, flow out of the window, return again with a flash of orange light. I lie resolutely; with determined vainglory, I tell her that I know all there is to know.

She sits up in bed smoking, silent for the first time since I have known her. Then she gets dressed and walks into the next room to wait for my mother's return. Not being able, I suppose, to bear the terrible storm of my tears. A minute or an hour later my mother's key turns in the lock. After a few whispers she rushes into my room, her face pale and disheveled with the fear of speaking truth. She wears the same black skirt, the same black crepe blouse, that she started wearing in France in June of 1940. It is a year, a few days over a year, since my father died, his plane shot down upon his very first mission for the Free French. Not until that night do I realize, with a flooding sense of my own monstrous cowardice, why she has worn black all the past year. My mother bends over my bed, we clutch at each other, our tears mingle for the first and last time. Why has she not told me earlier, I cry, why has she deceived me? Because she thought it would be easier with time, she sobs, because it is so hard for a child to understand. She caresses me, as we weep, with the dumb tenderness of a cat grooming her young. She stares into my eyes as into two cribs, still distrusting my capacity for achievement, wisdom, valor.

For years she would continue to look at me this way, with that searching yet evasive gaze, circumventing the truth of fact, refusing to face the harshness of its words.

When I grew up and became accomplished she began to trust me. When I achieved recognition she admired me, and we became great friends.

Most of us attempt, throughout our lives, to exorcise ourselves from the alluring spell of self-deceit. If we dare. But one illusion still haunts me, a dream I have had recurrently, since that June night, about my father.

Ageless and trembling, I lie on the floor of a room in Brittany, repeating, "When *did* he die, when *did* he die?" In this dream, I am rushing toward the end of my own life without remembering which stage of it was shrouded by his death. I sense that he has lived through my adolescence, has been cognizant of the chief turns of my life—graduations, marriages, the births of children—without giving me a sign of praise. He has abandoned me. In this dream, time shrinks plaintively like one note on the pleated stuff of an accordion; my childhood, adolescence, and womanhood shrivel into one moment of pain, I cram the quarter century that has passed since his death into one year in which, waiting for a sign, I received none. Toward the end of this dream, I try to open my eyes and I am aware only of a patch of blue sky, of the succulent purring of doves' voices, of stipplings of sunlight on the ceiling of Cécile's room at Saint-Seran. I strive then, as the dream ends, to forget my grief by sharing again the sweetness of her euphoria, her oblivion. She died, too, long ago, of an overdose of ether, a few days before she had planned to enclose herself within the walls of a Carmelite convent.

First Wings

1944

I

Two gym teachers in thigh-high apple-green tunics blow their whistles. We stand in two circles in the vast Lysol-scented school gym, our heads together, our arms stretched over each other's shoulders. In the circle opposing mine the brisk voice of my friend Janet Livingstone savagely leads those of her teammates. They scream, "White team, white team, rah-rah-rah!" My lips move mutely as my team vociferates its own cry: "Two-four-six-eight, who do we appreciate, gold team gold team . . ." The whistle blows again, chill as an air-raid siren, and the ball is thrown out. Janet plays a fierce forward. Her mastifflike face tightens into a predatory leer as she runs for the ball, her ungenerous mouth clenches into a hideous grin as she bends to wrench the ball from a Gold Team guard. I run behind her, my feet like butter. Her face puckers up into a disdainful smirk, her braces gleam savagely as she wheels around and jostles past me, she dribbles the ball triumphantly across the waxed yellow floor to flip it into the net.

We are thirteen. The athletic period dribbles by, time dribbles by punctuated by its familiar terrors: terrors of love and of not being loved, of speaking and of not being heard, of parents and of teachers, of never getting the ball and of getting it—what in hell would I do with the ball if I ever caught it? My arms are like noodles, my mind is with poor Lycidas. Weep no more O ye shepherds weep no more for Lycidas your sorrow is not dead sunk though he be beneath the watery floor. If I ever caught that ball I'd throw it out the window into the terrace of Miss Nightingale's School across the street, whence it would bounce into the façade of Miss Hewitt's ten blocks south, whence it would bang into the entrance of Miss Chapin's six blocks east, whence it would crash three blocks south into the stoop of Brearley's, smashing one window in each establishment to punish it for its team spirit. I'll break all your windows to punish you, for only the Anglo-Saxons, my beautiful Russian mother says, only the Anglo-Saxons make their women play team sports like men. And that is aesthetically unaesthetic, it is morally immoral. Women should be poetic, pacific, that's it, they should be made above all for individualism. I shall break your windows saying: with forced fingers rude I shatter your leaves before the mellowing year, bitter constraint and sad occasion dear compels me to disturb your season due, women should be gentle, pacific, nor yet where Deva spreads her wizard stream Ay me I fondly dream . . .

"Ouch!" I yell. "Foul, foul!"

Janet has tripped me, I lie on the floor inhaling an excruciating smell of varnish.

"She called time two minutes ago, you drip," she cackles. "Time to get off the moon, you sap."

And she runs into the locker room. The gym is empty. I rush in after her. Ah, relief of the locker room! Khaki gleam of locker doors, welcome odors of Mum, ammoniated footbath and dirty socks. Above the footbath stands a mysterious black box, the lovely desirable black box into which we drop slips of paper excusing us from three days of gym at a time. After gym even the school motto of Miss Temple's seems comforting, printed in green upon our blazers, in black upon our books, in yellow above the footbath: "NON SCHOLAE SED VITAE DISC-IMUS."

I stare at Janet's familiar body as she squirms out of her tunic. She is a product of Miss Temple's in its most aseptic form. She holds the records for the best posture, the greatest excellence in athletics, the fewest sick absences, the best citizenship, the neatest handwriting in the lower school. The fastidious rigidity of her posture, the savagely obedient backward thrust of her shoulders has given her an unpleasantly swayback figure. She stands over me, braces gleaming, thin white arms up, wriggling into a yellow sweater: "You're the slowest runner in the class, Stephanie, you drip. I bet you were thinking poetry, you sap."

"You make me sick," I answer calmly. I submit serenely to her castigations. She needs me, too. The exclusive friendship of this esteemed citizen is exchanged for my frequent class help. When I sneak answers to her in math and Latin tests she thanks me with a clandestine note: "You're my best friend. I'll love you 'til Ivory Soap sinks."

But toward the end of the eighth grade my two-year friendship with Janet Livingstone had begun to fade. She simply tortured me too much. For two years her thin cool hand had imperiously clutched mine as we lined up for assembly. For two years she had made me sit next to her through prayers, hymns, admonitions and classes as I stared with a mixture of envy and disgust at the chevrons and insignias, gleaming on her blazer, that rewarded her unsurpassed team spirit. Her cool reptilian hand continued to clutch mine on weekends. We sat together at endless birthday parties held by our classmates in the main dining room of the Carlyle Hotel (creamed chicken, bullets called peas, prestidigitators). I watched her ride and earn more insignias at the Ninety-fourth Street armory. (Was riding too expensive for me or was I scared of horses? Both.) Or we sat in some classmate's drawing room, trading cards, and this is where Janet exerted one of her subtlest tortures. "Trading cards" was the in game for girls from misses' classes in the nineteen-forties.

Trading cards was not a hard game—you collected jokers from your mother's, your aunt's, your mother's friends' bridge packs, and you tried to build up a bigger, lusher pack of cards than any other girl at Miss Temple's, Miss Hewitt's, Miss Chapin's, Miss Nightingale's. However, the status symbols were strictly delineated, the gradations were firm. The championship cards in the nineteen-forties were Gainsborough's *Blue Boy*, *Pink Boy*, and *Lady Hamilton*; Van Dyck's portraits of Charles I and James I on horseback; Sir Joshua Reynolds' portraits of Lady Bamfylde, of the Duchess of Buccleuch and of Colonel George C. Coonsander of the Grenadier Guards; Thomas Lawrence's *George IV*; and every Romney child available in bridge pack. These images scored ten points—they expressed the spirit of formality, gentility and Anglican opulence which it was the ambition of all misses' classes to emulate. Worth eight points or so, because though noble and depicting animals they were not of Anglo-Saxon stock, were Goya's *Marquesa de Montejos* and his *Family of Charles IV*, Velásquez's portrait of Philip II with his dogs, and any infantas by the same painter. Equally desirable were all cards with good pictures of animals: Potter's cows, Constable's landscapes if they had cattle in them, and, above all, any careful, fawningly photographic depiction of horses. Stubbs! Landseer! Hennings! I'll trade you my *Charles I* for your Masked Marvel. I'll trade you my *Duchess of Buccleuch* AND my *Lady Bamfylde* for your North Star. I'll even trade you my *Blue Boy* for Sir Galahad III. The young Protestant Establishment was horse-crazy, the Junior WASPs were obsessed by these beasts. Horses pranced on their bedroom wallpapers and across their Saturday blouses; fixtures in the shapes of stirrups and saddles supported their shoes, their bathroom glasses and their toothbrushes; the smell of leather and of saddle soap suffused their homes. They sat on the living-room floor, bickering, braids waving, and their little pelves quivered at the sight of a card with a purebred horse.

The first year Janet brought me into this game, in the sixth grade, she had me as she wanted me: submissive, impoverished, a sidekick. My pack was pathetic. I was hampered by the facts that my mother had rarefied, abstract tastes in cards and that she worked hard all week, like most refugees from France, and played a little less bridge than the other mothers. But my own sensibility was equally at fault. The little collection I'd built up was all wrong. I loved my Degas ballet dancers ("Ugh, too arty," Janet said.); my Frans Hals portraits (ugh, *poor* folk), my Botticelli *Birth of Venus* and *Spring* (ugh, they're naked), my Fra Angelico *Angel* (sissyish, icky-pooh). Above all I loved my Renoir picture of the girl sitting in the opera box, *Première Sortie;* I had a secret passion for the opera which I indulged in furtively, buying standing room on some Saturday afternoons when Janet was in a riding contest. This girl's soft, rounded beauty, her look of tender expectation, the reverent attentiveness which she bestowed on this greatest of spectacles, fulfilled all my ideals of womanly beauty. But the little braids waved disdainfully, the wiry shoulders shrugged impatiently, at the sight of Renoir's girl. She was "just plain icky-pooh," and I regretfully traded her for some desolate image of polo players, having assessed that the sensibility of all misses' classes were directed toward athletic feats, rigid social barriers, a more frigid elegance.

Janet was dictatorial, stingy, a sharp trader. "Buy yourself a decent pack at Dennison's," she ordered me one day early in the seventh grade, "something with horses in it, trade it in for one *Blue Boy*, a *Lady Hamilton*, a *Charles I*, and you can begin to build on that." I invested three weeks' allowance on a pack of Potters. Out of her desperate desire for love the only Jewish girl at Miss Temple's (one per misses' classes was about the average those days) gave up her *Blue Boy* for half my pack of Potters. With the rest of the pack I gambled on my classmates' growing sense of American citizenship, and gambled well. I acquired Copley's portrait of Benjamin Franklin, Inness' view of the Hudson, Leutze's *George Washington Crossing the Del-*

aware, and a large assortment of maudlin hunting scenes. I was in business. But in the eighth grade, when I had a top-quality pack, Janet began to get tough with me. It was her material supremacy over me in every domain that had cemented our friendship. "Don't you dare trade your *Red Boy* for Steph's *George Washington*," she whispered to Katrina, a glacial, exquisite blond athlete with whom she rode on Sundays. "Her *George Washington* is chipped, there's a grease spot on his horse's hoof." By the end of the eighth grade, when I could have played a top game without her deprecating tactics, Janet's comments about my pack had become downright humiliating. She made me sick.

The trading sessions were frequently held at the Livingstones' home, an aseptic apartment in the East Eighties where I often spent Saturday night. The Livingstones discussed makes of watches, bridge-bidding situations, jewelry insurance, safety locks, burglar alarms, the Truth about Meat Tenderizers, and other people's money. Mrs. Livingstone spent a good deal of her time commissioning custom-made plastic covers for her cars, typewriters, Gramophones, shoes, hats and Georgian tea sets. Coasters, lace mats, and crewel doilies were distributed throughout her rooms so as not to stain the polished genuine mahogany surface of her life. I took particular fascination in staring at the Livingstones' master bedroom. Its twin beds, covered in prune-colored silk, sheathed in clear plastic and set at a glacial distance from each other's, made me wonder how on earth Janet ever came to exist. She was an only child, born one January late in the Livingstones' marriage. And I calculated she must have been conceived between the changeover from winter damask table cloths to the summer's lace ones, during the week when winter clothes were meticulously shifted from clear plastic bags to quilted mothproof ones; on some spring day when, giddy with the delight of guiding her maids in the placement of new covers, Mrs. Livingstone had forgotten to put an obstacle between herself and nature's impulsive, staining sap.

But as Janet grew up she was as meticulously programmed, scrubbed and sheathed as every object in her surroundings. She closed doors with savage force, locked handbags, put caps back on toothpaste with the force of a wrench, shut off water taps with a vengeance. Her Christmas presents were bought, wrapped and stored by Halloween. A box of Kotex had been on her shelf since she had been ten years old, with a bulletin issued by some guidance service reassuring young females of the seriousness and inevitability of this event. No one at home had ever talked to me about puberty, and I read the bulletin with fascination every Saturday night: "You are about to face one of the *grand* experiences in woman's life . . . it is something that *every* woman must face . . ." When we were twelve, in the seventh grade, she got the curse. "*I* used up the *whole* box of Kotex over the weekend," she said superciliously. I despaired in silence. It was one more asset she had over me. She had always had pretty clothes, popularity, all those chevrons, pots of money, the best pack of trading cards in town, and now she had the curse.

Janet enjoyed flaunting her supremacy. After trading sessions we prepared for the evening and sat together in a tub filled with Friendship's Garden bubble bath. "My, Stephanie, you're in bad shape," she'd say, clucking her tongue. "Flab flab flab. Exercise is what you need. More exercise, less icky books." Then, splashing the bubbles onto her flat chest, she commented on the different fortunes of our classmates: "Puggsy's parents are very *wealthy*. . . . Katrina's parents are *rich*. . . . Audrey's parents are not *rich*, you old drip, they're just *comfortable*. *You're* just plain poor," she added with satisfaction. Then we got dressed in her horse-patterned flannel pajamas and lay on the floor listening to *Ellery Queen*, Rudy Vallee, *Inner Sanctum* and *Truth or Consequences*. After we'd gone to bed, Janet's voice continued whispering in the dark: "Puggsy's parents are so wealthy they've rented a whole movie theater for her birthday party. . . . Katrina's father has twenty-seven horses. . . . We're going to wallop Chapin at that basketball game next week. . . . If you're not nice to me, you frog, I'm going to get Katrina as my best friend. . . ."

Our friendship ended one day late in the spring of the eighth grade. Janet was a poor reader. I had humiliated her in English class, where she had misread a Shakespeare sonnet. "Shall I compare thee to a thummer's day," she lisped through her braces, "thou art more lovely and more temperature . . ." There was the usual cackle. And she saw me, clearly, leading the hilarity that followed her mistake.

She found me in the locker room, where I was staring at the black box after having dropped in the standard slip excusing me from three days of athletics. (Sometime in that past year I had begun to lie to Janet and pretend I had it, too.) Little black box! It held all deliverances (from childhood), all secrets (of womanhood), all eternal delights (of sex), all liberation (from gym). O Kaaba, black sacred rock, rectangular treasure suspended over the ammoniated footbath, when shall I stop lying to you? When will Stephanie become "a perfect woman, nobly planned, to warn, to comfort, and command"? . . . Janet burst into my incantations, her wrath whirled around me like a tornado. "Pink sunsets summer days poetry pee-ooh!" she screamed at me. A ray of light from the stark overhead bulb struck the metal of her braces, transforming her mouth into the hissing jaw of a predatory robot. "Pink sunsets, poetry opera that's all you think about, you drip!" Her braces blazed again over me, their brash gleam hideously offset by the moist stretching rubber bands that reinforced them. "Ickety-pooh you're nothing but a drip," she yelled. And she spat violently into the ammoniated footbath which we were urged to use daily to prevent athlete's foot. It was the only lawless thing which I ever saw her do. She then ran triumphantly into the gym, green pleats waving exultantly over wiry thighs, chevrons of achievement gleaming, face clenched with the determination of victory. My long friendship with this esteemed citizen was over. She went to camp that summer, to ride, of course, and we did not communicate. I was left alone with all the raw nostalgia, the incommunicable terrors of a thirteen-year-old romantic misfit. I was left free for the love of Joan Riley.

11

Two gym teachers in high pleated skirts blew their whistles. It was the sign to take partners for assembly; it was eight-forty in the morning of a September day. We were commencing the Upper School. The Upper School! That long-awaited period which, it had been gravely predicted, would prepare us for womanhood. And the new girl and I gravitated instinctively toward each other across the large yellow gym like two young, lonely animals.

It was Joan Riley's first day at Miss Temple's. It was I who must have sought her first, attracted by her extraordinarily large, round blue eyes, and by her total difference from any girl whom I had ever seen in that vast scrubbed gym. She exuded, at fourteen, an extravagant sexuality which pervaded any room in which she stood. Her figure had the grotesque exaggeration of calendar girls: a tightly cinched waist, broad hips, large breasts made ever more preposterous by the chaste white shirtwaist of our uniform. She had a small pug nose, a round face framed by glossy chestnut hair sleeked into a thick fat pageboy. Her dreaming cornflower-hued eyes were luminous, speckled with gold, fringed by outrageously long and thick lashes. But however arresting her eyes were, the most singular feature of her face was her round, fleshy, pouting mouth, a mouth that sucked voluptuously on a fat and lacerated thumb.

Sucking her thumb, she stood alone, with the inevitable shyness of a new girl, and then with some visible effort of willpower she withdrew it, and freed her plump mouth to smile at me. I asked her her name and we held hands as we stood in line, silent and shy among the autumnal twitter of greetings and recognitions. Janet, a few rows ahead of us, had lined up with her new friend Katrina. "You poor drip," Janet snickered. She stuck her tongue out at me. I stuck my tongue out at her. The new girl's hand was plump and warm in mine.

The music master strikes up the strains of the processional. We march: "O beautiful, for spacious skies, for amber waves of grain, for purple mountains' majesties, above the fruited plain . . ." A gavel knocks. The headmistress urges us to keep our voices low, our shoulders back, our heads high, our minds clean, our pockets ever ready for the poor, our actions team-spirited. Our class in particular is warned that it is beginning that year in education which will prepare us for woman-hood: *"Non scholae sed vitae discimus."* The Bible reading for the day is "When I became a man I put away childish things. For now we see through a glass, darkly; but then face to face . . ." Hymn time begins, and Joan's clear, chesty voice rises powerfully beside mine: "The church's one foundation is Jesus Christ our Lord . . ." The stark overhead light glosses her chocolate hair, the chaste white shirtwaist heaves with her breathing. It is clear that we both love music! We exit from assembly to Mendelssohn's "Wedding March" and stare at each other with deepening sympathy through Latin, math and history.

And then we get to English class. Joan's lovely eyelashes flutter wildly at the announcement that our term's study will consist of Romantic poetry! Our new English mentor in the Upper School is Mrs. Peters, a beady-eyed tyrant whose method of outlining literary movements is famous at Miss Temple's. She stands over us, her feet squarely parallel to each other, and violently bends the fingers of her left hand to illus- trate her points. "Romanticism: *One*," and her right hand pushes her left thumb until it almost touches her wrist, "an adulation of individual freedom, an impatience with social restraint. *Two*," and here her index bends back like a wire—Joan and I hold our breaths in suspense, "an unleashing of the well of personal emotion. *Three*," and her middle finger creates the most amazing arc of all, forming a perfect U with the back of her hand, "the renewed interest in natural landscape, in the manner and speech of common folk. *Four*, a distinct liberation of ethical standards." The ring finger stays twisted high in the air, Mrs. Peters' eyes are suddenly fixed critically upon Joan's chest. She pounces. "Read, Miss Riley, please, page twenty-two." The thumb pops out; Joan smiles with pleasure. She reads melodiously, mouthing each word with delight:

> "Blue isles and snowy mountains wear
> The purple noon's transparent night
> The breath of the moist earth is light
> Around its unexpanded buds . . ."

I watch with delight Joan's sluggishness, her helplessness at sports. The flesh of her indolent thighs waves like blubber, her small plump feet pat duck-footedly across the gym as she tries to defend the goal. She is all roundness and softness, all languorous curves. Wiry Janet jostles past her, dribbling the ball. "It must be jelly," she cackles, "'cause jam don't shake like that."

"Ooh, I hate gym," Joan moans to me during the next time out, her mouth puckered up like a baby's about to cry. "Ooh, how I hate it." My sympathetic look reassures her. "Stephanie, will you have tea today with me?" she ventures. "At Rose-Marie's? That rhymes," she adds tenderly.

Tea at Rose-Marie's! It was such a glamorous female offer. Until the Upper School our most sumptuous after-school release had been the boisterous drinking of milkshakes at the Seventy-ninth Street Schrafft's. It was a fine day, we walked a good part of the way, down Fifth Avenue. And Joan's womanhood purred beside me like a little motor. It was 1944. The posters on public buildings still said, "Keep Your Secret," "Buy *More* War Bonds," "Give *Your* Pint of Blood."

Rose-Marie's in 1944! Sad-eyed wives of Bulgarian psychiatrists, Hungarian dentists, White Russian generals, Viennese sinus specialists, Berlin violinists. Alabaster-skinned courtesans with ruby mouths, ruby claws, flowered turbans and Chihuahua dogs. Whipped cream, steaming chocolate, *Dobosch-Torte*, Ponchielli's "Dance of the Hours" oozing from the Muzak. Red velvet, red crystal, red satin, heart-shaped chairs, heart-shaped plates, heart-shaped cakes, everything as red and heart-shaped as Joan's sweet greedy little mouth. "This place is so *sensual*," she exclaimed as we sat down. "Are you in love?" We regretted that we were not. We cemented our friendship with a plateful of heart-shaped petits fours, we baptized it with cups of smoky tea. Oh, how Joan loved to eat! She ate voraciously, with short grunts of pleasure. I had not seen that thumb freed from her mouth so long all day.

And then we turned our attention to each other, discovering delights which we had missed in all our other childhood friends. She sang and painted and wanted to be an actress, I danced and wrote and desired to be a novelist. We both hated sports. We loved poetry, the opera, the ballet. We were both lapsed Catholics, and professed we were snobs. Goodness, how different we were from the other girls! The Temple girls had photographs of horses pinned to their wallets, what did we have on *our* wallets? A photograph of Igor Youskevitch taking the final window leap in *Le Spectre de la Rose*. Our favorite reading of the past year (and Joan had lived in Cincinnati all her life before this fall—it *must* have been telepathy) had been *The Stories of the Great Operas*. It did not matter whether we'd seen these operas in full or heard them in snatches, whether we saw them once a month or knew we could never see them. We had memorized their plots and the names of all their heroines, however obscure, as if the fierceness of their passions held the secret to our future happiness. We even knew the plots of Gounod's *La Nonne Sanglante*, of Meyerbeer's *L'Étoile du Nord*, of Donizetti's *Linda di Chamounix*, of Berlioz' *Les Troyens*, of Puccini's *Le Villi*, of Verdi's *Luisa Miller*. We pledged to go together to see *Lucia* that Saturday afternoon. We baptized the Temple girls "Tiny Teemies" for their team spirit. I thrilled at Joan's prettiness when she laughed. She reminded me, with her bangs, her pout, her flowerlike face, of that Renoir girl whose beauty the Teemies had disdained. As I took up my wallet with the leaping Youskevitch she said, "What artistic hands, oh my so delicate, I mean you must be a *creative* person!" I was gawky and flat-chested, almost fully grown to a height of five feet eight inches. I still wore high knee socks and was made to curtsy, and her compliments gave me more self-esteem than I had ever had. We parted on the corner of Seventieth Street and Fifth Avenue, in front of the Frick, where we decided to meet the following Saturday before the opera.

Joan insisted on taking a taxi to the Metropolitan. "My father's a mess, my mother's a nothing, my grandmother's the only interesting one," she confided on the way. "I can't wait to leave home." We sat entranced through *Lucia di Lammer-moor*. "Oooh, they love each other so," Joan groaned. "Don't you love passion?" We showed off to each other by whispering the names of the oncoming arias. "Here comes 'Il pallore funesto orrendo,' " I'd say. "No," Joan corrected, "it's going to be 'Quando rapita.' " Then Joan's eyes wandered nostalgically to the boxes above. "Wouldn't it be wonderful to be seated up *there*," she waved, "in a box, at *night*, with a man who wants you, after a beautiful dinner?" But our center fifth-row seats seemed magnificent to me. They had been bought for Joan that week, at the spur of the moment, for what must have been an enormous price. And I decided that the Rileys were the most liberal people I had ever heard of.

The Rileys consisted of a newly rich, buck-toothed father and a dumpy art-student mother whom Joan called "Shawn" and "Mary," in the manner of her former progressive schools;

also of a rouged, lascivious, coquettish grandmother whom everyone called "Dearest." The features of the three Riley women were so similar—their round faces, their bangs, their blue Irish eyes, their fat breasts, their thick short legs, their gaudy clothes—that they looked like a set of those gaily painted wooden dolls that fit neatly into each other. And they contrasted strangely with the trim, tweedy mothers of my other schoolmates. The Rileys' affluence was a creation of the war. Shawn had been 4-F and had made a fortune in Cincinnati manufacturing linoleum for battleships. He had retired at the age of forty. Whenever Joan, Mary or Dearest saw anything she desired—gourmet food, a dress in a Fifth Avenue window, a house on Long Island—she screamed, "I want it, I want it!" Her fat little feet drummed violently upon the floor. And then she bought it. They ate voraciously, discarded clothes after two wearings, indulged in erratic courses of study and sloppy, massive doses of psychoanalysis. The Rileys had no friends in the big city, and eagerly adopted me. I was a foreigner. So different, so creative, so sensitive! I wallowed in their permissiveness, their naïve greed for sensibility.

Adieu, trading cards! That golden October Joan and I spent our Saturday afternoons seeing *L'Elisir d'Amore*, *Norma*, *Madama Butterfly* and *Manon Lescaut*. And we lunched on tins of brandied peaches and improvised ballets to a recording of *Le Spectre de la Rose*. And we read Kahlil Gibran. And we memorized seventeen positions from Van de Velde's *Ideal Marriage*, with reverence, without our classmates' sneaky giggles. Dearest had told Joan that sex was beautiful, desirable, lovely, and she passed this assurance on to me. So to be ready for it we concentrated on becoming Beautiful Women. We sent mail orders for plastic contraptions to squeeze out our blackheads; we lathered our faces with masks of grated cucumber and puréed strawberries; we tightened our pores with nourishing egg yolks followed by astringent egg whites. We dieted and rested like courtesans in Joan's ruffled bedroom, snubbing Puggsy's movie party at Loew's, Janet's riding party at the armory. Joan was as generous as she was spoiled, as liberal as Janet had been stingy. She showered me with flowers and twice-worn dresses, with perfume and books of poetry. The only trouble with Joan was that she was so impatient about love.

"Shelley. *One*," Mrs. Peters said, "his conception of human nature: goodness and perfectibility. *Two*, the stress of instinct: The sad still music of humanity must be felt before it is comprehended. *Three*, his *unconventional* ethic and his *tragic, tragic* end." Joan and I sighed, we dashed to the library to write long papers on Shelley. "Shelley was said to be an atheist," she wrote, "but no one who believed in the things Shelley believed in could ever be an atheist. Shelley was deeply religious in his own way, he believed in goodness and nature and beauty, in the utmost freedom of the mind, he thought that everything that came from nature was right and good." "Shelley loved animals and children," I wrote. "At the age of fourteen Shelley already had his beliefs; he would sit for hours by the river, preaching to his charming companions about the vulgarness of marriage, the supremacy of nature, the beauty of things in their natural state."

We suffered in gym together. " '*Ah, morire potesso adesso,*' " she moaned to me at a break in the basketball game, as she leaned, panting and flushed, against the window. " '*Protegga, il giusto cielo,*' " I murmured back, " '*solitgo errante misero.*' " One day as we were changing from our green gym rompers, and the other girls were out of earshot, I confided to her about my lies to the black box. Her reaction was infinitely tender. "*Everybody* gets it," she said, "especially you, you're *so* feminine. Start later, you'll last later." She winked knowingly. We began to time our menstrual periods to each other's in order to have gym-free afternoons together. We made our periods last six, seven, eight days. We went to Rose-Marie's, to the

Frick where we were enamored of Bronzino's *Man with a Gauntlet*, to the Modern where we stood in awe of Tchelitchev's *Hide and Seek*. Later in the fall, stunned by the ease of it, we were indisposed for ten, twelve, fourteen days. We went to Arden's for massages; to palmists, tea-leaf readers and astrologers to find out if Joan would soon find love; we met Dearest at Bergdorf's to shop for Joan's luxuriant wardrobe; and when winter came we spent afternoons helping to plan Shawn Riley's feverish parties.

Saturday night at the Rileys'! Joan and I stand in front of the mirror in her ruffled bedroom, preening with Dearest. Joan is attired in some new garment of deeply cleaved red satin which grotesquely exaggerates her precocious curves. Her hair is fluffed into an outlandish pompadour and held back with a fake rose. She wears high tight pumps to minimize the width of her plump feet, and little folds of flesh hang sadly over the rims of her shoes. The outlandish makeup which Dearest is painting on Joan's babyish pouting face—rouge, kohl liner, umber eye shadow—gives her the tinsely glitter of a carnival queen. I stand alongside her wearing one of her twice-worn dresses, guilt weighing from my network of lies. My mother and stepfather, like all other Temple parents, won't hear of the Rileys: the Rileys are gauche, vulgar, *à côté*. And I sneak out most Saturday nights in my habitual drab plaids and high knee socks —with the pretense of a double-feature movie—to be transformed by the Rileys into a burning Cinderella. Dearest paints me too and instructs us how to wear perfume—"Here behind the knee, above your slip, where it is most seductive." We take a final pose in front of the mirror. "You are beautiful women," Dearest cries, "perfectly beautiful women!"

The guests begin to arrive. They are a motley lot gleaned by Mary from her painting, pottery, weaving and recorder classes; by Shawn from his classes in furniture refinishing and his psychiatrist's waiting room; by Dearest from her volunteer work at the USO and her language classes at Berlitz. They are art students, lay analysts, ski instructors, decorators, hairdressers, lesbian *diseuses*, fashion models, manicurists, sailors on leave, teachers of Portuguese and Swahili. A few adventurous juniors and seniors from misses' classes appear, accompanied by pimply private-school boys eager for the Rileys' notorious largesse.

Shawn Riley stands behind his makeshift bar by the piano, serving Martinis and champagne in highball glasses. "Want a drink, Steph honey?" His red shirt looms above me, open low onto his hairless, pudding-colored chest. "Have a drink, the well-balanced personality appreciates a good drink." His buck-toothed smile becomes arrogant and challenging. "Don't be a baby, I'm one of the kids."

The hairdressers titter, the sailors weave, Dearest and Mary, grotesquely dressed in girlish flounces, mince among the decorators. Joan and I parade in our sad womanly regalia, the champagne going to our heads. Then Shawn bellows, "A little something for the oral stage!" and we pass on to the dining room, where some caterer has spread a lavish buffet. There is black-market caviar, sturgeon flown in from Alaska, goose liver in the shape of policemen, fish molds in the shape of swans. Champagne corks pop to the ceiling, the lights are dimmed in the Rileys' living room, the seniors from Miss Nightingale's, Miss Hewitt's, Miss Temple's are throwing up in the bathrooms. The Victrola blares out and we dance to "Praise the Lord and Pass the Ammunition," "Eliminate the Negative, Accentuate the Positive," "Chattanooga Choo-Choo." Joan dances as in a trance, her eyes closed, her Pekingese nose flattened at the passionate contact with some new cheek, paper flowers tumbling from her hair, nipples straining against the tight satin of her gown, will this be love? Dearest hugs her Berlitz instructor. Mary sways in the arms of an eighteen-year-old potter. A ski instructor is squeezing the life out of me. Never never ask a man you're dancing with, Dearest always says, " 'What are those large keys you carry in your pocket?' " Never ask anything. Just dance on. We dance on we tango we waltz we paso-doble. There's an intermission, thank God, and someone sits at

the piano to imitate Burl Ives singing "The Foggy Foggy Dew."
Someone else imitates Alec Templeton's imitation of "The Ride
of the Valkyries." ("*Hiya towhoe-ho! Hiya towhoe-ho!*")
Then the conga line begins and the party has become one huge
snake, one-two-three-kick, one-two-three-kick, the snake winds
through the empty maids' rooms, through the dining room
where the vanilla swan has melted over the remains of the
sturgeon and the liver policeman, Shawn leads the line screaming, "Hey Dearest the kids are having a good time!" And
Dearest's eyes glitter as she points to the couples breaking away
from the conga line, then drifting toward the dark empty
maids' rooms.

But Joan returned disheveled and dissatisfied from those
dark rooms, mascara running down her fat cheeks, running
down onto that thumb which she had reinserted into her mouth.
Poor Joan, chaste Joan! She promised so much and gave so
little. Men did not ask her out again after the brief tussles in
the maids' rooms, and she was outraged by the lasciviousness
of their advances. Joan returned to school depressed on Mon-
days.

Monday was the day to begin a new poet at Miss Temple's.
"Coleridge. *One,*" Mrs. Peters said. "Early revolting against
tradition, Coleridge became an apostle of the French Revolution. *Two:* Addicted to opium, his production was mostly a
series of splendid plans with fragmentary performances. *Three:*
an interest in the supernatural as the tool of revelation. Read,
Miss Livingstone, please, page forty-four."

Janet was president of our freshman class that year. She had
sprouted small, pointed breasts and discarded her braces. But
her little face was as mastifflike, her lips as thin and mean as ever,
and she still could not read.

> "The shadow of the *dame* of pleasure
> Floated midway on the waves,

Where was heard the *mangled* measure
From the fountain and the cave . . ."

Cackle, snicker, titter. Mrs. Peters brandishes a theme paper.
"Some of you can't read," she barks, "and some of you can't
write. Let not those who cast the first stone . . . I have a paper
here by Miss Riley saying that the poetry of Coleridge is sensu*al*.
Now, Miss Riley, you may mean sensu*ous*, but you do not
mean sensu*al*. How many times have I told you"—her supple
finger waves metronomically over Joan—"sensual means the
evil desire of the *flesh*."

But poor Joan's sensuality, her sweet, mawkish sensuality,
hissed anxiously that year among the busts of Dante and Gabri-
elle d'Este, under the color posters of Mont Saint-Michel and
Stratford-upon-Avon. It swelled aimlessly under the melancholy gaze of the original Miss Temple, in the oak-paneled
library where we wept over the death of Keats, in the waxed
brown corridors that smelled of formaldehyde, library paste
and perpetually cooking meatloaf. It simmered in the damask-
draped drawing room where we sat waiting for our lunch
(knees never crossed, feet together) in the genteel dining room
with reproductions of the *Pink Boy*, the *Blue Boy*, *Lady Buccleuch*. Joan and I stared at Janet and Katrina, who had spent
their first Upper School Christmas whirling at the St. Mark's–
Groton and Junior Assemblies, they had even been once to
Larue's. And something novel in their demeanor—the pomade
glistening on their smug lips, the smile like a yawn, the pre-deb
glaze—signaled that they were getting precisely as much as
they wanted out of men. "But we're so much prettier," Joan
moaned. "When are we ever going to be in love?"

Summer came. The Rileys left for their new house in Montauk, where I spent a few weeks of the vacation. It was a fine
eighteenth-century house with broad beams and narrow stair-
ways. Joan and I swam and played croquet—our one conces-
sion to athletics. We took long walks on the Montauk beaches,

our hair free and wild behind us. We sat on rocks discussing God; our pantheism had grown firmer with our winter's reading of the Romantics. " 'The world is too much with us,' " Joan recited with a sigh. " 'And nothing can bring back the hour,' " I answered, " 'of splendor in the grass, of glory in the flower . . .' "

We sunbathed like pagans. Shawn made lamps out of driftwood and refinished furniture. Dearest read novels about Madame de Pompadour and Empress Theodora, Mary wove baskets and played the recorder.

"You have such a beautiful influence on Joan," Dearest would say when Joan was out of earshot.

"Maybe you can even get her through school," Shawn quipped.

"Well, Joan has such a lovely voice," Dearest said, "she's too creative to be disciplined."

"She's so warm," Mary agreed, "she has such a beautiful soul."

"She needs a man," Dearest sighed, "she needs a man badly."

It was the following fall, at some Glee Club concert, that Joan finally found romance. Love came in the form of a tall, slow, heavyset Southwesterner called Bill Moons. He had been born in China, where his father had held a small post in the Foreign Service, and this touch of exotica may have sparked Joan's fire—along with the fact that he was wild about her. He had little else to recommend him, except his height, a sizable allowance, and a plump bland baby face which Joan must have considered beautiful. He was six foot two or three and reminded me of those four-inch-long strawberries, those ten-inch wide tomatoes, which win prizes in American agricultural contests but have no perfume or savor whatsoever. It struck me then, as it does now, that such exaggerated and precocious bodies as Joan's arouse the appetites of slow, lymphatic men. Bill was eighteen, a freshman at Columbia, played limp renditions of Puccini on the piano, and needed three daily grains of thyroid to stay on his feet. His most frequent expression was "my lands." He loved to eat, and Joan easily wheedled him into taking her to the most expensive restaurants in town. "My lands," he moaned the next day, "the bills that girl can run up! Caviar, quail, raspberries out of season—my lands!" Bill Moons had an extraordinary fund of unnecessary and irrelevant information which we called, in our nineteen-forties lingo, "serendipitous." He knew the height of every mountain in the Himalayas, the name of every ship on the Grace Line, and the schedule of every train in the United States. "If you've got your heart set on going to New Orleans," he'd drawl, "the way to do it is to take an eight-twenty-seven at Penn Station on the New Jersey line as far as Philadelphia, transfer to the Southern Limited and catch a one-thirty-four to Richmond, there you sashay down to the Southern Pacific line and you catch a seven-thirty-four for New Orleans, and, my lands, you're there just a few hours later." Joan listened to him reverently, her thumb in midair. He was the first man, truly, who had lusted after her body and her soul.

Joan and Bill dreamed and ate together that Christmas, and sometime after Christmas they began to sleep together. I accompanied them for a few winter weekends to Montauk. "Safety in numbers," Dearest had said, winking, knowing precisely what it was all about. I slept alone on those weekends in the steep-roofed room which Joan and I had shared the previous summer. But when I saw her, at times, coming out of Bill Moons' room in the morning, I realized that love had not yet touched her, and perhaps never would. She emerged from their bedroom in an expensive lace nightgown, her chestnut hair rumpled, looking thoughtful and dissatisfied. She'd stand at the edge of the bathroom door or at the top of the stairway landing, sucking her thumb and stroking her throat in her old way, her plump feet blunt and childlike under the lace of her gown. I knew she felt some gnawing disappointment in the attainment of her dream. She stood there in her strange isolation, too en-grossed to greet me, and the smell of her warm flesh was potent and sour.

"How was Act Three?" I asked.

"Just fair," she answered. I had a way of jolting her back to reality, and her laughter pealed again like that of a tickled child.

Later that winter my habit of spending Saturday afternoons with Joan had to be abandoned. She grew increasingly dis-traught and glum. She was terrified, I suspected, of losing Bill Moons' lumpish burning lust for her. Bill was possessive about Joan, and wanted her to himself. But I was happier in school that year than ever before. My work was going well, I made friends with other girls, and even went to Janet's skating party at Rockefeller Center, and to Katrina's swimming party at the Junior League. However, Joan still needed me. That spring she became pregnant, and she begged me to attend the news-giving.

Shawn was irate, Mary inert, Dearest was tearfully lenient.

"Moons is a goon." Shawn banged on the table, and his buck-teeth protruded farther than ever in his flaccid face. "From the start I've thought he was nothing but a goon. And when do you think you're going to finish your education? What are you going to tell them at Miss Temple's?"

"I'll cross my fingers and hope it doesn't show before the end of the term," Joan wept.

"Next time just cross your legs."

"But Bill is beautiful," Dearest whined. "He'll take good care of Joan."

"He's wealthy," Mary said, chewing her dinner.

"Well, he's not wealthy, but he's comfortable," I said, and I suddenly realized that I was aping Janet's vocabulary.

"He loves nice things," Mary said.

"I got married when I was fifteen," Dearest said. "What's wrong with getting married young? She'll make a beautiful bride."

In the last weeks of school Joan grew terribly nauseous. Her work dropped miserably, she failed every subject except English and singing. "Ooh, I'm going to be sick," she moaned to me, usually in Latin class. Her face puckered into the red, fist-like scowl of a five-year-old; I grabbed her hand and rushed with her to the bathroom. "Ooh, those smells," she moaned as we ran down the waxed brown corridors. But the Lysol, the formaldehyde, the library paste, the cooking meatloaf suddenly seemed sweet and reassuring compared to her predicament. I stood over her as she gagged. She pleaded an intestinal virus with the school nurse, and spent most of the remaining days at home.

We stood at commencement singing "Gaudeamus Igitur," staring at the senior class on the stage of the assembly room. They wore long white dresses and clutched red roses. The headmistress admonished us that the senior class had learned not for school but for life: "*Non scholae sed vitae discimus*." She hoped that we would all become, like them, "a perfect woman, nobly planned, to warn, to comfort, and command." " 'And now we see through a glass, darkly,' " she continued, " 'but then face to face . . .' " The seniors smiled, they yawned, they sang "Out, Out in the Cold, Cold World."

Graduation was over, and the Rileys went quickly back to Cincinnati to get Joan married. They left the big city as suddenly, as nomadically, as they had arrived in it. Joan and I clutched at each other and wept as we parted, and promised to write—but never did.

But there were other girls, and there was my new sense of assuredness, and my new love of power. The fall after Joan left I became president of the junior class. My best friend was Puggsy, the girl whose parents rented Loew's theaters for birthday parties. I went less to the opera, and succumbed to Puggsy's obsessive passion for movie magazines. We combed our hair like Veronica Lake, as Janet and Katrina did, and tried to dress like Linda Darnell. I joined the Stage Crew, the Camera and Science Club, the Debating Team, and even won a chevron for field hockey. At the end of the junior year, Janet and I ran against each other for election as president of student council. She won by a narrow margin—ten votes or so—which made me vice-president of student council on top of being editor of the school paper, *Temple Tempo*. Puggsy was president of the senior class, Katrina was captain of the White Team. It was a busy year. We all went on to the colleges of our choice.

In my cursory glances at Miss Temple's alumnae magazine I always hunted for just one item—news of Joan Riley Moons, class of " '48x." The "x" means "not graduated," but most girls who have attended Miss Temple's retain such devotion to the establishment that they go on reporting their news even if they went on to graduate from Foxcroft, say, or Madeira. I had no other means of finding news of Joan. The Rileys had left no forwarding address and we had no mutual friends—the Rileys had just been too different. The trouble with alumnae magazines is that you're always hearing news of precisely the girls you're not interested in hearing about, the girls with the most predictable futures—Janet, for instance. When I went to Radcliffe Janet went to Finch Junior College, and she married the year she graduated—a Dartmouth man whom she'd met years before at the St. Mark's–Groton dances. She is the first one to report to the alumnae magazine, of course, with such reassuring statements as "We are still in Riverdale, and my name is still Mrs. Wilder Throot III. I am kept busy as ever by the antics of Wilder Junior, 2½, and one-year-old Arlene. Other additions to the family are Chicago, the Boston bull; and Pixie, a hamster. Between children and charities, time really flies! Involvements include Back Bay Boys' Club, Green Grass Ball, Neighborhood Youth projects, fund raising for Mental Health and Hepatitis drives." The alumnae magazine was replete with such accounts, but I kept on looking, without success, for news of Joan. She had given me something important: tenderness; security the year I needed it the most, that uncertain year between childhood and puberty; the tinsel glitter of my first wings.

At Twenty-three

1954

I

On one of the nights Louis Bonaparte said he was leaving me I decided that I would commit suicide in a tributary of the Seine. There would have been something showy about doing it in the center of Paris which he would have been the first to find in poor taste. Just imagine the headlines: 23-YEAR-OLD AMERICAN JOURNALIST FOUND DROWNED OFF THE ÎLE DE LA CITÉ . . . NEAR THE CONCIERGERIE . . . UNDER THE PONT NAPOLEON III (that would really have been the end). So the problem was to find some more discreet place, farther removed from his office and from my mother's friends, who all seemed to congregate in the vicinity of the Dior Boutique. During that last recitation of his ("I am totally corrupt, you torture me too much, I cannot stand your purity," etc.) we had both been quite drunk. After he left I had taken a double dosage of my sleeping pills—Nembutal, Doriden, Luminal, Seconal, I forget which, in the nineteen-fifties I used to alternate them daily for maximum effect. And the next morning the downstairs neighbor must have knocked at my door for half an hour before I woke up, to complain that my clogged sink was dripping into her bathroom.

By the time I did wake up I was in too much of a stupor to go to work or to suicide. It was just one of those days when I had to hold the cold compresses up and the hot tea down as long as possible, wondering how long I could last in this ghastly city, why I'd ever come here in the first place.

So, no search for a discreet suburban river bank after all. Good girl, you're improving your ability to change your mind gracefully, without any of last year's existential claptrap about radical decision-making, either/or, et cetera. After all, I should make another try at being happy with Louis, he's made to order, he's everything my mother ever wanted for me. She had always made me feel so boring, now that I'd hit the jet set, she might perk up and find me interesting. Prince Bonaparte—not the oldest title available, obviously, barely 150 years old, but Mama was not choosy that way. Fanatic rebellion against my mother's precepts for two years, followed by docile compliance, then back to rebellion: that had been my life since I'd been at Miss Temple's and all through Radcliffe, and here I was back in the obedience phase, all meek and tame again. Just think, eighteen months ago I was in "the vanguard of the Beat generation," as they called us at Black Mountain, an anarchist artists' commune where I spent the summer—I was a gypsy with shorn tomboy hair bursting into my parents' cocktail parties from Cambridge or Greenwich Village or North Carolina to spout Karl Marx and Kenneth Patchen. Amazing. That was only last year, and today here I am picking up the phone in my little Paris apartment, saying, "I'd like to speak to the Baroness de Rothschild. . . . Oh, she's not in? Could you leave her a message that I'll be absolutely delighted to come to dinner three weeks from Monday?" Next: "Givenchy Boutique? Miss Monique? How are you, angel? Listen, do you have a little *numéro* I could borrow for just this evening, I fit into your size-six mannequin samples, as you know. . . . Black chiffon would be absolute perfection. . . . Oh, you're always such an angel. Goodbyyyyyyyyyyyye."

So. No headline. Anyway, when they found me drowned under that bridge they might not even call me "journalist," just "working girl." "You're not a journalist," Coco Chanel had just told me a few months before when she'd had me to dinner with my mother, "you're just a poor *child*." That rodent face, those mean little teeth. "Screw you, Coco," I mumbled to myself over her creamed codfish, "someday I *will* be a journalist, and what are you anyway but a dirty old collaborationist." Very pleasant, the prospect of returning to the rebellion phase, when I can yell such things out loud **again**. Soon, maybe soon!

Louis works at the Paris branch of General Electric, placing orders for shipments of household appliances to other regions of France. Evenings, he goes home to the sad old apartment where he lives with his mother and sister, where he has lived since his birth. In his spare time he writes Surrealist prose poems in which I glimpse evidence of some talent. What an existence for the descendant of a conqueror! Yet there is wisdom in the ridiculous way he still lives with his mother and sister at the age of thirty-six, choosing not to dine out more than two or three times a week "so as not to hurt their feelings," as he puts it, terrified of not being found in his own bed in the morning when his mother sends the maid up with his breakfast tray. L. and I share a major phobia: the fear that permanence drives all ecstasy to decay, forces all bliss to putrefy. Is there any better preparation for the boredom of marriage than L.'s monumental doses of family life? What savvy. What an absolutely splendid husband he will make, gliding into the tedium of the tribe with all axles greased, able to smile serenely through family dinners whose conversations go: "I love apricot tarts with almond filling." "Do you really? I prefer them with apple glaze." "You do not! You've always told me you preferred them with almonds!" "Well, that's the way I like them in winter, when there are no fresh apples, but in autumn . . ." Actually that's similar to L.'s favorite scene in contemporary literature, a passage from Ionesco's *The Bald Soprano* in which the family conversation goes: "Well, it is nine o'clock. We have eaten soup, fish, potatoes with lard—potatoes are very good with lard, the oil was nice and fresh . . ." L. recites that scene with delectation as we study restaurant menus during our weekly dinners together, his face swathed with that haughty, fatuous smile which protects him much of the time from strong emotions, meaningful conversations. I well know that he does not find me "presentable" enough—on his mother's terms—to ever invite me to the theater where he rehearses his script for life's tedium. So I take great pleasure in imagining him declaim phrases of equally majestic monotony concerning the cooking of peas, rabbits, hams, camels, rutabagas. I also enjoy wondering whether his family gives him hell, as I do, when he drinks the seventh Scotch in a row, whether they make him wash his hands before he sits down to dinner. Out in the world, it is in part L.'s unkemptness that attracts me: unbarbered hair falling helter-skelter about a yellow collar, tie perpetually askew, the ruffian air of tobacco-stained teeth. He acts as if the sheer historicity of his name absolves him from all criticism, as if he is the only man in Paris who can afford to look like Ben Barka unwashed and still have hordes of women clamoring after him. L. is a tall, solidly built man whose powerful, mastiff-jawed head tends to look too large for his body. When he smiles the network of lines around his green eyes makes him look like a dissolute Buddha. There is something Levantine about the thick arch of his nose, his sensual and indulgent mouth. I find his eyes extraordinarily green, jade green, Nile green, lyrical in their cynicism.

"I wish I could have ecstasy all the time!" he once says to me. "Ceaselessly and unabatedly, do you hear? Every day of my life!"

We are sitting by the river on a rainy Sunday afternoon. Since the evening before we have made love six, seven times. It is the first weekend he has spent a whole night with me, having invented an elaborate excuse to his mother about a Saturday pheasant shoot.

"Perhaps you do have it," I reply sourly, "but you don't know you have it."

"I adore you," he cackles. He says that when I amuse him.

"You think of happiness as one continuous blast of sunshine. I think of it as scraps of blue sky constantly killed by the next cloud, tiny scraps I can hold on to no more than a few seconds. I'm quite happy going about like an alley cat, hunting down those scraps."

"Is that what you want of men, dear girl?" We are sitting listlessly in the rain, not touching each other, like overfed children.

"Precisely that. Scraps of ecstasy."

"Well, I'm not satisfied with scraps, do you understand? Not satisfied with those scraps you give me, with those scraps I give you." He stretches his arms to the river. "I would prefer the absolute! Bliss everlasting! Palaces besides! Fortunes to spend! Eternal felicity!"

Notre-Dame looms its backside at us, its buttresses stark and swollen, like the ribs of a dinosaur.

"You worry too much about your ecstasy," I yawn, "it's dangerous. You're so afraid of your bliss decaying that you'd rather stick with family boredom, and that way *you*'ll decay even before you ever get any ecstasy."

"But I'm terrified, Stéphanie, don't you see, terrified of becoming too attached to you, and then disillusioned." This is what we mostly talk about, *his* fear of all attachment, I can seldom get in a word edgewise about *my* fear of it. "What if you were Cinderella, what if I'd found in you the only woman who can wear the slipper? Just think, what an awesome notion: the notion that there is one single person in the world who suits us better than any other human, that we have finally found the other half of that primal being Plato writes about. What happens if something goes wrong *then*? The whole universe collapses! By the way, have you ever pondered the erotic implications of the Cinderella story? For one thing, that slipper was not made of glass, but of fur. The word 'glass' came out of a semantic confusion: *Le soulier de vair*, the *mink* slipper, was stupidly translated as *verre*, or glass. I abhor imprecisions of language."

A petulant, disdainful shrug. God, how the French can talk. About a stew, about a fly on the parapet, about death, about anything.

"One little foot in the kingdom," he continues, mincing, "is the one best fitted for my fur slipper. This pornographic tale has been lovingly told to children of all ages for many centuries. What erotic riches our folklore holds."

"You're so goddam romantic."

"I am not," he howls, as if I were stripping him of a Legion of Honor. "I am a quintessential cynic!"

"Is that what you fear about women? That your love might decompose the way the fur slipper might decay?"

"Of course. Because decay haunts every passion of our life. Once the ideal woman is grasped, handled, kissed, fucked, she necessarily runs the risk of degenerating into a mangle of meaningless flesh. That's why we must not try to last together for too long, why I must not touch you too often, because our touching is so perfect."

"Perfectly correct."

"Besides," he adds, giving my hair an amiable tug, "I abhor left-wing intellectuals."

"I'm not complaining. I adore my garbage cans."

I throw a pebble into the river. What polite lies I tell him. It's part of my courteous nice-to-Mommy phase, oh boy am I ever congenial, docile, subservient in this incarnation. The truth is that L. has found in me the two things he fears the most: poverty and a capacity for passion. Whereas I have found in him all that I desire the most in this particularly lunatic phase of my life: the glamor of history, the flash of his Paris *monde*, torture. Ah, yes, he certainly tortures me, he tortures me by denying me what I have never wished from any other man: to be totally subservient. I would not only have married him—the first time I ever desired that servile state—I would be happy to be his official mistress, his official slave. Something holds him back from offering me the abjection I secretly crave. Not enough love? The convolutions of his sadism? His mother's dominance?

Once, while skating on a winter day (so begins one of the literary fragments L. sends me in the mail almost weekly), *a young woman rushed up to me with a lightning stroke of her skates, stopping by me in a voluminous spray of ice. The weight of her gloved hand rested firmly on my shoulder. We skated off together arm in arm, and for the first time I was able to fall in love. The absence of the expected repulsion was in part due to the uncommon hardness of her torso, which gave my fingers the illusion of touching an object of metal or of stone. She reminded me of those statues which seduce me by their half-virile femininity.* To condense L.'s plot: The narrator and his austere beauty become engaged and travel together to Naples. During one of their many drives together in the city, the hero, observing Bettina as she reclines in the back of a horse-drawn carriage, notices that her beauty has grown singularly flawed since that first encounter when she had appeared to him on the ice, austere, severe, cloaked in black like a dagger. The southern climate and the maturing of their relations has made her into a woman. "I asked myself," the writer ponders, "what funerary fate was next due her: sickness, maternity, death?" Bettina falls ill with malaria. Her lover is so repelled by this further corruption of her flesh that he abandons her to die alone. "And yet," he meditates shortly before dying himself, "if Bettina had remained the marvelous statue she had been when I met her, would I not have defended her unto death, would I not have defended her until the extreme limits of my strength?"

Perhaps I am in small part that boy-girl L. describes—bony,

independent, fiercely proud, easily wearied of the flesh. Maybe that's why he tolerates me so much better than most women (or so he says); why he has abstained from his lesbians and his whores for a while.

From early on I know that we cannot last together for very long. For L. is fearful of our enacting any event more than once, as if any repetition would spoil the fragile felicity we had known the first time, as if every parcel of experience were as corruptible as the heroine of that morbid tale. Our brief life together is like one of those summers of early childhood furnished with didactically single archetypes: *the* rose garden, *the* grandmother, *the* well, *the* dark forest beyond the house. So with us: *the* one weekend spent at my flat, *the* one night at a country hotel, *the* one luncheon with L.'s adored spinster sister. Seducers are fetichists, obsessed with preserving the magic emanation of objects and events, searching for untapped sources of ecstasy. Yet L. is not incapable of extreme sentimentality, he may even be fiercely fighting it. Think of that valentine of a gift he brings the first week we know each other: a tiny alabaster heart hung on a gold bracelet chain. "I can do things nicely, with old-fashioned style," his eyes mock me as he presents it in a velvet box. "Let us have a name for making love," he says another time, as we stand by a florist's window. "You know, like in Proust."

"You mean when Swann and Odette called it 'catleyas'?"

"Yes, that's it." He smiles, the crinkles gathering fiercely about his eyes. "I adore your literary side, you little left-wing intellectual, as much as I abhor your politics. We can call it columbine."

When L. is not being literary, which he relishes, he talks mostly about the grandiose "style" of those French aristocrats whose wealth he envies. The plague of his life is not to have enough money to honor his name "with a *style* appropriate to its historicity." His own words. So as we sit at the Flore, on river banks, in public parks, on museum benches, in between long exegeses of André Breton and René Char, he talks about the Rochefoucaulds' castle, the Mouchys' fox hunts, the Montesquious' extraordinary chef, the Caraman-Chimays' sublime collection of Charles IX furniture. At times he talks out his envy with rage, after much drink he whines it out like a child, once he takes me to the country to see a ruined structure that had been his family's castle, he leans his big head against a heap of rubble as against the bars of a crib, sobbing his heart out. "The pigs, the pigs, they destroyed it all. . . . Well, soon I shall marry into money, and have it rebuilt." All of this with genuine pathos. He wants even *more* of that world of the high aristocracy. It is a universe I crave to enter but have too much pride to beg entrance into; one in which even L. navigates like a leaking ship the two nights a week he is not with me or with his mother, snubbed by many for his relatively modest means and the recentness of his title (which Paris wits say is the source of his drinking). What I envied that world's inhabitants most were not their houses or their horses or their money but the serenity and repose of their historic stature. I admired what I thought to be their Olympian tranquillity, a lack of that striving, clawing, charming, showing off which marked my mother's family and most all society I had known. How sublime to possess their prerogative for that brusqueness, rudeness, arrogance which were a repressed part of my own character, how sublime not to need charm! In Paris the gaze of these personages often reposes haughtily upon me—the women's malicious, the men's inviting and lascivious—at the kind of parties at which I met L. Now here's the subtlest torture L. tries to effect upon me: he does not want me to enter that world by my own means. He rants and rages at my independent incursions into it. He occasionally invites me to accompany him to the Mouchys', the Rochefoucaulds', etc., and then calls it off at the last minute. I am a trifle too independent, too much of an actress, to satisfy his whims of torture. He is annoyed when I feign casual indifference about an evening's cancellation. Our relationship is made imperfect by my incapacity to satisfy his profound sadism. Of course! That's why he keeps returning.

And then the sister! When L. is not talking about literature or "the top one hundred," as he calls *le monde*, he talks about Princess Amélie. He is mesmerized by her. She seems to spend most of her time aggrandizing her collection of cut-crystal boxes, ordering his meals, finding special little bargains for him: a Dior tie on sale at the Printemps in some bargain basement, first-rate English shirts reduced by half at some boutique off the Place Vendôme, a marble-topped night table with Sphinx legs in the 1810 style which he adores. Often L. calls me at the office to say little else but "Amélie has finally fired that terrible old cook of ours and found someone much better for only fifty francs more a month!" Or "Amélie has cut her hair, it's in a lovely gamine effect this week." I visualize Amélie as slender, dryly elegant, imbued with that studied gaiety with which wellborn spinsters often hide the suffering brought them by a tyrannical mother.

Sayings of L.'s, aphorisms scribbled on scraps of paper (no doubt a welcome solace in that dreary office of his, where he worries about the last shipment of refrigerators to Lyons, losses on the breakage of light bulbs in Grenoble, how many defective toasters remain in Marseilles, etc.):

Only mistrust those you love. Only they have the strength to hurt you. By all means avoid all contact.

It is certain that those who love us are the ones who harm us the most. They flatter us away from eternity. They exercise the worst of all possible influences on us, by seizing upon the grandeur of our solitude.

Love is a chain of cowardly complaisances and of perfidious attacks upon our privacy.

Simultaneous scribblings in that journal of mine which awaits

the awakening of Stephanie the writer. This entry in the form
of a self-questionnaire:

"*Are you sensuous?*" "*You bet.*"

"*Are you physical?*" "*Alas no, hopelessly cerebral.*"

"*What do you want in life?*" "*Ecstasy and tenderness. And
to be heard, eventually.*"

"*What do you fear the most?*" "*Insomnia, still. Waking up
alone in the dark without my daddy, my bottle.*"

"*What is love about?*" "*About talking.*"

The *fin-de-siècle* furniture of our gilded, brocaded hotel
room emanates a savor of clandestine love. Champagne is already waiting in the room. L. has brought me to one of those
classical country inns where, for two generations, men whose
style he covets have held their weekend bacchanals. There is
a bouquet of columbines on the table. I've secretly studied that
soft spot, he's a hopeless sentimentalist, that's the last thing he
would ever admit about himself. "You must admit, my dear
Stéphanie, that I am style incarnate," he cackles as he opens
the window into the spring night. Toward dawn he becomes
suddenly thoughtful, childlike. "It's admirable," he says. "I
have friends married for twelve years who came here last
month and made love a half-dozen times in one night, as we have.
Could anything be stranger?" We discuss it for several hours,
we talk about how terrified we are of that morbid descent
from bliss which any permanence entails. But once he has
dabbled in his favorite bit of metaphysics (need for continual
ecstasy! continual terror of its degeneration!) L. ascends his
stage again and struts about in that silk bathrobe his sister has
just found for him on sale at Dior, declaiming his other in-
satiable needs. 7 A.M.: "I must live in a certain style without
which I perish. *Of course* I'm a materialist. I *am* style. I am
style *incarnate*. You must admit I do everything with style."
8 A.M.: "Why be loved, when it's so much easier to be hated?"
9 A.M.: "Why don't you wear real jewelry? God, those dreary

politics of yours. There is something fabulously seductive about the clang of real pearls upon the night table, good for an immediate erection." 10 A.M.: "And of course to live in style I have to marry an heiress. Don't worry, I've already found her. It's been arranged for many years, we're just waiting for her to grow up." 11 A.M., after more champagne: "Why don't you desire *things?*" he howls. "Jewelry, fur coats? So many men must be offering them to you constantly! You always refuse! You're constantly refusing the only things we could give you a bit of! No, mademoiselle wants my tenderness."

In between, great fits of chest beating, recitations of how wicked he is, how incapable of fidelity, how profoundly conservative, how materialistic, how corrupt. God, how marvelously the French can talk. I lie in bed smoking, adoring the sheer volume of his verbiage.

My father teaching me the theme song of the French girl scouts: *"Ne pleure pas, Jeannette, on te mariera, on te mariera,/ Avec le fils d'un prince, tra-lalalalalalalalalala-la-la . . ."*

A brief notation in the mail from L. the following week:
My definition of the fall from grace: It was to lose our ability to forever retain the first passionate flush of love. Only its permanence would have enabled life to retain a perfect continuity of the impossible and the possible.
Birth trauma? The human condition? Always that obsession with the loss of love.

Orgasms, orgasms, I never know what to make of them. I can come several times in a row with a man who loves me and when it's over turn away from him with amicable boredom. I can fuck a man like L. with whom it's over in a few minutes and desire to spend the rest of my life with him. What is it all about, the howling and screaming with pleasure? I like the way L. never asks such questions as did you come sweetie, what was it like for you, why didn't you come, he doesn't seem to care. The inexplicability, the cerebrality of it all. With L. I celebrate the cerebrality of love, with him I know that we are pure consciousness and little else. Up to now he has been exhilarated by the barely obscene, the classically renegade: orgies with groups of middle-aged lesbian duchesses, visits to Oriental prostitutes whose mouths he considers exquisitely skilled. He likes to tell the story of the Japanese whore who deftly channeled his sperm into a tiny box and wrapped it before him in ravishingly pretty papers, to preserve it as a souvenir on her chest of drawers. He is not able to go much further than that with deviation. He keeps reciting voluminous passages from Sade, Verlaine, Baudelaire. But how could he have the revolutionary splendor of many men who are truly depraved, since he is unable to shed centuries of family precepts? Lacking that passion for human liberty which led his heroes to seek prurience, he is a Sade *raté*, a real failure as a pervert. His playing at evil is but another role to hide his monumental fear of freedom; of choosing himself; of shedding the carapace of prejudices history has encrusted him with. Actually L. makes love with conservative docility, not extraordinarily well, his frequent drunkenness is not conducive to the heavens of invention. He is too lazy to adopt the intricate *Kama Sutra* business I've learned with Americans. Frenchmen on the whole are lousy lovers. L. comes by himself, fairly swiftly, missionary style, like a whirlwind, and afterward he often weeps. Yet I know little more about ecstasy than to have been at the center of his storm. He always goes home at about 3 A.M., so that he can be in bed when his mother sends the maid up with breakfast.

How happy Mama must be in New York, saying over the canasta table, "You'll never guess whom Stephanie's living with!" It could be the Grand Prix or the Prix Goncourt, as long as it shines she's happy. I'm still not sure how much it affects me, the prince business, outside of my need to impress her. Beyond the beauty of his body and of his eyes, the volume of his words, he has also the unreachability, the fundamental glacialness of the classical seducer.

When he is very drunk, L. tends to weep again, or else to talk about death. "The most rational human act in the world is to shoot into a crowd at random—Surrealist Manifesto, 1922." Hands on hips, he lurches down the street outside Jimmy's nightclub, shouting, "Bang, bang, at random, into a crowd!" He plays at death, at poetry, the way six-year-olds play cowboy. Another time, as I am at the wheel of his car: "I shall put my foot on yours," he says, "press on the gas, place my hands over your eyes, as we go to encounter those utterly splendid trees we shall be in the same state of blindness as is achieved by a kiss that has no end." A game to which I do not accede, obviously. Listen, dear, I say, I often think about that, too, but when I'm ready for it I'll do it my own way, in the river.

Every morning in Paris I go to an office where I help to publish one of those trilingual magazines found in the offices of sinus specialists throughout the Western world. It is a dusty room in a seedy building near the slums of the Bastille. I translate articles from French into English about the coming-out parties of Princess Margharete de Holschwig-Holstein, the raising of lambs in Sardinia, the jewelry of the Maharani of Jaupurmutal, the building of new resorts off the coast of Madagascar. My editor, B.G., is a puffy-eyed, elegant Englishman whom I often see drinking late at night in Montparnasse, scanning the bars for boys. He detests the French more than any other people and has lived in Paris for more than thirty years. I constantly hear him dictating cables to England—letter for letter, as one must for Paris operators—maliciously using the first letters of French historical disasters: "*W pour* Waterloo ... *O pour* Ontario ... *U pour* Utrecht ... *L pour* Laval ... *D pour* Dien Bien Phu ... *V pour* Vichy. ..." Every three weeks he remembers there are galleys to be corrected at the printer's. He grabs my arm and we rush to the suburbs to rescue an issue from a month's delay. "Be an angel and drive like the devil," he yells at the cab driver. On the way back we go out for a drink and swap hostile stories about my Parisian compatriots. My best woman friend in Paris, I tell him, is a Sorbonne student whose father is a high government official. Over the last year I have introduced her to her first lover and been responsible for her deflowering, later introduced her to her husband-to-be, and all along have frequently fed and lodged her in my frugal one-room flats when she was too lazy to go home. I have never been invited for so much as a meal to her large family apartment, in which she lives with several servants. Listen, love, B.G. says, the profile is good enough to be fed into a computer, you've just described the quintessential inhabitant of this city. Ah, well, you probably did not flatter her enough. Have you noticed that the French find everything boring except the sound of their own voices or that of others' praising them? If we stopped flattering them, Parisian ears would go the way of tonsils and appendixes. Have you ever encountered a people more rapacious, greedy, inhospitable, more stuck on their families, more obsessed with style? Oh, yes, I say, they sure are obsessed with style. The reason I have lived here for thirty years, B.G. says, is that I hate them so. It relieves me of many aggressions I could direct against myself.

Apart from our enjoyable conversations, the tedium of the office work is relieved only by B.G.'s occasional attempts at suicide. Once he ties a noose around his neck and jumps from three telephone books stacked on the floor of his apartment, ending up with a severe sore throat. Another time, noosed again, he stands on a foot-high block of ice and waits for it to melt while reading from the Koran, whose violence he enjoys. My work is lonely. The paycheck is thin. This city seems to hate me. Its damp winds and smogs are giving me chronic bronchitis, its men trying to make me in taxicabs, its women hissing gossip that I'm a lesbian, the food of its lousy bistros giving me diarrhea, its pipes bursting wherever I live. For those who are not rich, for those who are not made of steel, this most splendid of cities can be as lethal as that statue of Don Juan which drags one into the earth's glacial bowels. How I miss my last job in New York! Midnight at the wire service: reek of tobacco and Scotch hovering over the din of typewriters. News of McCarthy hearings drumming on the teletypes. Heat of pavements under my naked feet as I walk barefoot to Times Square in my last, rebellious incarnation. The kindness, the cheer, the warmth of my adopted Americans! B.G. says I remind him of a boxer who wants to prizefight after having practiced for twelve hours instead of the necessary twelve hundred. "If you want to survive in Paris, love, you've got to learn how to box." He says I am here, of course, to "find myself."

In an American strip-tease joint down the street from the Dior Boutique, my mother's sobs were muffled by the clanging of a rhumba band. "Life is too short," she wept, in Russian, "perhaps life is too short to *ever* be separated at all." I was beginning my first winter alone in France. Mama had gathered her pals together to mourn her separation from me and the end of her yearly summer stay in Paris. "But at least," she continued, "at least I shall leave you in the care of such good friends." The next day we were accompanied to the railroad station by the clamorous band that followed her wherever she went in Paris—directors of glittering shoe boutiques, dress designers, glove and bag designers, window designers, jewelry designers, unsuccessful song writers supported by aging Latin-American heiresses. They all vociferated their adoration of Mama, reiterated their pleas that they would watch over me as if I were their only child, that they would each become my best friend in Paris. Laughing, shouting, smoking, hugging, kissing their affection, they took hold of me by the sleeve, by the elbow, pushed and shoved me out of Mama's sight. Her head out the window, she still shouted endearments at me in her native Russian. Indeed, her friends did try to alleviate my chosen loneliness, they were on the phone every two days. B. was the motherly director of a couture house in whose exquisite river-view flat I spent my first alcoholic weekend. M. was a former fashion model a few years older than I ("She will take *special* care of you") who nearly managed to give me my first lesbian experience on a particularly lousy Sunday afternoon. Countess V.T., the wife of a metal-rich German noble ("She'll be a *great* pal"), invited me to lunch the very next week. At her Sèvres-laden table five women compared the taste of sperm. Like pea soup, one said. No, more like fish chowder, another commented. A must for the complexion once a week, a third insisted. "Dear Mama," I wrote to New York to cheer her up, "Your friends are divine. They are taking such marvelous care of me."

Madame Bourdel's marble-white face was dominated by heavy-lidded, glacially pale blue eyes. Her Empire apartment overlooked the river. She lived off the revenues of her dead husband's seldom performed plays and her own ventures into literary pedantry. She had decided, that season, to rent out the room of the defunct playwright at the back of her apartment. It was a small, fecally dark chamber, mahogany- and pomegranate-hued, hung with photos of the dead one receiving the Legion of Honor, being knighted by the Queen of Sweden, being made a member of the French Academy. "It is sad but elegant," my mother commented as she urged me to take the lodging. "The address is impeccable, you will meet the right people here." In the dim brown corridor that led to my room hung nineteen-thirties photographs of Madame B.'s literary coterie—Cocteau, Bérard—indulging in opiate revelry. Every few days, a thin plume of pungent smoke was profiled against the exotic navy-blue walls of her bedroom. When she was not traveling with her maid to the homes of titled friends in warm climates ("What is a rest but a change of fatigue!") Madame

B. held a salon the first Thursday of each month. Actors, fading courtesans, desiccated academicians, a scattering of Nescafé society, mingled with aristocracy whose first names sounded like Zouzou, Baba, Néné, Lolo. A famous mistress of nineteen-thirties vintage gave me motherly advice about who's who in Paris. "Third diamond bracelet from the mantelpiece, look carefully. An interesting study in good manners. A Portuguese millionaire once offered her ten thousand dollars a month to live with him for precisely ten years, and she stayed to the day, do you understand, *to the day!* That is what I call correct, that is style. Almost next to her, two emeralds down: a man you might enjoy if you like the kind who beats you in the dark, but if I were you I'd start with simpler types unless you absolutely must have his horses. By the way, never, never, never stay home at night. Make yourself perpetually seen. You're too ladylike, too proud!" Three months at Madame B.'s. How she regretted when I left! "You were so calm, so courteous." Next, two months in a one-room flat sandwiched between a fish store and a cheap bordello, three months in a seedy hotel off the Quai Voltaire, ten weeks in another on the Rue Bona-parte. I turn and twist in this city like a patient with skin sores shifting in a hospital bed. Skinny, gay, ravishingly affable in my borrowed gowns, I go out almost every night to be wined and dined by lecherous bankers, window designers, publishing tycoons, cold-cereal kings, international hostesses. Every few months I stand on a street corner at dawn to hail a cab, my dress rolled into a pocket of my coat, not having waited for the sentiments, the how-was-its, the when-do-I-see-you agains. That's the way it was in Cambridge and New York, that's the way it continues to be here, until I meet L.: unease with the flesh, horror of sentiment, dread of permanence. Sitting alone in a cab at dawn, riding to whatever dreary room I am living in, a phrase from *The Story of O* constantly runs through my mind: ". . . the cool expanse of the plastic cab seats under her naked thighs."

Why is it hard, perhaps impossible, for women to describe lovemaking with some grace? It is one of our nights together in Paris, L. and I have drunk until early in the morning, arguing about how evil, how corrupt, how materialistic he is. *"Mon pauvre enfant,"* I say, "you are such a teddy bear, you are really an adorable, sentimental, home-loving, terribly puritanical boy." He gets so angry. Oh, how I laugh. Scotch after Scotch at Jimmy's, four drinks for him for every one of mine, in between setups we make a sight of ourselves on the dance floor. He likes to show off that way at times, he has to keep his reputation as a womanizer rigorously maintained, he holds his blond alley cat to him so tight that even Countess V.T. phones me the next morning to give me a talking-to on manners. We drive home and walk the two flights up to my flat, he hugs me to him with low moaning sounds. It is amazing the way he can still make love at all even when he is quite drunk. He undresses me immediately, he wants to have me totally naked while he is still dressed. He insists on fucking me just like that, with his winter coat still on, "as if I'd just found you in the Bois." He likes to sit on a straight-backed chair, holding me on top of him, guiding my naked hips with his hands, biting and sucking at my nipples as I glide up and down on him. Then I thrust down upon him the other way, my back turned to him, his hands guiding my hips even faster. Down on the floor, the rough carpet chafes at my chest, his rough tweeds chafe my back as he comes in me with great fury, moaning, moaning. Later he has undressed and is sitting on the edge of the bed, I sit at his feet gently sucking him as he rubs his hands through my hair. The sudden ecstasy, always the great surprise of that cataract. Impossible to know when it is coming, a thrill that, the thrill of the unexpected. Simple things really, much tenderness. The isolation, the solitude of sex. The only place we are totally together, totally ourselves, more solitary than ever.

One day L. decides that he wants me to meet his sister. We are to lunch at a small restaurant she likes behind the Opéra, on a commercial street in which she hunts for many of her bargains. Imagine my surprise: Princess Amélie is not the fine-boned spinster I had imagined, but a small dumpy woman whose very haughty, mirthful face is a rotund caricature of her brother's. Her hair is carefully arranged into a vulgarly teased and curly mop. Much of the time a condescending, fearful smile guards her privacy, causing a network of crinkly lines—as in her brother's face—to surround her shrewd green eyes. Throughout lunch the two talk about furniture, upholstery, cousins, vegetables, vacations, Maman is not pleased with this and that this week. Maman is critical of how Amélie plans to open the summer house in Cannes this June, what shall we do about the fact that Maman does not like the new cook Amélie has hired, also Maman is unnerved that the fee for repainting the entrance hall has risen so high this year. There is total serenity on L.'s face when he converses with his sister. "What are you having for lunch, my dear?" "The *blanquette de veau* with onions sounds very fine." "I thought you did not like veal in sauces!" "Whatever gave you the curious notion I did not like veal in sauces?" "Well, that's the impression I've had for thirty years, that you did not like veal in sauces." "I may have said I did not like veal in tomato sauces, but I certainly never implied sauces in general." "Yes you *did*." "No I *didn't*." I gather that they lunch alone like this once a week, feigning business appointments, to outline plans of defense against their terrifying mother. Since the mother, quintessence of purity, and the mistress, symbol of defilement, still cannot meet in L.'s world, I have to compose her portrait. I imagine her as stout and purple-lipped, with small greedy eyes and messily rumpled black stockings, a woman totally preoccupied with oppressing her servant, recounting her linen and her silver, poking about the lives of her married daughters, visiting widows her age, writing dour family news to cousins, going to Mass. A scowling woman who holds sway over her children not through the force of pity or of the wealth she could deprive them of by changing her last will and testament, but through the sheer mythological power of that abject trinity that is still the buttress of many Western societies: the family, the fatherland, the Church.

My closest relative in Paris is my mother's sister, who is married to a duke. In fact he's not really a duke, he's a Frenchman who was earlier married to a Spanish duchess. When that Spanish duchess died she left him her title through some matrilineal prerogative peculiar to her family, the way one would bequeath, in a will, a jewel or a dog. As for my Aunt Olga, when she was trying to be a coloratura soprano in the nineteen-thirties she was married to a hotel keeper who owned an establishment near the Opéra called L'Hôtel des Trois Mondes. Olga and my mother had arrived in Paris from Russia in the late nineteen-twenties, two great beauties dressed in rags, vociferating their desires to meet nobility and wear splendid Paris clothes. Baboushka, my great-grandmother, who had come to France a decade earlier, had met the two girls at the train station. And her summing-up of their arrival became a family classic: "All that Communist garbage fills their minds, but they also want to be countesses." Olga and my mother had hated each other since childhood. It is rumored that they had each tried to set fire to the other's crib. Upon their marriages the sibling rivalry became all the more morbid. My mother partly realized her ambitions for nobility by marrying my father, a moneyless viscount, whereas Olga had acquired a Frenchman without a *du* or a *de* in his name who ran a hotel with the name of a bordello, down the block from an opera house which refused to hear her try out *Lakmé*. In most White Russian communities, what with its men's extraordinary lack of ambition, their indolent tendency to gambling or to drink (my grandfather was a case in point), most social mobility was thrust upon the women. It was their function to climb the icy ladders of Paris—that particularly hieratic city—by becoming noblewomen, actresses or courtesans. So, with the quixotic dukedom Olga acquired in her fifties, she finally enjoyed her revenge upon her sister, and her long-awaited arrival to the Elysian Fields of Parisian success.

"What, you're not married yet?" she comments jadedly when I go to see her every few months. "And you're not even *attached* to anyone interesting? What kind of life do you think you're leading?" She clucks her tongue disapprovingly.

She usually receives me lying in her tufted white satin bed, her big round baby cheeks gleaming with cream or frozen in clay masks in preparation for her evening's outing. Her face, her breasts, her hips, her ears, her nose have been lifted and resurrected by so much surgery that there is little left for me to recognize as the warbling, Meissen-pretty aunt of my child-hood. Let us say that occasionally, when I study her very care-fully, there is a greedy gleam in her little eyes which reminds me of that personage of twenty years ago. At the age of fifty-two she is a surreally youthful pickle of a person, monstrously embalmed by her lotions, her gymnastics, her diets and her bouts of drugged sleep, like some preserved creature that stares out of a brine-filled bottle. She inevitably commences our visits by bitching about the past, and then we go on to discuss ir-resistible men: the Ali Khan and, in particular, Porfirio Rubi-rosa. For the men Olga admires even more than self-made millionaires are the ones who best mirror her own graspingness, the heiress hunters who milk women for every cent they have. "What a *raté*," she exclaims on the subject of B.L., a noted Paris buck. "You call that a career? No woman has left him anything, no woman has left him as much as a single piece of jewelry! What did he get from that last millionairess? Sand-wiches! Nothing but sandwiches!" she cackles.

I can stare at Olga for hours with a kind of perverse curiosity. For in her vulgar aspirations I glimpse the germs of my life's most insane phases—such as the one I'm living through now. It is as if in this tough woman totally different from me, from my ambitious but infinitely tender mother, from that callous scheming mother of theirs whom I shall never meet, some common germ could be discovered which would explain all four of us, like the curlicues of a virus diagnosed in a bottled culture. It is a pattern I peek at with perverse desire for self-defamation, the way we stare at ourselves in the grotesque distorting mirrors of country circus shows. And Olga in turn half welcomes my visits, with the meddling curiosity of the child-hating, barren woman whose only niece has totally flunked decades of family precepts.

"Nothing but sandwiches!" she repeats with a raucous laugh. "You call that success? I bet that's all you're getting, by the way, nothing but sandwiches!" When she laughs her jowls shake like two bowls of gelatine, her tiny porcine eyes are almost obliterated by the assault of her round glistening flesh.

Staring at her as she lies in her sea of cosmetics, I am awed by the generation of women it took to shape her ambitions. I am obsessed with the monstrous battlefields behind us littered with china, crystal, silver, calling cards and other sinister baubles documenting these women's attempted upward climb. Shall I become one of these monsters? How to break the vicious expectations of the female tribe? How much of life is worth wasting to engrave a card that says: "The Duchess of so and so will receive from five to seven, blah, blah?" And staring at Olga I realize that I have come to Paris to relive the ambitions she and my mother held toward this city three decades ago; that their aspirations lie still implanted in me like some organ grown obsolete in evolution yet large enough to infect and kill me; that this city may yet destroy me because of the lingering presence of these infected tonsils. In Olga the tonsils are still full-fledged and functional, as monumental as her jaws; she is tough, she is a boxer, she has survived.

"Now, if you want another man of success, a true *aristocrat*," Olga continues, "look at my husband, Eugène. An aristocrat of the *heart*," she adds briskly. "Isn't that true, my darling?" She turns toward the fulfillment of her entire life's ambitions, the duke. He is a frail, doddering septuagenarian who spends most of his time nodding over a newspaper, waiting for her to wake up from her drugged sleeps, and inevitably begins his clauses by mumbling the last words of her last sentence.

"Of the heart, of the heart, of the heart, the heart, the heart, of course, my angel, of the heart," he mutters, nodding over his *Paris Soir*.

"And isn't it true that I am tenderness itself, I who was so wronged by my first husband, tenderness itself?"

"Itself, itself itself itself itself, tenderness itself, you are tenderness itself."

They are known to be particularly stingy. Whenever I phone Olga she spends ten minutes pretending to be annoyed at my months of silence, then one time out of two invites me to lunch.

"It's so agreeable, agreeable to see you," the tiny duke mutters as he shuffles into the living room in his carpet slippers, his hand flashing an enormous sapphire inherited from his last wife. "Agreeable, agreeable."

"We are so busy this season," Olga whispers hoarsely, offering her gleaming oiled cheek, "the season is more hectic than ever, that is why I am left voiceless, I have lost my voice talking politics with ministers of state, I cannot tell you how many diplomats I have entertained in this room this week." At the lunch table a few unpeeled radishes are served as first course, followed by a small piece of burned gray beef reminiscent of those dusty pieces of hide seen in provincial churches that are claimed to be a part of Saint Matthew's sandal, a handle of the true cradle. "I have my receptions all figured out for the rest of my life," Olga says. "I have them carefully formulated. We are always thirty at the table, never less, never more, that is precisely how many gold plate settings I have. Tonight, for instance, we are having the Nicaraguan ambassador to Luxembourg, the former Argentine Minister of Health, the Portuguese Minister of Public Works." She notices that the Christmas present she last gave me is not working. It is a rusting jeweled compact inherited from the last duchess's estate that has never even opened properly. She starts fiddling at it with a table knife.

The absent, gentle duke suddenly becomes a lion, the Frenchman's indomitable sense of property inflames him to action. He waves his arms like a windmill, the glory of pure matter moves him to start a sentence by himself. "Careful with my fruit knife," he hollers at my aunt the duchess. "Don't you dare to ever do that again with my knife my knife my knife!"

More in the mail from L. this week. A new style of writing, mysterious, aphoristic, more lyrical. As usual the theme is the simultaneous absoluteness and impossibility of love, etc. I never know whether the words are his own or someone else's.

"We shall never be rid of our wishes for a golden age. Recently I dreamt that I was being transported, within the limits of a park, to that heart of the world where conditions of mutual tolerance permit the harmonious gathering of all individuals. Orpheus passed through here, leading the tiger and the gazelle side by side. Drawn curtains . . . caressing eyes of felines punctuating the sky with lights . . . the delirium of absolute presence. How could one not continue to love perpetually, at the heart of nature reconciled? Love, carnal love, only love there is, I have never ceased to adore your evil shade, a day will come when man will recognize you for its only master."

"Well, now, Mélanie," L. says, "what a surprise to see you! How do you like this beautiful day! Why aren't you riding your horsie this afternoon? Is he happy in his stable?"

We have been walking in the Park Monceau. Suddenly a child some twelve years of age has come along the bend of an alley, twirling her shiny new hoop. Her long black hair, held back by a little circlet of gold, falls in gleaming torrents of curls about her shoulders. Her placid eyes are of the deepest blue, like detached cornflowers. Her tiny snub nose, her ringlets, the dimples surrounding her prim, tight little mouth, lend her a certain cherubic glory. She wears a starched pink dress with a waist ribbon of a deeper crimson hue. Under the starched ruffles of her bodice, her tiny breasts are like lilac buds swelling under the ice of a March day. Just behind her stands a very formal governess dressed in heavy British tweeds. The child looks at us with surprise and pleasure, a little curiosity. As she stands there holding her hoop under the flowering chestnut tree, I know, I do not need to be told, that this is the unsullied, wealthy being for whom L. is reserving his boredom and the continuation of his name.

"Yes, how is your horsie?" he says. "Why aren't you out riding him on this beautiful day?" He stares at her dreamily, and beyond her, as if into the park.

"Charles is very well, thank you, my dear Uncle," she says in her crisp, barely accented Britannic English, "but Papa says that I must rest him for a week, for last Sunday when we were riding at Saint-Cloud we missed our mark at the last fence, and I went tumbling over his head, and he gave himself a slightly sprained ankle."

L.'s face feigns great horror.

"Oh, my poor Mélanie, my poor angel! Are you sure you did not hurt yourself?"

"Oh, don't worry, Uncle, it was just a very little fall," she says with a crisp laugh. When she speaks French it's with a faint British accent, like the Natasha of *War and Peace* who spoke her own language with a hard, rolled French *r*. She heaves a sigh, looking longingly at the riding alley, twiddling the ribbons of her hoop.

"And how is school? I hope you are doing well in your courses," L. continues. "Naughty girl, your papa told me how badly you did in your Latin last term. I hope you are improving."

"Oh, Uncle, you are always pushing me so hard to work," she says with a pout and a toss of her curls, whose wealth heaves over the somnolent lake of her face. "Why is it you want me to work so hard?"

"Because I want you to be a very perfect young woman, as I'm sure your papa does."

"And you and Papa are always conspiring against me," she says, patting her hair into order. "Latin is so boring."

"But it is essential, my dear, if you wish to develop a clear and lucid style, an elegant way of expressing yourself in letters, for instance."

"But that is all so boring compared to riding," she exclaims. "Tell me, are you coming up for a weekend to the castle soon?" She twirls her hoop again. "Papa was just complaining that you had not been up to hunt for a whole month."

"Oh, I shall come soon, very soon," he says, his eyes still plunged into the beyond of the park. "Tell your papa I shall be there within the month."

"When you come I'll show you how well I jump a three-foot hurdle!" And she begins to skip down the alley, her little baton tapping faster and faster at the hoop. "Goodbye, goodbye," she cries, her pink ribbons flying in the wind, "I'll see you very soon!"

We continue gravely walking in the park. "We chose her, you know, when she was only seven or eight years old. An angel. And all the money in the world."

I know. Woman as angel, woman as beast, the ancient divisions. Venerable and hallowed mothers, sisters, brides versus the harlot mistresses, who particularly trouble men when they are purer than they. Our enslavers segregate us into zoos, with our full consent. Never let the blame fall on the enslavers only. It is all becoming clearer, very slowly.

One principle of dazzling clarity dominates the psychology of oppression: the oppressor tends to characterize his victim by those very traits which he is most ashamed of in himself:

hysteria, dependence, feebleness, irrationality. Growing up in the fifties is already made dreary by men other than L. who exemplify this deceitful tactic of control, who pester me the way women are accused of pestering men, pleading for permanence, respectable households, constancy. Paul, for instance, a lover from my college days at Radcliffe, travels from Boston to my Paris apartment every three months as punctually as some migratory bird. He leans against the door, or a wall of the airport, a tree in the park, wherever we meet, and says, "Someday you're going to marry me, Steph. . . . I'm going to faint now." And in a slow rolling motion he slumps onto the floor, all six feet of him. He comes to within ten minutes or so, looking refreshed, a little surprised. I spend twenty-four hours playing the rules of his game, admitting some admiration for his candor—how many men accede to their surely frequent desire to faint before women, without suppressing it with out-dated myths of virility? But soon afterward our ways part again. For however many books Paul has read, however many degrees he has accumulated at Harvard, he threatens me with that sheltering security which terrifies me more than being a whore, a cocaine peddler, a tramp. With him I can predict what Caribbean island we would frequent at the age of thirty, where we would send our children to school when we were thirty-seven, where we shall go for our divorces at the age of forty-two. I can hear his deep voice whining, "Can't you make soup out of all those lovely zucchini wasting away in the garden?" and "God, darling, when shall we ever get a decent summer bed cover?" and "I'm going out to get organic molasses to make some lovely dark bread." Dutifully home-loving, devoted to his parents, overly domesticated, Paul belongs to that race of house husbands, of Father Earths, who will be the loneliest victims of the magnificent sexual revolution which is beginning to sweep the Western world. He follows me about with the lowering manner of a mother cow, remind-ing me to eat on time, ordering me to put my hat and boots on, using those simple tactics of domination which go under the guise of shelter. Otherwise, his decision to respect my privacy is admirable. Once, after our beautiful affair during my last year at Radcliffe, we slept in the same bed for three months without ever touching each other. Finally he had bet again on the American myth of the supremacy of the shared orgasm, and he had lost again. I was infuriated each time by our virtuosity. The cerebrality of the flesh, its need for constant discovery! Perhaps, as L. says, that is the truest meaning of the Fall. What with Paul's gigantic silences, his meticulous quest for the better restaurant, we started off at the wrong end of the telescope, as if with an aging marriage. For a year he walks beside me with his architectural degrees, his dogs, his Korean war medals, his tweeds, his loving parents, his quiet country house, tall, tanned, skilled at inducing shared orgasm—the American dream. But I already know that I do not like myself, that I need to be reborn, that in order to go on living I must break myself apart in order to put myself together again, and Paul will never let me break apart.

When we are together, his knotty, powerful hands are constantly clenched with that repressed rage which he never dares to put into words, which causes him to faint every few months. "Blackmail, emotional blackmail!" I mutter to myself after those bouts of candor. "All right, talk, talk," he says after recovering. And I talk as into a tape recorder, seldom corrected, seldom interrupted—that's why it's so boring—saying that happiness is not my goal, should not be anybody's goal, the goal . . . Jesus, didn't he remember my college thesis on Kierkegaard?

It is the fourth and last time he has come to Paris. I smoke throughout the meal, barely eating. He flashes me that perfect-toothed smile which shelters him like a mask.

". . . he said the goal is a much more tedious task of discovery, self-exploration, shedding of parental values, bringing death to the old self, being reborn—oh, God, I forget what else."

"Sure you forget, Steph. You've been through seven cycles of rebirth just in the few years I've known you."

"Okay, explain this one to me, precisely because it may have to do with forgetting: Everything has been written that needs to be written about physical frigidity, but what about the emotional kind? I'm a case of spiritual nymphomania and emotional frigidity."

"It's because you're so goddam literary." The pegs they find for you, always their refuge.

"I can have perfect sex, but it means nothing unless it's textured by a fascination for power, for adventure, for suffering, for the impossible . . ."

They don't understand a word of it. Those damn sex manuals have taught this generation of Americans such reverence for women's orgasms that they are emotional illiterates. Their next step is always a return to the sheltering tone.

"I can't stand to see you living in that hovel."

"I want to live in a hovel for a while. I want my filth, my solitude. I want my despair, my floundering."

"This city is killing you, Steph. You've lost ten pounds in the past four months."

"Well, maybe I want to almost die. Maybe it's my destiny to be almost killed by this godawful city."

It is a cold or a hot night in Paris, I don't remember, I remember little of these last months save the stupor in which I go out to dull the edge of my solitude, the increasing brutality of my barbiturate hangovers, the growing tightness in a stomach that can barely digest anything, my bouts of rage at my impasse with L. I only remember that in the middle of that last evening with Paul I turn away and stare at an American couple dining by candlelight whose beauty harasses me. The man looks disturbingly like Paul, with that buffed, burnished aura of Ivy League and good tobacco. The woman is about ten years older than I am, with ashen hair pulled back into a soft bun. She smiles, and rests her chin on her slim ringed hand.

There is a serenity about them which I know I shall have to achieve someday to avoid my own destruction. Oh, save me, God, but not quite yet, as we used to say in the seminar on Saint Augustine. But not quite yet.

The next morning, to remain true to his image of me—what else can I leave him?—I compose a literary note for Paul.

"I have tried so long to love you! But in wanting to give me so much aren't you cornering me, aren't you protecting me from those encounters with fate which women are so brutally deprived of?"

Colette. How well she understood our ambivalent need for solitude, the blackmail tactics of men who offer oppression in the guise of shelter.

"As a vagabond, how many times will I turn toward that strength of yours which is both my repose and my deepest wound? Perhaps you had not counted on the pridefulness of poverty, and the banality of happiness."

He takes the plane back to New York that day after scribbling his own little note, in which he appreciates the "sensitivity" of mine. A few months later, just after I've fallen ill, he writes me from his parents' home in Massachusetts that he misses me, and that all may be over between us. I alternately weep and rejoice at his letter, fearing and missing his shelter as the canary misses its cage.

When I was a child my father—in an attempt to part me from my governess—once sent me to a winter camp in the French Alps ironically named "The Sweet Nest." Every afternoon scores of children were bedded in metal cribs upon an outdoor terrace for their nap, their hands tied behind their backs to deny them the comfort of sucking their thumbs. I used to lie there in the brilliant cold, staring at the detested snow, my ears ringing with the shouts of children deprived of this great solace. My convalescence in Switzerland now reminds me of those afternoons. Terminal despair, the air about me like the bars of a crib. Some weeks before I came here a doctor stood at my bedside in a Paris hospital, saying, "You will be saved by altitudes."

Five thousand feet up in the Alps, my windows overlook a Wagnerian landscape constantly washed by monumental sheets of rain. The furniture of my hotel room is finished with a uremic glaze particular to tubercular resorts: the chest of drawers, the chairs, the beds, glisten with a brash yellow veneer applied between occupancies as a disinfectant. Alone, alone, finally I am totally alone. In this dismal season sandwiched between the end of the skiing and the opening of the golf the hotel is almost devoid of guests, the ground lies like mangled flesh between thin bandages of filthy snow. I have been ordered to spend eighteen hours out of each twenty-four in a reclining position, to walk an hour in the morning, an hour in the afternoon. After breakfast I walk as far as my strength allows me upon country roads dotted with sanatoriums. A few hundred yards above me men in striped pajamas stand on balconies, waving and shouting lewd appellations. My days are measured by medicines, my walks are attended by the hooting of owls and the yelling of these pale, striped men. Everything here is minutely portioned out, as in an infant's diet, doled out in tiny dosages. The little walks, and every two hours the little white pills that will bring my crazy white corpuscle count back to normal, every three hours the pink tonic that will help strengthen the red ones, every night the yellow barbiturates that I repeat three or four times in the dark to bring me another bout of sleep. Some mornings I reach for the wrong bottle, take a yellow barb instead of a pink tonic, force myself to vomit it out to deter the terror of another sleepless night. The lunchtime medication is the trickiest bit of the schedule: amber-brown, faintly anised drops—most effective when accompanied by a great deal of wine—which put me to sleep for two hours of the afternoon. All right, darling, I say at twelve noon sharp, drink yourself to sleep, afternoon is the most painful time of all, like the sound of those children screaming in their cribs. Finally, lunch is finally arriving. *Le petit bifteck, encore du gros rouge, les pommes frites, le cantal du pays.* The brown drops toward the end, with a bite of apple and the fifth large glass of red wine to wash them down. I rise from my chair and keep my spine very straight, trying not to stumble before the guests at the other tables, trying to be dignified. There is always a handful of transients to watch me, a few tourists passing by on their way to Zurich to admire the rain pouring down on the Wagnerian landscape. *Schön, schön.* A pretty, neurotically thin young woman with long blond hair rises from the table and carries a cup of decaf to her room. One foot carefully ahead of the other, there, very slowly, so as not to stumble in public. They must think I am here to recuperate from some disease of the spine, the way I stare straight ahead of me so as not to miss the lowest step of the stairs. Or that I am catatonic, or hypnotized. Stairs after lunch, the most difficult part of the day. The first week I was here I kept stumbling on the seventh step, spilling the brown medicine all over me, laughing my head off, reeking of anise, but it was all worth it, worth two and a half hours of this month's most blissful deathlike sleep. Always the dilemma of the borderline alcoholic: to drink enough to feel good without letting the world know how good you feel, to keep that a secret, a deep inner secret. To be secret. To be alone. That is the alcoholic's secret, the alcoholic's loneliness. That's the whole fun of it, to walk through a room keeping that secret secret. I fall often upon the shit-colored stairs, but what a deep sleep I have, passing out on the Lysol-scented sheets . . .

Upon my waking, the mountains loom about me like the bars of an enormous crib, I feel five, six months old, my mouth is sucking for comfort, I lie in my bed whimpering for my next fix, my next bottle, my next sleep. More dosage upon waking: a cup of strong tea with lemon to startle me into reality again, a slice of raisin cake for the sugar energy that will take me on my walk. Outside, a group of Swiss tourists ride brown mares into the rain-gorged golf course. Tea, cake, horsie, I am still waking up. As I start walking, the terror of insomnia looms again. Every hour I am awake I dread the next night's solitude, every hour is obsessed by the desire to be returned, with minimum struggle, into that dark maternal night. I pass the terraced sanatorium where men stand in striped pajamas, calling and waving. That's what men are, cripples shouting obscenities, never able to give me what I want: both tenderness and ecstasy. Two English spinsters sit beside me in the tea shop where I take my four-thirty pill. God, we are all so pale. "It's that foul English air of ours did your lungs in, dear," one says to the other. It's those foul Paris drawing rooms did *me* in, sweetheart, that foul middle-class disease passed on by women, to rise, to rise. You bitch of a city, you finally did me in.

One afternoon before tea L. suddenly steps out of a taxicab, just like that. I have heard from him a few times since I was in the hospital, notes to the effect of "Why did you do this to me, you are torturing me again," etc. We go to the hotel bar. He sits with his back to the Alps, his chair separated from the abyss by a slim mountain fence. He is drinking something red, a gin and Campari, I think. "Why did you come here?" he asks. "I detest mountain views." "Why did *you* come here? That's more interesting." "I may never see you again! When will someone drum some sense into you? . . ." In a few hours the fever returns. I am weak, weakened by wine, weakened by sex. Our first and last illness. Our first and last mountain view. Our first and last trip abroad. He stands by the window, declaiming, "I need a certain way of life . . . style . . . don't you think there was a certain style about the way I just appeared here . . . you must admit that I am style incarnate . . ." Style incarnate style incarnate style incarnate yes yes you are style incarnate. Suddenly I rise and run out of the room, I decide to run away, to run so fast and so far that I shall never be found.

. . . high up on the mountain a feminine figure ran down the path in great haste, but the way was steep, and it constantly seemed as if she hurtled herself down the mountain. She came nearer. Her face was pale, only her eyes blazed terribly, her body was faint, her bosom rose and fell painfully, and yet she ran faster and faster, her disheveled locks streamed loose in the wind, but not even the fresh morning breeze and her own rapid motion was able to redden her pale cheeks. Her nun's veil was torn and floated behind her, her thin white gown would have betrayed much to a profaner glance, had not the passion in her countenance turned the attention of even the most depraved of men upon itself. Where does this woman belong? In the cloister? Have these passions their home there? —In the world? This costume?—Why does she hurry? Is it to conceal her shame and disgrace, or is it to overtake Don Juan? She hastens on to the forest, and it closes about her and hides her, and I see her no more, but hear only the sigh of the forest. Poor Elvira!

I run and run and fall under a pine tree, the stars throbbing at my skull like needles of light. I feel as if I have been devoured by maenads, as if my limbs are scattered all about the forest, hundreds of yards apart from each other, and all the flesh left to me is one enormous muscle of a heart that is about to explode. I grasp for breath, ten or twenty seconds elapse before each breath, my mind is as light and clear and giddy as if I were whiffing pure oxygen. Hooray, hip hip hooray! Baby has finally fallen apart. Dolly is broken. Stephie went boom boom. But all Stephie's horses and all Stephie's men will help to put Dolly together again. One or two things are brilliantly clear: She wants desperately to live. She is not her mother, or her aunt, or any of the female tribe before her. She is herself. So that's what we have to do, break out of everything we've been taught, allow ourselves to scatter apart and try to pick ourselves up again. Like that quote from Kierkegaard which I kept repeating just last year, in that world I'm about to return to for good: "So then choose despair, for despair itself is a choice. And when a man despairs he chooses himself . . . in his eternal validity." Oh God, there comes that Parisian creep, his face screwed up like that of a big rubber doll. "You're putting me into terrible states . . . what if we would have been happy together, it would have been too ghastly . . ." He wipes his eyes with a corner of his table napkin. Suddenly he looks just like his sister, a fat-faced, pathetic baby.

"I suppose you'll soon be going back to New York and those ghastly leftist friends of yours."

My first and last insult. I rise on my elbows, feeling stronger than I have for weeks, the new me starts talking, the one that may be here to stay for a good long while: "Listen, Bonbon, not only am I going back to West Fourth Street, I'm going back there on the first plane I can catch next week. You should look in on that scene sometime, you'd have the screaming heebie jeebies in five minutes, you'd be scared so shitless of those friends of mine you'd be yelling for your little sister in five minutes flat. About a half dozen of us live in one room in which we all eat sleep piss and shit leftist lingo, people who all said beddy-bye to their mommies long ago. By the way, isn't it time you straightened out? I'm so fucking tired of your crappy Paris life, of your so-called Paris *monde*, a bunch of cock-sucking creeps and collaborationists. Listen, brother, I mean it, why don't you straighten out and leave that tight-cunted family of yours before they devour you altogether? Families are the most intense cannibalistic machines in existence, aren't you hip to that? They'll pull you apart limb from limb if you don't wean yourself away from the nipple before the next Pentecost comes around. . . ."

By that time we are back in my hotel room, L. is brushing his teeth, gargling over the sink, his green eyes roll with amazement in his large face. Well, I must say he is doing relatively well, hiding some surprise at that last aria of mine. Masks upon masks of style, masks of cynicism, God how they're skilled at it.

"I adore you," he gargles. "I adore potatoes with lard. Do you like potatoes with lard? I detest mountain views. I detest the middle classes. I need style, admiration, brutality, perpetual bliss."

According to a mutual friend, L. proclaimed, years later, that he had found me insufferable because he could not communicate with me in words, but that I had offered him the greatest "ecstasy" of his life, whatever that is. I, on the contrary, found the mechanics of our sex indifferent. I was in love with him because of the gods I later forswore, because I loved the sheer volume of his words, because he made me feel pure consciousness, because I was fascinated to discover the next turn in the convolutions of his mind. How little people understand of each other. Or of love, which after all is mostly a process of reconnoitering, of exploration, of communication, i.e., a system of information-gathering.

I did not see L. again until years later—a decade after I went home and married Paul—as he strutted on the boardwalk in the south of France in the company of his large family. The old princess, looking precisely as I had visualized her years ago, led the regal file like an aged chicken. Bloated, bejeweled, hobbling on a cane, her fat legs wrapped in sagging black stockings, her small greedy eyes swiftly roving left and right to see what suspicious new faces were about. Then followed L.'s sister Amélie, her plump little face more chapped and chilblained than ever, her eyes screwed up into that wince of fear they assumed whenever she thought of her mother, as if she might even be scolded for the logistics of this particular promenade. Behind her, of course, came L., resplendent in a yellow turtleneck. He was vastly fattened, his cheeks had reddened and turned even coarser, displaying those capillary patches that give away the most indulgent life. His face was scrunched up into that feignedly stupid smile which sheltered him from the ridicule of emotion, his eyes lewdly scanned every woman who passed by, his head seemed larger than ever as it doddered on his overfed body like that of a monstrous Buddha doll. What a waste, what a waste. Finally, behind the three, walked the young Princess Mélanie, her prim little mouth set into an expression of extreme displeasure, her former beauty almost destroyed by what one assumed were arduous years of child-bearing, seeing that she had three young ones in tow that day and was barely twenty-three. Nothing much was left of her beauty, really, save the vacant cornflower-blue eyes that hung upon her drawn face like waning lamps on a dark, still night.

What a beautiful and moving greeting L. sent me for my birthday recently, as he does every November. Over the years I have found that his messages grow increasingly classical, senti-mental, meditative, unhappy, and I am surer than ever that the words are someone else's, not his own. Here is the latest:

On the ocean path, along which are seen no trees, no villages, no steeples, no monuments: on this road devoid of columns and military tombs, which has only waves as boundaries, only winds for com-passes, only start for illumination, the most beautiful of adventures, when one is not in quest of uncharted lands or seas, is the encounter between two vessels. They discover each other on the horizon through the looking glass. The two structures approach, lower their flags to half mast. When all is silent, the two captains, placed at stern, hail each other on their bullhorns. "The name of your boat? What port? The name of the captain? Where is he from? How many days at sea? Latitude and longitude? Goodbye, good luck!" The sailors and the passengers of each boat stare at each other as they retreat, without saying a word. Some are off to search the suns of Asia, others the sun of Europe, which will equally be witness to their death. The passengers signal each other from far away. "Adieu! Good luck!" The common port is eternity.

Long accustomed, as L. must be, to the bitter compromises of marriage and of what society calls "happiness," and in memory of our blissfully lengthy conversations of a decade ago, I send him messages admittedly gleaned from literary classics which often refer to that city where I freely admitted to despair. Such as this one:

"So there is an either/or. If you will continue to divert yourself with the trumpery of wit and the vanity of esprit, then leave your home, go to Paris, devote yourself to journalism, doze your life away in the glittering inanities of the soirees, forget that there is an immortal spirit within you; and when wit grows mute there is water still in the Seine and gunpowder in the store and traveling companionship at every hour of the day. But if you cannot do this, then collect yourself—respect every honest effort, every unassuming endeavor, and above all have a little more reverence for woman. Believe me, out of a hundred men who go astray in the world ninety and nine are saved by women and only one by immediate divine grace."

—Sören Kierkegaard, 1842

Holiday for Cannibals

1 9 6 3

I

"It's a perfect day for the beach!" my mother cries. Her voice rises over the succulent, slapping noise of her morning massage. "Get hold of the fisherman, call off the fishing trip, and let's go to the beach!"

She lies on the sun-drenched terrace, her magnificent body gleaming with oil, quivering with the excitement of morning planning. "All three generations finally under my roof," she says to the masseuse. "Can you imagine my happiness! My daughter, my son-in-law, my adorable grandsons—I've finally gotten them all to the South of France."

I am at the laundry line, picking at dry bathing suits. At every turn of the garden some ancient self of mine sits up suspiciously and sniffs a recollected odor of childhood and of war. "We're going to the Côte d'Azur!" my mother said to me in that summer in 1940 when the Kommandant had given us visas to leave occupied France, and I was disappointed to find that the grounds and the rocks were not a bright cerulean blue.

"Love," my stepfather is saying on the telephone. "L-O-V-E

—Lucien, Octave, Victoire, Émile. *Cable direct pour les États-Unis. C'est ça*—'Love.' Lucien, Octave, Victoire, Émile. . . . *Merci beaucoup.*"

He hangs up. The phone jangles angrily again. The fisherman is calling back. The fisherman is annoyed.

"We're terribly sorry," my stepfather's suave voice says, "You've already bought all the fish for the picnic? . . . Of course, we wouldn't have caught any anyway, there are almost no fish left on this coast. My dear friend, you make us feel even worse."

"Buy his fish!" my mother shouts. "Buy all his fish!"

"We'll buy all your fish. . . . Twenty thousand francs? It's a pleasure. . . . Not at all, *we* thank you. . . . We're here for the month. We'll talk again soon."

"Next call Zozo," my mother cries. "Next call Minou. Tell them to meet us at the beach!"

"I can tell your liver is tired," the masseuse is saying. "Oh, but you can't hide anything from me. *Vous avez le foie très fatigué aujourd'hui.* All the clients from America seem to have a tired liver."

The north wind rises, the doors bang, the wind whistles through the white shell of my parents' house. My stepfather's courteous voice explains to Zozo, Néné, Micou that we shall meet them at the beach, at the café, at the nightclub. A bulldozer mangles the neighboring mountain. Radios shout, cars roar, Vespas whine, brakes screech, sirens moan on the highway two hundred yards below. A gaiety of petunias and geraniums suffuses the narrow garden. My mother loves all that is open and cheerful. She named this house Villa Come-and-Go. It looks out upon a blue, boat-filled Mediterrannean bay. In 1940 there was the same abundance of large zinnias as now, the same smell of eucalyptus and of ripening figs. Food was rationed, scarce. We sat at dinner in 1940 and played a game: we conjured up horrible combinations of food to assuage our hunger. "Sardines with hot chocolate sauce," I said, and won.

"They are superb, magnificent," my mother says tenderly this morning, watching my two sons play.

"They are sublime," my stepfather agrees.

My mother takes the children on her lap and forecasts the delights of the day: "First we go to the beach, and we lunch at the beach, then we have a drink in Saint-Tropez, then we have dinner in a restaurant. . . ."

"Daddy's still asleep," Jeff says. "Why is he always asleep?"

"Because he hates the South of France," Tommy answers.

My mother looks hurt. She puts the children down and starts trimming her geraniums. Whenever she's sad she trims her geraniums.

The children run into the garden with an explosion of make-believe machine-gunning. "Rat-tat-tat-tat-tat I'll get you, you terrible German!" Jeff shouts.

"I can't understand why those children play war so much," my stepfather mumbles. "I suppose they hear too much about the war."

"On to the beach!" my mother cries. "We're all ready to go to the beach!"

I go into the house to wake my husband. Paul lies on our bed sprawled out like a large child, one knee curled toward his chest. His eyes are swathed in a black silk mask, his ears are filled with wax earplugs, a pillow is folded over his head, a bottle of red sleeping pills glimmers on our night table. Paul is an old-fashioned man. He believes in the Realm of Spirit, Family Life, and Peace and Quiet. We live in New England because big cities are Dirty, Noisy, and Crime-Ridden. The Riviera is Crowded, Noisy, and Crude. He lifts his pillow. A tired blue eye appears.

"How was your night?" he asks.

"Just fair."

"I figured out at 3 A.M. that this house is built upon a rock above the highway, with the acoustics of a perfect Greek amphitheater."

"It *is* noisy."

"Stephanie, I detest the Riviera."

"You're the one who wanted to come."

"We had to. They've been asking us for years."

"We haven't had a good talk in days."

"Well, when do you expect to talk? At that packed beach we have to go to every day, at those cafés where you can't hear yourself think?"

"Let's try again today. And get dressed. It's time to go to the sea."

"How original. I thought we were finally going fishing."

"Mother says it's a perfect day for the beach."

"What date is it today?"

"July third."

"Three more weeks here. Steph, you know what my grandmother used to say when we wanted new bathing trunks for the summer? She'd say, 'What do you want new trunks for? June, July, August, September, and the summer's over.'"

He gets dressed, and wears that polite, frigid smile he prepares every morning for his vacation with the in-laws. We walk to the driveway. The children agitate with sand pails around the family car. We pack into the Peugeot station wagon.

My mother is happy. "This is the only immortality," she says, "to have you all here under one roof, in a place I adore." All her eggs in one basket, she adds, all her chickens in one coop. She praises the color of the sky, the temperature of the water, the whiteness of the sand, the invigorating air.

The children's voices rise over her banter like the twittering of sparrows: "How do you say 'hole' in Spanish?" . . . "How do you say 'the whole wide world' in French?" . . . "Are all Germans bad?"

My stepfather is at the wheel. His silver hair gleams in the morning light, his moustache twitches with emotion. His happiness glows in the precarious balance of our morning harmony.

"It's so wonderful, so beautiful, to be here all together," he says. "Hi, big shots," he calls out to the children. "Darling Stephanie," he says to me. "Are you happy, my love?" he asks my mother.

"Finally," she answers. "We must do this every year." And the look in her eyes conveys her image of a family united, unanimous in all its pleasures and opinions—get out the camera, heads together, smiling, click. . . . My husband's cheek twitches. His white teeth shine like a keyboard in his tanned and tired face.

We drive along the bay toward Saint-Tropez. Here where the new camping site begins, my friend Minou and I used to turn inland on our bicycles at dusk, that winter of the war, to fetch milk from a farm. I was nine, and too scared of the dark to enjoy my independence. The pine copse rushes past with a sweep of bittersweet recollections. Across the road, several hundred campers' tents stretch down to the sea. Billboards loom over the pine copse, advertising Coppertone, Nivéa, Ambre Solaire. Gigantic billboard girls bare their teeth, thrusting brown breasts and bottles of brown liquid at the driver. Campers swarm among the orange tents.

"Goodness," Paul says. "How they spoil the landscape."

"You are a snob," my mother says. "Statistics show that the height of the average Frenchman has increased by two and a half centimeters since camping has offered them more sun."

"Well, their growth hurts the eye."

"Please be more democratic," she commands.

Convertibles speed past us, filled with young, sadistic, grimacing faces. The girls' manes fly in the breeze. A violet-colored Simca shaves by and closes in in front of us, its driver shouting at the driver ahead of him. My stepfather slams on the brakes. The children scream with delight.

"God, they drive badly," Paul says. "The French have got to be the most godawful drivers."

"Well, no worse than Americans," my stepfather says.

"Nonsense. Americans may be slower, but they're more responsible."

"Driving is based on fast reactions. All good drivers are fast drivers."

"Statistics show that one out of every four French drivers is hospitalized for a car accident," I say. "Statistics show that they *are* terrible drivers."

"It's that lust for power," my husband says. "They've lost their colonies; they take it out on the roads."

"You're all so psychiatric," my stepfather snaps. "They're young, they're on vacation, they're having fun."

We are on a dirt road now, following a line of Opels, Renaults, and Mustangs to Pampelonne Beach. My mother continues her praises of Saint-Tropez. She has read in *Match* that this beach averages four more hours of sunlight a day than any other European resort. She has read in *Elle* that children brought to the Mediterranean suffer twenty percent fewer colds than children taken to the Atlantic. We reach the parking lot. Some three hundred closely packed cars gleam in the sun. My mother inhales the salt breeze ecstatically as we get out of the car. We walk toward the sea, and she stands on top of the dune, looking affectionately upon a seething mass of bodies on the sand. "How amusing this is!" she cries. "How I love this beach. Come quickly, children!"

We change on the beach, demurely swathed in large towels. Paris friends greet my parents. Beachboys and bartenders swarm around them effusively. The children run to the sea edge. My husband and I shuffle toward our umbrella. He collapses on his mattress and buries himself in the Paris *Herald Tribune*. I hide in the hot shade and survey the scene. We are daily taken to an establishment called Tahiti-Plage. Its bathhouses are built of rushes in emulation of African or Polynesian huts. The name of the restaurant where we eat lunch, the Madagascar Bar, is printed in fuchsia letters on a lemon-yellow awning. The sand is sugary white, orange and turquoise umbrellas thickly pack the beach, we lie on candy-striped mattresses. My allergic skin is a mottled pink, Paul's peach-hued in the orange shade of our umbrella. Above our heads waiters parade with trays, wearing tight peppermint-striped trunks. At our left a middle-aged woman, her flesh bursting out of a tiny bathing suit, slowly massages her stomach. Girls in doll-sized, fruit-colored bikinis rub amber-colored grease on the backs of their companions. Hand in hand or half entwined, lovers of all ages sprawl in the sun. I discern French and Swedish models, German steel magnates, British starlets, Paris fashion designers, Italian film directors, American decorators. Long-haired teen-agers, thighs rotating, breasts bared, parade slowly at the edge of the water, scanning the beach for encounters. And the expanse of oiled flesh gleams in the sun with the sad splendor of quartered meat.

There is a clatter of voices and provocative giggling, the roar of motorboats and helicopters. An African rhythm starts pounding from the restaurant jukebox. A woman's voice screaming, "You're going to get it!" is followed by a long, sustained child's howl. An Arab in burnoose stands over me, wailing the praise of his roasted almonds. I try to talk to Paul.

"What is it exactly you don't like about this place? I mean how would *you* define it?"

"The fecklessness of it all. Everybody on the make." His pale puritan eyes critically survey the surrounding flesh. "All those bodies lying in the sun, like in some ghastly rotisserie."

" 'Fecklessness' is the perfect word. You always find the perfect word."

Our children are whooping by the sea edge, throwing pailfuls of water into the moat of a sand castle. He takes my hand. We admire the beauty of our offspring.

"The monsters," he says. "They like it here. What a trap."

"Well, it doesn't *have* to be a trap. Perhaps we should make more of an effort. Perhaps we're being pills. . . . I can't stand hurting anybody's feelings."

"O.K., I'm a pill." He strokes my arm. "Stephanie darling. I'm sorry, this place tires me so I barely have the energy to talk to you."

"Well, you never talk that much anyhow, sweetheart."

We hold hands. We apologize to each other. We whisper future plans for northern vacations—a lonely house on the Irish Sea, on the Scottish moors. A few yards away from us my mother patrols the beach. She is statuesque, jeweled, coffee brown, golden-haired, dressed in barbaric colors. Her rich and deep voice booms over the beach. She laughs with friends, predicts the lines of the next Paris collections, roars lunch orders at the waiters, commands women to oil their children, builds sand castles for her grandsons. My stepfather lies gleaming and placid on his mattress, his eyes half closed with contentment, looking with admiration at his little family. "Hi, big shot!" he calls out to Jeff. "How do you like our beach?"

"Well, it's all right," Jeff answers, "but it's a little noisy and crowded."

My stepfather pretends to be amused. "It's so funny the way they repeat everything their father says."

My mother continues to pace the beach, Cinzano in hand, greeting and expounding. A tune sung by Les Playboys starts up on the jukebox. She shuffles her feet and swings her hips, singing, "*Watu-si—comme c'est drôle le Watu-si . . .*" Then her voice booms over us: "You may complain about this place, but everyone comes back. The most interesting people in Europe are here this morning. Over there in the green bikini is the editor of the most influential women's magazine in France. Next to her is the film director who is going to get the prize in Cannes this year. Then there's Tiki de Benzeville, the man with the most beautiful jewelry in Europe. And the top model for *Queen* magazine, and the former girl friend of the Prime Minister. One does not argue with winners." She swigs her Cinzano down defiantly. "It's so international, so gay."

Two women twenty years apart in age come toward us, greeting us in shrill polished English.

"Here is my Zozo!" my mother cries. "Here is your Minou!"

Zozo, a cigarette clenched between her lips, has a round, wizened chocolate-brown face familiar to me from photographs taken with my mother in the twenties. Her daughter, Minou, has the same mop of bright-red hair which I used to help her braid when we were children. We all rise, we all kiss.

"But how you've grown!" Zozo exclaims to me.

"Isn't it fantastic to have them here!" my mother cries. "You and I haven't missed a year, but them, all three generations—can you imagine my happiness?" The two women link arms and prance toward the bar.

Minou comes toward our umbrella. She is a successful businesswoman, still unmarried—one of those compact little Frenchwomen whom one sees at the wheels of sport cars, briskly dodging traffic in the thick of Paris rush hours. She settles under our umbrella with a diffident, pouting smile.

We exchange the ritual greeting of our childhood. "Moumoute!" I whisper to her. "Dear old moumoute," she answers. And for Paul's benefit we clarify our greeting: "Moumoutes" was a club we founded when we were nine years old. We sum up the conditions of membership. Moumoutes move furtively, soft-footedly, they are feline, secretive, mysterious, hearth-loving creatures. Sleep, childhood, shade, privacy, corners, fogs, rainy days are moumoute. So are eating jam with a spoon, licking chocolate off the cooking pot, crouching by the fire, hiding at length under the covers. Cats, seals and bears are moumoute, dogs and horses are not. Moumoutes are mysterious, selfish, and adept at imitating purring. We still say, whenever we meet, such and such a person is moumoute, such and such a place is not.

"This beach is not moumoute," Paul suggests.

"But he must be one of us," she whispers. "How could he have learned so fast?"

"I'm a supermoumoute," he says with a smile. "What are you doing, Minou, in this most unmoumoute place in the world?"

"It's a duty tour." She curls up snugly under the umbrella, wrinkles her freckled nose. "My flapper mother! Her gayest days before the war were spent here. It continues her youth. She adores that crowded, noisy little house of hers."

"How well we know. Will they ever get disillusioned?"

A group of teen-agers behind us discusses heatedly the relative merits of the new French cars—the chassis of the Peugeot, the acceleration of the DS, the trunk space in the 404.

"In the nineteen-forties Frenchmen discussed politics," Paul says. "In the fifties, food and sex. And now it's nothing but cars, cars, cars."

"Of course, it's the new French obsession. The roads are impossible."

"It's sheer hell. They're so rude. They drive so badly."

"Stéphanie, do you remember how empty the roads were in the summer of 1940?" Minou exclaims. "No one had any gasoline, so there were no cars. We were allowed to bicycle all day long on the main highway. We especially loved that part of the road where that ghastly camping spot is now. Do you remember that ride every night for milk?"

"God yes, there was a dark copse of pine woods to go through. In the fall it was already dark by milking time and I was terrified of the ride back. The big pine branches waved at me like scythes. I hadn't been told about Papa's death yet, but I dimly suspected it. Ever since then I've imagined angels of death hovering over the roads here. Minou, do you realize that Papa's death traumatized me so I've never even dared to go back to Saint-Seran to visit his tomb?"

"You don't mean it. You've never been back?"

"No. I'm still terrified. Anyhow, Minou, you used to laugh at me so because I didn't like to ride down that road at night."

"You were such a melancholy girl," Minou muses. "So unlike your children! They're so gay! Look at them play."

"Our parents are much gayer and more frivolous than we are, too. They make me feel quite old."

"Well, we're that odd war generation," Minou says. "I just want to survive and be left alone. . . . How are you surviving the family experiment?" she asks Paul.

"I adore my in-laws," he says laconically. "They keep saying how good it is for the children."

Minou laughs cynically. "As if our mothers ever knew what's good for children. Do you remember ever spending one summer vacation with your mother? We were always sent off somewhere with our governesses."

"Lunch!" my mother calls out. "Lunch, everybody!" She waves from the table where she and Zozo have been sitting, growing increasingly voluble over their cocktails.

"I tell you Néné *has* lifted her face," Zozo is asserting as we walk toward them. "But you never did believe anything I said."

"Well, I tell you she has not. Why should I believe what you say? You've always exaggerated everything."

"I know her better than you do."

"You do not. She confides everything to me. No one ever confided anything to you."

"What are you talking about?"

"Everyone knows you're the soul of indiscretion."

"Well, I simply refuse to discuss this anymore," Zozo says. She glares into her whiskey glass.

We sit down. "Steak for everybody!" my mother shouts. "Salad for everybody! A lot of wine for everybody!"

The men in peppermint-striped trunks set plates in front of us. Paul cuts the children's meat. My stepfather savors the wine. The children sink their teeth into their steaks.

"Look at them eat," my stepfather says. "Have you ever seen them eat so marvelously?"

"One's the image of the father, the other's the image of the mother," Zozo says.

"They are superb, beautiful," Minou says.

"This is the only immortality," my mother says, "to be all lunching together at my beach."

"They are fat, lovely, like ripe peaches," my stepfather says. "We must do this every year."

"When the Germans occupied France," Tommy asks, "did they bring their whole country over?"

"When a country occupies another country," Jeff asks, "how come it doesn't fall into the sea?"

"Boys," Paul says, "come out of the sun. Don't eat your lunch in the sun."

"But you're going to kill those children with lack of sun," my mother moans. "It makes their bones grow."

"There's nothing worse for kids than too much sun at midday," I say.

"You used to love the sun," my stepfather says. "You used to spend hours and hours just lying in the sun."

"Well, I can't take it anymore. I've changed."

"You certainly have."

"They've had too much sun and that's all there is to it," my husband says.

"But how you've grown," Zozo says to me. "You're still taller. How old are you?"

"Thirty-two."

"Impossible!" she screams. "You are lying!" She frowns, her head bending over her Scotch. "Of course, you're Minou's age. Perhaps you're thirty-two after all. You came to us with your father for a weekend in 'thirty-nine, do you remember?" Her face turns malicious, she tantalizes me with memories, as if offering candy to a child. "You were the little Stéphanie he had to tuck in every night. Then he knelt at the bottom of your bed to say prayers. It was the spring before the war. How he adored you!"

"Yes," my mother says curtly, "he adored her."

"And I made fudge in your kitchen, do you remember?" I said. "And there was an invasion of caterpillars on your terrace. And my father ordered me my first pair of slacks."

"All that I don't remember," Zozo says vaguely.

The candy is withdrawn. I stare, defeated, at her curved and predatory toenails, painted deep ruby red. At the neighboring table a former husband of Brigitte Bardot teases a marmoset. The animal is dressed in miniature bathing trunks and pulls pathetically at his leash. The ex-husband's entourage shrieks and laughs over the animal's antics. A voice wails on the juke-box, *"Qu'on est bien dans tes bras . . ."* Zozo continues talking with my mother about the old days. The time they won the Charleston contest, the day they swam across the Bay of Saint-Tropez, the time they drove to Rome without stopping to sleep. There was that Jewish banker crazy to marry Zozo, the American lawyer who wanted my mother to divorce for him, that Russian prince who was so poor and so handsome that they spent their evenings with him riding the Paris subways. . . . I conjure up photographs of pale-faced, cupid-mouthed women in fedora hats, reclining, swathed in smoke, against the tufted banquettes of nightclubs or leaning on the gleaming sur-faces of Ferraris. Their marcelled hair waves low over their brows, silver-buckled belts swing low on their hips, pointed shoes terminate their slender legs. Minou and I stare warily at our flapper mothers. The gay, gilded past of the twenties and thirties floats past us like a perfumed barge. . . . I shut my inward eye, weary of comparisons. They continue to argue.

"You're wrong; it was the summer of 'thirty-seven that we drove to Rome together, not 'thirty-six."

"I assure you it was the summer of 'thirty-six," Zozo says. "I was with my second husband. We met on this very beach on the way back."

"You weren't with any husband at all. You were with that André de something or other."

"Whoever I was with, it was the summer I had my motor-cycling accident and you had your car accident."

"You've got the summers all twisted."

"Well, I simply refuse to argue with you any more!" Zozo

exclaims. "You're too stubborn, and besides I think your memory's quite gone." She turns to my husband. "And you live in the United States? In the country? You are not bored to death? And I hear you do not like our South of France?"

"Well, there's nothing much to see here except all these bodies." He smiles glacially. "The interesting part of Provence is terribly far away."

"He's an architect, he loves to look at architecture," my mother explains. "Crypts, ruins, and all that. And also he loves nature. All Americans love nature."

"My son-in-law believes in the Dignity of Man and in Peace and Quiet," my stepfather gibes. "He does not find them here."

"I might if I could sleep."

"Insomnia is a state of mind, nobody talked about insomnia in my generation," my stepfather says. "I think I'll call you the Tired Generation."

"And he does not dance any of the new dances," my mother says sadly. "He stopped with the waltz. He refuses to set foot in a nightclub."

"Just like Minou." Zozo sighs.

We sip our coffee silently, dazed by the lunch wine. There is a mournful, very old Piaf record: *"Il était blond, il était beau . . . il sentait bon le sable chaud . . . mon lé-gion-nai-ai-re. . . ."* The tables are vacated, the gleaming bodies lie at new angles, like needles of compasses, to absorb the rays of the slanting sun.

"I'm going to my massage," Zozo announces.

"I'm going to take a cozy little nap," Minou says.

"I'm going to take a walk," my mother says.

"Rest, my love, lie down," my stepfather says. "It will do you good."

They go to their mattresses and lie hand in hand in the sun. My mother's free hand continues to tap agitatedly on the sand to the rhythm of the jukebox. Minou has curled up under our umbrella like a cat by the hearth, her knees curled up against her chest. Paul lies on his back, arms akimbo. In his exhaustion he is the shell, the discarded rind of a man. "I can't work here,

I can't read here, I can't sleep, I can't fuck, I can barely write a postcard," he mutters. "June July August September and the summer's over," I whisper. It could be three, four, five o'clock —who can say? I lie in the timeless umbrella of my family summer. Around us the sun worshipers have begun to intertwine. Bleached heads rest on male stomachs, sleek arms enlace with hairy thighs, men's heads repose on half-naked breasts, nipples emerge from the flimsy stuff of brassieres, thighs rotate in the waning sun. The beach swells with oiled, flailing limbs, like an estuary gleaming with fish at mating time. The sight of the flesh, of the bared breasts, begins to fill me with nausea. My head is throbbing, my skin itches from the reflected sun of the umbrella, a cicada sings violently above the buzz of voices and the thud of the small waves.

One of my flushed children appears, his face caked with sand and salt. "How do you say 'neck' in French?" he asks. "Everybody on this beach is necking."

"Lie down in the shade, Jeffie darling," I plead weakly. "You've had too much sun."

But he's off again, staging an attack on his brother's sand castle. Peace, family peace, family love, it took me years to get it, let's hold on. We must preserve it. L-O-V-E. Lucien, Octave, Victoire, Emile. Family love, through rage and war, war and peace, lies and fornication, boredom and disaster, marriage and madness. Stay sane, Stephanie, stay sane, stay snug for a while in your nice warm nest taking care of your birdies, and try not to suffocate. . . .

A shout from Tommy stirs us: "You're my prisoner! You can't escape!" He has thrown himself upon the back of a helpless, peeling German tourist, who acts politely bewildered. "I've caught a German!"

We leap to our feet. We scold and apologize profusely. The German disappears, with a show of exquisite courtesy.

"This is too much," my stepfather says. "Why bring him up this way? I'm disappointed in you. Why bring him up with hatred?"

"Well, I hate the Germans, too," Paul says.

"What kind of an answer is that? I'm disappointed in you."

"Isn't France wonderful, darling?" I ask Tommy diplomatically. "What do you like the best in France?"

"The accidents," the child says. Then his face puckers up and dissolves into a howl. I pick him up. He is a baby again, clutching at my shoulders.

"I've said before that these children are getting too much sun. We've been on this crazy beach for six whole hours; it's almost evening."

"Well, what's wrong with being on the beach?" my stepfather says. "I work hard all year, I'm on vacation, I want to enjoy my vacation. Can't you enjoy a day at the beach?"

We gather towels, moist bathing suits, sand pails, anti-sun lotions. My mother has a hurt look in her eyes. Her photograph of family unity is shattered. Zozo looks at us cynically, cigarette smoke swathing her leathery face.

"Why don't *we* take the children back?" Minou says. "It's right on our way, almost next door."

"Can't we go home, too?" Paul whispers to me.

"We're supposed to meet those people for dinner at Saint-Tropez. Please, one more little show of togetherness."

Minou and I say goodbye. "Au revoir, moumoute. I'll take good care of the children."

"Thank you, old moumoute. Tell the maid to put them to bed very early, and I'll call her at eight. See you tomorrow, I hope?"

"Perhaps." She shrugs, with her little dour smile. She goes off to her mother's car, holding a child awkwardly by each hand. We walk back to our station wagon.

My mother consoles herself by making plans for the next day. "Tomorrow Néné is coming for lunch here, and Renée, and Mimi. I must order a table for twelve or fourteen. . . ."

We pack again into the Peugeot. The brilliant, raped landscape reels past us once more as we follow the thick line of traffic to Saint-Tropez. Pink stucco villas, gas stations, more campers' tents, billboards of bronzed breasts and thighs dot the sparse groves of olive trees. Paul sits stalwartly in the back, arms folded on his chest. He is like a picture in the medical books depicting the nervous system: ganglia rawly exposed, neurons taut as violin strings. He may scream at any human touch. . . .

The sky is turning the pink of cyclamen. We circle in the port of Saint-Tropez, looking for a place to park. The little mooring bay is filled with opulent yachts. The quay is lined with fishermen's houses transformed years ago into awninged cafés. The houses are blue, green, melon—confectioner's colors. Brightly hued pennants fly from the masts of the boats.

My mother heads toward the most crowded bar. "This is *the* place," she says. "This café always was the place in the fifties, and look, everybody's still here!"

A waiter salutes my stepfather's tip. We sit down and take in the sights. Movie actors cruise the port in mauve-colored Opels. A crowd congregates around a French singing star. Jeweled men sit over cocktails on their yachts, scanning flesh through their binoculars. The in crowd pushes at the bar, jostling to be seen. The men wear tight pants and embroidered shirts. The girls wear thick false braids down their backs, white paint on their upper lids, pale pomade on their lips that exaggerates the cultivated Negro hue of their skins. Thighs rotate in the neon lights, the stuff of clothing is stretched drum-tight over breasts and buttocks, the crowd ogles and appraises itself.

"Isn't this fun," my stepfather says. "So gay. So attractive. The girls are splendid. . . ."

We sip our Dubonnets. Paul has buried himself in a new issue of the Paris *Herald Tribune*.

My mother returns from her examination of the port. "Let's go, let's go," she calls. "I've reserved a table for dinner in a divine new club. Voom-Voom—isn't that a brilliant name for a nightclub? Voom-Voom!"

"We're going to go home and have a sandwich and go to bed," Paul says.

"But just come for a drink, then!" she pleads. "Come see Voom-Voom!"

We walk down the port, passing shops filled with artists' supplies, jazz records, tropical fruit, paperbacks, fake antiques, sandals, postcards of breakfasting nudists, plastic housewares, straw hats. Voom-Voom is in a narrow back street, a cave built into the cellar of an old fisherman's house. The agitated African rhythms of 1963 thrust out of the cave. A few couples have already begun to gyrate.

"I have a headache," Paul says. "I'm not going in there."

He has backed up against a shop window, and rows of fruit-colored, dwarf-sized bikinis frame his head. An alternating neon light pulsates through the beachwear shop, flushing the street with hues of peach, apricot, fuchsia. My mother is at the entrance of the blue cave, beckoning, swinging her hips to the rhythm of Les Playboys.

"Come! Come!" she cries. "Come to Voom-Voom!"

My husband stands stalwartly on the pavement, pale-eyed, American, priggish, determined, firmly clutching my hand.

"I am not going in there," he repeats.

"But just come for a look, then," my mother pleads. "It's so gay, the décor is so amusing."

He does not budge.

"I have a headache. I can't take that noise and that smoke. We're going to find a taxi."

"Leave them alone," my stepfather says gently. "They want peace and quiet."

"I'll tell you all about it tomorrow," my mother promises. She waves regretfully as she disappears into the cave. "And perhaps tomorrow you'll change your mind."

Then we are in a taxi. The port sways behind us, pale masts against a violet sky.

" 'Steamer balançant ta mâture,' " I murmur. " 'Lève l'ancre pour une exotique nature! . . .' "

"Mallarmé?"

"Right."

"I wouldn't mind raising *my* anchor. Goodness, family vacations can be exhausting."

"But necessary."

"It'll be great to be quiet and go to bed early for a change. Back to Come-and-Go." He sighs. He takes my hand. "Sweetheart."

I squeeze his hand in return. We ride back in the dark to our selfish peace, our quiet caves, to his beloved refuge from the century's noises. And across the bay, through the navy-blue Mediterranean night, wafts a tomtomlike sound of music, to which I suppose my mother is dancing, dancing.

Tribe

1966

I

"What about Suez?" Aunt Charlotte asked. "What about Algeria? What about Vietnam? Twenty years! We have a lot of catching up to do. How curious of you not to have returned sooner!"

A very heavy woman, her flesh accreted like uncontrolled lava, was welcoming me back to Saint-Seran. I had finally gathered the courage to visit my father's family again. Aunt Charlotte's silvery hair tumbled over an exorbitantly pink face, she held on her lap a piece of tapestry work and a large album of collected stamps. Inured by age and willful isolation, her mind swung giddily among historical cataclysms and recitations of family chronicles. All of my father's brothers, including her husband, Uncle Jean, were now dead.

"Are there roads in America?" she continued. "Do you eat bread in America? What kind of bread? What is the speed limit on your roads? Did you do your studies in English or in American? Do you remember how you used to skim the foam off the raspberry jam in our kitchen before the war? Do you think you could send me some African stamps from the United

States? Possibly you could find me some from Zaïre. . . . Listen, dear child, we have all the room in the world for you."

And she pointed to the proliferation of bedding scattered about her living room and the entire house. It was the most startling feature of this dwelling I had not entered since the age of fifteen; it made my long absence seem all the odder. There were army cots stood up helter-skelter against the eighteenth-century *boiseries* of the old library, folding beds crammed in the hallways, sleeping bags strewn about the little dining room to which Aunt Charlotte hobbled to take her meals, more beds stacked against the delicate Louis XIII staircase that wound upstairs from the front entrance hall. This proliferation of sleeping arrangements contrasted bizarrely with the bleak gray walls hung with portraits of ancestors, the forbidding crucifixes dominating a wall of every room, the austerity of gray stone floors left uncarpeted since the German occupation. It gave Saint-Seran a warm and profligate bohemianism, testifying to the enormous number of grandchildren, great-grandchildren, nephews, nieces who flocked back here every summer with an eagerness which I found mysterious, seeing how terrified I had been of my own return. When my father was shot down over Gibraltar from the Spanish coast, presumably by German gunfire, he had been buried in the British cemetery. Nine years later his body had been brought back to France and reburied in the family vault near Saint-Seran. I had never dared to visit his grave. I had spent a good part of my life denying the reality of his death. And now as I finally sat facing Aunt Charlotte I was crippled by another fear that had haunted me for decades: that my family would bear me too much rancor after my long absence for any return to be bearable, that I could never return.

Rancor? Quite the contrary! My aunt's gentle, inquisitive eyes seemed filled with gratitude at my visit. She lived all year long in this ancient house where I had spent some of my happiest childhood holidays. Seventy-six years old, rooted to the first floor of the dwelling by her great weight, she was as frenetically curious about contemporary events as she was reluctant to witness them at first hand. And she treated my arrival as if it were the most precious of gifts—a marvelously riskless exposure to the modern world.

"Don't you dare think I'm out of touch," she announced emphatically, pointing to her large RCA television set, "even though I've not once been to Paris since World War Two. It's only a three hours' train ride from Nantes nowadays, but there is something about the capital which most of our family has always disliked and feared—the many new ideas perhaps . . . the modernism . . . the size . . . the craze for novelty . . . the foreign visitors . . ."

Her fingers fidgeting with a corner of her stamp album, her cane tapping agitatedly on the floor, she stared at her foreign visitor with the furtive, taunting excitement with which we sometimes stare at a tiger safely caged in a zoo.

"You're not going to tell *me*, in *this* house," she challenged me within ten minutes of our first embrace, "that Algerian independence was not a monstrosity. Just think of your great-great-granduncle, General de Lamoricière, who dedicated his life to conquering Algeria for France, and your father's brother, Uncle André, whom independence left totally destitute at the age of sixty-seven. And now it's the Algerians who are bankrupt; we gave them freedom much too early for their own good, not even to speak of ours. What's all this idea of liberty for children who don't even know how to read, who barely know how to make a little camel drawing instead of their signature, how can they vote? That's one point on which I broke totally with our great de Gaulle, but God bless his soul, he may have been forced into it, he's beyond reproach on all else. Tell me, aren't you afraid of an invasion of Chinese into the United States?"

No, I said, there were many things to fear, but that was not one of them.

"Well, I'd watch out if I were you, I think you're overly optimistic. They just might turn out to be like the Africans in England or the Arabs here, drive you out of job and home. And what about Vietnam, what could you think of that atrocity? How did you manage not to learn a lesson from our history and immediately get out? What a frightful decade you must be living through!"

Yes, I said, I had been arrested once for taking part in a demonstration against the war in Vietnam.

She clapped her plump little hands, and appeared to feel increasingly safe in my company. "Bravo, bravo! You're one of us down to the last straw, that's just what many of us would have done. Risk! Acting out one's conscience always entails some risk. I must tell you that several of your second cousins who were in the underground have never really recovered from their experience in concentration camps even twenty years later. Foreigners tend to forget how scarred we still are by the war, how many generations it takes for these wounds to heal. By the way, I suppose you're going to visit your father's grave tomorrow or the day after?"

Yes, I said, it had been very much on my mind to do that.

"Well, Stéphanie, there is something you do not know about him that is very important for you to know. You see, after we saw you here last we heard from the chaplain in Gibraltar that all the men on your father's plane were still conscious when they crashed upon the beach, that they were all able to receive Extreme Unction."

She watched my face closely, waiting to be rewarded with an expression of gratitude, which did not come. For the first time, she seemed irritated with me.

"But you live in a world of delusions, my dear! You don't seem to realize what joy it gave us to know that he had received the last sacrament! Just think how ghastly it would have been if the plane he was on had fallen into the sea like the others, if we hadn't been able to eventually bring his body here. You see,

God always gives us something to be grateful for, if you look at life in the right way." And she crossed herself with great cheerfulness.

I stared at the crucifix hanging above the television set alongside a picture of de Gaulle, and the family's hallowed dead, thinking yes, this was the kind of grim detail I must be prepared to face here, that I had felt incapable of facing up to now. At such times my mind took refuge from her chatter in safely historical, encyclopedic meditations on the verdant countryside about me: "Vendée, a maritime department of western France adjoining the southeast boundary of Brittany, one of France's most conservative districts, was the region which most fiercely resisted the Revolution in 1793. The Chouans, peasant bands well documented in the Balzac novel named after them, instigated a series of Royalist insurrections which lasted well into the nineteenth century. . . ." The landscape out of Aunt Charlotte's window was as flat as any in my memory, there was not a hillock, not a rock, to disturb the monotonous platitude of its horizon. A serene, dead-straight alley of luxuriant chestnut trees stretched from the little castle to the country road. To the left stood some dilapidated buildings that had once served as stables and servants' quarters. The old greenhouse to the right of the entrance had also been abandoned since the war, when the family fortune declined sharply. In the flower beds circling about the castle's entrance only the simplest and most tenacious of flowers—hydrangeas, geraniums—fought their way nobly through tall clumps of weeds.

"Now for the family albums," Aunt Charlotte was saying. "Let's start with 1936, we'll do 'thirty-seven in the afternoon, and perhaps 'thirty-eight after tea if we're not too tired. Well, here you are, aged five, with your cousin Daniel, who's coming from Nantes to lunch with you. There you are with Louise, your oldest cousin, who is coming from Paris tomorrow to see you. And look at that sweet picture of you with Catherine, who is coming to meet you here this afternoon. Ah, here's one of you with your father and all five of your Saint-Seran cousins, mercy how they adored him, he was their hero . . ." She lingered with particular affection upon a photo of my father surrounded by a pack of children—we were swarming and climbing up his limbs as if he were a huge oak tree, gamboling on the stoop of the ancestral door which I had avoided for so long. Cousins, cousins, I never knew anyone could possess as many as I did. Throughout the day they tumbled out of Aunt Charlotte's albums as prolifically as the camp beds set out to accommodate them, testifying to the redoubtable fact that in other parts of France my father's other three brothers had each borne a minimum of five children, most of whom had also had five or six of their own, and that all thirty or forty of them came back here every summer. It was awesome, this proliferation of shared protoplasm, to someone who had been brought up kinless in the New World. Every few hours some new batch of my tribesmen would arrive, each greeting me with different tones of curiosity, irony, emotion.

"It's very nice of you to come back after all these years," my cousin Daniel hollered at me from the front door, by way of greeting, "awfully good of you to finally come back!"

I stared back at him with particular curiosity, for he was depicted in one of the few childhood photographs that had followed me to America. It showed us together at the age of eight or nine, both sucking on lollipops and dressed in white for someone's First Communion. My arm was linked through his, and he looked miserable under my possessive embrace—I had been madly in love with him at that age. He was now a tall, angular businessman in his thirties with great fangs of tobacco-stained teeth.

"You could have given us some sign of life earlier, you know," he continued to roar. "Awfully strange behavior. Strange notion of family you have in the United States. We've always heard you had no great sense of family or of the past.

Well, my dear, you're a living proof. So you've finally decided to come back. We were never about to spank you or anything for staying away. Your father was one of my best friends when I was a child. A hero to us all, God knows. Every few years our magazines still ask for a picture of him to illustrate another story on the early days of the Resistance. I'd have recognized you in a crowd a hundred yards away! Ah, well, give us a kiss, it's good to have you back!"

And he embraced me powerfully, exhaling pungent odors of Gitanes. It was almost time for lunch. On this August holiday—the Feast of the Assumption of Mary—young cousins from Nantes, from Rennes, from Brest, kept flocking unannounced to the family house, arriving on motorcycles and in *quatre chevaux* with the suddenness with which a lover surprises his mistress on an idle afternoon.

"Yes, here they are," Daniel said pointedly, *"they*'ve got a sense of family. Properly brought up people. You can't keep them away."

The helter-skelter village girl in charge of Aunt Charlotte's housekeeping scurried about, peeling more potatoes, picking more tomatoes.

"It's always like this in the summers," Aunt Charlotte grumbled good-naturedly as she hobbled about, masterminding the frantic resetting of the table, "sometimes we're three, sometimes eighteen. I wish they'd let me know with a little phone call, I who try to build my life around accurate and precise reception of world news, lunch at twelve sharp so I can get the one o'clock *informations*, dinner punctually at seven so I can see the best of the evening reports . . ."

With an entrancing blend of formality and confusion, a long series of courses—melon, fish, chicken, a vegetable, salad, cheese, fruit—were served separately, on seven changes of slightly chipped two-hundred-year-old family china.

"We hear you're a writer. So what do you write about in America?" Daniel shouted over the table. "Oh, my God, current events? I don't know how you can keep up with them, where you live."

"Where's Dayton, Ohio?" asked a young cousin who had arrived from Nantes on his motorcycle. "In the center of your country or on the coast?"

"You have only two children? Why such a small family?"

"Do your sons play soccer, rugby, or football?"

"Hasn't Dr. Spock had a terribly pernicious influence on your young people?"

"What are the speed limits on your roads?"

"Absolutely monstrous of you to pressure your President Johnson with those filthy antiwar demonstrations," Daniel broadcast over the fish course. "You elect him with the greatest plurality in history, and then you make life hell for him. What's all this hysteria? I repeat, you have no sense of history. You should have avoided the whole mess by profiting by our example, but once you're in, full steam ahead. All your puritanical nonsense about corruption in South Vietnam, it's so naïve. What do you think politics are all about? Did anyone raise an eyebrow when Napoleon pillaged Italy?" He washed down his fish with a large mouthful of Montrachet. "Did anyone protest when Louis XIII had his opponents jailed? How else can you run a country? In messing up your Johnson you're thinking of yourselves, not of world order, it's very selfish, it's not very elegant."

It was the hottest day of the summer. Some twelve of us were crowded into the tiny dining room furnished with frayed, weathered Louis XV chairs and piles of sleeping bags. All the windows were tightly shut. The crucifix hanging over the door to the kitchen was ornamented with dried palm and bay and surmounted a receptacle for holy water. Everyone except me had gone to Mass that morning. The three nieces I had acquired at lunch that day were large and pretty, with that high-toned, Irishlike complexion typical of the Vendée and Brittany. The prettiest—one of Daniel's daughters—wore a thin-strapped mini-skirted gingham dress that looked like an elongated bathing suit.

"You should have put something on top of that décolleté today," her father grumbled. "Monsieur le curé almost had a stroke when he gave you Communion this morning."

"Don't worry, Papa," she minced saucily, putting her arms over her large and beautiful breasts, "I crossed my hands over them so that the Host wouldn't fall in between."

Her father guffawed. What an unpredictable lot, I thought, I rather like them. I fancied their blend of conservatism and earthiness, their extraordinary fear of fresh air. Halfway through coffee, almost fainting from the heat, I pleaded the beauty of the midday light on the castle's façade and went out to take a photograph and breathe. The pretty niece followed me.

"Stop, stop, don't take it yet!" she cried as I focused the camera. "There's a window open on the second floor, it looks so awful!"

She ran up to close it and quickly ran back. "*Now* take it," she ordered, staring beatifically at the pale symmetrical structure surmounted by silvery slopes of gray mansarded roofs.

I obeyed. *Click:* my ancestors' home. With all its windows shut, the little castle, glimpsed through its alley of chestnut trees, looked as impervious to the flow of history as to currents of air, like a structure out of a Perrault fairy tale, like a picture in a coloring book which each of us could fill in with our particular obsessions. Papa had spent his childhood here, had helped to nurse his mother through a dreadfully lingering cancer. I had learned that detail only today. The Benjamin of the lot, he had been nine when she died, the same age I was at his death, and had remained alone with his older sister Colette while his father and brothers were away at the First World War. Had those years of sorrow and of solitude helped to shape his need for heroism, for early death? Here we had slept in the same bed, during some weeks of each summer, in that second-floor room which I refused to visit. And two years ago the last of my surviving uncles had died here, quietly sitting in his armchair; a wave of sorrow suddenly filled me for not having seen him one last time, there was no one left now of my father's generation except Aunt Colette, whom I was to visit tomorrow. Too late; always too late; perhaps not always totally too late. . . .

The pretty cousin hollered to a bevy of her contemporaries, and we all took a walk in the park. It struck me that there was literally nothing to do at Saint-Seran but wallow in family history and walk through forests. There was not a pond or a river to bathe in or a movie to go to, no horses, no tennis, no town to shop in within a half hour's driving distance, nothing, nothing, nothing. Nothing but *la promenade dans le beau parc*. And here were these hordes of young persons in their late teens and early twenties who had the means to go to the mountains or to the Côte d'Azur, but who preferred to lounge about this sweet dormant structure; with nothing else to do but study Aunt Charlotte's family albums, glue into them the weddings and baptisms of the year, or walk through alleys of trees, commenting on the beauty of sunlight as it hit the oaks, a stand of elms, a cluster of chestnuts, a grove of pines or poplars. Occasionally, when filled with a sense of adventure, they employed themselves by cutting down some brush to enlarge the park's old alleys, or began the grave task of tracing the beginnings of a new one.

"So you come here every summer for your vacation?" I asked the pretty cousin.

"Of course," she exclaimed, as if I were mad to ask such a question. She worked as a bank clerk in Brest, and had five brothers.

"You like it better than the sea, or the mountains?"

"We come here to recapture our childhoods," she said as if announcing something totally uncontestable. "Don't you like to recall your childhood? What is there more beautiful than bathing in the past?" she added dreamily, hitching up a strap of her bathing suit–church dress. "Oh, I can't tell you how attached we all are to this place, every single one of us. Look, it is so pretty from here, why don't you take a photo now?" She squinted her eyes to admire the silvery structure, whose gray slate roofs sloped gently down to its long, narrow closed windows.

History, loyalty, continuity. It would take me some time to realize that my cousins' attachment to Saint-Seran was dictated by a quest for roots that was also a reassurance of immortality, that they achieved some peace by bathing in the aura of the ancestral dead. And if there were an occasional glance of defiance, of irritation, admixed with the burning curiosity my cousins bestowed upon me, it was because I was the only descendant who had refused to continue this linkage, who had once attempted to scrub myself clean of family memories, who had tried to forge a false innocence by shutting myself off from the griefs of the past. Destroy, New World immigrant, destroy, destroy, destroy. Destroy the forest, destroy the past, be free again from the pain of history.

There is a recurring nightmare that has haunted me in various forms, over the years, since my father died. I dream that he is still alive somewhere, and hiding; that he is avoiding me, that he has just reasserted his refusal ever to communicate with me again. The dream recurs one night that very summer in Nantes, where I have taken a hotel room, twenty minutes from Saint-Seran. I dream that my Aunt Colette and I are on a plane that has made a crash landing. We are not hurt but seem to be the only survivors, and massive debris is scattered all about us. We receive a message that my father is alive and well in some distant country, that he is crippled and confined to a wheelchair but still strong and magnificent, that he is happily married to a much younger woman and refuses more adamantly than ever to communicate with us. "Traitor!" Colette and I scream together upon receiving the news. "Traitor, traitor!"

On the morning after this dream—the day I was to see Aunt

Colette again for the first time in twelve years—I took a long walk on the banks of the Loire to shake off the obsessions of the night. And I tried to remember that time twenty years ago, after the war's end, when I had returned to Saint-Seran and found my father's absence there so insupportable, and had fled after twenty-four hours. During the war years in the United States I had romanticized the family house—the way my cousins did now—as that place where reality was unsurpassed in its perfection. And I had rushed there alone as soon as traveling became possible. I was fifteen, childishly unaware of my relatives' suffering or of the toll of the war. The pain of the visit was bound to be augmented by the fact that my mother's anxiety about the past had kept her from ever mentioning my father to me, and that I doggedly continued to believe he was still hiding in the Resistance underground long after I had learned he was dead. And pain still reduces my memory of the visit to images of catatonic brevity: Saint-Seran is a crumbling structure set in a stretch of stagnant fields. My Uncle Jean is thin. My Aunt Charlotte is fat. One of my cousins is in the colonies. Another one is trying to leave for the colonies. The oldest cousin, the wan pious Cécile whom I used to visit in her tower room, had died a few days before she was scheduled to enter a convent. Nantes is one of the three French towns most brutally destroyed in World War II. Aunt Colette lives in one pathetic room overlooking the rubble of the bombed-out port. We sit down to a prisonlike supper of watery soup in which float stony hunks of dry bread. The next morning I am taken to visit the place where my father will be buried when his body is brought home from Gibraltar. The cemetery is overgrown with brush, and the dank family chapel is filled with the tombs of ancestors whose history is meaningless to me. I remember little but the high grass, the dampness of the chapel's stone walls, my dumb pain and anger. With anger I stared at what would be his final resting place, raging at him: Why, why did you abandon me? I think I needed to break down right there and accept the reality of his death, I needed to lie on his tomb and flail my limbs about in some grim but necessary exorcism of emotion, demanding to pierce into the earth, to be reunited with his bones. But they were not even there. The absence of his body was like a double treason, further augmenting the treason that was his death. I had insisted on taking the next train back to Paris and had wept for days, refusing to eat, unable to stop crying, not knowing precisely why I was crying—a minor breakdown, perhaps.

When I had come to live in Paris eight years later, at twenty-three, I had steeped myself in my mother's world and elaborately steered clear of any contact with my father's immediate family, as my mother always had. Eventually I ran into Aunt Colette, the adored older sister who had taken care of him when their parents died and who had been one of the idols of my own childhood. I met her by accident at the home of distant cousins. Since it was her only trip to Paris since 1947, when she had come to receive a Legion of Honor for her work in the Resistance, I suppose she had come in great part to try to see me. She was very poor. The trip was difficult for her. Her eyes had devoured me across the room. I did not have the honesty or kindness to return her gaze. I was terrified of this proud, gentle woman who had worn mourning since my father's death, who was my last link to my total childhood. "It would be so nice to see you, even here," she had said, intimating that she would prolong her stay in Paris if I could grant her a few hours. But I had lied and said that I was going away that same evening to Italy. Those were years when I could not bear to hear the mention of my father's name. And I had rejected her as crassly as I had avoided the rest of his family—more crassly, since she was so totally alone in the world, since along with me she had mourned him more deeply than anyone else.

Walking through Nantes today toward Aunt Colette's apartment on a summer day in the nineteen-sixties. Past the great castle of Anne of Brittany, where white swans glide tranquilly in deep lily-filled moats. Past the monument to Jules Verne, born in this city, past the factory which manufactures the nice biscuits Petit Beurre Lu, Lu Lustucru. The city is bathed in that silvery light of the upper Atlantic coast, we are in Gaelic, Celtic country here, the light is like the gleam on a pear, all seems spun in webs of fragile silver. Past the docks famous for the drownings of the Revolution, when some two thousand Royalists, their hands bound to their sides, were marched into boats that were sunk in the River Loire. Past the house where Aunt Colette and my father were born. My grandmother was a great beauty and painted with talent; during World War I, my grandfather died of typhoid; I am thirty-five and have learned that only yesterday. I suddenly need to see and own a picture of them, very well, all's easy now, I'll ask Aunt Colette. A student in theatrical peasant costume hands me a pamphlet on the Breton liberation movement. Another Breton liberationist, incongruous in blue jeans and formal white lace headdress, hands me an antiabortion pamphlet in Gaelic. Three hippies with angelically long blond hair sit on the sidewalk in the morning sunshine, washing their feet in the gutter as they would on a summer day in any town in Europe. World War II has ended, Dien Bien Phu, Suez, Algeria, have come and gone, and the dead are coming home from Vietnam, and I am walking down a street called Cours John Kennedy. Some new courage buttresses me this morning, making all kinds of new emotions and meetings possible, as if this visit has finally thrust me out of childhood. I come to the address Aunt Colette has given me, to the door of a ground-floor apartment in a pale seventeenth-century building a block from the cathedral.

An extraordinary face stares at me through the window. A delicate face as fragile and carefully painted as a moth's, ruled by enormous and melancholy eyes. All over the moth's face large furry tufts of silvery hair grow in mad, erratic spurts, as they might on some wood sprite, on a creature half human,

half tree. Aunt Colette so clearly has my father's and my eyes—
ironic, sad, gay eyes with deeply chiseled lids—that this is the
way one of my cousins had found me at the airport: she had
simply walked up to me, extended her hand, and said, "You
have Aunt Colette's gaze." The moth's face leaves the window,
and a few seconds later a person weighing some seventy
pounds, with the frail, erect, boyish body of an aging ballerina,
opens the door. She is eighty years old. She has still a different
way of greeting me. She falls into my arms, her body shaking,
her face shaking, yet some stoicism keeps her eyes quite dry.
"Well, here you are at last," she says during our long embrace.

I am shaking, too. "Forgive me," I want to cry, "forgive me
for my lies and my evasions." But I know that I can never use
such terms with her, that this frail, subtle, solid woman prefers
not to resort to words, that everything between us will be
accomplished as in a choreography of insects.

Very soon thereafter we sit down to lunch. One must always eat. Among the decorous, the diffident, the French, much
pain and joy is punctuated by appropriate mundanities over the
solemnity of a five-course meal.

"Did you do your studies in British or in American?" she
asks, her eyes devouring me, our gaze meeting straightfor-
wardly across the table laden with fragile Saint-Seran china.
"Do you eat much bread in America? What color is the bread?
Do you have Trotskyists in America? How many of them
do you have? They are responsible for many of our troubles
here, aren't they responsible for your black uprisings? What
do you think of the Pope? I hear from Aunt Charlotte that
you receive dissident priests for tea, it has become much the
fashion here too, deplorably. Have you reread Sainte-Beuve
lately? Don't you agree with him that the progress of civilization is accompanied by a terrible degeneration of morals in
mankind? Is your stepfather Catholic? Oh, he is Jewish. Ah,
well, the Pope has forgiven them. . . ."

In this willfully remote province, reality seems to filter

through prisms that block out many aspects of modern civilization yet enlarge others into obsessive proportions—Trotskyists, speed limits, the color of bread. Aunt Colette's voice is as light and striking as her person, thin but powerful, with a silvery tint to it recalling the light that bathes her city, frequently punctuated with pealing, boyish laughs. She retired fifteen years ago from her work as a librarian, and lives in a modest but dainty three-room flat filled with remnants of Saint-Seran as frail as her body: odd teacups, residues of Sèvres porcelain, miniatures of ancestors on fragile Louis XVI tables, spindly chairs covered in worn petit-point rose patterns that seem as if they could support no more than her weight. Even the crucifix hanging on the wall by the inevitable photograph of de Gaulle is spindly and ethereal. She shares her flat with a childhood friend, also a spinster, and by pooling their resources they have somehow reconstituted comfort out of their postwar poverty. And I rejoice in Colette's ease and her lack of solitude, as if these amenities—those of her own resourcefulness—could reduce my guilt.

Perhaps desiring to emphasize our birthright to decorousness, she feasts me, as Aunt Charlotte has done, with a procession of courses served on five different sets of china. I protest, in midmeal, that one could eat the vegetables *with* the meat instead of separately, wouldn't it make her dishwashing easier? "Oh, no," she rebuts, her voice crackling with indignation, "eat like the Germans, who heap meat and potatoes and vegetables on the same plate? The most disgusting custom I know. Why, even when we go on picnics in the forest we bring at least four changes of china."

I am regaled by tales of her frequent trips to the country, of her vociferous reading, of her prodigious passion for bridge. She plays bridge at least four afternoons a week, being, like most members of our family, "of a nature driven to excess." She frequently entertains groups of ten friends in her flat for two-table bridge parties; since they are all quite old, she explains, there are always two players dropping out and napping in the other room, resting up for their turn to play. She goes every August to vacation on the island of Oléron with a few friends her age. Over the years they have chosen a particular hotel for its proximity to beautiful trees and also to a church where they can go to Mass every morning. "I adore forests," she says, "the joy of my life is to walk in lovely parks like that of Saint-Seran or Oléron, and observe the play of sunlight on different kinds of trees. In Oléron we always carry a folding card table into the forest and spend the afternoon playing our bridge match there, enjoying the effect of afternoon sunlight on the leaves. . . . Tell me, do you have insomnia?"

Yes, deplorably so, ever since a certain period of the war.

"Bravo, then you're really one of us!" she exclaims, acknowledging the reference to my father's death with a wise, sad look but preferring not to dwell upon it. (For she, who knows more about him than anyone else, never offers any detail more telling than "He hated his braces as a child," or "He passed his exams marvelously.") "You might even have had insomnia *without* the war," she continues. "That's a trait from the Lamoricière side which plagues most of us. For instance, your grandfather, a colonel in the professional Army, read and reread Taine through the night, whether he was stationed in Annecy or in Algeria. Your Uncle Jean used to read Michelet from two to six A.M., he slept three or four hours a night and hunted five hours each day; he lunched at ten and dined at four . . . as for my white nights, I reread de Gaulle's memoirs."

"Why this anxiety?" I ask. "Are we romantics?"

She nods her head emphatically with an ironic smile. "Oh, yes, indeed, we've always been romantics."

"In what sense?"

"We're concerned with heroism," she ventures slowly, "and the future of our actions, and how they relate to the past. Oh, by the way, have you been there yet? No? You are going tomorrow, with your cousin Catherine? Very well. Do you like de Gaulle?" she asks hurriedly, as if to get ourselves back on safer ground.

"A great man," I answer carefully, "perhaps a little astigmatic, more skilled at seeing long-range consequences than immediate ones."

"But you *do* think he is great?"

"Oh yes."

"Thank God," she simply says. "All these modern trends, I just don't know about them . . . these Cabinet ministers whose wives allow themselves to be photographed in bathing suits . . . these birth-control pills handed out by the state to anyone . . . those hooligans who salute you with clenched fists. . . ."

She noticed, before lunch, that I looked longingly at a photograph of my father on her bedside table. And after taking a brief nap to rest for the afternoon excursion we have planned, she comes out of her bedroom, swiftly handing me an envelope. She gives it to me between one room and another, with an air of contraband and one of those infinitely sad, wise looks of hers. Our sorrows flutter, hover about each other like languorous moths. We look at each other with that melancholy, ironic gaze that belongs to her, to him, to me. We link arms and start on our walk. We stroll in the Botanical Gardens, and admire the play of sunlight on its elms and oaks. She wears a gown of watered silk, a sweater reaching halfway to her knees, long pearls, her legs are like matchsticks, her nails are painted the color of fading tea roses. She helps me to feed the swans in the moated castle of Anne of Brittany, as she did when I was a child. I take her photograph on the cathedral steps as she clutches her extraordinarily flowered hat in a gust of wind, saying, proudly, "We have the highest nave of any church after Beauvais."

At day's end we drive to visit distant maiden aunts of mine whom even Colette refers to as "the guardians of the past." They have lived totally alone since the end of World War I— when both their parents died—in a magnificent Louis XIII castle they have dedicated their lives to preserving. Smell of damp wood, splendor of moldings not painted since the war of

1870, resplendent alleys in a park designed by LeNôtre. One aunt is seventy, the other is eighty. Bent and elflike and totally eccentric, too poor to employ a servant, they live and cook, each one for herself, in different floors of the great house, keeping vastly different hours and savoring totally different styles of life. One cultivates the flower garden and sweeps the castle's thirty-six uninhabited rooms, the other spends her day doing the heavy outdoor work, maintaining LeNôtre's alleys with a John Deere garden tractor. They have not been to Nantes in three, four years. It is a twenty-minute ride away. Before an array of harps and ancient harpsichords, the peeling dank walls of the grand salon—which they open only every few years for special guests—are hung with pictures of great dead Frenchmen. We are briefly left to ourselves while our cousins make tea.

"Ah, look, there's de Gaulle," Aunt Colette jubilates as she advances slowly into the salon, unfolding her lorgnette.

"No, Aunt Colette, it's Pétain," I correct her.

"*Merde alors*," she exclaims, "I must admit that I haven't been in this room for years and that I've never mentioned de Gaulle's name to them, they might think I'm a Communist."

After tea we stroll out into the park and walk in the alleys designed by LeNôtre. "Look, what an exquisite oak, of the species *Quercus virginiana*," Aunt Colette murmurs, "and what a noble elm, of the *Ulmus procera* species." Our seventy-year-old relative rides past us on her electric carriage, dressed in boots and ancient riding jodhpurs, a khaki army hat set cockily on her head. "What dedication, what sacrifice," Aunt Colette says. "This house is their child, their martyrdom, their immortality. You see, perhaps that's why we're such insomniacs in the family. We're romantic enough to dedicate our *lives* to any cause we believe in, however small or great."

"Do you believe in grace?" my cousin Catherine asked me as we drove through the flat, flat countryside outside Nantes in the direction of the family chapel where my father was buried. It was her way of being mundane, I suppose, of diverting me from the trouble that might lie ahead. She was a singular woman, this husky, serious cousin who had undertaken to accompany me on my first visit to my father's grave: the only spinster of her generation in the family, tall, powerful, with short gray hair brushed back in mannish fashion and steel-rimmed glasses framing the family's melancholy, straightforward eyes. She was the cousin who had met me at the airport, and I had immediately sensed that as the spinster of the family she assigned herself the more disagreeable and awesome family tasks: helping to cook and keep house for her aging mother, my Aunt Charlotte, meeting strangers at airports, accompanying them on delicate missions such as this one. As if it were her way of punishing herself, within this family hell-bent on procreation, for failing to reproduce God's image. She was a government social worker, with a fairly high-placed job in the federal system which entailed attending a monthly meeting in Paris. And she was utterly consumed by her duty toward others. She lived in a phoneless two-room flat in Nantes. Anyone attempting to find her there in the evening would learn that instead of going home to put her feet up and do her laundry, as she constantly announced she was about to do, she had gone to check on some particularly bereaved family in the suburbs, or rushed to Saint-Seran to make sure that her mother's dinner was properly taken care of. Her manner had that balance that characterizes the finest members of her profession—those equipped with enough diplomacy and toughness to deal adequately with drunks, drug addicts, the orphaned, the handicapped. And she had asked me, in that diverting tone appropriate for the day's excursion, whether I believed in grace.

"I'm not sure that we would see eye to eye on that." I was trying to avoid the severe cultural shock that some of my answers evoked among my relatives. "I mean I've quite lost my faith in Christ as the exclusive vehicle of salvation. I think grace can be attained through the visions of many other great religions, and also outside of them." How flat the countryside was on the way to the chapel.

My answer seemed startling and novel to her, but not totally shocking. "Ah, how interesting, Stéphanie," she exclaimed. "You do *not* believe in Christ as the hinge, the joint that relates God to man—you think one can reach grace through Buddha, or the Hindu deities, or some curious Moslem sect?"

"And why not *without* them, since they all stress that He is in us already? I think there are many persons untaught in any religion who have grace because they are able to live totally for the other."

"Total sacrifice for the other, certainly, as you find in all our saints," she agreed. "But how would you recognize a state of grace among the unbaptized?"

"Well, their sainthood might remain quite obscure, totally unrecognized. I can't think of any surer sign than their willingness to risk going into death for others. And I'm not sure that such grace can be reached without the most scrupulous self-knowledge, and it is this knowledge, this total givingness, that is of the essence, not the contact with any religious system."

She was frowning.

"Look at all the lies we invent to protect our self-esteem and self-respect," I continued. "I talk about this a lot with a great Jesuit friend of mine. He's always stressing our unwillingness to face the reality of death, our arrogance in thinking that we are Godlike and immortal."

"What do you mean, *thinking* that we are immortal? We *are* all immortal! I am immortal! You are immortal! That is precisely how we differ from animals! What does our catechism say? 'Because I have an immortal soul'!" ("Really," her eyes were saying to me, "you Americans go too far, even your priests!")

"Well, perhaps our beliefs are more similar than you think, and we just phrase them differently. I'd say that we differ from animals by our awareness of death, and that this awareness of death might be the sign of our potential for some form of immortality, a manifestation of some kind of immortal world soul."

Stopping at a red light, still frowning, she offered me a package of licorice and mint candy drops which she kept in a pouch in her car—along with comic books and a manual for self-defense—for the adolescents she had to transport back and forth to the rehabilitation home.

"To get back to grace," I continued, trying to soothe her back into the conversation, "I am trying to document a story about a humble nineteenth-century servant girl who rescued a child and then died herself as a result. She was so devoid of illusions, so completely willing to cross into death for the sake of another human being, that she was a perfect example of a state of true grace. Do you get to see any Ingmar Bergman films in Nantes?"

"Oh, we get very few foreign films," she said. "As a matter of fact we get very few ideas of any kind from the outside. While you in America, on the contrary, must be veritably swamped, inundated, by fresh and novel ideas. How curious that must feel!" She ran her large hand through the stubby hair with a gesture that communicated impatience, some envy. "Doesn't this profusion of new ideas, this perennial invasion, sometimes make you feel . . . out of balance? To be perpetually bombarded by such a stream of novelty?"

"Yes. It's a country where it's sometimes hard to keep track of reality. Everything flows by us so very swiftly—fads, allegiances. Your brother Daniel loves to attack me for our lack of any sense of history."

"Do you know, Stéphanie, that in the ten years I have had to make monthly trips to Paris I have spent the night there only once?" She said this with a certain pride. "Even though it's only three hours by train, I did it only once, when my sister Louise offered me a ticket for a performance of the *Saint*

Matthew Passion in Notre-Dame. But I felt so guilty for having offered myself this luxury that I took the six A.M. train back to Nantes, and then I worked for twenty-four hours around the clock to get rid of my unease."

I stared at her with the same intense curiosity with which my French cousins often stared at me. "You see, darling," Aunt Colette had said, "we are all so nutty, so excessive . . ."

"Go on, talk some more," Catherine said, "you're such a breath of fresh air. Tell me how you really feel about this place, why you finally came back when you did."

We would be arriving at the chapel soon. The ancient fear gripped me. I sensed that I could talk freely to her.

"Well, I'll tell you, I've been terrified of this visit to Papa's grave. It's as if . . . well, as if he could drag me down with him, as if he had the power to force me to join him in death. And so I was too much of a coward and a louse, too small and ungenerous to honor his memory. It's as if—to get back to what we were saying a minute ago—as if I dared to think I could never be touched by death, and refused to acknowledge any aspect of it. If it weren't for the advice of my Jesuit friend, Father Gregory, I'd never have dared come back. I was equally fearful of some ill will on the part of the family here, fearful that they might bear me a grudge for never coming back. And every year it grew worse, every year I feared it more. That part of it was silly, you've been so marvelous to me."

She gave me a proud, forthright grin. "Well, perhaps we're more understanding than you thought we'd be. Not necessarily about Buddhism or foreign films, but about things like pain and death and a child's emotions toward them. Do you know, I understand your fears totally. Someone once wrote— who could it have been, Mauriac perhaps?—that upon the death of a parent, a child is like a reed bent by a heavy storm. He may straighten up in time, or he may not. He may have to live perpetually in a stooped position, in a condition of enfeeblement. Also, what happened in your particular instance is quite clear—a child who is not properly acquainted with the facts of a parent's death may suffer from powerful delusions, complex feelings of guilt. One, you feel guilty that you did not join him in death. Two, you feel guilty that in some vague sense you are responsible for his death. Three, because you were not given the chance of going through the proper rituals of mourning—these things exist for the sanity of the survivor, you know —in some sense you may still refuse to believe that he is dead."

Her conciseness stunned me. Cartesian clarity, one, two, three, like a prize-winning French high-school essay. And so much briefer, clearer, cheaper than the shrink. I could not speak.

"What about life after death?" she asked in the same conversational, mundane tone with which she had ventured into grace. "Or the resurrection of the body, things like that? In a system of thought as progressive as yours, what would you have to say?"

"Oh, I don't have any great problems with it. It's the *transfigured* body, after all. I've always been absolutely obsessed with that concept. Remember how in catechism we used to ask, 'What is the transfigured body?' and they'd answer, 'Ah, my child, that is a mystery.' I don't admire the notion because the Church teaches it but because it's such a brilliant historical solution; after all those centuries of pre-Christian quibbling about body versus soul, they had the genius to come along and say, 'You can take your body too.' Anyway, there might well be a residuum of self that is not reducible to material quantities, the nature of which science may never be able to decipher. And if so, why not a continuity, or even a resurrection, of this selfhood?"

"Well, speaking of *that*, here we are," she said, putting on her wide, comforting social worker's smile. "Here's the town where they're all buried."

It had come earlier than I had thought, a bare half hour from Nantes and Saint-Seran. I felt a kind of numbness. That blunt wisdom of Catherine's had made everything much easier than I had expected.

"Look," I said, "I might break down, okay? I just don't know yet. I hope you'll understand."

She made a casual gesture of dismissal, as if to say, "If you only knew the real breakdowns I see everyday."

My great-great-granduncle General Louis-Christophe-Léon Juchault de Lamoricière, who helped complete France's conquest of Algeria and briefly served as its governor, is so revered in his native Vendée that no one is quite sure which part of him is buried where. His heart—that much is certain—is preserved within a gigantic black marble cenotaph in the north nave of the Nantes cathedral. It is said that at the insistence of the very first colonialists another parcel of his mortal body was buried in Algeria. One of my aunts suggests that still another slice of the General reposes in a Paris church. But whatever remains of him after these cannibalistic acts of veneration is buried in his native village of Saint-Philbert-de-Grand-Lieu, in a family chapel built by the General's sisters. It was here that my father came to rest some seventeen years ago.

As one drives into Saint-Philbert, the General's connection with that town is announced by a twelve-foot-high bronze statue that shows him striding into battle, his bearded intense face—not unlike Lenin's—surmounted by a towering kepi, his long sword held high to the sky as if giving the signal of attack. Below him a Zouave soldier in native robes bows in deference and blows his war trumpet. At the General's feet sits Marianne, symbol of French glory and justice, naked to the waist, her large and perfect breasts surmounting the noble flow of classical draperies below. And to the left of Marianne an Arab woman kneels in tribute, offering her a large basket of native fruit and flowers—the fruits of the Algerian colonies for France. The family's burial chapel stands two blocks from this martial statue, in a village cemetery dotted with marble or stone crosses

of varying degrees of grandeur, and with the purple and crimson ceramic flowers that adorn many French tombs. It was
this site, this building, which I had been trying to avoid for
over twenty years.

What a goddam bitch reality is, I thought as I walked in,
will she always remain as elusive and stingy with her symbols?
Entering the chapel that day with Catherine, I experienced the
same anger that had swept over me two decades ago, when
I had come here before my father's body had been brought
back. For I was looking forward to a physical sign of his death,
I wanted a tomb, an indenture in the earth, a sarcophagus, a
glimpse of his coffin even, something real, something tangible,
something that would knock me over the head with the reality
of his death. The chapel offered none of that. It was simply a
sea of names engraved from top to bottom of each wall, gold
letters on black marble slabs, and the dead were buried below
or around it, I did not know which at first. The only change
from my last visit was that my father's name had been added to
the left wall, near the entrance, underneath the names of his
parents. First came his father's name: "*Mort pour la France,
1918.*" And then my father's: "*Mort pour la France, 1940.*"

"So here we are," Catherine said cheerfully. "Would you
like to be alone?"

"No, no, no, no." And I wandered about the chapel with the
casual air of a museum visitor, whispering the musical names
of ancestors commemorated on its walls: "Marie-Laure de
Hauterive . . . Clotilde du Maistre . . . ah, yes, Anne-Marie de
La Laurencie . . ." Would there never be an end to my cycle
of anger, delusion, anger? He might not be here. He simply
might not be anywhere to be found. He might have abandoned
me even more totally than I had thought. What a cheat life is,
always to be deceiving me that way. I would go, I must go to
whatever place his body really lies in, to make absolutely sure,
to see the coffin bearing his name. I wanted to break down in
the presence of his corpse, to affirm the reality of my grief, to

confirm my sorrow to him and to myself, and here there was nothing but names, a sea of names, there was no one to cry to, no one to talk to, and inside me there was an anger that verged on boredom, on void.

"So," I asked Catherine, "where are they?"

"Below, naturally. Actually, if I remember accurately, your father is almost underneath and to the right of the sealing stone, just a few coffins away from the General. As for Papa—his oldest brother—he is to the left, and their mother is directly above them. Over toward the apse you have the Montmorencys," she continued, as if seating a dinner party, "the du Maistres, the Saint-Marceaus, the branches of the family that have become a little more distant. You're sure you don't want to be alone?"

"No, please stay. What does it look like downstairs? How are they buried?"

"It's not unlike the . . . you know, the cubicles in which you check your bags at the railroad station," she said, pushing her spectacles onto her nose. "A long deep recess in the wall into which the coffin is placed lengthwise, with a plaque outside."

"How does one get down there?"

"Right through here." She gave a familiar pat to a large stone in the floor, just to the right of the entrance. It had a large, rusting metal handle.

"Can't we go downstairs?" My voice sounded faint and piping, like that of a child fighting back its tears.

"Certainly not, my poor girl, that's a very complex proposition," she exclaimed, lifting an arm up toward the sky to indicate a very annoying chapter of family history. "We are never supposed to go down there except in the company of a witness—a judge, a clerk of the court, an official of that order. It's a very difficult business, breaking all that cement around the stone, unsealing it, then lifting it. I know all about it, I'm the only old maid in the family, and I get all the wretched jobs. Ten years ago the vault became totally filled and we realized that to be practical we'd have to do some clearing out, some pruning and weeding if you will. And wouldn't you know it, I was the one who had to get the stone unsealed and go down into the burial vault with a witness." She gave a little shudder.

"Merde alors, tu sais, c'était très impressionant. It was dark in there, very dark, and . . . Listen, are you sure you don't want to be alone for a moment? All right. It was dark, it was not a pleasant task. We had held a family council the night before and decided exactly whom to get rid of. We decided not to stick to chronology, that would have been a bit didactic. We simply got rid of those strains of the family we like the least—the Cassons, the Du Bourgs, all distant cousins, and there were a few bad marriages in those branches of the family anyhow. We did some selecting, in other words, and put them into the common grave still farther underneath. What else can you do, when you get so crowded? The whole planet is getting to be that way. Can you imagine what it will be like at resurrection time?" she added gaily. "Not an inch of elbow room! What a mess!"

She was twisting and turning her car keys now, eager to go, as if she really had seen quite enough of the place. "I think we're all right down there for another twenty years or so. But you just wait and see," she added, throwing the car keys defiantly into the air. "If ever it gets filled up again, I'm the one who'll end up having to go down there again!"

And with that we drove back to Saint-Seran for tea. On the drive back my husky Charon had the brisk and tender manner of those nurses assigned the midnight shift to deal with the more complex textures of loneliness and pain. "You're quite all right, aren't you?" she would say, giving a reassuring, sideways look. "Would you like a licorice, a comic book? Ah, I forget, you're too old for that, in my mind you're always my little cousin. An aspirin? I always keep them for the drunks I have to transport to the tribunal. I haven't told you, have I, that Nantes has the highest percentage of alcoholics of any city in

Europe. Worse than Dublin, can you imagine? Actually we're so alike, we and the Irish, all wild Celts. So. Tell me more about America. Did you do your studies in English or in American? What do you do for your insomnia? I find Teilhard good at those moments. I hear you do not eat lunch in America. How is that possible? What do you do all that time, from twelve to two? Perhaps it's why you get so much accomplished over there, you're less sleepy in the afternoon. Does France seem like a very small country in comparison?"

And she said that her oldest sister, Louise, who was waiting for me at Saint-Seran, swore she remembered and loved me like a sister, and had driven from Paris a day ahead of schedule to catch me before I flew back to New York.

Alone, alone, I thought, as Catherine's chatter lulled me like a midnight hypodermic. I must go back there tomorrow alone.

Louise was waiting for me at the front door, an enormous woman with the body of the *Venus of Lespugue*. Having rushed toward me as I got out of her sister's car, she cupped my face in her hands and stared at me intently, exhaling strong odors of garlic sausage.

"After twenty years I would have recognized you from a hundred yards away," she cried, "from two hundred yards away, do you hear, if I had so much as passed you on a street in Paris!"

And she leaned back to study me more attentively, smiling beatifically at her little cousin. She had a round and shiny face, abundant brown hair pulled back in a messy bun, yellowed teeth that went at crazy angles to each other, an expression of great kindness. Her enormous breasts were barely covered by a flimsy printed challis dress. "Well what's taken you so long? What's the idea? Oh, if you knew what a shining memory we all have of your father! He was our hero, you know that. What an extraordinary man! What brilliance! What charm! The best-looking man of his generation, on top of everything else!

What an impression he made on us! How he stamped our memory! How indelibly, in-del-ib-ly he marked us all! How he adored you! And how you adored him! Do you remember him well?"

"Very," I said faintly.

"And, of course, you're one of us down to the tip of your little fingers! Well, welcome, welcome!" And she hugged me to her large chest, rocking me back and forth like a small baby. Behind her stood a bevy of her children, a new batch of nephews and nieces for me to meet—five sons and daughters between the ages of nineteen and twenty-four who had come to spend the week at Saint-Seran.

"Yes, how he adored you, how you adored him," she repeated. "What a pretty couple you made, always hugging and kissing, never separated, he couldn't stand to have you out of his sight for five minutes, and you couldn't stand to ever let go of his hand. No one else really mattered for you when you were little, isn't that right? No, I know, no one, no one! How you must miss him!"

She squeezed me again to her bountiful chest and began to whimper, quite genuinely. The sweet bitch, I thought, when will she stop? "Poor little Stéphanie," she moaned, "left alone at such an early age, and by such an extraordinary man, by such an extraordinary parent. How different, how different things would have been if he had not died—what a different destiny you would have had! Even our own destinies might have been changed, too. Do you remember when he took us all to Nantes to see *Three Little Pigs?*"

"No, I don't, quite."

"You don't remember *Three Little Pigs?*" she wailed. "But how could you forget? I was fifteen, Catherine was twelve, you and Daniel were eight. Then do you remember that time he took us all to the circus in Nantes?"

"No, not quite."

"But how can you not remember? There was this lovely

clown you enjoyed so, but when he came toward us and your father said, 'Don't you want to shake hands with the clown?' you burst into tears and said, 'No, I can't, we haven't been introduced.' "

She laughed uproariously, shaking my body back and forth.

"You were always such a formal child, always so strictly brought up by that governess. Almost too strictly, I'd say. A very complex child, that's for sure, very precise, very sensitive. I remember you used to brush your hair one hundred times in the morning and one hundred times at night even when you were eight years old. You were always our little princess, even though you didn't come back all this time, you've remained our little princess in America. Oh, my God, I haven't even shown you the photographs of my daughters' weddings! Such marvelous weddings! How could you have stayed away!"

An album was already set upon the table next to us, carefully prepared for my perusal.

"Ah, here's the wedding of my oldest daughter, Poupette. Yes, how could you have stayed away from such a fine event? We sent you all our wedding announcements, we all did, for years, and you never responded to them. She married a very good name. Not that much money, but a very old name, that's still what counts, after all. And an excellent piece of land in Picardy. The wedding at a private chapel of the bridegroom's parents' castle. Not many of us have that anymore, a private chapel! Four priests officiating. Dominicans. Can you imagine! *Four* Dominicans! Then an orchestra from Amiens played Strauss waltzes. Six attendants in Alençon lace, carrying bouquets of roses and stephanotis. How could you not have come back to such a splendid wedding?"

"Oh, my little treasure. Hello, my sweetie, sweetie, sweetheart." Louise's daughter is already wheeling a baby carriage at the end of a stroll in the park. Aunt Charlotte, my cousin Daniel, Aunt Colette very slowly walk alongside her, making pretty noises at the baby. More celebration of the propagation of protoplasm. Another offspring to revere Saint-Seran, to come back each summer to admire its shuttered windows, its mysterious and sleeping air.

"Oh the beautiful little doll, the beautiful little soldier," Aunt Colette is cooing into the carriage. "Don't you love babies when they're tiny tiny, when they can almost fit into the palm of your hand? Look at those teeny teeny hands, those teeny teeny feet. Can you imagine, even de Gaulle once had feet as teeny as those."

The family gathers about the beautiful chipped porcelain. Tea is brought out. Debate rages about the chocolate cake. The recipe has not left the family for two hundred years.

"You do *not* add the egg yolks to it, you only put in the whites," storms Aunt Charlotte. "I know that our cousins on the Lamoricière side add the yolks, but that's a deformation of principle. Yolks make it too heavy, I assure you."

"Maman, I agree about the yolks," Louise rebuts, "but I don't agree about the flour. Some of our cousins put in five tablespoons of flour and you don't put any in, but I compromise and put in three tablespoons for measure. It needs the binder."

"My sweet sweet dolly," Aunt Colette continues to purr at the baby, as she may have purred at me in my carriage, "my rabbit, my little treasure . . ."

One last family picture, outside the pale dwelling bathed in the shimmering Vendée light. *Click:* here they are, poised for my own slim slice of eternity.

Aunt Colette in her watery silks, her tufted face pointed in the direction of the forest, says in her twinkling voice, "We had a glorious stroll this afternoon, the afternoon sunlight is so beautiful today on the stands of elms at the northwest corner of the park."

"Mozambique," Aunt Charlotte says, pouring tea out of the gilt and crested Empire tea pot, her album of stamps on her lap. "Listen, dear child, you're going back to America tomorrow, surely you can find me one from Mozambique. And listen, next time you return, there's more than one bed for you, we expect you back next summer."

"So you're going to go back and give more hell to your President on some other silly puritanical principle," Daniel roars across the tea table. "Did anyone raise an eyebrow when Napoleon pillaged Egypt? A little more high-handed authority, that's what the modern world needs."

Catherine is looking anxiously at her watch, straightening her spectacles, saying, "I really must get back to Nantes by five, there's a very disturbed child in an alcoholic family . . ."

I almost do not get there—back to the chapel alone. I feel an ambivalence of desire and terror toward that last visit which is more confusing than any emotion I have ever known. Yet I manage to go. I am booked on a one-o'clock plane from Nantes to Paris which connects with a three-o'clock flight back to New York. I hire a car for the morning and set off very early, my bags in the trunk, for Saint-Philbert. I am possessed by one principal fear: that I shall again feel emptiness, the absence of him, the absence of pain, the same numb hollowness I felt before, the void and boredom that so artfully mask rage. I find my way without difficulty. Turn right at the post office, turn left at the bakery, turn right again at the General two blocks away from the Saint-Philbert cemetery. On the side wall of the bakery is an enormous sign: *"Gordon's Gin."* The General looks fiercer than ever in this morning's sunny light, his sword rising threateningly above the bands of petunias, forget-me-nots, geraniums, that grow in impeccable circles about his feet.

One more block and I am at the graveyard. I park the car, walk out and take a picture of the cemetery. The ceramic flowers blaze crimson and purple about the gray monument. An albinic light envelops it all. Once inside the chapel I walk up the tiny nave, reach into my pocket for a notebook, and feel driven to take notes on my ancestors' names. So and so

and so and so and so and so, Amélie de Pommery, Isabelle de
La Varende, such pretty names, names of champagne and mus-
keteers. The notebook is a hedge, a chastity belt, a haven of
safety. Stephanie's the reporter, she always takes notes on
whatever comes within her range of sight, she's seldom moved
by the subject matter at hand. Still, they all had insomnia, that's
very touching. Grandfather reading his Taine, Uncle Jean his
Michelet, Colette her de Gaulle, my father spending seven
years of his white nights authoring a tract on the radical reform
of the European economy. He lost the only copy in the back of
someone's car. Whence this anxiety, dear history nuts, whence
this agitation? Here you sleep at last, new friends, sweet insomniacs, here you sleep at last after centuries of turning in
your beds. . . .

A woman in dun-colored dress walks into the chapel, quietly
comes up the nave, crosses herself and starts to trim the gladioli
and dahlias at the altar with slow deliberate strokes of her
pruning shears. She bows again, returns to a back pew and sits
down. I am still scribbling, scribbling. The gold letters an-
nounce that one of our great-granduncles died in 1838 while
directing the French Navy's assault on Vera Cruz, Mexico;
that the General, after leaving his post in Algeria, was exiled
from France for opposing Napoleon III's Italian campaign, and
chose to serve on the other side—as head of the Papal troops.
Militarists, imperialists, colonialists, just the men I would take
part in protest marches against, and yet I am beginning to
understand them, to be proud of them. What a good tribe I
was born into, defiant, eccentric, pigheaded. Created for violence and romance, for heroism and early death. Nantes—the
highest percentage of royalists of any city in France, the highest
percentage of alcoholics of any city in Europe, perhaps the
highest percentage of insomniacs. The Brittany liberation
movement is trying to make it the capital of a new independent
state. . . . I sense by the silence behind me that the woman with
the pruning shears is praying, that she must be a nun. I hear

her footsteps retreating, I sense by some slight rustling of her clothes that she is making the sign of the cross as she leaves the chapel.

I put my notebook back into my pocket. I don't quite know what to do next. Now that I am alone again I turn around and walk down the nave toward the back pew. The nuns must come to tend the flowers every day, there is a heavy but clean scent of roses on the air. Outside the chapel the light is fresh, inviting, bland. Shall I leave now, exit into the sunlight before it happens? But through some instinct made possible by the rituals of childhood, I kneel down on the sealing stone which stands between me and the dead, the stone I had so desired to break open the day before, the stone that separates his body from mine. I kneel on the stone, scratching shyly at the cement that seals me off from below. It resembles all the other bands of cement that intersect the gray flagstones of the chapel floor, but it is slightly darker, different in texture. There is some difference, some difference that makes me keep on scratching, scratching, to make sure that it is indeed as immutable as Catherine said, to make sure that I cannot break through it. And then suddenly my liberation comes. I am free now, kneeling on the stone, suddenly free and shaking, my head resting against the rusty metal handle that could be lifted for our reunion. I weep, I shake, I pound at the floor with my head, I kick it, I beat it with my hands. I feel no unease or shame at my behavior, I know that society is sick for forbidding us such liberations any more, for obstructing the channels of our grief, for not letting us properly mourn the dead. I know that I am inconquerably sane and that society is mad. I lie prone on the floor for a half hour, crying abundantly, my hands bruised by my knocking, my head aching from hitting it against the stone, my jeans drenched as if I had sailed a boat into a storm. Yet I do not feel any more rage. Nor do I feel void, or fear. I am ready to die, but not now, not in a violent or untimely way, I simply have no more fear of dying, I want to die the way

I want to live, I have conquered some fear of both. I am crying my heart out, free at last. He is there, he is there, he is there. I finally know that he is there, down below. But that is not the point. He is both there and not there. Above all else he is now allowed to live in my memory, totally restored and whole now, as if resurrected, the reality of his death accepted, faced. After some time I begin to raise myself up to my knees. I have no more need to hammer at the floor, I know he is there, may he sleep at last. May he rest in peace. May he sleep at last.

As I start to get up I see that a plaque above my head, a few feet away, commemorates one Julie de Lamoricière, wife of that martial conqueror whose remains were so voraciously preserved by his admirers. It says:

> Julie-Amélie d'Abeslard de Lamoricière
> Died in Paris the 26th of April 1885
> Her body reposes here
> Next to that of her husband and her children
> Awaiting the resurrection.

Think of that.

Marriage
and Madness

1 9 6 9

All that is temporall is but a caterpillar got into a corner of my garden, but a milldew fallen upon one acre of my Corne.

—JOHN DONNE

I

A winter weekend in Atlantic City, that was Paul's idea of a nice way to spend New Year's Eve. He said it would remind him of his childhood, he was dying to go back. We booked a room in what he remembered to have been the grandest hotel there. But the suites he'd stayed in as a child had been closed for decades, we were relegated to what used to be servants' rooms, little cubicles in which I mostly remember piss-stained rugs, rusting yellow bathtubs. I sat in bed much of the weekend reading George Eliot and thinking, Why am I here, swigging from a miniature whiskey bottle the evenings he wanted to make love, so that I could do it better, make him happy. On the way to dinner we passed through the hotel's large abandoned drawing rooms, whose peeling walls resembled third-degree burns, maps of the moon. Paul passed under a cracked chandelier and said that he remembered walking through that very room holding his mother's hand on New Year's Eve. "And she whispered, 'It's going to be 1930 tomorrow!' " I knew the details of that euphoric memory without asking: her perfume, his childhood, the gleam of her newly acquired jewelry and furs. I on my part was thinking of what good radicals unlike us, good radical Jews, used to do in resort hotels in the nineteen-twenties. When the management had been rude to one of their people dozens of them would run the bathtub water and silently leave town, closing the door, leaving the taps to run. Perhaps that's how our room had been messed up—that was one consolation of the weekend—perhaps some offended Jews might have turned on the bathtub taps and silently left town. That New Year's Eve we went to small restaurants in the neighborhood, we mostly talked about our children, I loved him, I drank my boredom down. The next day in the abysmal cold of daylight we strolled on the boardwalk, sleazy now with bowling alleys, cheap clothing stores, taffy candy shops, more decaying hotels. Filled also with old people in wheelchairs from neighboring rest homes, people who did not have his deathly desire to turn time back, who simply wanted a few more scraps of sky to glimpse. "In the old days one could rent a wheelchair and a blanket," he said, "and an attendant would push you up and down the boardwalk, *whatever* age you were." My husband was more silent than ever this weekend, not ready to admit his disappointment with this slice of his beloved past. The old days, the old days, that's what he talked about often when we traveled. What a decline in the quality of resorts, of art criticism, of political ethics, he said that weekend, what a decline in the quality of human values. In the old days he could buy lovely fresh fish for his dogs at seventeen cents a pound, help was easier to get, what a good life Renoir must have had. And there were all those things he said with his eyes only, which he never spoke audibly: in the old days children stayed with their parents until they married, whether at the age of twenty-nine or forty-five, in the old days women were predictable and docile or else they were stoned, maybe to death. We both have insomnia, his is more acute than mine, it was worse than ever that weekend. I take light pills for it, he does not, he says he is already depressed enough without them, instead he takes naps in the afternoon, almost every day when we're home the house is hushed, hushed while Daddy is napping. In the first years of our marriage when we could not sleep we made hot Ovaltine in the middle of the night, played chess or backgammon, now we are too fragile for that, even on vacations such as this our light sleeps rustle next to each other like animals panting on a hot night. Every New Year's Day as I try to fall asleep I recall the seasons of the preceding year, the rumble of the snow plow slicing through the first great January storm, the late muddy winter, the fetid smell of dead animals suddenly surging under the melting snow, the swollen streams, the glossy, lemon-yellow willow buds. Summer, our children growing, the sweetness of their naked bodies, the triumphant splash of their urine against the large oak behind the pond. On a fall day when the trees ooze colors like syrup, I have often thought that on such a day when my beloved children are grown I would not mind dying, ending all contradictions and desires, driving my car into a copse of crimson maples to the strain of my sweet radio jazz. But one must wait, one must wait until the birds are grown. Nurturing, nurturing, that is our beginning and our end. In a December storm I love to see our little boy standing immobile in the snow, arms stretched out as he watches the silent flakes settle on his hand, on the dog's long fleece, on the stippled birches. We are punctilious parents. The tree is bought before anyone else's, the carols are learned and the crèche is in order two weeks before Christmas. Thin high voices soaring. *Ces voix d'enfants, chantant dans les coupoles.* I want everything to be a precise opposite of my own lonely childhood. Theirs will be all laughter and companionship and normalcy, I fear to leave them for more than a day, we are the prize-winning little nuclear family, oh what a show of unity, we never quarrel before them, we never quarrel behind them, that is a part of our manners, perhaps that is why we are insomniacs. When I go to bed on New Year's night I wind my watch, thinking, If I have to turn it less than twenty times before it locks I'm going to have another affair before the summer. But by the time it locks I'm so slowed by Nembutal I've forgotten whether under twenty or over meant trouble. So that's that. After a few years of seeking shelter in marriage, before I started writing, teaching, seeing other men again, I pondered a great deal on death while gardening. I detest gardening, I did it out of docility, the way I froze forty quarts of beans in summertime, to satisfy Paul's expectations of me. I worried about my potential for suicide; spading up the earth of his flower borders, I kept seeing my death in the face of the peony, in the pistil of the lupine, there was a great emptiness, a great terror glimpsed through the fissure of this calm act. I grew formal and decorative dahlias, double begonias, pompon zinnias, Madame Butterfly snapdragons, Giant Pacific delphiniums, I saw destruction in the face of each flower. Every spring, stomp, stomp, my naked feet wallowed into the sumptuous freshly furrowed earth, pressing down the seeds of snow peas, bib lettuce, fennel, Hubbard squash, there was that funny day the first summer of our marriage when a friend from Paris came for lunch in a chauffeur-driven limousine, one of those dashing magnates my mother used to thrust upon me in hope of getting me well married early. We gave him a simple lunch, buttermilk soup, lots of cucumbers from the garden, he left with a puzzled expression on his face, the new me stomping about the vegetable patch must have seemed very odd compared to the doll in borrowed Chanels wandering through nightclubs in search of love. Yet within a few years I knew I would rather die brutally, prematurely, than lead the life my husband would have preferred for me, he would have liked me to garden more, bake more bread, count my linen, never travel alone, attend fewer antiwar demonstrations. Puppy, puppy love, he used to call me in the first years when I fulfilled his image of happiness the way he at first fulfilled mine. And I called him Father Earth because along with his work and his family he loved his property, his garden, his home beyond all else, he was always so sweet and eager to help me out. "Stephanie darling, where's that silver serving spoon my mother gave us, we're already losing our wedding gifts, it's incredible, I can't ever find anything. . . . The garden isn't weeded, sweetie pie, you're losing all that lovely lettuce. . . . Would you like me to make some nice curry for dinner, there's all that lamb left over from the weekend going to waste, and I could add some of our own zucchini. . . ." We go to PTA meetings. We have breakfast, lunch and dinner together every day. Our parents spend all the holidays with us. I have been analyzed once, not long enough. At a Christmas party last week a Radcliffe classmate asked me what kind of life I had, I said the year after I came back from Paris I married a successful architect whom I'd known for years, we own a nineteenth-century house and forty acres of land in Massachusetts, my husband is the original Mr. Marriage, my marriage is so solid and substantial it could be made of kosher chicken livers. Yet the funny thing is, I continued, I have these recurring dreams that I'm a middle-aged spinster pining for a family and a home, isn't that hysterical? The liberation movements of our time give most of us a profoundly ambivalent attitude toward permanence, she said, to which I replied, Aren't women great, I would never have thought of that all by myself. On that New Year's night in Atlantic City I dream again that I am middle-aged and unmarried, homeless, with nowhere to sleep but the steps of a primitive Mayan shrine on which I have been waiting eight years for a bridegroom, dressed in long white robes, my hair cut short as if for surgery. I am hungry, lonely, where is the bridegroom? Finally he advances, holding an executioner's ax. He neatly decapitates me, I am metamorphosed into a casual observer, as the former me becomes a human sacrifice, my former head rolls down the steps of the altar in a pool of nectar.

The power with which the human male for the first time overwhelmed the human female marked the end of woman's ability to choose . . . the primal rape was a phallic, sadistic act.
—Gregory Zillborg

Rain beating down, sheets of water sloughing up against the black windowpane, the car cutting through the sheets of rain like a surgeon continuously sopping up the blood that spouts from his incision. Whatever the weather, he drives a car the way he provides for his family, with utmost silence, resoluteness, assurance of his worth, occasionally giving me a sweet, paternal smile. Until a few years ago I hated his silence, I resented it, I remember writing in my journal phrases like "Our silence festers," "Our silence swells," "Our silence lies between us like a heap of garbage." I resented the boredom and the muteness, it reminded me of the wordlessness with which my mother had stifled my childhood. But lately, tonight for instance, our vacuum has taken on a quality of refuge, almost of pleasure, it is my way of remaining separate now that I have lost that sloppy romantic desire to merge. "Being part is an exertion that declines," that's Wallace Stevens, I think, I do not want anyone to drag me down now that I am finally raising myself up, up. Nights like this when we drive home through the Massachusetts countryside, that's when the silence is most satisfying, especially if I'm a little stoned, then riding through the black rain is like being born into the night, borne, born through tunneled darkness on great waves of amniotic fluid. I particularly like to get stoned when driving home in the dark like this, I like to have fun alone inside the silence, play inside it all by myself. In this car similar to the silent living rooms of my childhood the same loneliness prevails, the darkness is full of ghosts to be charmed and exorcised by games and word tricks so it can become as tender as the licking of an enormous black tongue. Tonight for instance I think of death and the afterlife, my last lecture on John Donne, the influence of alchemy on Donne's notion of the resurrection of the body—the alchemical ruining of the body effected by a quintessence of privation, of *nothingness*, is necessary to the glory of the resurrection, what a thought—and I think of some event in one of my children's lives that I am telling friends about, and about two or three students in freshman English who need an extra tutorial, and of how I'd like to be alone more, be able to disappear for a month, yet remain still loved (will that ever become possible, this marriage is so big and kosher it's like a government, we have our State Department, our Ministry of Defense, our Health, Education and Welfare), and I think of how I need another glass of wine to better survive the silence of this drive, about how I haven't felt like fucking anyone for months, and I wonder why I don't masturbate the way other women say they do and whether they're putting us on with their talk of how often they jack off—jack off, funny words for us, but the proper terms for our bodies don't exist yet, so we have to borrow them from men for the time being, go in drag as it were, drag our way through their language until we forge our own—and just think, I did it for the first time only last year, in my thirties, on a day when I had a bad cold and was reading in bed thinking about Claire, thinking of how beautiful she had been at that last peace demonstration when I lay on the grass with my head on her lap, and she stroked my hair like a mother panther grooming her young, telling me, "You look like a swan, you have the heart of a lion," that's what I like most about love, the unclouding of the mirror of self, very narcissistic but what can you do, it's true, and it's what I miss the most in this marriage, I'm never told what I am, never given a mirror, because that needs language and he seldom dares to talk about us, that would be taking off his mask, words are shit, he once said, and we never discussed it again—anyhow, thinking of Claire, I tried it, and it brought only the gentlest sensation, pathetic compared to the real thing, no more than a little sigh, a tiny puff of pleasure, like seeing the Parthenon for the first time after having heard about it all one's life and finding it to be a pretty little building thirty feet long, and yet it did offer a resolution, the fantasy was abated by rubbing that unctuous triangle, and it was curious to do it in that bedroom which I painted dark green years ago, green for the repose, the refuge, the shelter marriage provided for me, it has become like a childhood room because I spent the childhood of my marriage there and I have changed so much since then, and here I was jacking off next to those dolls my father gave me a few years before he died, the beautiful nineteenth-century wax dolls with the blond curls and satins and laces and gilt ribbons whose glass domes I have never dared remove because I was afraid they would crumble at my touch, there they were looking at me like kind nurses as I felt the lovely little warm rush in my groin . . . and come to think of it I've got to do something about this silent man I love sitting at my side, I'm fed up with all our excuses about backaches and insomnias and headaches, last Tuesday we'd been married fourteen years and when we came home I thought, Anniversary, it can't go on this way, we've fucked twice this month and I'm beginning to see the pale anxiety in his eyes, this is what I hate most about marriage, the chattelizing, the obligation, the damn duty, duty—duty really is his bag, he's into duty the way others are into grass, duty to me, to his parents to his genitals to his mouth, God how miserable he looks when a meal or a fuck isn't on time, that's what an orderly life is about I suppose —anyhow although he's the best lover I've ever had I can't stand being merged, fused, entered right now, so I said, "Can I do it for you?" and he said, "Yes! that's what I like the best anyway," and I started stroking him, but my arm got tired, I couldn't get the variety of speed he needed to get off, I got bored and lazy and said, "Do it yourself please a little while and tell me when you're close to coming so I can put my mouth to you," and as he pumped it himself I was struck by his beauty, the elegance of that head framed by thick wavy barely graying hair, the youthfulness of his long body, the beauty of that penis, as alabaster fresh and brawny as if he were eighteen, he pumped it mightily, but it was too late, my fault, we were both tired and had had a lot of wine, I'd already taken my sleeping pill, we turned over and hugged each other and said, "What an anniversary, thank God that only happens once a year," and I fell asleep. . . . The rain beating, the car slicing through the sheet of black water and silence. . . . This is what I think about a lot in these dark night drives, how to fuck, how to fuck better, how to fuck several men at the same time, how many cocks could you fit in all at once, and how things look, how bodies look in various positions, for instance when he is over me, thrusting his cock into my mouth, the view of our green bedroom-cave is circumscribed by the hulk of his buttocks, by his golden-blond ass as palely fuzzed as the landscape at my favorite time of year, at that dawn of spring when the growth is not any color yet but a pale gloss, an evanescence—to stare at the horizon of those buttocks is also like staring eye level at a gigantic apple, at the beautiful cleft in the middle of the fruit from which thrusts the upright stem—the golden spring landscape falls and rises, falls and rises over my head, almost strangling me, obscuring all else in the room except a speck of green ceiling, nothing but the lovely apple-hill rising and falling like a breathing mountain over me . . . when we turn over and do it sideways I get the full beauty of his cock near my eyes and it becomes metamorphosed into the face of a sad, wise man, it has a character, it has an expression, it is the face of a terribly wise ironic man with the beauty of an El Greco portrait—eyes slit with pleasure at the top of the long narrow face, the lips way below at the fold curled into an ironic smile, the face of a mystic contemplating the irony of creation—and this is what I think about often when I ride home in the dark, how I have loved his cock and that of other men, how the best fucks have been with him or else the times when I've fucked two men on the same day, there's an amplitude there, a thrill at the thought of two identities of sperm mixing a few hours apart, how glorious it would be to treat ourselves to six, seven men in a row, to have a constellation of semens twirling about in each of us, but we women have not been allowed that for the past ten thousand years or so, we the dispossessed, we who were disenthroned so that men could inherit the vile stuff of property, we who can reach it without trouble twenty-seven times in a row, we whose gigantic needs were suppressed to make this stinking so-called civilization possible, we who can only live out our sexuality in fantasy, in dream, in religion . . . and this is what he will never understand, this is how men have enslaved us, precisely by looking at our bodies as objects of worth, I have not any awe for my body neither do I wish him to have any, what is my body but an impoverished appendage of my spirit, Buddhism, the whole East is beginning to bring that home to us, I think it was John Donne who called it "a bracelet of bright hair about the bone," what is the body but a modest hostel to be cleansed, enjoyed and shared with increasingly simple, austere, communal ways of housekeeping . . . and whoever looks on it differently, with possessiveness or uniqueness, debases us to chattel, keeps us as morbidly encased as those wax dolls under glass that stand in my bedroom . . . the dark night flows, flows about us, he drives on silently, I am always alone.

I I

"And forever, and forever, and forever," he sings. The man I love that day stands by the window toying with a tacky hotel-room curtain sprinkled with apples, grapes, laughing cherubs. He hums along with the cassette of Handel's *Messiah* we are playing on the little tape recorder I keep in my shopping bag. We play Bach, Vivaldi masses, mostly religious music. "I need either a brothel or a conversion—the two interchangeable—" I've been writing something like that in my journal every few months for years. Need for more religion, different fucking, need to have my mind blown rather than my body, that's the gist of it. Well, dearie, try again, it's not this sparrow academic who's going to bring you nirvana, but the privacy is great anyway. This could be Paris, Cambridge, Milan, in a hotel room I forget all, I have a passion for transiency, if I ever get rich I'll rent a motel room for the afternoon a couple of times a week just to be alone and think and read and get away from the Chicken Livers Kastle we call home. So this is better than nothing and yet, poor prigs, we drink Scotches neat at twelve noon—his office lunch hour—to relax ourselves for adultery. In my shopping bag some delicate little lunch is always rattling about along with the necessities of the trade—cucumber sandwiches, Pouilly Fuissé. Going to market, going to market for love. As the affair drags on, my fear of his boredom centers not on my flat chest or our waning repertory of novel positions but on how weary he must be of staring at that same canvas shopping bag, it must be as boring as his wife's nightgowns, why hasn't *Vogue* mentioned this aspect of the seduction business? "Have a variety of shopping bags for your daylight affairs! Try Art Nouveau decals for a refresher!" We need guidance on that point and on the hairpiece problem, whether to take it off before or after your clothes. Not that the professor is himself unwearisome with all that talk of his tenure, his children, his vacations, his macroeconomic aggregates, I still don't understand Keynes after hearing about him twenty times. It's crazy how much more we think about sex than care about it, *Post coitum omne animal triste,* as the Church Fathers said. With this sparrow there's mighty little of the discovery which is the crux of any pleasure, the physical stuff is just medium, but that never matters to me anyway, there's just that delectation of privacy so direly lacking in modern life, in which we are constantly checking up on each other, able to reach each other by phone or jet at any hour of the day, what an FBI, what a nuisance, what a loss of civil rights. That's why I prefer to make love when I'm undressed and he still has his raincoat on, his shoes, all his clothes, at least that way I still get a touch of transiency and freedom. "God, kiddo, family life is dreary enough," I say as I struggle to put on my hairpiece in time to catch a cab ride with him back to college, "you manage to make affairs even drearier." He mumbles one of his fashionable open-marriage slogans about how I'd probably prefer to make it with his wife. Sure, I say, I'd vastly prefer to make it with Claire, but I'm not liberated enough yet in these matters to approach her. How do they do it, bookstores are full of manuals for gay men but not one in sight for women, there again you're way ahead of us, what does one say, when does one say it? During a dinner party as we giggle and pee together in the bathroom? Over lunch hour, as we try on Levis at the Harvard Co-op? After he's dropped me off at my office I think of her milky blonde's skin, of how I envy those full breasts with nipples like little pink saucers. "I love you, I love you," she keeps on saying, but where do we go on from there? How beautiful she was that time we got busted together during a peace demonstration, and she stood clutching at the bars of her cell, not singing or lolling about on the benches and yakking like the other sisters but just standing clenching the bars, chain-smoking her Turkish cigarettes, her topaz eyes smoldering with rage like those of a caged lioness, eyes singed with an anger which could be that of all women, the anger of nuns whose eyes are caged by the snowy frames of their starched coifs, of those Moslem women whose eyes look out upon reality with an anger equaled only by desire. They'd taken away our watches, our spectacles, hairpins, wedding bands, all we had, while the men in the other compound had been allowed to keep even their penknives. Typical.

Each time I went by Claire's cell on my way to the bathroom I put my face to the bars and we exchanged a long deep soul kiss, women's mouths are so much more unctuous than men's, that's to be expected, all soft and juicy like sinking your tongue into a little bowl of mashed-up peaches. I have this recurrent dream about her and her dreary husband, she is sitting in their bedroom dressed in a purple Orlon bathrobe, he makes her lean over the chair, he fucks her from behind as she screams in joy and pain, next we are all three together on the floor, much younger, children again, gamboling and humping each other in turn in a large army-surplus sleeping bag, every inch of our bodies resurrected into sexuality and narcissism like those of babies . . . wanting to rebecome androgynous, to share more men, women, men/women, to be both, to become what Claire calls good socialists of the body, that's my fantasy, we all have the right to one . . . as for that husband of hers you can have him, he's so dull that I fall asleep even before fucking as he talks about cycles of recession, cycles of depression, I perk up only when he starts saying things like you are this, you are that, you are a curious amalgam of hyperfeminine lyrical intro-version and aggressive masculine drives. All ass is grass. Orgasm is for the birds. Carrington loved Lytton Strachey so much that she committed suicide the week after he died. They had never had sex. They had lived together for twelve years. That's what love is about. Think about that.

He sat in the vast courtyard lit by April sunshine, a man in early middle age nursing his dying dog. He had taken one of the ladderback chairs out of the dining room and sat over the animal, his hand soothing the old spaniel's chest, straining to let her live as long as possible into the sunny morning. The chair he sat on was of maple, its caning as rumpled and mangy as the dog's russet fur. They had lived together in the intimacy that only the most silent men can offer their animals. The spaniel lay on the same spot where she had lain for many years and had bared her fangs at anyone who disturbed her master's peace. She panted quickly, her brown eyes stared straight ahead with resignation, occasionally twitching at her master in a conspiratorial blink. Paul crouched over her, his head on her neck, a man in his thirties crying his heart out over the body of his dog. I looked at him out the window, not daring to intrude. Oh my God, the last of his dogs is dying dying dying, how will he get over it? My younger child sat on my lap doodling, prattling. "When I erase a letter does it die and go to heaven? Does it, Mom, does it?" There outside was his father, a man who loves us as deeply as he hates words, a man who dislikes much of the world about him, a man often tired, difficult to live with. I walked toward him and put a hand on his shoulder. A tear rolled down his furrowed cheek. His eyes are pale blue, both tender and severe, when I describe them to myself I often refer to them as "judgmental." My husband has judgmental eyes. This was the last of the dogs with whom he had spent twenty years of his manhood. The moment I finally decided to marry him he was walking through the corridors of that big Massachusetts house he had mysteriously chosen to share with his parents, a man in his thirties living with two parents and three dogs. He came toward me as if through a long corridor, walking through his study, through the dining room, the golden dogs whirring at his feet. He was handsome as a movie star, everyone said he resembled Jimmy Stewart. I kept wondering why no one had grabbed him yet, what was wrong with him that no one had yet stolen him from his mother, she dominated the house, her whines of worry about china, pearls, silver, the winterizing of her furs, hummed through their rooms like ultrasonic beams. For years I'd wondered how he managed without women, living like that in New England, seldom going anywhere except to look at some new architectural site, just designing those buildings and reading and gardening and taking care of the old house, how often did he jack off, what was wrong with him that he sought such refuge in the past, that he did not love today and grab it more. One day after I'd returned from that crazy year of being twenty-three in Paris, his parents went on a trip and we made love again in his house, briefly and simply, nothing extraordinary that time. I wanted to marry Paul because I needed his growing tenderness, his need of me, his frequent and protective smile, those fireplaces, I suddenly wanted to have his children, I wanted to bring up his children in that house. That's love. His parents eventually moved out and took a flat in Boston, after much difficulty. In the first years of our marriage we often discussed the following question with great seriousness: who had left us a more spectacular mess, his devouring whining mother or my devouring vociferous one? We mended each other piece by piece, ever so patiently, as if we were wounded animals or anemic children, in those early days we were constantly nuzzling, caressing, praising each other, our I-love-you's were coming out like the ticking of a clock. He even talked me into some of that bourgeois finery I'd always detested, china, monogrammed towels, a little silver even, it seemed to reassure him, it gave him a sense of permanence, his mother's sense of material permanence. I sorted his socks, I made blackberry jam, I hung his Harvard summa-cum degree over his desk, I spent five hours making one *pâté en croute,* I did little else, I was a blast, I was a housewife. Goddammit, this was the fifties. I waited for him at lunch every day, I set his place at the kitchen table with the new silver, waiting for him to return from his drafting board, looking forward to seeing his fine hair curl over his strong neck, to his smell of dark ink and lemon soap. Dammit, how much fairer to him if we had brought each other up in the seventies, and I'd be a lawyer or a doctor coming home at eight most nights and going away to monthly conventions, how much easier life would be for him now. In the beginning, we sometimes drank a bit at night, and cried at the thought of each other's death. I also wept when I learned that I was pregnant, after two years of constantly trying. "We're never going to be alone anymore," I sobbed, and the three dogs licked me as I stood by the fireplace weeping at that thought.

When I had first slept with him years ago I discovered that the dogs were inseparable from him, an extension of his body and of his chosen loneliness, sleeping on top of his bed, on top of his clothes. He protected himself with those dogs the way he protected himself from the century with his sad parents, his property, his compulsive ten-hour-a-day working schedules, his dull, mournful country acquaintances: rich Wasp country gentry, two decades older than he most of them, with whom he could decry the loss of human values, talk about the old days. He seemed to prefer them to his contemporaries, the few artists or writers he saw were older men who he felt had been left behind by the stream of history, he was always singing their praises over those of the young twerps who had made it. A man perfectly sexed with no society of his own, only one or two friends in the world, he reminded me of a splendid but unidentifiable tree in a forest of birches, or a beautiful unidentifiable forest animal. Perhaps that's why I'm still unable to put together the pieces of his character, the picture-puzzle pieces are still jumbled in the brown paper bag, little details of the design come out, like here's the well, here's the kitty cat—he is brilliant, loyal, loving, secretive, self-righteous—but even after all these years I can't make out much more than that, I'm left ignorant of the larger landscape, maybe that's why I'm still in love with him, he's so mysterious. The evening I'd said, "Yes, I'll marry you," I had gone out for a walk alone and stared at the brilliance of the trees hanging over his country road and thought, That's it, my life is settled, all is in order now, I shall have order at last, order order order, none of Louis B.'s or my parents' brilliant disorder, I shall have that quiet country life of Paul's which my friends warned me would drive me crazy—something more on the order of Saint-Seran—lots of dogs, a country gentleman for a husband, meals on time. Somehow I had always imagined it occurring in England rather than in America, I'd once had an English boy friend who called me Poppy, I'd imagined a household like those photographed in *Country Life* magazine, Sir and Lady So-and-So are shown here with their German shepherds and their two delightful children, Sebastian and Bartholomew. A bookish, donnish man with a little title and an unused degree in theology from Cambridge with whom I could discuss the influence of John Donne's sermons on Marvell's conceits, that would have made it perfect for my mother and me. "What was the theory of afterlife among the metaphysicals of Cromwell's time?" I could have asked him as I pruned the rosebushes, and he would have replied, "Well, Poppy dear, one could say it is exemplified by that poem of Donne's in which he refers to the body as 'a bracelet of bright hair about the bone,' a quite fundamentalist view actually, very obsessed by the resurrection of the body with considerable stress on the Transfiguration. . . ." But notwithstanding his summa-cums, the man I married prefers to stand about the lawn in his pajamas, volume of Proust in hand, talking to his dogs, saying, "Do your peepee, Sahara, do your peepee, darling, that's a good girl, ouisee ouisee, that's a good puppy." "Words are crap," he had once said. We live on in considerable calm and silence. Like most others we were at our happiest when we were still building our little nest, when we scheduled our lives around our babies, like that time we went to Spain with those elegant, gay American expatriates. It was just like that summer in Saint-Tropez, after a few weeks we barely talked to our chic friends or relatives, we relished only our purring peace, we stayed in our little room most of the time playing with baby, the mattress was set on the floor to aid Paul's ailing back, Tommy was eight months old and beginning to sit up and ask for things, we could watch him bouncing on the mattress for hours on end going, "Whee, whee." Paul was always the exemplary father and husband, up early doing the first bottle and diaper shifts, taking pride in whatever little bouts of writing I could get done, poring over my Master's thesis for hours, penciling all my papers and articles so meticulously, always so helpful, never complaining, those are the most difficult men, the ones who make you feel grateful for so much. That time in Spain we once took a train to spend two days in Madrid, leaving Tommy in the country with a sitter, what a major expedition that was for us. I was already pregnant with a second child, with Jeffie. We walked too long in the Prado visiting those paintings we both love, the Hierony- mus Bosches, the Grecos, the late dark Goyas in the museum's basement, art is something he can always be eloquent about, especially about the use of materials, the formal design. We had a lot of wine with lunch and made love afterward, that evening we were terribly worried about the baby inside me. "You're going to have another baby," he said as we rode back on the train. "I must buy you a fur coat, you've never had a decent winter coat." Respectable mothers must have a fur coat, the silver must be kept polished. A protective, tender hug, a flash of the movie-star smile that shields his identity like a mask. I said I couldn't stand fur, it was a symbol of death, but he repeated, "You must have a warm, decent winter coat." He brushed back my hair with so much tenderness that serenity and fulfillment flowed mightily through me, those were sweet days, sweet days.

Marriage like the Sea of Azov! When I used to study geog- raphy with my Russian governess that was where I wanted to go more than anywhere else in the world, the Sea of Azov. I like the calm, the platitude, the intimacy it implied. Azov, that's the way marriage is with a man who paces his life and others' according to certain ineluctable principles: Respectable women own a string of pearls. New York at night is dangerous. Stay away from philandering men. Confucian devotion to parents. The perfect wife is the Indian goddess with thirty-seven arms who spends her summers taking the children swimming, driving the children and their friends all over the map, entertaining her husband's clients, getting an hour's work done on her own manuscript before cooking a meal for twelve, grooming the flower garden, putting the anise out in the vegetable patch so the deer won't get at it, writing letters to newspapers about political prisoners in Chile, raising funds for war resisters . . . Mother earth, I love you best as Mother Earth, his eyes are most often saying or else they say, Be patient, everything has its place. Ah, yes, place. At times I try to sit on his side of the kitchen table, I adore a change of view. But he takes that poorly, he takes it as a revolt. He moves my plate and spoon out and puts his plate and spoon back in their usual position, he insists on keeping the same place year after year, at the south side of the kitchen table overlooking the lawn in which he buried his last spaniel. Well, I could have said it along with Sigmund, order is a compulsion to repeat which "spares indecision and hesitation," or something like that, anyhow it's another tactic to avoid anxiety. I'd wanted order, and order, order is what we're eating at this table, civilization and its discontents right along with our Grape-Nuts. There are times when I walk into the house and the calm, orderly anguish of Paul's life is summed up by the sound of his chewing. He is a lean man who loves his food, who looks anxious at parties when food does not arrive on time, not because he is truly hungry but because conversation bores him and food reassures him, and he wants to fall into bed as soon as possible to return to his books and his attempts at sleep. And sometimes when I walk into the house I am surrounded by the crisp angry sound of his chewing on something dry and brittle—toast mostly, toast or crackers—a sound like that of an army of squirrels fervidly chewing. Being of an elegant and delicate nature, he will not vent his anxiety on meat or rich matter, only on austere thin dry objects, wafers, toast. And over the years the sight of his chewing obsesses me as the symbol of his mysterious aloneness, his estrangement from his century, his peers, his colleagues, from everything except his family and land—oh yes God, that family and land which give him all the roots he has. It is like the chewing of one of those squirrels one sometimes observes in a forest, separated from their tribe, standing with a worried look in their eyes but munching vigorously on their twigs, as if the working of their jaws was the best protection against the fullness of their solitude. And as I foray into his den, that unshakable north seat of the kitchen table, the pale, worried blue eyes seem to convey the following message over the indomitably moving mandibles: "These are frightening times. I believe in human dignity, private enterprise and the sacredness of marriage. I know that you chafe a bit in this calm life of ours, but I demand your loyalty and patience. We married because a time came when you seemed as afraid of solitude as I was, and when you leave me for even two days I get intensely depressed, I shall not shy away from using the blackmail of my depression. I can lean against the icebox and faint again the way I used to in Paris, I shall give you considerable freedom from criticism in order to avoid that blackmail or the bargaining for truths about our pasts. So let us live on as serenely as we have lived for the past many years, let us never shift the breakfast dishes at this table. . . ." Meanwhile my own eyes are saying something like this over his genuine hewn-pine kitchen table: "Threatening blackmail, preserving the sanctity of home and of ancient rules, just like a woman! What a decade, now *we're* the ones who want adventure, independence, transiency, a new place to sit at. . . ." His own eyes are very beautiful, pale eyes filled with the self-righteousness of his beliefs, standing like cold lakes in the fine, chiseled face. They dominate that portrait of him someone did when he was in his twenties, a terrifying painting that hangs in the hall by his study: It shows the hard-etched face of a Cromwellian minister or of some New England divine willing to ostracize those who differ from his beliefs. Over the years as I become more playful, freer, I salute it increasingly often as I saunter down the corridor. "Hi, Cromwell dear," I say, or "Good morning, Oliver," "Oliver, dear prig, how's business today?" It's another little magic trick to soothe the loneliness, to survive. For even those times when we take our evening strolls there is terror in the blue eyes of my shelterer if I think of a line of poetry and start walking a little ahead of him (he likes to walk up the same road every night with a little military step, his arm tenderly around my shoulder). "Why are you walking ahead of me?" he barks, tugging at me sharply from behind, back into history, into subjugation. "Don't walk ahead of me like that!" It's like Vietnam, or the *Mayaguez*, they've got to show us they're *men*. "Hell, fucker," I say, "I don't give a shit when *you* walk ahead of me," but I say it inaudibly, most of our anger lies unsaid, we spit it out in the pantomime of our eyes, and when pulled back like that, smile women smile, the way a prisoner smiles at his guard, hoping for a better deal next time around. Often he calls me by his doggie's name by mistake, "Come here, Sahara darling, here, sweetheart, come on, puppy love," how many men must wish we were like that, staring longingly at them through the window, saluting them with bounces after a few hours' absence as if they'd been gone for days.

WITCHCRAFT / WITTGENSTEIN, Ludwig /
WLADYSLAW II, Jogi / WOHLER, Friedrich /
WOMEN, Status of / WOOD and Wood
Products
        —*Encyclopaedia Britannica*, 1974 ed.

If I were ever to go mad it would be on Thanksgiving Day, that day of guilt and grace when the family hangs upon you like an ax over a sacrificial victim, like the oven's heat on that poor bird. What a perfect day to go loony. In comes the turkey and out I go, borne on a stretcher into the cold maternal night, smashing all that crystal and china of theirs, howling, "Liberation from this shit! Freedom!" "Eat your turkey, darling," Gwammy says, "Eat the lovely turkey Gwammy and Mommy cooked for you." "What's that funny dress you're wearing Gwammy?" Tommy says. "That's called a kimono," Gwammy says, "your Daddy brought it back to me from Korea, he always used to bring me such nice things in the old days." Jeffie wants to know how Gwammy likes the stuffing. Gwammy says, "Hmmmmm, it's not too bad, but I prefer the bread-and-cream kind I used to make for Daddy when we lived in Westchester, you remember dear how I used to make it in Purchase, cream-and-cornbread stuffing?" "Well, this is almost as good, Mother," he says, "I don't mind her apricots at all." (This is what I dreamed of all through high school, when we had no dining room and I ate off cupboards, standing up, I dreamed of sitting down for Thanksgiving dinner in candlelight, of meals on time.) Tommy wants to know whether Dad has heard about Billie Jean King's press conference. "Sure I've read about Billie Jean, what's she trying to prove, that she's just as strong as any man?" Tommy says that's *not* what she wants to prove, she's just saying that women are underpaid. And Mommy says she made it perfectly *clear* that that's what she's talking about. Daddy says, "Nonsense, that women's lib movement is always trying to prove that they can do anything as well as men." "That is *not* what the feminist athletes are trying to prove (stay with my college podium jargon, keep my cool), they're saying that their performance could be improved to a degree if societal attitudes . . ." "I hate hate hate that women's lib," Gwammy says, "I hate everything they do, everything they say." Poor sweethearts, how they always side together on the lib business, how they miss the good old days when there was better weather, better ice cream, docile women. Last night I had another funny dream, that I was longing for a man whose mother had locked him in her room, I found the way to his bedroom and she was there at the door, saying his name was Ockham but I mustn't touch him because he is too frail, he would crumble into dust at the slightest touch. Ockham, William of, razor's edge, I manage to pursue him down a long, steeply curving staircase which transforms itself into a water chute, a steep down-winding stream. He hangs on to the staircase, he escapes me, but I have a good time alone in that scene of birth and freedom, I slide down the long water chute as unctuously as a puppy slithers out of the tomb, oops I mean womb, that's the way I said it to my shrink and he was fascinated by the slip—tomb, womb. (So he's not born yet? Still hanging on to the Cord, in your opinion? Maybe it's strangling him?) Almost every night I have similar dreams—I am unmarried, unloved, have nowhere to live. Then I wake up and find that I am still young and beautiful, that I have two perfect children, a brilliant and adoring husband, that I am saddled with the matter of affection. What do they mean? "Remember those lovely little carts with white awnings the Negroes used to pull us in when we went to Florida," Gwammy is saying, "they were so comfortable, those good old days are gone. . . . Remember how well the clematis grew right on our terrace in Westchester, just a little handful of bone meal at the roots and it had flowers up to the roof. . . . Your linen's in terrible shape, you should go to the July white sales at Altman's, that's where we used to go for our linen, you remember. . . ." She loves to rub in the memories of that past of theirs which he wears like a scar, and almost every Thanksgiving Paul's back corset makes funny little bulges under his shirt, upon arriving at her flat for the weekend he is inevitably stricken with some ailment, usually his back. It is the subtlest proof of his distaste for the visit and of his determination to suffer through it, they must have had pains together the way some couples have children. "How did you sleep last night, Mother?" "Oh terrible, I took a Tuinal at two A.M." "I did even worse, barely three hours of sleep." "I woke up with the funniest pain in my wrist." "Well, I should tell you my ankle is really killing me." This apartment of hers we're sitting in always reminds me of a funereal bird's cage, with its hair-parlor Louis XV décor, bisque statuary, tragic cousins in graduation pictures, custom-made lace tablecloths brought to the house in little suitcases by Mr. Rozensweig, gilt-framed photographs of loved ones mostly dead. Paul's father, dead of liver troubles and intemperate diet two years after our marriage; Paul's older brother, killed in his thirties in a homosexual crime of passion; Paul's younger brother, dead in his thirties of a stroke induced by drugs after ten years of massive analysis. ("Death at an early age?" That's what I try to have my eyes say in our inimitable dumb show when he's bugging me with his solid old values: "Death at an early age, is that what you want for us too?") And then pictures of Paul still alive, so different, so composed and disciplined, his fine angular beauty so unlike the rest of his thick-limbed, thick-lipped family that he seems to have fathered and mothered himself, gone through an admirable process of self-birth which exhausted him for life. Every Thanksgiving when I stare at those baby pictures of my husband, that's when I decipher a bit more of him, when the landscape beyond the rosebush and the well begins to crystallize like the image in a Polaroid shot: Perpetual guilt, that guilt the shrewdest mothers of the species know how to instill into their sons for ever leaving them at all. Perpetual need for tribe; and since he had always hated his aunts and cousins and brothers, found them coarse and vulgar, his tribal loyalty had all devolved upon this lovely blond mother whose mind is exclusively furnished with crystal, silver, furs, children, and ailments. Ah, yes, maybe that's what you're most afraid of, my beloved squirrel with the anxious eyes, afraid of being left without either a mommy or a wifey. . . . There were days after one particular affair when I reached for a Bufferin in the early morning and swallowed a Seconal instead by mistake, following it with an emetic to throw it up. Well, here we are, kiddo, downing reds in the A.M. like in Paris and Switzerland, we've come right back to where we started. I am unfaithful because I am lonely, because I want to be a boy,

222

because I want to be punished, because I desire to desire my husband again, because I want to know who he is, because I am starved for transcendence, because I rebel for all women, because we are killing each other in our dolls' houses, because . . . The night he learned about that one he confronted me with the face in the portrait, the paleness of his eyes blazing like ice in the moonlight, he said never again, I want those children, things like that. He left for two days and I slept druglessly those nights for the first time in years, as if I had brought my life to some needed resolution, and the next morning I desired him again for the first time in years with the full force of those early days. How we made love after that reconciliation! Love of my life, I have never wanted you as much as the time I hurt you the most, because it was the only time you let the being caged inside you rage, the only time I fully grasped you as a person, the only time you were about to kill me, the only time you really talked to me, the only time the reality of your manhood overcame the sheltering stranger who sits at the other end of the Thanksgiving table talking about our children, our mothers, our property, our dogs, our recipes for spinach. Last night after the birth-in-water dream I had still another dream that I was growing older and lonelier, that I sorrowed for never having married: My bedroom has a huge glass wall overlooking a pool through which I see a beautiful blond child swimming, one of those Park Avenue nymphets like Janet who made me miserable at Miss Temple's. During a ten-second swim she metamorphoses into a woman, she sprouts breasts and pubic hair, a large screen over the pool flashes an announcement of her forthcoming wedding, a glamorous event to which I am not invited and at which I stare again through a glass wall, the perpetual outsider. . . . A wedding dance, maids of honor with gardenias in their hair. . . . The pool metamorphoses into a frozen pond (marriage as a freezing of the impulses, as sleep and death?) . . . Everyone is skating, dressed in white ermine muffs, long white fur dresses. My mother stands beside me, singling out a tall silvery stranger as a marriage partner, saying, "You're married to Paul, but it doesn't count, it's not enough, you must have *another* one." Claire, my dearest mentor, if only she were here today, with her I could discuss this dream or anything else, God, Kafka, the resurrection of the body, instead I'll drink on, I'll drink to her, I'll drink to remember and forget. To remember that day last month I spent in jail in the cell next to hers, watched by slender matrons whose pistols rode like jockeys on their pointed hips, talking about death, the Rosenbergs' innocence, the meaning of Kafka's *Metamorphosis*. "*Hypocrite lectrice, ma semblable, ma soeur*, what does *Metamorphosis* mean to you," I asked her, "is Gregor Samsa a symbol of original sin? Or of the resurrection of the body? Or is he a symbolic victim of our parents' sloth and selfishness? When he wishes to assert a separate identity they hate him to death, they kill him!" "Gregor's loneliness," she answers, "is based on the fact that he does not belong to this security-minded illusion of life but to the mystery of a final vocation. That might be a lesson to all of us, Stephanie love! You and I and all our sisters must remember that like men we have before us many lonely tasks of liberation. Our mothers have taught us to be the retarding and conservative force, to cling to the corrupt finery of civilization rather than fighting our servitude. Because we are slaves we have misshapen our children by clinging to them, we must regain our power but use it more carefully, we have been given the historic vocation to rebuild society, always remember that there was a time when we were more free." Yep, that's what she said that day. Well, maybe next year at this time when I wake up I'll be metamorphosed into a turkey, I must jot that down in a postcard to Claire, they'll open the door to my room, like in Kafka, and see a large turkey parading her bright feathers and put me in the oven. This Thanksgiving has been as dreary as ever, with everyone clutching and embracing our beautiful children, and Paul hovering as tenderly as ever over his new dog, and my mother-in-law laughing like a hyena over her bourbon as she tells her forty-year-old son to cut his hair. Actually she has become relatively quiet and tranquil since the other sons' deaths, when there was only one to go she became very relaxed, nicer than ever, she seldom meddles in our affairs, we get on marvelously well. She smiles, she hums, she pouts no more, she whines fifty percent less. She enjoys more than ever those radio commentators popular among right-wingers who urge the government to destroy North Vietnam, get tougher with the longhairs, crack down on druggies, kill the kids. It is her way of requiem and liturgy, after Thanksgiving dinner in Boston we sit by the fire nursing drinks, listening to some guy saying on the radio, "The pinko peaceniks are lying through their teeth, the longhair student pot-heads are undermining the nation's heritage." "Look at the sun," she mumbles, "look at the beautiful sunset." The good boy who excelled at Confucian dutifulness says gently, "That's not the sun, Ma, that's the moon." "You're wrong," she says, "that's the sun." "No, Mother," he says, "I assure you it's the moon." "Ooooohoooooo, the moon," she warbles pleasantly, "what's the difference?" She's so right, what's the difference? What's important tonight, I try to say with my eyes, is which comes first, Chronos or Oedipus? To eat or to be eaten, that is the question for Thanksgiving night. Oedipus was left on the mountain to die even before he had the impulse to kill his father. Reread mythology, dark devouring parents, reread it constantly. You ate up my old friend Louis B. and you almost got me.

III

Our neighbor John Burtz was found swinging from the ceiling of his farm shed last week by one of his seven children. He had wound a noose around his throat, then pulled the hydraulic lift of his bulldozer. He was a laughing, brawny man with meat on his breath, it was said that he loved machines excessively, that he was gadget crazy, deeply in debt. At the funeral, his two brothers come into the church trying to support his widow by each arm. A useless gesture, since she walks steadfast and crisply, supporting them if anything, with no outward show of grief. At the cemetery they stand very close together in front of the grave, huddled together like cattle seeking warmth, the raw November air pierces like needles, the sky is of the low, unvariegated gray that precurses snow. The dead man's mother, his widow and his brothers link hands behind each other's backs and again in front, with a looping gesture that resembles an ancient peasant ritual, as if they are about to stomp their feet in a ritual dance. The widow suddenly breaks loose from the mesh of intertwined arms and, standing at the pit of the grave, stares down at the coffin not so much with grief as with anger, with a certain disgust. That week my son had asked me to get a pollywog from the nearby pond. After I get home I break the ice of the pond to get the animals, put them into a pail, take it into the kitchen sink to get more water. The child climbs eagerly upon the sink to see the operation, my hands shake after the funeral, I am careless, the two parcels of life slither like so much refuse into the sewage. The child's face screws up into a wail of despair, he stares at me with distrust for many days. But the widow Burtz's attitude to death! That's a different cup of tea. The day after the funeral she stands at her door with a pot of geraniums in her hand, waving at me with elation. "Hi! How nice to see you! I've had company all day!" Inside her candy-littered house, kids are tumbling before the television, stuffing themselves on Cracker Jacks, arguing about what they're going to wear to the restaurant that night. "Mom, can I wear my green-and-white polka-dot pants?" "No, you can't, Sally you fink, they're Doris'!" "Mom, when are we going out for chow?" "I'm taking them out to supper to this nice new Italian place where they make a great lasagna," the widow says cheerfully. "Oh, don't worry about me, John and I had a good life together, fifteen years, what more can you expect? I don't know what I'd do if anything happened to one of them, but him . . ." She smiles again, looking relieved. Deliverance, he must have been at her day and night, she looks relieved. For months to come, the town pastor—a Congregationalist with a minted breath—keeps cornering me by the vegetable counter at the village store, saying, "That's the trouble with our church, no way for men to talk out their problems, we can't give them as much help as you Romans can. It must have been a snap decision, there were thicker and more efficient ropes he could have used if he had planned ahead. In your church the confessional takes care of all that garbage of the unsaid, you're lucky to have that channel of communication." He said it while choosing tomatoes, a man with a late vocation who had once played the violin on a New York stage, he said it with definite bitterness. Wise words. I kept thinking of them during those years of relentless search for man and God, God in man, man in God, brotherhood, whatever that means. Need for more religion, more communion, more conversation, the three interchangeable, need for a conversion or a brothel. Every few years I return to confession, sometimes out of the starkest of duties—in memory of my father—sometimes to see how it's changed, what they're up to, always with a thirst for talking. That's how I come to sit week after week in the room of Father Gregory Hillsman, a friend from college days in Cambridge, who now receives me at the Jesuit compound wearing summer shorts, sipping beer, his long lean legs crossed nonchalantly.

"Resurrection, Greg. That's where it's at. Ever since that visit to my father's grave I've been very moved by that notion."

"Yes, but it's the resurrection of a 'glorified' body. We can't possibly conceive its nature."

"Then what is the relevance of moral behavior to a theology of the afterlife?"

"Relativism has its traps, since every action of ours that pains another disturbs the order of the universe. Take the notion of fidelity in marriage, Steph. Until society changes radically how are we going to avoid the painfulness that infidelity can cause? Yet modern anthropology tends to show that the ideal of fidelity debases womanhood, it's based on men's need to assure paternity so that they can pass on property to their sons. I don't need to tell you how important that could be for your women's movement! By the way, kiddo, do you want to confess? I'd love to talk to you until the Parousia, but I know you've got to go home to get chow for your kids."

He downs his beer. A sly smile. "Just like my sermons. A lot of foam and no body. Let me get another one, okay?" He settles down with his Budweiser and I stare out the window into the street below.

Whenever I go through this process I feel little emotion, little guilt or sorrow for whatever I recite, but I feel an ardent pleasure in participating in this historic process, in this ritual of purification that precedes the cannibalistic feast, I feel a high exhibitionist pleasure in recounting sexual fantasies to this man I have come to desire. His lean hound dog's face resembles that of the young Teilhard, I watch it for a sign of surprise, but he is as much of a cool con person as I am, the high icy dome of his forehead never twitches at any recitation, the thin mouth remains tightly clenched, I could be talking to Sade's analyst. "Uhum uhum," he says occasionally, just like the shrinks. I enjoy staring at his high-laced basketball sneaker, Keds size eleven and a half, particularly at the large red emblem accompanying the words "All Star" on the instep. Two decades ago we had lived across the street from each other in Cambridge, the year he had decided to go to the seminary. We had sat together at the library, we had gone down together to work at the Henry Wallace headquarters. I had loved him secretly, with that burning love we can have only for those with whom we cannot experience the flesh. Now as I stare out at the street below I think, Let's not kid ourselves, this jazzy modern church stuff isn't going to work, at first we were all so excited by it—the grape-juice-and-cookie guitar Masses, the abandonment of the Latin and vestments and the dank confessional booths—but like all the other liberal solutions it's a mess, it's like the dribbling of token funds into the rotting cities or the Uncle Tom handouts to women, it won't do, it's all got to be totally torn down and rebuilt again from cellar up, these new padres with the basketball sneakers and the swinging ethics grooving on the newest radical fads won't do either, all you'll do is get drunk and stoned with them and fall in love, and then the goddam sexist will leave you gasping like a fish out of water, retaining control like most men, what a tease these priests have gotten to be, if anything they're more destructive than ever. His eyes are hazel, speckled green and brown, careworn, the deeply chiseled, almost cavernous lid folds heavily at the outer edge. "Okay, absolution?" he always says in a weary, gentle voice when I am through. And there is a blur of ritual words while I turn away, clutching at a button of my shirt, embarrassed by my lack of emotion, by the mood of curiosity dominating all of me.

There are long oak tables, lazy susans of pickles and ketchup, a faint smell of beer and baking bread in the Jesuit refectory where I often join him for lunch. "What were we talking about earlier? Ah yes, Christianity is the most physical, the most sensual of all faiths." There is a teasing, cynical curve to his wry smile as he opens another beer. "I'm interested in the deepest implications of this physicality, Steph, in the instinct lovers have to possess each other, to eat each other up. That's what attracted me to the priesthood in the first place —the anthropological reality of it, the cannibalism. *Hoc est Corpus Meum*. Daily cannibalism, can you imagine? You've read in Lévi-Strauss about how savages eat their most beloved heroes, in order to be saved by their *mana*. Isn't that what the Eucharist is all about?"

Once as we sat on a park bench he touched my dress, took a fold of it and rubbed it gently between his fingers, as if to remind himself of what a woman's garment felt like. Another time, while we sat talking in his car after he had driven me home after an antiwar meeting, he clutched a lock of my hair, twisting it softly with his thumb. Nothing else. "How many people are we going to try to get for this demonstration," I ask him as an excuse to phone him every day, "did you call the local papers about next week's talk-in, have you put the newsletter together yet?" I take Communion from him twice, three times a week, I am temporarily at peace, never giving a thought to the flesh, I am sweeter than ever at home, as calm as the Sea of Azov, I am temporarily stoned on Christ, stuffed with religion. I want to cook and sew and scrub for Father Gregory, ah yes, that keen erotic pleasure of serving forbidden men which nuns have always treasured.

"The psychological tests show that I need constantly to seduce people," Gregory says one day as he paces his room. While pacing he repeatedly tucks his shirt into his lower back. "I know I'm a flirt. I can't stand missing out on anything. I'd like to experience all that the world has to offer. Visit every country. Sleep with every woman in the world. Ah well, civilization and its discontents."

"Well, you don't think marriage is any easier than the priesthood these days, do you? Isn't it just another form of celibacy, since it involves a constant repression of instincts?"

"Right on. You see, the problem is that fidelity or celibacy would only be truly moral if we could choose it instead of having it imposed upon us. That would be the only truly ethical way, since choice is the only ethical condition of any act. I wouldn't mind being a monk if it was a choice within the priesthood. One could choose celibacy or fidelity as a preference *over* sex or promiscuity. That's a rather beautiful idea. The way one prefers one woman to another."

"Well well, Father, do you think we're ready for such freedom? Ready to kick the Grand Inquisitor in the ass already?"

"And what do we get for our good conduct the way our system stands? Do you still think it gets us better mansions in heaven?" He gestures cynically toward the bed, upon which a pile of linen has been neatly folded by the nuns—three handkerchiefs, two undershirts, three boxer shorts neatly aligned below the crucifix that hangs by his bed.

"At times I think I know what I get from so-called good conduct, Greg. I'm getting shelter, protection. Maybe the shelter I needed to grow into freedom."

"But that's precisely the dilemma Freud left us with: Is your shelter worth it? Is civilization as we know it worth the discontent it causes? Do you remember one of the last lines from that incredible book? 'Man's judgments of value are nothing but an attempt to support his illusions with arguments'!"

Six months later Gregory left the Jesuit order and I went on to other things, other obsessions. He came to dinner once shouting that civilization was not worth it, we must dare to be playful and unleash our instincts, rebecome polymorphous perverse. Due to the stranglehold he had over me I was still occasionally going to Mass, would continue doing so for some time. "How can you still go through that stuff?" he cried out a little hysterically, waving his arms about. "I have a veritable disgust for it." This is My Body. Before leaving Boston he gave himself a swinging super-ecumenical going-away party, with Jewish folk songs, Sufi sayings, bouts of Zen meditation, a veritable smorgasborg. He moved on to California, where he became a controversial figure in academic circles and acquired still another doctorate, this time in medieval history, while teaching transactional psychology. Renounced by the Church for seditious writings, he publicly declared his decision to remain in the priesthood and maintain all its rules—except obedience to Rome. Then he moved on to live in ashrams and convents in India and in Africa, where he steeped himself in contemplation.

In between bouts of confession-going I think of new ways to fuck, in ways as anonymous as possible, with strangers whom

I'll never see again, with whom I'll never need to share what I describe in one of my journals as "the fetid burden of sentiment." Other lines from journals of the past years: Age twenty: "I analyze myself with an incestuous precision." Age thirty-five: "I feel sanctity and wholeness only when I am two persons." A few years further on, after Gregory: "Unification of my dual selves: That's the mysterious center where I can start writing, that's when the story can begin."

> *Her dominant idea and goal is freedom without responsibility, which is like gold without metal, spring without winter, youth without age, one of those maddening, coo-coo mirages of wild riches which makes her a typical product of our generation.*
> —F. SCOTT FITZGERALD, *The Crack Up*

I keep remembering how once, in Spain, my husband and I drove for eight hours through a black landscape that was like the inside of a gigantic onyx bowl, through fields of copper, barite, corycium, that had the sinister splendor of garnet and of jet. Our silence was as heavy as the devilish blackness we traversed. You drove your machine responsibly and silently, modern man, with such grim intensity. For eight hours there was no relief in sight, no relief of human voice. That dark valley used to remind me of our marriage, there were times when your silence and dependence wound around me like pools of darkness, when our void was like earth thrown upon my still live body. Particularly after Gregory left there were days when I felt, Nothing has worked, nothing can work, I am broken. But those days are past, I have gone through centers of darkness in which I was purified, I have begun to heal. And so, dear love, I have abandoned the image of that valley.

I am determined that our marriage must be like the life of the old lady who lives alone over my workroom in the barn. I hear her every motion, she is a lesson for life. From 9 A.M. on, her prayers are said, her high heels are on, she scuttles about her room as if she were tending an enormous household. I hear her above, clickety-click, scrubbing her tub, doing her breakfast dishes, down for a catnap with her missal. And then she takes her two-hundred-yard walk to the mailbox, that is the expedition of the day, she gets dressed up in her best clothes—hats with butterflies, jeweled pins, the shoes with rhinestone buckles, also a beaded bag, lace gloves, lots of rouge. And she minces to the mailbox dressed as for a glorious Easter service, tripping on her heels and picking herself up again, each day a holiday, a carnival. Every night the old lady cooks as if expecting fine company, delicious odors waft down to me, stuffed peppers and cabbage, osso bucco, saltimbocca, they take hours to prepare, I saw her eating once, extraordinary show, there she sat alone in front of her lace doily and her tiny wineglass, smiling at the lonely meal. What manners, what discipline, what illusions! Truly an existential heroine! Solitude and death yawn at her like a lion, and how she defies the gravity of despair, as we all must do, acting as if each day offers unbounded delight and hope. Is that the way we must adorn our realities? Are our characters to be attired like her poor body, either with silence or in masquerade, so as never to show ourselves in our nakedness and truth? Perhaps, dear love, you're right to talk so little, perhaps no two pilgrims must discover each other too well. And at times we do connect and re-create the ancient feast, clutching at each other in the night, always the great miracle and great surprise that it can happen again, that it can happen at all. Your reticence abated, you thrust down upon me like a turbulent animal, calling me your baby, your little girl, you tear into me more fiercely, you give me more pleasure than any man I've every known. How mysterious that force is in its rareness, its equally great simplicity! Afterward, our limbs still locked, we lie in the dark exchanging simple declarative sentences, such as "A snow plough, the last of the winter," or "The pussy willow's out, the first of the spring." At such times nothing else is needed. At other times so much more is needed that I don't know, I don't know how to proceed. Marriage is like the Church or the stranglehold of property, institutions full of the brutality and deceit of the past which we cannot repair in patches, which must be reconstructed from the bottom up in order to survive, we must cut the forest down and replant it, leaving many homeless animals in our wake. . . . On days when I have returned from one of my brief solitary trips I pass behind your chair as you sit hiding from the world behind your reading, and brush my hand over your forehead. You close your eyes and throw your head back at the touch, and the longing in your eyes fills me with anguish. In a terrifying century you stand for all that is noble, nourishing, repressive. But your goodness is not the stuff of innovation and we must always move on, move on at increasing speeds in order to avoid decay. Perhaps it is you who are right and the century that's crass. Perhaps the other way around. Only history will tell. You fill me with guilt, eternal boy, you too aren't loved the way you'd wish to be, you'd have done better with a wife who peeled your apple, mended your clothes, worried about your silver and your china, shared your love of land and little tribe, your fear of people and of loneliness. But I with my searches, my nightmares, my causes, my need for crowds and solitude, what a burden I must be. Who are you? Can we really ever know each other? Is it dangerous to ask?

The house sleeps, my love sleeps, marriage is a long sleep, a large life, a long gestation. My love sleeps in that room I painted forest green in the first months of our marriage, when I swabbed my way through his house, obliterating the dowager escorts and dank wallpapers of his bachelorhood, his mother's laces, the musty cigars left behind by his father, the

234

past. I painted it green like a cave, green for the long estivation of marriage, green for the shelter in which we both hibernated away the scars of our childhood, in which we shall gain the strength needed for our freedom. In this cave where we conceived our children, where he often seeks repose from the exhaustions of the twentieth century, there my great love still sleeps, his breathing calm and even under the acrylic coverlet, his knees thrust up to his chest, a pillow sheltering his head, dreaming perhaps of the solid beauty he will create in stone and steel. Seen at eye level, the green blanket that covers him seems made of moss, its spikes and spears resemble the tiny promontories of some spread of lichen, and so he seems to be as in the pit of our dark-green cave, in the warmest bottom of our animal hole. On the edge of the mantelpiece stand mementos of our passing enthusiasms and happy childhood days together, little painted stones, alabaster elephants, inch-high marble mushrooms, music boxes in which white-ruffled Pierrots dance under tiny domes. These childhood toys are what I would like to leave behind me, I desire instead to enter the Chinese painting of a plum tree which he hung by my bed early in our marriage. Its branches could be the design of my own life, they gush upward and northward, becoming more concentrated, narrower, more intense at their upward ends, they are full of knobs and promontories, of beautiful islands to rest in, I'd like the end of my life to resemble the superb branch at the upper left which is segmented like the limb of a rearing horse and tapers to a fine hoof at the painting's uppermost frontier. For up there at the top blossoms proliferate, rewards for my patience and hard-won freedom, blossoms as succulent as globes of fat floating on the broth at Jewish weddings but suspended on branches as austerely thin as the streaks of light that jut from prisms. And the second half of existence should ideally be like that painting hovering over us, all of one's life-stream leaner and sparser, less people to see, less food to eat, less flesh, the body austerely kept, the house as emptied of stuff as a Zen monastery—that would be the beginning of the liberation from pain, desire, contradictions—nothing but the works of our imagination proliferating like the rich blooms on those sparse limbs. Upon the mantel of this room where we have spent the childhood of our marriage the wax dolls also hover over me, staring at our incubator like kind nurses through their glass panes. The smaller one is in blue taffeta, the larger in pink satin. The larger one has an air of compassion, she holds a wreath hung with silver ribbons which she thrusts out to me today like a muse awarding a prize. At her feet, in a crib of fern flanked by pink flowers, lies a baby-sized replica of herself the length of her two hands, an infant doll dressed in lace on whose chest a sparrow perches, its beak poised toward the baby's mouth. I do not know what leads me to do now what I never dared to do in my childhood, to lift the dome of glass, to touch her and end her immaculate protection from all history and change. The house is still in its sleep, as still as my marriage, the dogs stare at me with those great plum eyes of the Fayum women, with the anxious eyes of Moslem brides behind bars. I have placed a bouquet of purple iris and pink peonies by his bed, the whole house sleeps, his body rises and falls gently under the lichen of his blanket, he is the landscape of my life, the creator and obstructor of my freedom, I need him the way we need our daily bread, I miss him the way the sequestered bird misses her mate/his mate in the next cage, I would die both for him and for my freedom, which is now to be found elsewhere, outside this room, outside my body, outside our mothers' illusions of security, in work, in dreams. The house's rhythm is slowed to the rhythm of his breath, every inch of it is slowed, the dogs move as in a slowed-down silent film, the cat's whiskers twitch only once an hour, all is as slowed and paced as a sleeper's pulse, I lift the dome very carefully, I stroke my finger across the doll's forehead, fearful until the last moment that she will crumble and dissolve like ancient flesh. And indeed my touch leaves a train of darkness on her

236

brow like the touch of embers on Ash Wednesday, the passage of my finger was more brutal than I expected, it could be the beginning of her destruction. And, terrified of this decimation, I put the dome back, sensing some magical connection between this green shelter and her future and mine. I worry about you as I leave the room, eternal boy, men like you who are so fetal and so rooted, where will you rest if your shelter is altered or rebuilt? I leave the sleeping house and walk out into the terrifyingly sunny day, toward the nearby forest, all smells assail me at once, the sky is blue, my children are grown, I can walk in and out of the cave, the lupine does not frighten me anymore, I can die anytime now, I become part of the oak tree and am carried beyond it, I am distilled into some severe essence of that tree, this dream is my knowledge, I am fragmented on the altar of light, the sky sings of streams and rivers to the ashes of my body, I am drunk with emptiness, my bitterness tastes sweet and my spirit is clear, I inhale the smoke that I shall be, my body is debased to humus, I shall survive it in some way, freedom is near, to be hunted like a treasure, to be measured in milligrams because of its dangers, to be taken in tons because of its beauty, to be transcended. The dream floats in and out, in and out, moving like fish on the surf of memory. Stephanie is choosing herself at last, walking off the ground, above the ground, sucking herself up, she can walk with death, rejoin the dead who have loved her so, whom she shall love again when she shares their humus. She is a child and free again, playing games in a large stand of oaks. She runs through the luminously beautiful forest, which is neon green, screaming green, the green yells and glows, claps its hands and sings, celebrates its harshness. She clutches at the largest leaves, she chases birds with branches of ferns, she snares butterflies with sprays of laurel. She moans with thirst after tasting all those mushrooms, she stumbles and falls, she is a savage again, in the dense brush she crawls on her knees, eating wild berries off the bushes, her lips as purple as a drowning man's. She runs up a hill, the wind sings through the trees with a swelling, rolling sound like that of heavy surf. The smell of spring grass is rampant, the ground is brilliant with the fire of new poppies. She comes to a river bank and for a second Stephanie cannot see, she is struck as though blind, a wall of blazing whiteness faces her, filling her eyes like a sheet of white-hot metal, and a wind rushes through her as she knows it will at the moment of her death. The water below her is as black as a diamond and as still as a shroud, the trill of the thrush is like water pouring out of a narrow-necked jar. She wades into a bank of orange lilies, face to face with a flower she moans her love for it, she wishes to enter it, to make love to it and be drowned in it, to explore its fuzzy caverns, its cloying recesses, its honeyed interstices. The lilies are up to Stephanie's waist, she wades among them as into a sea, asking for entrance and for burial. Crouching in the bank of flowers, Stephanie rocks back and forth, back and forth, crying her wishes to be at her mother's breast, in her father's arms, to be reborn, to be a boy, to be free, to be God, to be permitted everything, to be allowed the universe, to re-enter the paradise we once tasted and never forgot.

Stephanie

1 9 7 -

I

(The first scene, that of Elijah Stewart and Stephanie in their hotel room, must be very intense, with a certain psychological violence to it. Elijah has the rock station on full blast. He is stomping, stomping about the room, his long hair flying about him, chewing on a very large wad of gum. He is in his early twenties, very tall and very lean, with long, curling light-brown hair, a light growth of beard, deep-blue eyes with very long dark lashes. His features have a classic beauty, the nose is aquiline, there is a certain hardness to his thin, crisply chiseled mouth. He is wearing a flowered chiffon shirt, black leather pants. The black leather jacket that matches it is lying on the bed next to Elijah's cameras and his shoulder-strap bag, out of which spill an assortment of grass and hash in plastic baggies, airline tickets, films, exposure meters, a copy of D. H. Lawrence's *St. Mawr*, issues of *Fag Rag* and *Gay Sunshine*. A recording of Edgar Winter's plays on the radio and Elijah sings along with it, head down, stomping on the floor violently. "Well, if you wear funny clothes/ and you travel on the road/ You can bet they'll call you an animal/ And if you're spaced out/ and like to stand up and shout/ they'll call you a premature brain child/ a savage run wild/ . . ." Stephanie is lying on the bed, drying her hair under the clear-plastic hood of a portable dryer and combing out a hairpiece. She is also lean-limbed, blue-eyed, with a long, fine-boned face and curly ash-blond hair a trifle lighter than Elijah's. Her cheekbones are high, her skin is pale, she is wearing an Indian caftan of mauve cotton. She is in her forties now and she looks her age in the room's harsher lights, thirty-five in others. Their hotel—somewhere between Tucson and Phoenix, Arizona—is near a guest-ranch-turned-meditation-center at which Stephanie and Elijah are reporting on a week-long symposium.

While dancing, Elijah seizes Stephanie's hairpiece and flops it on his head, secures it with bobby pins and continues to sing and dance all the louder, absorbed by the music. "If you drink and you curse/ cause your life is so complicated/ they'll call you an animal/ some kind of animal/ a savage running wild/ . . ." Stephanie's hairpiece makes large circles about his head. He goes to Stephanie's pocketbook and takes out her lipstick. He stands in front of the mirror, puckering up his mouth, pouting like a fashion model as he puts on her lipstick.)

God, you look like Joplin having one of her tantrums, Stephanie says. I may look like Joplin, but don't you start telling me I look like a fag this way, Elijah says, we don't use that word anymore, what do we call it, Steph? Okay, Lija you're gay, but I still wish you wouldn't act like a queen. If you call me a queen, Steph, I'll call you a matron, how do you like being called a matron? About as much as you like being called a pansy, Lija, and I bet that's not very much. Watch out, he says, standing over her and holding her arm, I'm very strong, I'm going to turn into a Hell's Angel any minute. Ouch, she laughs, let go, let go, okay, you're just gay. Jesus, that bag of yours kiddo, you're still carrying an SDS manifesto around, that's incredible, you hang on to the sixties as if they were your balls or your virginity. Don't you attack the sixties any more, he says, starting to dance again. You can give that to your stuffy middle-aged liberal Boston friends but not in this room with me. I came of age in the sixties, the sixties liberated me from my mother, my father, my military school, everything that had laid shit on me all my childhood. I took twenty acid trips in 1969 alone, the year I got my scholarship at the University of Chicago and joined the SDS and first read Genêt and Burroughs and Frantz Fanon, hey listen Steph I'm starved, when are we going out to dinner, I'm famished. Well it's only seven Lija, that's very early for dinner even in the Southwest. I don't give a chic shit when the fashionable hour is, I'm hungry and I want to eat. I fed you lunch only four and a half hours ago Eli, you ate three shrimp cocktails, spaghetti and a whole chicken, you can't be hungry. Don't use those words 'fed you,' Steph, I can't stand your mothering act, I mean I like it and I don't, okay? all I know is that I'm hungry, maybe I'm still growing or something—how do you know what's going on in my stomach? I could order you a hamburger from room service. Will do, but listen Steph, let's split in about an hour anyhow and go to a really nice place tonight, I'm fed up with the Buddhist pabulum in that meditational dining room, I want to go to some place really nice where I can get a steak and a good city view, okay, I want to take pictures of Phoenix, why don't we go to the Biltmore, for instance, it's supposed to be the most elegant place in town. It's also the most expensive restaurant in the state, she says, that's a funny hangout for a supporter of the PLO. Come on Steph lay off, will you, let me live with my own contradictions and you live with yours, okay? You want everything, don't you Lija—men, women, expensive restaurants, being a Communist, working for fashion magazines.

Pablo Neruda had all that, Elijah says, why shouldn't I?

Stephanie is lying back on her bed staring at the ceiling, thinking, I'm even aping his language, talking like him, I guess that's part of what I wanted, freedom, return to childhood. Well we've reached it, baby, we've reached the gigolo stage, that wasn't expected—the little breakdown, the hysterectomy, the separation from Paul, that was all in the books, but not the gigolo trip. Yet maybe it's okay after all, maybe my hangups are based on the old crap about men having to pay and dominate, so what's wrong with reversing it and having us do it, the women's movement might take up the gigolo gig as the grooviest thing going, wouldn't that be hilarious? . . . Stephanie picks up the phone and says *pronto*, room service—could you bring me a very rare hamburger with an order of French fries. Thanks U.N. Elijah says, listen, I just thought of something, you promised to call that magazine editor, you said you'd phone her to see if they could use a picture story on this meditation shtick here. I'm tired Eli, I worked all afternoon and talked with Gregory for the first time all year. I'm really exhausted, let's do it tomorrow. You don't love me at all, Elijah says. Stephanie closes her eyes, saying, I'm tired. I'm sorry, honey bun, Elijah says, I'm driving you too hard, making too much noise, being a brat again. He turns off the radio, he lies down next to her and lays her head on his shoulder, he strokes her hair, her temples. I'll call the operator and you just do the rest, Steph, all right? She smiles. I already called that editor for you at noon, Lijie, she's away on vacation until Monday, we'll call then. You called, you called already? Oh, you're so sweet, Stephanie, I love you so much. L-O-V-E. *L* like Ladybird, *O* like ozone, *V* like venal, *E* like Elton John. Tell me you love me. I'm very fond of you, she says, love is a big word. She brushes the curls off his face. Don't say that Steph, I want your total and complete and absolute love. Do you remember what I said to you when we met last month at that Third World rap in Ohio? I said fantastic, we look like twins. It's very narcissistic, but it's true, I was struck by how alike we were, tall thin bodies, the color of our hair. You said out of sight, Lija. Well it sure was that Steph, it's not every day you meet some-one whose book you ripped off two months ago. You never told me you ripped off a book of mine, Lijie, which one did you rip off? The last book, the one on women. I was real broke Christmas Eve, I needed to give a present to my mom, I wanted one that would raise her consciousness. I ripped off your book at the University of Iowa bookstore. The week before I'd ripped off a whole set of Conrad and an edition of Proust from the University of Southern Illinois bookstore—that was a good month. Did you ever buy anything, Elijah? Hell no, you're so proud of how well-read I am, how else do you want a college dropout to get an education, how many peanuts a month do you figure I'm making right now as a *Free Press* photographer? We have every right to rip off the liberals' bookstores when we're oppressed. You are not oppressed, Eli, stop that nonsense. Look Steph let's not argue about politics, okay? I've gone through enough Maoist study groups to make mincemeat out of you, and don't try to make me into a liberal. I may become a conservative like my old man or else I'll become more radical than ever but I'll never be a liberal, never never never never. I guess that's about the only thing in life you don't want to be, a liberal, right, Lija?

Right.

My shrink used to say that the sixties radicals have a streak of infantile regressiveness, Stephanie says, they want the whole world as if they're still at their mothers' breasts. Oh don't lay that shrink trip on me Steph, I can't take it, all shrinks stink, they're as bad as those freaky guru friends of yours, freaky fratres, that's what you surround yourself with, shit Steph when are you going to get off this meditation gig and write about something more relevant, like rock, movies, a novel? You've barely met Gregory Hillsman, she says, he's one of my closest friends, I'll be upset if you don't get to know him better tomorrow, and Reed Weiss is a sweet guy, he wouldn't hurt a fly. Well he might not go for your fly but he sure is eager for mine, Elijah says, the way he looked at me this morning I felt he was unzipping me from head to foot, actually I don't mind if he does, his body is incredible, I love guys with great bodies. He's more apt to try unzipping your mind, Stephanie says. He loves the idea of getting everyone to meditate. Well well we'll see if it's just the mind Stephanie dear, we'll see. Hey Steph what do you think, let's have an affair. Don't be silly Eli darling, that's the silliest thing I've ever heard, you wouldn't be my Ariel anymore. Well just as long as we don't have a relationship, Elijah says, I can't stand that word. Elijah laughs, his pretty teeth gleaming over his lipsticked mouth. I'm going to write a letter to Ann Landers, he says. Dear Ann, I'm so in love with a woman twenty years older than I am that I'm ready to give up my gayness, which up to now has been my most precious jewel. What shall I do? Signed, Lord Byron. And I'll write her too, Stephanie says. Dear Ann, I'm madly in love with a homosexual who is madly in love with me, but we can't decide whether to have an affair or not. Should we try the *I Ching*? Signed, George Sand. Hey darling, he says, do you want a joint before we go out to dinner? No thanks, Lijie, after four weeks with you I feel as if I have grass coming out of my ears, my nose, my ass, I really can't stand it more than a couple of times a week, it makes me feel miserable. What a generational gap, he says, if there's one place in the U.S. where it's easy to get Acapulco gold, this is it. What's it like with boys, she says, stroking his hair, what do they like, what was it like between you and Joel for instance— how often did you do it? At least once a day in the good times when we weren't fighting too much, I'll never forget the time we did it on top of a cliff overlooking the Pacific, that was out of sight, he came in me and then I in him, and there was the roar of the ocean below. . . . God Steph you know it's very strange, since I've been with you I'm not as obsessed as I used to be about sucking cock, you know most of the time for me it's just sucking cock, blow jobs, and making love with Joel was incredible, his sperm was so sweet, it had a very special taste, as if it carried no semen, no reproductive matter, as if it were just a nectar. After Joel there was Conrad, and then Fred, nothing seems to last more than three months or so . . . hell Stephie, let's get off that subject, Stephie you know what I enjoy most, after love? After the sentiment of love, my favorite emotion is that of irony.

So let's speak about ironic situations, Lijie.

Look, Steph, I don't believe in fidelity, but which would upset you the most, if I were unfaithful to you with a man or with another woman? Well that's one of the oldest questions around Lijie, it's a tough one, you never know until it happens to you, if you went for women it would make me feel like a success, as if I'd been able to give you something. It was worse for me when Joel or Conrad went with women, Elijah says, it was much worse, a couple of times I wanted to kill myself. There you are, she says, there you are saying it, it's the worse of the two pains because you feel you don't have what they need that day. Maybe you want to be bisexual to be more like Joel and Conrad, to take their kind of revenge, eventually. Oh God Steph there you go with your shrink stuff again, it's too heavy for me, I'm not ready for it. I don't want to look into myself yet. I'm a child of nature, okay? . . . I'm sorry, I didn't mean to snap at you like that, you've been so perfect, Steph, the way you haven't pushed me into anything, if you knew all the dames who've thrown themselves at me since I was sixteen, all boozed up coked up or just plain horny, I hated them, hated hated hated those women you understand, and here you are you've just let me be, you've just let me hug you and lie down next to you, oh God you're such a friend. Hey Steph, have you ever loved anyone enough to die for them? Sometimes I think I'd like to have that just once before I die she says, have one powerful love that possesses, annihilates me utterly . . . actually maybe not, like most things that are frightening it's yes and no, I want it and yet I don't. I guess that's the way the taco crumbles Stephie darling, one more thing, why do you write?

He puts his hand on her breast as tranquilly as if it were her arm, her head. She stares at his feet. For such a big man he has very little feet, and they have a sad way of curling down and out over the coverlet, looking like small wounded pigeons. It's the only part of him that is not beautiful and full of bravura. He has told her that his funny flat feet were his father's fault —he blames everything on his father—his father took him to a crazy doctor who did a botch job on his arch supports, and his feet turned out strange. A bisexual friend of hers once told her that the men who were gay because they hated their fathers could change more easily than gays who were attached to their mothers. This friend also referred to homosexual love as ultimately inferior because it was of a "parodic" nature, that was an extraordinary word, that was an interesting lunch, that friend went on to talk of his great love for his wife and child . . . Why do you write? Elijah is asking, softly stroking her breast. Art is both a vengeance against reality and a reconciliation with it, she says. I hadn't thought of that he says, explain it. All art creates an alternate reality, maybe my pen can be my penis, my vengeance for not being a man, how do you like that, shnookums? Jesus Steph, that's heavy, have you ever had a lesbian experience? Not all the way, I've tried but I can't really get off, it just stays playful and sweet and that's not enough, it doesn't seem to possess me enough. Tell me one dream Stephanie before I go and take my shower. Okay, she says, very simple, just last night. I'm on the beach and a very beautiful young man rises out of the ocean. He's like a twin brother I haven't seen for a long time, he's a long-lost part of me, someone with whom I shared a precious unity in childhood, like my long-lost other half. He tells me to meet him in a town in South America, and I do, and we have this idyllic life together, we don't need to make love, we just live together and are each other's other halves. When I wake up from this dream

I am muttering the words resurrection of the body. That boy was me, Elijah says, thank you darling that was a very beautiful dream, upon that I shall go and take a shower.

As Elijah goes out of the room Stephanie is at the dressing table brushing her hair, singing a Bessie Smith song everyone sang during the summer workshops at Black Mountain twenty years ago or more; "Black Mountain, where the babies are screa-ea-ming for liquor . . . and even the birds sing bass." Hey that song is outrageous, Elijah yells from the shower, where'd you get that? That was in the fifties Stephanie says, the other song that was popular was "Come o-on my house, co-ome on, I'm gonna give you Christmas tree, candy, everything," do you remember, Oh my God of course you don't remember Elijah, you were still wetting your pants. I still wet my pants when I think of you Steph, you're cosmic. Oh that's terrific kid, that's a big change, and also you said cosmic. In college we used to say cosmic the way you say cool or far out. Like love-making in the early dawn is cosmic, Mahler is cosmic, particularly early Mahler, *Des Knaben Wunderhorn,* and this Thunderbolt is cosmic—that was a cocktail which was one-third gin, one-third rum, one-third bourbon, oh my, did we get stoned on that . . . Elijah is singing Springsteen in the shower and Stephanie lies back on the bed, thinking that for the first time in two years it's like those summers before her children went away to college when she spent much time loading a car with all the things they had asked for—cookies and sodas and Frisbies, hamburgers and paperbacks—after years of that rich thin nurturing life in which every day was sliced up like a pie she had so needed to be alone, without any of the familiar tyrants about her, and yet here she was again, saddled with this beautiful bossy kid . . . Stephanie, having exhausted the decoration of her nest, has gone about the psychic overhauling of Elijah Stewart, a twenty-three-year-old former-SDS-er, former-rock-singer photographer. God. The process is exhausting,

249

he has to be fed, soothed, scolded, supported, taught, gotten jobs, edited, everything, adult ambition and gross motor activity working all at once. Make me a milkshake, call this editor, teach me Spanish, let's go swimming, I'm going to the library make me a list of the twenty best contemporary Russian poets. After a few weeks of it she feels exhausted, done in. Every morning after having listened to Elijah talk until 4 A.M. she stands in front of the mirror looking for the lines from mouth to nose, the little crows' feet or whatever they're called that have deepened since her operation six months ago, the fine new webs that appear in the face of a woman past forty when she has had only a half night of sleep. For Elijah is at her like a suckling babe until the early hours of the morning, asking her for food or conversation or a combination of both, the two seem interchangeable to him. Oh God, this oral generation, brought up in front of the idiot box and getting instant gratification for every one of their desires, posing for photographs after each rebellion dressed up in their revolutionary costumes. Thank God her own children are out of the storybook seventies, sweet sunny boys who talk about graduate schools and party politics and biology and architecture, they are so different. . . . Elijah comes out of the shower, a towel wrapped around his waist. When his back is turned she looks at him while pretending to sleep, he is very quiet and thoughtful right now, tiptoeing about the room and respecting her medical need for rest, the rock station turned off at last. There is a violence about his beauty which has to do with the fact that one cannot possibly conceive of him as ever getting older. He is perennial youth, therefore he will die still young, therefore his very youth and beauty have something violent about them. Could he be Nihil, the angel of death? There in the room putting on a flowered shirt stands Nihil, who has asked her to keep him from dying alone. "I don't want to be only a homosexual," he has said, "I don't want to end up a lonely old man like Aschenbach." She is to give rebirth to one already adorned with symbols of death. Elijah is putting on the shirt she bought him two days ago. "That's what I always wanted," he'd cried out, and she bought it for him, and the next thing she knew he was fingering an edition of Tolstoy, wanting that too, and she gave him that also. In the books she has read about these kinds of affairs, the women were the aggressors, but Elijah demanded to live with Stephanie the first week they met as adamantly as he demanded everything else, he is very imperious, bossing her about as few men have, she feels very ambivalent about whether she likes that or not.

Stephanie gets up, starts dressing. Do you know what Narcissus was looking for when he drowned in that pool Lija, he was looking for the image of his dead sister—that's an interesting version of the story. Hey that's neat, Elijah says, I've never heard it that way, listen Steph, I want you to put on that bright-red caftan and I want your hairpiece nicely done up right now and that's an order. I want you to look really gorgeous tonight. I love to step out with you, you can still be so beautiful if you try a little. "*Still*," she thinks. "*Try* a little." Hurry up please Steph I'm starved, and I want to see those early-evening lights on the town, so shake a leg, will you, kid? God Lijie she says as she puts on her hairpiece (he loves to help her with it, put the curls in the right place, put the pins in) God I've had a lot but I still haven't had anything that I could call freedom. Do you know whom I envy more than anyone else on earth? I envy a beautiful friend of mine called Claire who's occasionally capable of loving a man or a woman, who divorced long ago, she lives in a flat in New York with a woman friend and they travel together or with other people when they feel like it—men or women—and she's a prominent sculptor and doesn't have my crazy need to constantly burden myself with people who have to be comforted, taught, nurtured. God, what a good life Lijie, why can't I find Claire's kind of freedom? And she puts her head down on the dressing table, shaking a little. Just calm down sweetheart Elijah says, don't be so agitated, it's time for your Demerol, here's the water, would you like me to bring some Valium to dinner for you? Nurselike, often brotherly like that, so sweet. He makes her stand up and hugs her and kisses her deeply on the mouth, he hugs and strokes and kisses her all through the day and through most of the night, but notwithstanding that tender sucking mouth his hugs are frail and light, out of an afraid body, like the cool touch of a colt's limbs. Staring at his beautiful bony body as they finish dressing, she thinks at some point this week there might be a triangle between myself, Elijah and some other man. Classical story, new twist, meditation conferees fight over the body of beautiful Tadzio. Who really cares? One must be indifferent about all sex. Have you ever loved anyone unto death? Elijah asks her as they get into a cab. I've already told you, only my children I think.

Well that's the way I want you to love me, Steph, you hear? That's an order.

He lies down on the cab seat, his head on her lap, he closes his eyes and falls instantly asleep. She stares at the elegantly long slender legs, the narrow hips, the pale chiseled face, his body always has the fatigue of the adolescent too quickly grown, or of the young underfed revolutionary. He wakes up as the cab stops at a red light in front of a Chicano church. It must be a holy day, dozens of women are dragging themselves on their knees toward the altar, they look like lepers or war amputees as they drag themselves across the stone floors. God that's so beautiful, Stephanie says, their belief, their desire to still go through this ancient ritual. Elijah sits up and looks and bursts out come on, Steph, I won't have you saying reactionary things like that, do you hear, that's precisely the mentality that keeps humans from being liberated, we have to destroy all that kind of shit, we have to clean up society from the bottom up and rebuild it the way the Cambodians emptied their cities. I think people may have the right to remain unliberated Stephanie says, that is one of the great civil-libertarian issues of our time. I love you Steph but get off that religion stuff, you can talk that line to Gregory or your Boston liberal friends but not to me, it's only one out of ten people who will liberate themselves, so you have to force the nine others, you've got to impose freedom upon them.

On the pavement outside the church a woman is selling insects encased in bits of brilliantly colored crystals, in jeweled armatures like some creatures out of Hieronymus Bosch. Some of them have military outfits and little army caps, others have gauze tutus like ballet dancers, imagine the idea, Stephanie thinks, of creating Celliniesque outfits for these creatures who live for only two or three weeks, whatever the life of insects is. God, the transience of magnificence, the brevity of love. What were you like at my age? Elijah asks, looking up at her in the cab, were you like me? I order you to say you were just like me. I wasn't too unlike you when I was twenty-three, she says. I dragged myself from kick to kick, from pain to pain. Every few months I methodically destroyed every friendship, every love affair I had, as I'm sure you do. Stephanie he cries, sitting up, shaking her by the shoulders, I don't want you talking like that, I'm going to love you until the day I die, do you understand that? They have arrived. She pays the cab. Whenever she takes money out of her wallet he stares at it with fascination and greed; the gaze in his eyes is not unlike that in her children's eyes when they were still dependent on her, too little to carry their own cash. They walk into the restaurant. Stephanie feels reborn, eighteen years old again, with that young flesh beside her. Another Stephanie walks with her, he/she is so nice, both man and woman, she is feeling happy, feeling two, feeling more, feeling other. She is repeating to herself the phrase she has been muttering for the past three months: "My secular, historical life is over, my secular, historical life is over." She repeats it with the same sense of novelty with which she said to herself, when she was seventeen, "I am not a virgin anymore, I am not a virgin." How many more years are there? Since the operation she looks frailer, more drawn than ever. She knows that in certain lights, in twenty percent of lights, she still looks marvelous, in five percent of lights she might look frightening. And one never knows what kind of light one is bathed in. My secular historical life is over, this way no man will ever turn me down, I do not want any possibility of that attack on my pride. Hence, stop. Decision. Forget that rubbish of the perfect light. Tonight, however, she must look especially well, everyone is whirring around to stare at them, the world seems to be saying, "Who are they, brother and sister, husband and wife, friends, what?"

As they stand at the bar waiting for their table Elijah dances briefly to the pounding of the jukebox, he is pleased to be twice admired, he thrums furiously at the floor like a young eagle enamored with his own reflection who pecks at his image in the ice. Are you fed up with being looked at like that, darling, he asks as they walk to the table. Yes and no, I'm afraid of it ending yet I've had enough of it, you'll see yourself someday, it just might be another form of deliverance.

This table stinks, Elijah says in front of the waiter. I want to sit by the window, I want the best view over the town. Would it be possible for you to find us a table by the window, sir, please? Stephanie amends. Waiter, I want some ice water, Elijah says. May I have some ice water *please* she says. Could I have some ice water *please*, Elijah repeats with a sweet smile, okay Steph you do it, you give the orders, you're the one who was brought up in salons, my dad is a self-made man, made his punky money selling insurance. Hey Stephie, do you remember that line from *The Great Gatsby* when Daisy wants five bathrooms at the Plaza so they can all take baths on a hot day? She says, "What'll we do with ourselves this afternoon? and the day after that, and the next thirty years?" That's us Stephie, we have all these years to spend together. Elijah takes Stephanie's hand. I am your Lolito, he says charmingly. Look, how pretty. He hands her a gold cigarette lighter. For heaven's sake where did you get that Lija? Ripped it off at the bar while we were having our drink, very pleased with it, always needed one. Christ Lijie, I wish you wouldn't do that, really that's a terrible habit. . . . As they finish dinner Elijah cleans up everything Stephanie leaves on her plate. He's eaten her soup, two thirds of her meat, her potato, her bread. She orders a triple portion of dessert for him. Later when they go back to the hotel Elijah puts on her kimono to sleep in as he does every night. He says he does that because it is a part of her he can already have, he wants it against his skin. That new flesh exhaling her own perfume beside her.

To Be or Not to Be is on the tube. Carole Lombard and Jack Benny, Elijah says, oh God that was my favorite movie when I was taking film courses at Chicago, please Steph please stay awake so we can talk about it. I can't she says, sorry darling, I'm just too weary, too tired. He lies behind her, hugging her, his soft beard and his long hair covering her neck, he continues talking to her as he always does even after she's taken her Seconal. God if you knew how miserable I've been all these years he says, it was awful, from the age of twelve on I'd walk down the street and each guy I'd see I wondered what it would be like to love him, and I knew I was different, different from the rest of humanity. I remember the evening Martin Luther King was shot, I was in the gym playing basketball and the teacher blew the whistle and told us the news had just come over the radio, and I ran to the locker room and collapsed on the floor and cried and cried, but even as I was crying a guy whom I'd had a lot of fantasies about came in and started getting undressed, and there I was, big as life, and all the time I cried I somehow associated death with my desire for him, I knew it was destructive, lonely to love that way. It's been one long life of worrying, wondering, and Christ, you don't know what it was like, Steph, last week when I had an erotic dream about you, I've never had an erotic dream about a woman before, do you realize how momentous it was? Steph do you remember that beginning of *Lady Chatterley*, it's so beautiful, when he says, "We are among the ruins, we start to build up new little habitats, we've got to live, no matter how many skies have fallen . . ."? Steph, living with you is much better than going back to college. Listen, I'm possessed with ambition, do you understand, possessed, in the next few years I want to make a big name in journalism, both as a reporter and as a photographer, and then a few years later I want to be an actor, both on the stage and on the screen, try both for a decade, and then by the time I'm forty I'll settle down to my first novel, in ten years when I've made a fortune I'll buy you such beautiful presents. . . .

He lies behind her, leaning on his elbow, her perfume drifting from him. He usually insists on taking a Seconal when she does, but his drug-hardened body is so resistant the pill does nothing but make him more manic, more hungry for talk. At 2 A.M. Stephanie starts crying softly, in part out of sheer exhaustion but also because that's the way Seconal has been affecting her since her illness, she starts thinking of her childhood and cries because she wants to be a child again, and then she usually has to take still another pill to calm down. What's the matter honey bun, he says, tell your Lijie what's the matter and it'll all be better, what are you looking for, what are you searching for? I guess . . . I guess I'm looking for a new life Lijie, I'm not sure, I think that's it, each time I try to fall asleep, for instance, I think of my childhood and I start crying. For a few days when I was so sick and so afraid of dying I had these terrifying flashbacks into my childhood, it was like standing at the end of life and making a complete revolution back to its very beginnings. . . . Do I make it worse, Stephie, do I make you cry? Oh no you've helped me so much, Lijie, you're my Ariel, you're my freedom, you make me feel like a child again, you've helped to deliver me from the flesh, from time, from everything. Don't go to sleep yet Stephie he says, hugging her, burying his hair into the back of her neck, don't

256

go to sleep, and he continues to talk to her as she tries to fall asleep, saying, don't you understand Steph I could be totally transformed by that dream I had the other night, totally changed, Christ you're dense, don't you understand anything about liberation, ever since I was thirteen society has made me feel ashamed to be what I am, and suddenly here we are, I'm a man, you're a woman, Christ Steph don't you love me, Steph don't you realize how frightened I've been all my life, Steph can't you stay awake so I can talk to you. . . .

I I

I love you, I love my Stephanie Elijah hums during lunch at the guest ranch. His voice rises over the food like that of a child going "Dadadadada." Often when Elijah says those words Stephanie is reminded of the girl at Miss Temple's who had stood on the stairs at the midmorning break, repeating, "I love you, I love you." That had been equally mysterious, unfounded. "I like you very much, too," Stephanie had answered, but the fifteen-year-old had glowered fiercely into her chocolate milk, repeating, "No, you don't understand, I love you just the same way a man does, just like a man."

"Checking, checking," Stephanie speaks into her tape recorder. "Here we are in Arizona at another cafeteria of the Absolute. . . . Listen, Lija, how about this: Eastern methods of achieving Unity with the All continue to be the rage in the United States, tens of thousands of Americans are taking crash courses in contemplation as eagerly as they go to golf or tennis camp. Just this week the Tucson Institute spent several hundred thousand dollars sending for scholars from Beirut, New Delhi and Berkeley to give a seven-day symposium on Contemplation in the Twentieth Century. Sitting over there in the corner, in Princeton ties and Brooks Brothers tweeds, are some of the most interesting figures attending this event, a group of professors from Midwestern colleges who recently became Moslems in order to practice Sufi mysticism—that seems to be the newest trend. Headline: Conversion to Islam Might Soon Replace Buddhism as the Fashion among Hordes of Americans Seeking Authority of Religious Faith."

"Hey why don't *you* convert to Islam, Steph? I can just see the women's movement flipping out when you start walking behind your man. I swear, you sure have a taste for freaky situations. I've seldom been surrounded by such a bunch of creeps as I am here. Listen, Steph, how long do I have to set my shutter speed on these whirling dervishes from Illinois and listen to those fucking Indians drone on about eterrrrrnal rrrrreality? Can't we drive down to Mexico for the weekend, do you realize I've never been out the Midwest?"

"Dammit, Lija, I've got to stay here until I finish this story for the *Times*. We got this assignment because you asked me to, you needed the money and you wanted to be published in a national magazine, quote unquote—really."

"Steph, I'm sick and tired of the vegetarian slop in this dining room and of the little bistro down the road where it's so dark you don't know whether you're eating bats' testicles or dromedary shit and I don't want us to go back to the Biltmore. I want us to take a nice long drive tonight."

"All right, Lija, but for Christ's sake let's finish this assignment before deciding where we're going to go next. You know what the mama moth says to the little moth: 'Eat up your flannel and you can have mink for dessert.' "

Elijah leans back in his chair and laughs. His long light hair shakes over his face. His beard is about a four weeks' growth, full of soft, curly tendrils. He takes Stephanie's hand, and with his other hand he twists a lock of hair about his finger. He gives uncommon attention to his hair, often toying with it like a flirtatious schoolchild.

"Here's what I got out of today's lecture at the Tucson

Symposium—date, April twenty-sixth," Stephanie speaks into her tape recorder during a break in the afternoon conference. "Dr. Vehdemata, from the University of Benares. Basic Hindu doctrine, quite well put: the whole physical world is illusion— Maya. Mind is the sole reality. Vehdemata used a very revealing metaphor, he depicted Maya as the magic veil worn by Nature—the Great Mother Isis, as he calls her—which shrouds the reality of Mind. Break sequence, the next aside will be mine, not Vehd's. Here we go again with the sexism of most religious systems—as usual the female principle is being pictured as the irrational force, the great deceiver, like Eve. Typical. Okay, back to the lecture: Later Vehd used a good image from alchemy, something like this: The waters of Yoga separate the dross—ignorance—from the gold, which is Right Knowledge, and he who has acquired this Knowledge can determine his reincarnation."

She clicks the tape recorder shut and turns to Elijah. "Listen to this, Lija, this is what turned me on the most from today's lecture. Do you realize that three thousand years ago a theory of prenatal impressions had evolved in India just as complex as those of post-Freudians like Melanie Klein? They believed that we even carry the memory of the act of *conception* that forced us to enter a physical body."

"That bores me Steph," Elijah says while he aims his camera at diverse guests seated about the terrace of the guest ranch— Zen masters in business suits, NASA astronauts turned mystics in blue jeans and beads, students from a local university dressed in white flowing robes like those of Buddhist monks. "Do your thing, but don't bother me with that religious or psychiatric crap when we're alone, okay? Let's get stoned together and talk about love and death and Wordsworth and Jimi Hendrix, but let's not talk up the kind of regressive junk that's dished out here—opium of the people, yuk."

Stephanie shrugs, thinking God we're so lonely, the solitude of it all. . . . "End of the world, end of creation," she dictates, picking up her tape recorder again. "As a spider spins a web from his own substance and draws it back into himself, so Brahma has evolved the Creation from itself and again will absorb it. This web of Brahma's is the Wheel to which we are all bound by Karma. Or, one could say, the Promethean rock to which we are all chained—"

"Prrrrrey to the eagles of Desirrrrrre," Elijah interjects in singsong Anglo-Indian. "I guess you'd better believe it, if you stay on a diet of yak butter all your life."

"Get this, Stephie, I am not converting anymore or being converted, and this is precisely the change I would like to see in you."

Gregory Hillsman is pacing up and down on the terrace of his guest cottage, knocking a clenched fist into the palm of his other hand in pace to his steps. His hair has grayed considerably in the past years. His swift hazel eyes glimmer like sentinels in his sparse, chiseled face.

"I'm not converting anymore, to either a new form of priesthood or another way of meditation or another liberation movement or another radical politics, as you and I were doing throughout the sixties. Since I've stepped halfway out of the Church I've purged myself of all those fads and searches, I'm getting absolutely stoned again from time to time on the Ignatian meditations I had in seminary, and occasionally I even mutter my breviary—but not dutifully, that's the point. Out of free choice, pleasure."

"And you feel grown up at last."

"Oh don't be that simplistic, Stephanie. We must never grow up, we should always maintain our capacity for transformation. I just mean that I'm fed up with the kind of cuckoo instant mysticism we see right here, with all the spirit-starved Americans who come to feed on the Zen or Sufi trough the way they fly to Iran for caviar. And I refuse to be like that Reed Weiss, who goes about like a shamus in a synagogue picking up scraps of our poor decade for his doggie bag. Just yesterday I asked him if he thought a community of wealthy Manhattan

Jews playing Buddhist could survive—he'd told me he does some twenty hours a week of Tantric Buddhist meditation—and he answered, 'Of course we'll survive, we've already been together for eight months.' "

Gregory's lean face widens into that expression of shaking mirth that possesses him in his moments of sarcasm. They both burst into laughter, but Stephanie suddenly has that pain in her groin which recurs since her operation whenever she exerts herself physically.

"That's looking at it *sub specie aeternitate*, isn't it? He's the drum majorette of the meditation movement."

She feels a rush of sweat, she puts her face down and quickly brings her handkerchief to her forehead. Gregory stares at her, his laughter subsided.

"I hear you've been in bad health. I was so happy to see you again yesterday that I didn't want to mention it. But you got over the operation marvelously, didn't you? Is the family well?"

"The boys are doing splendidly at Harvard. And Paul and I have gone our separate ways for the moment, he might have found another woman more to his liking." She wipes her forehead again. "And you, dear Greg. You're well settled in your new job at Berkeley? You're the fashionable former radical wildly attacked from both the right and the left—you adore controversy, you must be very happy."

"All goes excellently. I'm teaching just about every medieval course we have to offer. And occasionally doing a lecture on contemplation, as I'm doing here this week. Saint John of the Cross, Meister Eckhart, et cetera. It pays well, and I need the money to finish my book on the Gnostic heresies."

"Dear Greg, I came awfully close to it in that hospital. Paul was extraordinary, I might not have pulled through without him. The irreversibility of time. That's the hardest thing to accept at our age, that's the most violent aspect of death."

"Why see it as violent, Stephie?" Gregory whispers, suddenly gentle. "Why not see it as the greatest equality, eventually?"

She stares at the familiar beak nose, the curving, ironic mouth.

"Ah, the revolution bit. That's where we were years ago, Greg, when you urged me to go back to France and face my father's death. 'The most revolutionary act in the universe will be the resurrection of the body,' you said, 'the dethroning of matter by the spirit.' Quite beautiful, actually."

"I have something better now," Gregory says with his mysterious smile. "I get increasingly simpler with age."

"What is it?"

He spreads his arms out the way he used to at the peak of his sermons, when she used to go to his Masses in the Boston slums.

"Why not think of death as . . . as the great surprise?"

Stephanie looks startled. "I think I like that."

Gregory bows deeply from the waist, in that half-mocking, salaaming fashion he acquired during his years in the East.

Elijah crouches on a terrace of the Tucson Institute, twisting and turning his body like a large sleek panther as he searches for angles from which to photograph Reed Weiss. Weiss sits in the lotus position, the soles of his feet nimbly paralleled to the sky. His body has the voluptuous austerity of the meditational athlete, its every muscle is groomed to a perfection of litheness. In the past years he has been a Marxist labor organizer, a convert to Christianity, a Lutheran minister, a civil-rights and antiwar activist, an encounter psychiatrist. He is at present a meditational entrepreneur whose three-day crash courses in Zen, Sufi and Hindu mysticism are being enthusiastically booked by colleges, civic clubs, encounter, and consciousness-raising groups.

"You look cool, Baba," Elijah says, kneeling down while he changes a lens. "You're the coolest-looking baba I've ever seen. I hear that's what they call you—baba—you guys who come back from India with the Eastern gigs." "You've kept away from me most assiduously in the past day," Reed says, pursing his mouth. "I've been meaning to tell you that I'm driving to Mexico this weekend to check out a new Sufi commune near the border, feel welcome aboard if you're free to come." "Hold still dear and don't twitch like that, I'm going to open it up to one tenth of a second to get your gorgeous muscles on sharp in this almost-nothing light." "So you've made it, Elijah, you've made it with the great white goddess. She's such a beautiful person." "If you mean it that way, no, I haven't made it and maybe I never will, that's all this culture reduces things to, sex sex sex." "You don't seem to depend much on sex, Elijah, that's very creative, very liberated." "Sex spoils a lot of things. Celibacy isn't a bad bag, I like it." "You can take it or leave it, that's very liberated." "I don't have to go all the way to India," Elijah says with superiority. "Hey listen Reed baby can you spare me some of your hash, you'd be a doll. I haven't had a decent smoke all day, I've got an old lady now who's only smoked about forty joints since her Radcliffe days." Reed reaches into his pocket and throws him a small plastic bag. "Hey that trip to Mexico isn't impossible," Elijah says, putting down his camera. "I've always wanted to go driving outside of the country, I'm a real hick, I haven't been anywhere." "We'd be back in two days." "Listen, Steph is so enthralled talking to her hot-air friend Gregory for hours on end that I don't see why she'd mind my splitting for a little while, I really don't. God, those endless conversations of theirs —'Stephanie, the issue is whether Leibniz' monads are contingent or necessary . . .' Say Steph isn't that the way Gregory talks?"

He sees her walking toward them, opens out his arms in Gregory's theatrical, priestly way. "Each monad may be estranged from the other because of that eternal problem of windowlessness, and we must overcome the following unsurmountable obstacles. . . . Each monad is a Madeleine, and therefore the problem remains, can we still tell one monad from another after a coffee break? Are monads nomads?"

"Oh God, Lijie you're so brilliant," Stephanie laughs. "I wish you'd go back to college and get a degree in something."

"Cut out the schoolmarm trip, honey bun. I know twice as much about literature as all those creepy teachers in Chicago put together."

"But it's all so stupid. With your 150 I.Q. and your A average you could be so many wonderful things, you're so brilliant, Lijie . . ."

"Goddammit, woman," Stephanie writes in her journal later that day, waiting for Gregory on the terrace of his cottage, "why in hell didn't you start digging out, clawing out sooner? Why didn't you fight back earlier against the oppressions of your family, your men, your tribe? What in hell took you so long? You almost got snowed under, oh it was a close shave. Are you afraid of being on your own? What about trying it for real? Okay, it's been hard, very hard for a woman to shake free in our culture, all our biggest heroes are dropouts or bad boys, from Huck Finn to Norman Mailer, and when we women try it we get pelted. Imagine just trying to meditate in the desert for a year, the way Gregory did to get his wisdom—it wouldn't wash, it wouldn't wash at all. The guys who've done it like Greg come back saying, I'm a true socialist monastic, you can do no more than play with those ideas, poor little girl. The ones who don't want us to leave them in the first place say ootsie pootsie my baby wants to be a philosopher when she grows up. But times are changing, why not give it another spin? Is it so scary to be a dropout? Isn't that what I'm doing right now, in my own funny way, living with a twenty-three-year-old? Society's basket cases, that's what women are, born into tightly lidded little baskets through which we must claw and chew our way to freedom. And we've got to do it in proper time—the big danger is to dig out too slowly. Belated recognitions, belated arrivals, that's the essence of tragedy—Romeo at Juliet's tomb, Isolde at Tristan's bier, the epiphanies of deliverance can reach our bedsides too late for rescue. Christ, I didn't see any of this clearly until I was lying in that hospital. There I saw it: every woman's life is a series of exorcisms from the spells of different oppressors; nurses, lovers, husbands, gurus, parents, children, myths of the good life, the most tyrannical despots can be the ones who love us the most. What a late bloomer I've been all along—a little more time deceiving myself about my father's death, staying under the spell of my mother or of L. or of Paul's dollhouse, I might have gone really crazy. Why in hell have I always been so late, made it just under the wire? The voids of my childhood, I guess, they made me too greedy for love and shelter to risk being the bad girl which every true liberation still forces a woman to be. I think I might have a novel right here in these very themes: *One:* woman's life as a series of exorcisms from the spells of different oppressors. *Two:* We must name the identities of each jailer before we can claw our way toward the next stage of freedom. . . ."

"Dearest Stephie," Gregory says as he comes back to his terrace. "Always the compulsive worker. I bet you've already finished your *New York Times* article."

"Oh, no way, I'm so fed up with that kind of writing, Greg, I'm getting a regular block about it. 'Meditation has replaced drugs as instant ecstasy in the most affluent and spiritually starved nation on earth, blabla . . .' What more can I say about it after a year of writing nothing else?"

"I'm glad you're fed up with it. Why don't you give up the meditation bit and do that novel? I've been waiting for it since our Cambridge days."

"Well, I'm trying. I've refused all magazine assignments after this one on Tucson, I've started to work out some short stories that may blossom into something larger. I'm fed up with being a reality junkie, Greg—"

She stops herself, she's aping Elijah's way of talking again. What the hell.

"I've O.D.'d on reality, Greg, I want to invent. But I need to dig into myself a little further before I can begin, I need the courage to be a dropout."

Gregory stares at her as she sits on a bench in her blue jeans, her elbows on her knees, in that boyish position she assumed twenty years ago when listening to college lectures. She suddenly sinks her head into her cupped hands.

"But don't you see how much harder it is for women?" she whispers. "It's so much harder for us to shake free of conventions, of everything. So many of those attempts at conversion that you're knocking now are nothing more than our need for . . . hell, for all that transcendence we had when we were still nurturing, giving birth."

"Goddammit, Steph, don't take refuge in your inferiority as a woman!" Gregory says these words with a certain anger. "Do not seek shelter in your status as the oppressed, that's the worst cowardice there is! Get off that women's-lib bit, will you? I don't want to hear one more word about that from you."

He paces again. Typical Jesuit, he can have that pernicious buffeting manner. Like Zen masters. She knows that about him and bewares. Some years ago he pushed her toward the women's movement. And now that she's spent all these years analyzing herself as a member of that third world, oppressed womanhood, there he is about to pull her out of it again into something else. Well, dammit, she must hold on to herself, she mustn't let this particular tyrant fuck up her life.

"Stephie, what was it like? Last year when you were so ill? The big scare, I haven't faced it close up."

They are in Gregory's cottage, drinking tequila. Elijah and Reed are playing rock and talking loudly in the next room. Gregory's habitually ironic eyes are eager, intense. Stephanie stares at the clean white cotton sport shirt lying against his milky, priestly flesh. She lies down on the floor, her feet up on a chair.

"Well, let me tell you what it was like the month before the operation, when I had no one to talk about it to. We were spending August at our cottage in Maine, I hadn't told Paul and the boys anything, I was going to tell them the following month, a few days before the fact. That summer I wanted to glut only on the simplest, most childlike pleasures, to be obese with sunshine and the sound of my children's laughter—that Colette side of me which you don't understand. Alongside the writing I was finishing, those were days when the fullness of my family's happiness, the smell of my herbs, the quality of light falling upon a flower, were more important than all else. Here we were, the ideal little nuclear family I've always preserved notwithstanding all the darkness that often underlies it, having marvelous picnics at the beach every day and making fresh peach pie and beach plum jam, all this very oral, very childlike. Greg, it was like going back to a microcosm of everything I'd loved in the very beginning of marriage and rebelled against later, the bow-wow quackquack miaow-miaow dollhouse happiness. I remember going out to pick blackberries early one morning, that expanse of bush glistened in the low sunlight like a blinding expanse of stained glass, each little globule of each berry like a dark sapphire on a medieval crown. The pains I take to reach just one of those best thick berries gleaming at the top of the bush! I get huge gashes from the prickles of the thick old branches that always guard the best fruit, I bleed to pluck just one of those dark jewels, that's the way I felt about my time. I knew that every perfect day was one more wound in me, I wanted to glut on the beauty of one more berry, I wanted to give myself to those I loved for one more day, I was obsessed by the pain my death could cause them, I only wanted to gather, to nurture one more time. All those weeks, I drank at night to allay my fears and took more and more pills, hiding everything from everybody. But that's what life's all about, Greg. Garlic and sapphires in the mud. Quite a bit of anguish hidden behind our placid, blissful exteriors."

"And so—what in hell are you doing here, with that beautiful kid?"

The tequila is going to her head. She waves her hand at him, as if to say, It's too difficult, forget it.

"Well, I'm trying to figure that one out myself. Let's see.

Down here at this seminar and in all the religious documenting I've been doing this past year I'm looking for spiritual rebirth quote unquote, for a way of accepting death . . ."

She stares at the desert flowers blooming in the violet haze of the Arizona dusk, the green-and-orange-blossomed chollas, the white-and-yellow saguaro towering over the violet-fleshed cactuses.

". . . and up there in that hotel room, I'm playing Mother Earth again, involved in some symbolic birthgiving process."

"Perhaps your *own* rebirth into a beautiful boy, which is what your father wanted you to be."

Stephanie jumps up from her chair.

"I hadn't thought of that one!" She laughs. "You're incredible, padre. So much better than any shrink, and so much cheaper!"

Stephanie: "I had a dream that I was preparing dinner for my family, and as usual I wanted to cook only vegetables, and my mother had sneaked in behind me and put a large piece of meat in the oven, and I reached in and took it out and . . . it was a little, very rosy, very pretty suckling pig that looked like a human baby and I was very upset. I started to scream and physically attack my mother because of this baby pig, as if my own safety was totally at stake, I was threatened by what I saw as a cannibalistic act, I started to beat up my mother with broomsticks, chairs, everything I could find at hand."

Reed: "The ancient myth of the devouring mother."

Elijah: "Because guess who that little piggy was? You!"

"Peace," Reed says and passes another joint to Stephanie. "I love you, Steph." She takes a drag and passes it to Elijah. "I love you, Steph," Elijah says, passing it on to Reed. "I love you too, Reed." "I love you, Elijah," Reed says. "Everybody loves each other today," Gregory says, without lifting his eyes from his *New York Times*. "Love must be fashionable, like peace, Sufi, Zen." "You look down on people who smoke, don't you,

Greg?" Elijah says. "You must think it's childish, juvenile, barrrrrbaric." "We each have our appropriate opiates," Gregory says. "That's a sweet rhyme," Stephanie says. "Appropriate opiates." Grass goes to her head very fast now, like liquor, cigarettes, all drugs.

"The only one here who doesn't love me is Gregory," Elijah says. "He thinks I'm a barbarian. Don't you, Greg? Reed is a barbarian, too, but we're different kinds of barbarians, and he's the worse of the two."

"What do you mean I'm a barbarian? I didn't think Gregory thought of me as a barbarian. What kind of a barbarian am I, Greg?"

"You are a spiritual barbarian, dear Reed," Gregory says, finally looking up from his *Times*. "You are exploiting ancient spiritual traditions for the modern freezer, whereas Elijah is quite simply a materialistic barbarian, a rather harmless Genghis Khan."

"You're worse than I am," Elijah says, "You're a spiritual barbarian, Reed, I'm just a plain barbarian *tout court*—hey, listen to the French Steph is teaching me."

"Don't misunderstand me, Elijah," Gregory says with an almost affectionate smile. "You are a cynical, playful barbarian, like the little Maoists in Paris in 'sixty-eight. That's always better than the more serious kind. You're theatrical, you're amusing. Deadly serious revolutionaries, *non merci.*"

Elijah lies on the couch. In the late-night drug haze his face is the color of fine bone china. His mean seraph's head is thrown back like that of a drowning man's. Lying there, he looks the way Stephanie had feared one of her own sons would look someday—she had feared she would find them lying in a filthy room after a binge of drugs looking just this way, staring at her with indifferent eyes, all love, all meaning gone.

"Come here, my shake-and-bake goddess." He draws Stephanie toward him. "You know what?"

"What?"

"I'll tell you what, Steph. You want to make me into Adonis, and I want to be Mickey Mouse."

"Oh, go on, you dumdum," Stephanie says. "Let's all try to sober up. I want to talk to Gregory. Stephie's stoned and tired and wants to talk to Father Greg. Let's go into the other room, Greg."

It is near midnight. Gregory goes to the Instamatic machine in Reed's bathroom, makes a cup of coffee, hands it to Stephanie. She follows him into the next room and sits by him, her head on the settee.

"We're leaving in a few days," she says. "We're going."

"Where, what, with whom?" Gregory asks impatiently.

"I'm taking Lolito out for a ride," she says as slowly as she can so as not to slur her words. "Las Vegas. I'm taking him to Las Vegas."

"Why there?"

"That's where he wants to go. So that's where we're going."

"Well, why not."

"One more prince to boss me around. I'm afraid of the future, Greg, I really am."

"In that case, it might be a good idea for you to go home soon," he says softly.

She stares at him. The clean white shirt, the priestly milky flesh.

"You're hilarious. You helped me to get rid of all that bourgeois shit, and now . . . Good God, brother, back to quack-quack bow-wow? Christ."

"Someday you might return by free choice, as I did in a sense."

"You goddam Jesuits," she mumbles, "always wanting to surprise us, giving us nothing but riddles."

"Look, Stephie, otherwise you have to face, to a much greater degree than I think you are capable of facing, the possibility of . . . of nothingness. So far all your life has been structured, safely and rigorously structured by the womanly roles that society has assigned you. It's a grave step to deny them, to turn your back on them. Perhaps an important step, but a grave one. Do you think you're strong enough?"

"Shit, Greg, nothing works except getting to know yourself a little better every five years, does it, getting to identify a few more oppressors?" She closes her eyes, sips her coffee. From the next room come the muffled sounds of two men enjoying each other's bodies. Stephanie lets herself fall into a state of total indifference, as indifferent as she tries to be toward the stray thoughts that interrupt her meditations, she is mastering that art of taking mental Demerols. Black Mountain, Black Mountain in the fifties, that was a place ahead of its time where the same Demerol was needed, a whole dormitory of men and women humping each other like puppies at any time of day or night, men and men, women and women, men and women. At Black Mountain she once ended up lying in bed with Ron— he was her rival, the part-time boyfriend of the man she was in love with that summer—because someone else was stoned in her own bed. And as he started jacking off Ron said, "You know what this place sounds like at one A.M.? It sounds like dozens of grapefruits being squeezed." She acted out her greed for love with Ron, she dyed his shirts pink, loaned him money and made him birthday cakes; when she and their mutual lover lay in her room listening to *Kindertotenlieder* she combed and cut his hair, made him coffee. . . . So here in the next room is something else to be cool about, something of that casualness which she has always craved and never quite been able to get. Elijah and Reed. Like two grapefruits being squeezed. Why should sentiment ever be involved? What's that fine line of Auden's? The Platonic blow? What the hell. A Cat Stevens song is playing in the next room: "My bo-o-o-o-dy . . . has been a good friend. . . . I won't need it . . . when I reach the end." In the same room Gregory sits looking at her, softly singing a Mozart aria, in perfect Italian: "*Se vuol ballare . . . Signor Contino . . .*"

"Greg," she says, "you know what? You know one of the

troubles? I want to be a bad girl for a while, I don't want to be a good girl now, baby. And one of the troubles is that there just isn't a tradition in our society for women being bad girls, dropouts. That's tragic. We don't even have any bad-girl goddesses, for Christ's sake. Not even minor bad-girl deities. No playful pranksterish tricksterish deities like they have in India. Or like Puck, Pan, they're all boys. Greg, I've been a good girl all my life, I married a man my mom approved of, like Paul says I even used to fuck the titled goons she approved of, Paul can be so funny when he wants to, he says I should have worn that on a lapel button when I was twenty-three. Fucking Goons for Mom. And I've been such a good wife and mother, dammit, always there, it's so damn shitty, unfair, the way society makes it hard for us. Kerouac, James Dean, look at how it glorifies the men who drop out, they're our heaviest heroes, for Christ's sake. I want to be like them, Greg, free, free for a while, the way you are, the way Elijah is."

"Dear Stephanie," Gregory says with his wry smile. "Our friendship will always be complicated by the fact that you'd rather be me."

I I I

Elijah's body is beneath hers, Stephanie is staring at him writhing with pleasure as at a reflection of herself, he is still wearing her own nightdress, their nearly identical manes of hair are tangling and tangling, brushing like leaves in a heavy wind. And all the time he is whispering God it is so simple, it is so simple. She asks him to take off her dress, she wants to see his body, to put her mouth to his nipples, but he says no, no, let me be, let me leave it on. So the soft folds of mauve silk remain crumpled about his waist as he thrusts his strong buttocks up toward her. He commands her as usual, saying slower, faster, slower goddammit, ah, faster, faster now. What is it like compared to men, she whispers often, how does it feel? It is 3 A.M., they had lain together as they had all the previous nights in Tucson, Elijah facing her back, his face buried in her hair. God Stephie he had said again why was I singled out to have the brunt of all these fears, these guilts, these desires, why was I chosen to be so different, so alone? And then in the middle of his litany, which she listened to now as if with a third ear, knowing it by heart, loving him too much to be bored, but rabid, rabid in her need for sleep, in the middle of these words he had screamed out, God Steph I've got a hard on, and it had been just as easy as that, as easy as when it had first happened to her when she was seventeen. When he had first cried out those words she'd thought Oh God I'd sworn to myself that I'd do away with that whole business of the body, that's been the greatest discovery of my life's second half, it's been such a freedom to finally feel my body still, so still. My secular, historical life is over, my freedom is not of this body but in dream, illusion, imagination, I'd even written those words, and yet, goddammit, here it was all over again, the body and its tortures. Wouldn't you rather keep it the way it was, she whispered to Elijah, shouldn't we stop this, but as she spoke she felt his penis swollen hard against the back of her thigh, she impulsively seized his hand and guided it about her body. Then he grabbed her hand toward him, he grasped onto her shoulders while she stroked his penis, she felt him trembling behind her, for the first time she knew him to be cowed, fearful. He threw his underpants to the floor and she saw them lying there, childlike and threadbare as those of a destitute monk. Can't we keep it the way it was Elijah, she repeated, can't we? She was crying now and this made him stop trembling, he became very angry. Christ Stephanie you're not there just at the moment I need you the most, you're just not there, are you? His penis was rubbing against her thigh, his hand was exploring the soft furry part of her. When he became bossy, angry again, she stopped crying and then he rested his hand on many parts of her body with tender curiosity, saying God your breasts are so delicate, almost like a boy's, is that the clitoris, I've only seen it in books, does it feel good when I rub it like that, and there's that hole, there's that hole, your vagina. He thrust his finger into it very gently a few times and then like an infant finding the breast, he thrust his member into her, saying my God is that it, is that it, it's so goddam easy, and she said yes that's it, that's it.

So they started that way from the back, lying side by side. Next he ordered her to get on her stomach and he went at her fully from behind. She asked permission to turn over so that they could make love face to face but he seemed reticent to be fully seen by her in the act of love, as if he were still searching for a clearer reflection of himself. Instead he commanded her to get out of bed and lean over an armchair so that he could thrust at her from behind, which he did with a certain brutality. He condescended to be on top of her for a few minutes after they had returned to bed, and that's when she most clearly felt his latent maleness, she shoved a pillow under her buttocks, she put her legs up and wrapped them about his waist so that she could receive the angle of his violence even more powerfully. He thrust at her with ferocity, breathing and grunting like a savage in a tribal dance, while she wondered whether it was woman's fate perpetually to need being pierced, seized, entered, torn, how many times had she rocked in a man's arms screaming kill me, kill me, urging him to bite her nipples to the blood, to tighten the hold of his hand upon her throat until she felt her breath almost stifled, to put his teeth into her shoulder until she was branded. . . . In the last moments he orders her to get on top of him again and then she plunges into that good darkness for which she has delighted finding metaphors, she dives into the groin of the forest, into the crotch of the night, into the depths of the lake. She stares at him beneath her, her reflection, her mirror image, Stephanie is plunging in and out of the pool, lapping her own image, sucking her image, she is two people, she is man and woman, she is the great round ball of light before it divided into man and woman, she is Eve fucking Adam before she is detached from him, she is mouthing herself, thrusting her long tongue into herself. She has a penis at last and is fucking a huge orange lily, thrusting into its cloying caves, into its honeyed interstices, she is wading knee deep into her image, she gulps and swallows herself, drowning and dying with delight in her image, her long curls tangle with those of the creature below, the creature pants too in its orgasm, saying faster, faster, faster now, goddammit, there is the familiar tempest as they rage together, they crash together through the water's surface. They have passed through the glass wall of the lake and through to the other side, all has become still again, he is holding her very tight, whispering in her ear am I still Ariel, and she says no, no, now you're Caliban as well. Am I the best, he says, no I won't ask that, am I one of the best ten? You're wonderful she says. I want to have your child, he says. Sorry darling she whispers. Oh Stephanie I want it, I just want to hold it there in my arms. That night he falls asleep quickly, but she lies awake with no anxiety, she will fall asleep by and by, she wants to remember the brief moment his head loomed above hers while they were making love. And yet she lies there thinking it is sad, so sad that it has changed, that it has become reducible to the flesh, to time, to decay, to our sex-ridden society. Dammit, is this why we've been considered the dark, material principle, Mother, mater, matter, the great nurturer and devourer always suckling, extending, gathering? Stuck with our bodies, stuck with the flesh, and even when we're past the age of procreation we return to the flesh to give men still other forms of nourishment, of rebirth.

When Stephanie wakes, Elijah is already up. He is curiously peevish this morning, as if the pleasure of reassurance he received a few hours before was admixed with fear of the changes it might bring him. Shit, shit Stephanie I am *not* a heterosexual he cries out at one point, get off your Pygmalion wagon, will you? I may turn out to be bisexual, but I'm going to stay gay too, I want *both* sides of it. And while rearranging his photographic equipment upon the bed—lens, filters, caps—he smiles cannily at that word "both," he says it with a mixture of apprehensiveness and satisfaction. A half hour later he asks her again, couldn't they take two days off to go to Mexico, he's dying to travel across the border, he wants to do some photographs there, he knows he can sell the pictures. If she can't take him he might skip over there with Reed for two days.

"I'm staying here to finish my article, I'm not taking you to Mexico or anywhere else. Really! Sometimes I think that's the way I've been looked on all my life, as the big Earth Mother who's going to resurrect the wan young men and feed them every goody they ask for. Isis. Astarte. Well, I'll tell you something, I'm going on strike, that's going to be the slogan on my lapel button: Earth Mother on Strike, Isis Stages Walkout."

"Hey, that's none of my business, darling, none of my business how many times you've laid your Mother Earth trip on other guys." Elijah chews a big wad of gum, his teeth gleaming disdainfully. "Really, you make me feel as if I'm one of ten thousand guys lined up at the door of the temple of fertility.... You make me feel like a sex machine," he adds, tossing his brown curls forward as he brushed his hair.

He cannot understand why she laughs as hard as she does at that last phrase of his. It is the first time he doesn't hug and kiss her twelve times before going out of the hotel. There is little sentiment that morning in their relations, there is some bitterness. It has all started, love-hate love-hate. They go their separate ways that day, Elijah off with Reed to photograph some Indian gurus outside Tucson, Stephanie to the Meditation Center to continue her interview of Gregory. And as she drives up the hill from her hotel she laughs so hard at those words of Elijah's that the painful spot on her stomach throbs terribly, and she has to stop the Volkswagen. "You make me feel like a sex machine." She has to take deep breaths to ease the laughter and the pain, she stares out over the hills. That's another curious quality about this generation which fascinates her, which Elijah exemplifies—their asexuality, their androgyny. Perhaps it's the result of an overly eroticized society, or a healthy instinctual reaction to the overcrowding of the planet. . . . Getting back into the car, Stephanie jots a note about that in her journal before she drives up the hill to meet with Gregory.

IV

Stephanie lies in the dark alone a few nights later. She has a particularly acute pain in her side. It is the first night in a month that Elijah has not shared her room. Moments of her childhood flash before her as if a little kaleidoscope were being softly shaken in front of her eyes. It is at such moments of pain, when she takes Demerol and wonders how certain her "remission" is, that the personages of her childhood appear most vividly. The men and women she most loved float into her consciousness like loving nurses at her bedside—her mother, her stepfather, her father, her great-grandmother. She sees herself with Mama in the nineteen-fifties, walking down a New York street with her at the end of that stupid affair with L., Mama always so strong and fine in the face of one's needs, it was that time Stephanie had returned from Switzerland and she thought it was over for good with Paul—she had just opened a letter from him intimating that, depriving her of a shelter she had both rebelled against and needed for years. "Let's walk," Mama had said. As they walked down the street, never talking, Mama held her by the elbow, creating formidable support, ballasting her, healing all pain as long as she was beside her, giving her full knowledge of the pure gold she was made of. . . . Great-grandmother Baboushka rustles into Stephanie's memory with her odors of raspberry jam and eucalyptus, her spread of watered silks, the lozenge-shaped diamond brooches rescued from St. Petersburg gleaming in her old lace ruffles. How they had loved each other, in that special way the old and the very young can love, without qualifications or criticisms, in undemanding delight. . . . Even the governess, Mishka, the old demon, what love she had given in her own way. Riding back from catechism class with Mishka on one of their eternal subway rides, thick orbs of the governess' spectacles reflecting the white tiles of train stations rushing past —Louveciennes, Kremlin-Bicêtre, Porte d'Auteuil—the images of beautiful children advertising chocolate bars, detergents, underwear: Bébé Cadum, Eau de Javel, Culottes Petit Bateau, Chocolat Nestlé. Little Stéphanie knocks her hand upon her breast, clawing at her clothes. "I have sinned, I have sinned, I have greatly sinned." "What nonsense is this now," the governess asks, "you are ruining your best blouse." "I am a sinner." "Oh, not a bad one, not a bad one." "Well, the nuns tell me so. And so are you." "Ah, yes," cryptically, "if they say so." "You can purify yourself through sacrifice, Mishka." Her embarrassed laugh. "A charming idea, at my age." Javel, Etoile, Ambre Solaire, Du Dubon Dubonnet . . . She feels at peace with her and the rest of them, extraordinarily at peace, devoid of the old resentments, curious to find those loved ones again in that great surprise of Gregory's. She learned of Mishka's death a few years ago, Mama read about it in the White Russian paper she still received every day, there Stephie was in her forties still having nightmares about her old governess, terrified that she would reenter her life in some way. God, how many decades it takes us to crawl out of our baskets, to exorcise ourselves of our oppressors. Mama spoke about Mishka's death over Sunday lunch and Stephanie rode down a hill on her bike, the wind in her hair, feeling seven years old, thinking, Ding dong the witch is dead, I'm free at last, but the next hour she meditated on this death, felt guilt, felt pity and sorrow for the old woman's loneliness, cried about her, vaguely thought of going to church to light a candle for her, in that atavistic fashion of those early nourished by religion. . . . She reaches for a glass of water and wonders anew: Why is it that now, in what could be the last decade of her life, she has an increased fear of men, a strong new craving for all memories of earliest childhood, for her mother's arms, for the arms of women? She certainly will not be able to go to sleep this night, she vaguely knows what is happening to Elijah, he wants both men and women but is scared of both—this is what Norman O. Brown might call the polymorphous perverse generation, kids who want everything, won't accept any contradictions, want the universe. And Brown is all for them, he says they will create a more peaceful world because our levels of repression and of rage will be reduced, who can tell. Elijah probably has that deep terror of women's flesh which pervades most homosexuals, and who knows that it can ever be cured, that it should ever be cured. What terrifies her the most is the disdain she feels for him and for Reed tonight. Waves of spitefulness toward homosexuals sweep through her which she has never been aware of before, cannot control. The word "parodic" floats in and out of her mind as she stares at the issues of *Gay Sunshine* Elijah left lying about the floor of their room when he left for that excursion across the border with Reed. The nasty queens, fag fag fag fag fag fag that's what they are, these vile words notwithstanding her carefully culled radical politics, her support of gay-liberation movements—she had marched with them—the anger in turn makes her feel small, guilty, reactionary, God how hard it is to get rid of myths, attitudes, prejudices, however liberated we think we are. . . .

No sleep. At 2 A.M. Stephanie reaches for her tape recorder to replay a passage from the interview she taped with Gregory the night before.

"Gregory, what is your definition of a balanced civilization?"

"Certainly, one in which man can fully experience both his divinity and his animalness, one which offers ritual channels through which he can be possessed by forces larger than himself—as in Greece, or the high Middle Ages. The proper balance of Apollonian and Dionysiac is obviously what I mean. This is an aside, Stephanie, but what do you think your dear Elijah's deafening rock music is all about?"

"How did you come to these considerable changes in your way of thinking and your style of life—you who saw everything in such a secular light ten years ago?"

"Well, I'm not in the mood to share those various changes with the general public. But let us take one matter, the simple matter of celibacy: I am not formally bound anymore by the rules of the priesthood, and yet I remain celibate. My decision to renounce women is as intimate and uncommunicable as another man's decision to prefer one woman above all others—it is the result of an intimate and mysterious experience of the heart. I remain celibate the way I had always wished to be celibate—by choice. Which is the only ethical way to renounce anything."

"What is your comment on the conduct of those priests and nuns who took another way at some point—who married, let's say?"

"Dilettantes! If you're a priest in love with a woman you might sleep with her, but you do *not* marry her. Let's keep our manners utterly correct."

He had rolled his *rrr*'s mightily in that last word, adorning his face with his most disdainful Voltairian smile.

She shuts it off. Religion, the religion of her childhood, can it ever be possible again, can it be possible at that ultimate moment when she will need assurance that there is something rather than nothing? Stoned on the beauty of the Mass that spring Sunday in 1940 at Uncle Jean's, coming home from church to the smell of cow dung and roses, of sour milk pails and fermenting cider, to the din of those loved voices prophesying war. Earlier, aged five, going about presenting sacrifices to little Jesus, putting her favorite doll, toy, candy on the nursery table before an open window that looked upon a Paris court-yard, hiding in the closet, swearing she heard fluttering the wings of the dove that carries the gifts back to heaven. Sitting in the catechism classes over her coloring book, the nuns' minted breaths pulsating from under their white starched heads, coloring in blue the bodies of Saint Cecilia, Saint Stephen. . . . Childhood, early childhood, that's what she wants the most tonight, she wants it so badly that she begins to cry again, thank God Elijah isn't there. Always better to be alone in these moments, manless. Solitude, splendor and horror of solitude. . . . She floats into a still earlier memory: learning to walk, taking her very first steps, being what?—no more than fourteen, fif-teen months old—that's how early her recall is, psychiatrists have always been stupefied. A nursery, the crib behind her with its pacifiers and silver rattles, the old nanny from Poland guard-ing the door with her enormous coif of starched whiteness, and outside, sunshine, metal bars, the odor of dusty ivy and stewing cherries, other babies being wheeled in waxy black carriages, more nannies with great coifs of starched white wings. And on the other side of the room the great loves of her life—her mother and great-grandmother holding out their arms, saying, "Here, darling, here darling, *viens, mon beau bébé, viens, ma chérie,*" and she begins to waddle, to sway toward them, she recalls that at that moment of freedom she has a bandage about her waist—the nanny's archaic way of swaddling a child, or a deformed recall in which she sees herself as damaged?—any-how there is pain and fear and glory associated with this action, this sudden sense of flying. Mother over there beckoning, with her gleaming cap of golden marceled hair—it is 1932 or so—her flat, smooth platinum jewelry, her smooth white slender arms, her long red fingernails, Mother made all the more precious by her rareness, her absences, looking at this adored idol she starts swaying into nothingness and Mother claps, claps so hard she continues plunging into space, Mother laughs, she emits roars of laughter from between her gleaming ruby lips, and by Mother's side there is Baboushka, her chin quivering with emotion, her Vieille Russie diamonds glimmering on her lace scarf, her watered silks rustling with excitement like the wings of an agitated dove. Ecstasy, freedom, she walks! They roar, they clap their adoration. She waddles toward the women, screaming mamamamamamammam. . . . Oh, to be back in that state, to be sheltered, cribbed, held, to be at Mother's breast, to be One with All, to be loved while screaming, while in tantrum, to be back in that world of women, our first loves, our first loves!

Stephanie drops off to sleep for a few minutes, dreams about a lover of some years ago, wakes up, and continues remembering moments of that particular year. Stephanie-Persephone in the underworld, quite happy there, could have stayed a long, long time, as long as her demons chose to keep them there. Pete had powerful shoulders and a sweet Irish face that would have been handsome if less blurred, less bloated, he was eight years younger than she, putting himself through college by being a bartender. He lived in a room whose filth was not necessarily created by any debasement of character but by the death-trance disorder of his alcohol. Its smells of urine, nicotine, liquor, offal filled her with curiosity rather than disgust. Most of the time, when not in bed, they spent their hours sitting in the tiny space that served him as a kitchen, drinking straight rye, sometimes on a hot evening he would leave the icebox door open to bring light and a little freshness. They sat facing each other in two cheap kitchen chairs, he with his legs spread wide apart, her slender body encased between them, and by the light of the icebox he would talk to her, one large hand on her knee, the other fondling his bottle of rye. Yes, he said, his extra paycheck was coming in and if she could find a night to be free he would take her out to dinner next week to the seafood house where the bartender was a pal and they would give him a cut price. And she said don't worry Pete I don't ever mind paying for anything, God, we have such a good time together. As she had turned thirty-five and first sensed the possibility

of sexuality's end the Mother Earth streak had surged powerfully within her, that Mother Earth presently occupied with
the resurrection of Elijah. And this sense of sexuality's end had
also been simultaneous with a crazily increased potency, this
man held her buttocks in his hands as if they were a bunch of
lilacs, drank her like nectar, drained her of flesh through orgasm
after orgasm. She was never sure whether the ecstasy he offered
her came from the skill of his mouth and hands or from the
sharp way he had of ordering her about, suck me, suck me
harder he would say in the flat voice of the drunk, right up
there, babe, at the tip, ah yes, suck, suck, suck, ah, swallow—as
if she did not know. His semen was sweet, less acrid, less piscine
than other men's, its sweetness was in such strange contrast to
his dour, torn surroundings. The ecstasy was there even though
he was often too drunk to get off himself. He would fall asleep
before his own orgasm after eternities of fondling her body
with his hands, his mouth, oh God the memory of riding the
minuscule saddle of his tongue, the extraordinary delicacy of
that organ thrusting into her.

Seated encased by his wide legs, downing the rye by his icebox, she was transported in his talk to all the other lives he'd
had, to his two haggling former wives, to all the other broads
to whom he'd promised that he would take them to a show,
to the beach, when the next paycheck came. And of course he
talked about that novel he wanted to write, most men who
came to her wanted to eventually write a novel, as she did.
God, Americans and their desire to be novelists, the American
novel should be listed in medical dictionaries alongside Mega-
lomania and Obsessional Neuroses. He said to her, next week
if you can find an evening to be free—oh, please Stephanie
can you—I'll take you out to that seafood house and the dinner
will be on me. And she repeated, don't worry Pete, I don't want
you to ever mention that again, but he had a streak of stubborn
pride which made him resent all her givingness, and he would
sulk and sorrow about the fact that she could not spend more
than an evening or two with him a month, and that she could

never stay for the night, the darkest and loneliest part of his life, when his fits of drinking were at their most extreme. On the days she said okay we can have the evening together he would shower and put on the pink shirt she had bought him and look like a happy boarding-school child being taken out for dinner by his mom. Oh God, she thought, here I am with one of my own students, since I was seventeen men have been asking, Save me from this, save me from that, and I've often gone about it not even knowing whether there was anything there to save, wasting my energies upon men the way men squander their seed over the face of the earth. Nurturing, when we stop that we are as good as dead. That kind of education of women certainly should change for a better society to exist. . . . Most of the time she had to be home by five to cook dinner for her family and she left Pete glowering, with that scowl on his face which she knew signaled an imminent bout of drinking. You always have to go away, he said with anger. And she thought, I'm taking him just the way men have always taken women, on their off hours, the way men have taken women throughout history! What a turnabout, now it's the men wanting the permanence, the housekeeping, the little dinners *à deux*, the playing housey, it's the men saying, I'm lonely, I'm alone, can't you spend the evening with me. Not only husbands, but lovers too. Often when she walked into Pete's in the morning she would find him in the stupor of his most drunken sleep, cheap rye rising from his big body like a smog over a city, sometimes a disheveled woman whom he had picked up the previous night lay by his side. On those days she drank very heavily with him to retain his affection—he had the drunkard's hatred for those who did not share his weakness—and then she became like an animal, transcending that goddam delicacy, that breeding of hers which had always plagued and limited her, she wanted to crouch on all fours and be petted by him when he himself had already become an animal, she wanted to fuck only on the floor, on all fours, exulting in her fantasy of having three or four cocks in her at once. She had been writing a monograph on Verlaine that winter, and the French Romantics' *nostalgie de la boue* was clearer to her than ever, phrases from those poets floated through her mind as she sat on Pete's lap downing his rye, or lay in the tiny dirty bathtub after they'd made love. Thoughts from Verlaine perhaps: Our whole life is a search for that angelic excitation found in filth, command, debasement. To find ecstasy at the dark center, to make gold as in alchemy, only after reducing matter to its basest. A line from Verlaine, precisely this time: "All is drunk! All is eaten! There is nothing more to say!"

Stephanie twists and turns in her bed at about 4 A.M., trying to find a position in which her stomach will hurt less, unsure whether to take another Demerol or stick it out until morning, when the pain usually subsides. Ah yes, sacred and profane love, whatever that is. The honor and tragedy of an aging marriage. The vacations of her marriage. Gardens and solitude of Morocco, of Sicily, of southern Spain. Paul liked to sit and look, sit and look at landscape. From the earliest morning hour she would hear the sounds of his swallowing numerous cups of tea, it was that intimate, that oppressive, she was constantly obsessed by the sounds of things going down his throat as he sat on a terrace consoling himself silently with weak tea, hot milk, mint infusions. A little slurp, the slow appreciative swallow, the sound of his pleasure. Toward noon they might drive to the beach and sit in the middle of a few families in which the sad-eyed women had early turned to fat, and the men talked garrulously, secretively, to each other. When there had been a particularly long silence between them they exchanged smiles. His came first, patronizing, pitying, glossy with the splendor of his very white teeth. They were genteel together, seldom raising their voices, oh so genteel. His smile always seemed to say something like "Poor baby" or "Poor darling." Often he actually said the words "Poor darling," for she had that melancholy frailness, that alley-cat quality which he was tempted to patronize. After a few years of being touched by his protectiveness she had been driven up the wall by it. During their swim their smiles floated again over the turbid, weed-laden water, reassuring each other that they were enjoying their vacation. Solitude and grandeur of those Mediterranean places in the early afternoon: the plazas abandoned by a sleeping town, like the solitude inside Stephanie herself. Olive trees turning the silver underside of their leaves to a scorching wind born in the oven of the mountain. Pale parched plains, acrobatic goats climbing heaps of stones, sheep palpitating in the shade of scraggly oaks. Odor of dung, dust, thyme. White haze of noon heat over the plain. Chalk-white villages like crowds of surprised faces, the windows and doors like black gaping mouths. The scenery grenadine and violet and violent, her mind blank, blank with him. His neck seemed to turn red and bull-like when he drove, intimating all that inner violence which he kept locked inside him, which he never dared express in his work or his language, which caused him his migraines, his backaches, his insomnias. . . . Spain, 3 P.M., a vacation. The licorice gleam of the Guardia Civil's hats, the plaster madonnas clutching dried flowers, the calendar pictures of laughing, white-toothed Andalusian beauties. Electric fans creaking slowly over the dusty crucifixes of a dining room. Clink of wineglasses on the marble-topped table. Rasping of cicadas over their silence. Dutiful lovemaking after lunch, duty duty. She could not always "play the comedy," as her Aunt Olga had called it, Olga had always stressed how rare orgasms are, how you almost always have to fake them. They'd been walking on the beach at Saint-Tropez that summer of 1963. The women who get along best in life, Olga had said, are the ones who are best at faking it each time. "*Oh, ma petite, mais il faut jouer la comédie, mais constamment.*". . . Colors deepening on the parched plains. He reads Salinger, she reads D. H. Lawrence. The plain pink again as dawn, the mountains scarlet. He hates streets, towns, cafés, the animation she thrives on—classical situation. In the evening he likes to sit alone on a terrace again sipping some light wine drink, staring at the landscape, she hears anew the liquid sliding slowly, voluptuously, down his throat. Marriage. Dung and jasmine on the air. Olive trees as green as the jackets of the Guardia Civil, as green as that poem of Lorca's about everything being green, *verde yo te quiero verde*. The plain as vast as her solitude. Yet it had been the richest of lives, she would not change an iota of it. It had just been a life. She wonders about Paul now, she thinks of him with tenderness and gratitude, how good it was for them to walk out of the cave, live more on their own. They had often strolled together in Maine the summer before her operation, remarking on the town's fine eighteenth-century houses, picking blackberries, talking about the children, never saying "What happened between us," never confronting each other the way others do. They were circuitous, ever so thoughtful. On their last Sunday there, after the children had gone back to school, they had strolled in the thick fog past the pale gray of the old clapboard houses, the pale blue-gray of the hydrangeas, the pale gray-lavender of the clematis vines. What suitable colors for the last summer of one's life, Stephanie thought. Pale gray, pale blue-lavender. And the sting of that late summer air, especially when she biked fast down a sloping street, was like the smart of some disinfectant on the tongue. Back at the house Paul fixed lunch for himself—he was often fixing delicate little dishes for himself, little salads, little sandwiches with watercress and bean sprouts. What would it be like to make a beehive for one's own self, Stephanie thought, one's self alone, have no more offspring or any other creature to feed, have nothing else to do but feed oneself. God. "Can I make you some lunch?" Paul had asked. "No, I'm not hungry," Stephanie replied. Yet after Paul had eaten she had picked up his salad bowl and drunk the liquid left at the bottom, a curious sweet-sour mixture of melon juice and vinegar. Gall, it's like gall, Stephanie thought, why do I punish myself, why do I need to starve myself so, especially before an operation? The fog was beginning to lift. She got on her bicycle to get the Sunday paper. Halfway down the hill she thought of her governess, ding dong, the witch is dead, and she waved to a schoolmate from Miss Temple days whom she occasionally saw in town—a woman in perpetual tennis garb with intricately streaked hair and a round Doris Day face, still pretty at forty-four but preserved on an edge of hazardous plenitude, everything like a lovely piece of fruit about to get too ripe. I have chosen the other way, Stephanie thought, away with the body, away, away. Funny, funny that her lack of anger has brought her to such slickness, decadence. Better maybe to remain enraged.

Click: The light. The tape recorder. "I want to remind you of that phrase of Luther's," Gregory was saying. "*Pecca fortiter.* Sin boldly to enter the kingdom."

"But, Greg, look, how did you come to *your* illuminations?"

"Listen, Stephanie, you and I are two persons for whose consistency I have the most profound admiration . . ."

How he smiled. It was in his rare moments of revelation that he chose to speak in his most exotically convoluted language.

". . . and I am obligated to proceed in a way which embarrasses me *profoundly*. I must stress to you—and I cannot emphasize it enough—that the answer to a question such as you just asked me can seldom be stated in words and, moreover, that it may be dangerous to put it into words."

"All right." It was the day after she had first slept with Elijah. They were sitting on the terrace of Gregory's cottage. She put her head down dejectedly on her knees. "Let's stop right now."

"No, no, look, I want to help." He put his arm squarely on top of hers. "Look, I once had this illumination of . . . of nothingness. That will take me some time to explain. You see, there in Africa, I found myself in . . . in a beatitude of cultural poverty. Not able to speak their language and unable, for once, to even learn it—some Bantu dialect it was, one of the most difficult skills in the world to acquire. Stranded there, alone, silent, in the desert. Now, careful, all enlightenment involves a considerable amount of suffering. I came to realize, there in Africa, that we are here to witness the total relativity of human convictions in the face of . . ."

"Of what, Greg, for Christ's sake?"

"Of—perhaps of nothing!" Gregory shouted out, and he burst out in his most Mephistophelian laugh.

She paced the garden a few times before speaking up again, almost in tears, staring at the sumptuous, waxy yellow blossoms rising from the violet and green flesh of the cactuses.

"So you have no other counsel for me, padre. That's precisely what I'm heading toward for the first time in my life—nothing. No predictable future, nothing."

"I know that. And I don't know if you're ready for what you're trying to do, or for the meditation I'm going to give you—but here it is. You've asked. I'm giving. Throw these out at yourself: Think of an Unground that precedes any Being—think of it as absolute and original freedom, since it comes before anything in time."

Gregory closed his eyes and leaned his head back, as if to expose it to the fullest power of the sun's rays.

"Think that this Unground, this unfathomable will, resides in the depths of divinity, and before divinity—that this first divinity, divine nothingness, is before and beyond good and evil. Nothingness is prior to, deeper and more divine than Something. Darkness is prior to and deeper than all light."

Gregory opened his eyes. The speckled green irises gleamed luminously, almost maliciously, over his ironic mouth.

"This is all totally heretical, of course."

Stephanie grinned. "Okay, professor, why don't you give me one more exercise? Of a historical, not a personal, nature."

"Oh, that's easy. For hundreds of years classical scholars

have been attempting to determine the nature of the vision received by the illuminati of Eleusis—one of the most esteemed shrines of ancient Greek civilization. The initiates were put to sleep with some kind of herb potion in little chambers which one can still visit. Thousands of theses have been published, tons of paper and of scholars' hours have been consumed in the attempt to define the nature of the vision received at Eleusis. Well, I've recently come across some material—I hope to publish it soon—which I think defines the central symbol of the Eleusinian revelation. Do you know what was that central dream—later reported to a priest—which certified the dreamer as properly initiated? He dreamt of—a stalk of grain!"

The wide grin, the outspread hands, as if to say, It is so simple.

"Well, what does it say? Unity within multiplicity? The continuity of life and death?"

"Certainly—and many other things as well. The survival of the species. It also says that the illumination of beauty, truth, can be found in the simplest details of life, once one comes into proper relationship with oneself—cleaning a house, a simple marriage."

"Picking blackberries on a sunny morning."

"For you, perhaps. And so, Stephanie, I urge you to have your *own* vision. I urge you to imitate me!"

"Oh God, Greg, what an insane idea! Me imitate you. You with all your arduous climbs of the spiritual mountain, with the thousands of years of men's independence behind you—can you see society even allowing women to even leave for the desert as you did? And once we got there the Bedouins wouldn't let us in. . . ."

Stephanie clicks the tape recorder shut again. She had laughed over that last comment of hers, but, if she remembers properly, Gregory had shrugged a bit impatiently, as if to say, "You're offering yourself such pathetic choices, you're your own worst oppressor."

It is 5 A.M. Before making her last attempt to sleep Stephanie sits cross-legged on the floor of her hotel room to do her morning meditation. The intruding thoughts are fewer today than on many other nights, perhaps because she is alone. She simply concentrates on her breath, tries to be only her breath and nothing else, feels gratitude that she is still breathing, feels amazement that she exists at all, feels fully the beauty and the preciousness of life, life, life, there was that Russian architect who came to the house last year who said that back home he had a dog named Life. Life. Just simply that—Life. Paul loved that, that complex being who put such ultimate value on life's simpler aspects, the growth of his children, his flowers, his vegetables, the well-being of his beloved animals; that steady tenderness toward all that was alive was more essential than any talk, any words. Just think, a dog called Life, in Russia, where life must be so precious. Paul, life, breath, Paul is like life, with its unresolvable contradictions, its beauties and its tragedies, patches of blue sky coming two minutes a month through fields of clouds, that's life. . . . These thoughts are drawing her away from the business of concentrating on her breath, and in a very disciplined way she says to herself, as she was taught, These thoughts were not thought by me, not by me, not by me, these thoughts were in Japanese, in Portuguese, and then she starts the series over again, concentrates solely on the phenomenon of the intake and output of air into her slight body, one, two, three, four, five.

V

" 'Monoliths of red sandstone,' " Elijah is reading from the *Mobil Guide to the Southwest,* " 'tower as much as 1,000 feet over the valley floor.' Wow. 'Also outstanding are the weird and gigantic forms caused by erosion . . .' " He throws the book into the back seat, puts his head back on Stephanie's lap, his camera on his stomach. "Stephanie, listen, don't leave me, do you understand, I would collapse. I've got nothing, nothing. I've heard you and Greg talking about the beauty of nothingness and of solitude and all that crap, but it's so abstract, abstract, God how the two of you can theorize. Stephanie, talk to me, will you please?"

Elijah and Stephanie are driving through Monument Valley. At the last gas stop Stephanie wrote three postcards to Paul, her husband, telling him what the landscape reminded her of: ". . . most frequently I see figures from the dark barbaric ages, pre-medieval sacred figures, kneeling Carolingian kings, dying Merovingians brandishing their swords, Vercingetorix reclining against his dolmen . . ." She started out writing one small postcard to Paul, but it did not fit into one card, so she wrote on another and still another card. It was curious, writing him. It was pleasant. Stephanie has already taken her Demerol and is driving slowly, slowly through the valley, the concentration of driving is helping to ease her pain, she is enjoying the redness of the landscape, its emptiness, the dust, the haze, her freedom, her recovered childhood, her freedom from love, from responsibility, from all emotion, she is enjoying her indifference. They have been on the road for two weeks now, zigzagging all over the Southwest with no particular route in mind, led only by Elijah's whims for hamburgers and heated swimming pools. Every morning Stephanie wakes up happy and looks forward to the next slow dusty drive, to the quality of light on the desert landscape, to the next Demerol, to the next word game she will play with Elijah, to the next swing of the clock hands to 6 P.M., when she allows herself her first drink, to the sight of Elijah's strong white body diving into water, to the next motel room, to the next evening of sweet crazy vacant prattle with him. There is less pain this week and each morning she feels happier, freer, giddier, more stoned on beauty, more indifferent. She just wants to go on living with the redness of the landscape, with the warmth of Elijah's head cradled in her groin as she drives, with one more day of minimal pain. She keeps thinking of those nineteenth-century women who spent much of their lives drugged on opium, who stayed in a stupor of opium night and day. Especially in the New England coastal towns, where it was brought home in quantities by husbands returning from the Orient in their whaling ships. Day after day, walking high as kites down the streets of New England towns when their husbands were out on their two- and three-year-long voyages, keeping their body temperatures raised by opium in their freezing houses, administering it to their children to quiet winter coughs, taking a third dose at lunchtime to calm the beginning of a neuralgia, or to get even happier—just imagine those stoned matriarchies, those towns administered year after year by thousands of women as stoned as she is, imagine the beauty of that. . . . She stops at a red light in a small town. Elijah stares at her with his great amethyst eyes as if she is someone else, someone new.

"*Talk* to me, Steph."

"Okay, I had a dream about you last night, Lija. I dreamt that you've been locked up after a terrible street fight, I take an elevator to look for you, stopping at every floor, every floor is like a max prison, with men chained to the walls, I don't find you. When I come back to the ground floor a wizened middle-aged doctor with a European accent tells me, 'I've found him for you, but be prepared, he's in bad shape.' I go into the room he shows me and there you are in the top bunk of a double bunk bed, looking like an animal in a cage or a baby in a crib—squatting on all fours, your face chalk white like a clown's and absolutely blank, like a retard, as if you've been lobotomized—and I rush to you and cradle you in my arms and you start talking to me, but only in very short rhymed couplets, you say to me, 'I am free, I am free, let me be, let me be.' "

"Steph, I don't get any of that psych stuff, remember?"

"I guess it means that something's been freed both in you and in me—that up to now I've needed to keep you as a child but . . . that I'm worried no one else will . . . that I love and hate men, I guess."

"Steph, will you please continue the conversation I started ten minutes ago?"

She tries to remember what that was. Ah yes, the sixties' Movement, he had nothing to go back to, he was afraid of being left alone.

"So what's so new about being left alone, shnookums? You've split before, and other guys have split on you."

"But you're all I have right now, Steph. You're my big chance to make something out of myself *fast*, otherwise . . ."

"Otherwise what?"

"Otherwise . . ." He takes another puff on his cigarette, winces at the sun, throws the butt out the window with an angry gesture. "Otherwise shit, Steph, it might take me months, years."

She laughs, a high-pealed, unbound laugh that startles him, makes him sit up.

"So what am I supposed to be—Ms. Presto Magico, the queen with the golden fingers? I don't understand."

"Steph, you could teach me French and Spanish, you could teach me to write better, I want to be a writer and a photographer for the next few years, and travel at lot." His lips curl up in that pretty Mona Lisa half-smile. "Now that I don't have to die there anymore I want to go to Venice."

He puts his head back on her lap, and falls asleep.

Stephanie drives on for half an hour through Monument Valley and stops the car in the shade to rest. She continues her postcard series to Paul: "These shapes fascinate me because that was always my favorite period of history as a child, the darkest ages this landscape reminds me of, I envied the privacy of those profligate kings carried about in the curtained litters—

Les Rois Fainéants, as they were called in our French history books. Something to do with my love for hiddenness, caves, small dark rooms, subways, deep forests. Paul darling, it's so good to write to you again." She puts her head down, closes her eyes, inhales deeply the arid, pistol-cold morning air. The freedom of this drive, her frequent bouts of meditation, her frequent doses of Elijah's grass. There is a strange new clarity. She feels weightless. She stares down at Elijah thinking who's this kid always lying in my lap this way, he's lying on my groin, as if emerging from me. Good God, Greg wants me to go home soon. What a thought. If Paul would have me back. What a gamble.

"Steph, I'm thirsty," Elijah is complaining. He is lying there in her lap calling into the bleak landscape. "I want a milkshake. When are you going to finish your morning meditation?"

"In a minute, sweet pea."

He closes his eyes again. She pats his luxuriant brown curls, curls like those of the Olympic athletes in Hellenistic sculptures at the Naples Museum. Naples, eighteen years ago, a happy evening with her husband and her parents, dinner in a small bistro of the port, squid and a lot of wine for dinner, the navy-blue Mediterranean night, a guitarist singing in that heavy dialect, "*Shcallinatella, tella, tella . . .*" So the whole family is there, and they are watching her in that funny way they have when they are all together, the three pairs of eyes saying wordlessly, When is she going to break out, when is she finally going to be bad? She was like a smoldering little volcano with this family she adored, needing both their shelter and her freedom—oh God, those contradictions—seeking resolutions in long bouts of sulking, the family always staring at her as if she were a caged lioness. God, how fiercely and beautifully she made love to Paul those days when they were still building their nest, she'd never known anything like it with any other man. Those were the years in which she still clung to that doll-house happiness against which she so rebelled, in which she sometimes wanted to knock her head to death against the walls, often saying to Paul let's have another baby please, please, knowing that this was her safest refuge from adventure, self-discovery, other men, becoming a writer. And Paul who kept the key to the dollhouse wisely said no darling it's better not for you, better not. The autumn after Naples there was Kennedy's death, stranded in Texas and California on one of Paul's trips to some architectural site they made love in their hotel room in the glare of the television reports after crying their hearts out in each other's arms, the following weekend Jeff turned six years old and requested a picture of the dead President for Christmas, and nothing else, it was the beginning of that child's dazzling love for history. . . .

"When are we going to get out of the car?" Elijah mutters. "I'll drink anything, beer, iced spit, holy water." Elijah's feet are on the dashboard, small, dejected in that large elegant body, funny how men are expressed by their feet.

"Don't worry, shnookums," Stephanie says. "Lolito be a good boy. Humberta Humbert is going to stop and feed you very soon."

She drives on slowly, relishing the immensity of the red sandstone monoliths, the bone dryness of the air. "That's a funny one, Lija," she says, pointing to one of the monuments, "it's a man in front of a building. What does it remind you of?"

"Maybe it's Norman Mailer in front of the Pentagon, maybe it's the poisoner of love himself."

"You're so stuck on the present, Eli. Maybe it's Hamlet. Hamlet standing at the entrance of his mom's room, waiting for a nice warm cuddle."

"*Très recherché.*"

They have come to a small low shack in a dusty plain that borders on Monument Valley. A sign says it is called Ethel's. Ethel lives and works alone inside. She is very fat. On the wall behind the cash register she has pasted up pictures of famous towers—the Eiffel Tower, the Tower of London, the Leaning Tower of Pisa, the towers of numerous minarets. Here are all these pictures of towers hanging in the flattest groin of the Utah desert. Outside, one telephone pole is all that breaks Ethel's view of infinity, plus one electric wire, one outhouse. Stephanie sits down and asks Ethel whether she has ever been to Monument Valley. Ethel says no, she has never been there. My goodness, Stephanie says, it's so beautiful, and it's only an hour away. I was born *here*, Ethel says. Elijah orders two chocolate frosted malts, three hot dogs, two hamburgers, a bag of potato chips. Stephanie asks for tea. Ethel goes into her own icebox, in the back room, to give Stephanie the last piece of fresh lemon she has. She brings the lemon on a clean white plate. "Do you have God?" she asks Stephanie, shoving a picture of Jesus Christ alongside the plate. "God, yuk," Elijah says. "Do you have God," Ethel persists, staring at Stephanie. Her eyes are yellow, like those of a pale-eyed dog, a Weimaraner. "Sometimes yes sometimes no," Stephanie says, "you know what I mean?" Ethel nods, very satisfied. Her eyes soften. Without a word she puts a fresh tea bag into Stephanie's empty cup, pours fresh hot water into it. "Why did you come here?" she asks Stephanie. "I'm preparing for death," Stephanie answers, stirring her tea. The woman nods again, smiles. "Why do you live here?" Stephanie asks. "I was born here," the answer comes. "I love you Ethel, you're great," Elijah says thoughtfully. They go to the outhouse, they get back into the car, they drive again. Elijah's eyes are more brilliant than ever today, he has been clean for two days, drug free, she is the one who is stoned on her painkiller. "Talk to me Steph," he says, "I want to talk to you until the day I die." "Ah yes, that would be fun. Our last dying words, let's play that game. What would your last dying words be?" "I'm hungry, that's what they'd be." He bursts out laughing, pearly teeth gleaming. "How about you, Steph?" "I want to *know*—something that corny. You're nice." She pats his head, smooths his temples, the way he does to her every few days when she cries, lying in bed, her head buried in the crotch of his shoulder.

They have made love twice since that first time in Tucson, but each time rather indifferently, each time on nights when he had had a fit of anger, felt smarted by the world. Once, for instance, they had struck up a conversation at a bar with a New York editor who said that such and such a film Elijah liked was popular with fags, and that had been enough to set him off. The East Coast literary establishment was a bunch of cock-sucking creeps, redneck bureaucrats, jerks. Look at all the geniuses who had been gay, Michelangelo, Leonardo, Auden, Tchaikovsky. He lay in bed, smoking, raging. The motel room they were in that night was lined top to bottom with purple plush, the water in the toilet tank shone a bright cerulean blue. The upholstery and bed covering were bright-orange fabric shot through with gold thread. The chairs were sculpted of marshmallow-hued plastic, like gynecologists' furnishings. There was a cocktail dispenser built into the wall which gave out little bottles of brandy, whiskey, gin. She lay there trying to caress whatever part of his body was not flailing about the bed, every few minutes he rose and paced the room, still dressed in her mauve kimono. Oh I love you Steph but I don't know how we're going to make it, you're always analyzing me so. I'm not ready for that shit, I'm not ready to know myself, I'm not ready to face my contradictions, I want to hold on to them. To get him out of his sulks she called room service, ordered steaks and malteds at 2 A.M. Elijah had found slugs with which to rip off the drink machine, that cheered him up, seven, eight brandies in a row, he finally lay in bed more quietly, crooning with a Mick Jagger cut coming on the radio: "Let her talk— she needs to survive . . ." Well, that could be the theme song of the month after all those years of Paul's silence, Stephanie thought, that sure could be my theme song. The ceiling's surface was one enormous expanse of mirror. Stephanie stared up and saw their two bodies floating above her, those two heads of curls intermingled. Elijah talked for an hour about how sick society was, oppressing gays, imposing bourgeois capitalist values on everyone, he lay close behind her as usual, his soft beard against her neck, his groin against her buttock. Suddenly he exploded with the same phrase, Jesus, Steph, I have a hard on. And they made love, he seemed preferring to take her from behind or else on top of him, impatient with her search for more novel positions, and then stopping short of orgasm. He would say that he was tired from the drive, or had talked too much or had had one drink too many, that it had often been like that with Joel, with Conrad, with Jim So and So, and they enjoyed it just as much when he didn't get off. But she sensed a deeper reluctance in the matter, some reticence toward having his seed in her, as if he didn't want to shower it upon women, preferred to reserve it. So each time it ended with her on top of him, he ordering her to go faster or slower, and then he would arrest the motion of her buttocks, saying, "I'm sorry, darling, I can't, I'm pooped, too much traveling I guess, maybe next week."

In the mornings they rose and ordered breakfast in their room and resumed their drive toward Lake Powell and Las Vegas. She feared his boredom. He enjoyed playing the Who Am I game. He'd decide he was someone, Mick Jagger for instance. If you were a texture, she'd ask? Black leather. A drink? Tequila Sunrise. A flower? A green-dyed rose. Leaving Monument Valley, meandering on their way toward the Grand Canyon, they drove through the tunnels and the still towns of Utah, gaping at the grim gray state package stores, the empty streets, the dour faces. "Imagine making a state dry," Stephanie muttered. "Americans are so mad. This is the lousiest state in the Union. This is absolutely the most sinister place I've ever been in. This place is like terminal cancer. And I ought to know." Elijah's jewel eyes stared up, accusing and helpless, from her lap. They were low on grass and he often resorted to taking her Demerol. It put him into his own kind of stupor, something about him was softened on such days. She felt guilty for the abandoned look that hit his eyes when she said those last words. "You know what I'd do if I lived in this state, Lijie?" That was a duty, to cheer him up. "If I lived in this state, I'd dance stark naked down the street, brandishing a bottle of bourbon in each hand, wearing nothing but IUD's as earrings." His laughter pealed from her lap, high and helpless. "I adore you," he said. "You'll never know how I adore you, Steph." She felt very high that morning, she could not stop talking. "Mormons are crazy. A bunch of anal-retentive types. Just look at all these tunnels. That means something. Eli, do you realize that this state has the highest rate of alcoholism in the nation? Serves them right, stupid puritan bastards. Look at these towns at night. Dead, dead, dead, an exercise in necrophilia. God, Eli, I hate puritanism, Wasp puritanism, all kinds. Do you realize that it's puritanism got us into Vietnam? The myth of keeping society pure. Like hanging the witches of Salem. Read Arthur Miller's introduction to that play, a hell of a brilliant insight. Vietnam had nothing to do with economic determinism, that was a lot of Marxist bunk. It's mythological determinism, Messianic ideals, that are at the bedrock of the American psyche. You see, America is the first country ever founded by people who thought they were saints. They wanted to make Eden here. Oh, we were the sifted grain chosen by God to make his work perfect. But it won't wash, Eli, it won't wash. How can the depraved creature build the perfect community? One way to do that, brother, only one way, we're going to purify. We're going to clear the land of the infidel, that's the only way to create Eden. So there we go on our quest for the pure community. Burn the witches, the Indians, the reds, the Vietnamese, destroy, destroy, destroy. Oh wow, the arrogance of innocence, Lija, the filth of purity. Are we ever going to abide by the rules? Oh no, we'll remain frontiersmen, Wild West movie cowboys, shoot it all out as usual. Oh, I don't know what I'm doing living in New England, Elijah, God, the self-righteousness around me!"

"Let's elope to Venice," Elijah suggested. He sat up on his seat, clicking picture after picture of her as she sat at the wheel, her wan, classical face outlined against the pink desert.

"Hey, neat," Elijah shouted, "I've got an even better idea. First you adopt me, then we'll elope."

" 'Lake Powell,' " Elijah reads, " 'is a man-made lake which will have a 1,960-mile shoreline when totally filled.' Jesus, Steph, almost two thousand miles, the distance from Miami to Maine. That's outrageous. What a thing for the U.S. to spend its bread on when the blacks and the Third World are starving. 'Reaching out to hidden canyons, caves and islets, winding through towering red walls and cliffs, Lake Powell presents an ever changing scenery.' Cripes, Steph, it says here that this is where *The Greatest Story Ever Told* was filmed."

"The Bible as told by Hollywood," Stephanie continues on a postcard to Paul. "Creation renewing itself, *natura naturata*, frozen in an expanse of cold red stone. Man became God here, creating nature, sculpting mountains and bodies of water, Babel in other words. Red clay in the configurations of Meso-potamian domes, Assyrian ziggurats . . ."

Stephanie and Elijah sit at the bar of a hotel bordering the world's largest man-made lake, made possible by the presence of the nation's largest dam. The density of the windless air is like the water of the Dead Sea. The walls of the hotel's bar are filled with mounted fish that claim to be the largest of their kind ever caught, three-foot-long trout, thirty-pound bass. Stephanie puts her pen down and stares at the ten packages of salted peanuts Elijah has ripped off the motel bar. Would he ever get rid of that habit? Should he? At least she has stopped him from ripping off the bigger things as he did when she first knew him—expensive art books, portable radios, clothes. What a rip-off artist. How he prides himself on it. Frost-wigged waitresses in pink miniskirts strut about the floor, a jazz band dressed in magenta fluorescent coats sets up its instruments upon a tiny stage. Outside, the joyless playgrounds of the Lord gleam in the moonlight.

Stephanie is still talking about puritanism. "Witches of Salem. Clear the land of the infidel. Read all about it, Vietnam and the Myth of American Innocence, yours truly, January 'seventy-two issue of the *Saturday Review*. That's all I wrote for years, Lija, political and historical stuff about God, America, Puritan theology, resistance trials, the myth of innocence, the chattelizing of women in agricultural society, the Orientalization of American spirituality, our right to abortion, nineteenth-century French poetry, bla bla, wondering whether I'll ever dare to invent. . . . Oh God, the desolation of evenings in New England, Eli. My husband's a Puritan, he's the nineteenth-century lighthouse keeper, there he sits guarding his land, his home, his family, from the invasion of the infidel, that's where he guards his noble ancient values, I need to swim to the mainland every few days, it's exhausting, but that's where the action is, that's where I'm going to get the stuff to be a writer, I'm a Latin, I like to stroll around the streets for a couple of hours after dinner, listen to guitars, sit in bars, listen to the men talk about women and politics and join in the conversation, drink and talk until 1 A.M., that's where you'll get your ear for dialogue better than anywhere else, Lija, drinking in bars."

The band strikes up "Melancholy Baby." "*Baila vamos*," Elijah suggests. "*Vamos bailare*." "Okay, *vamos bailare*, Steph, dammit that's a fox-trot, the fox-trot is coming back, I want to learn it. I want you to teach me how to dance the fox-trot." They rise to dance. She has to pace his limbs, which flail about in the wild motions of rock. He presses her close to him. "That's called cheek to cheek, right?" That cool, angular boy's body next to her, sometimes when he is showering she sees his body not as a thing of flesh but of wood or mineral, his back, his loins have the lissomeness of a log worn by running brooks, or the cold sleekness of a porphyry statue constantly smoothed by the waters of a fountain. The movements of a colt, the texture of marble. "One two three," she says, "one two three, calm down, not so fast." All around them enormous tourists are swaying in dance, or seated at tables gorging on gigantic slabs of meat and fish. Men six feet tall and three feet wide, women dressed in red and blue sequins, ankles bulging out of their shoes, wearing little jeweled American flags in their lapels. The nation's largest tourists at the nation's largest man-made lake, feeding on the world's largest bass. Stephanie and Elijah glide softly about the floor past the fluorescent magenta musicians, as tall and thin as twins. Stephanie has gotten used to being stared at with Elijah, she feels none of the old excitement or pride, they can stop staring anytime if they want to, she does not care. He is a friend, she has loved him, the music is playing. In the past two days he has been eating a little less, he is quieter as they approach their destination, he hugs her from behind without talking while she falls asleep, the only thing he does more than ever is stare at her with those great dark-fringed amethyst eyes that constantly say, Don't leave me, Stephanie, don't leave me. "One two three, one two three," she whispers. One more person afraid of her death. What right does she have to impose upon one more human being the pain of her possible death? "Let's play making pretty phrases," Elijah says, "let's play that game. You start." "All I have to offer you is the simplicity of my emotions, and the complexity of my desires." "Dear Stephanie, you honor me by honing to even greater diamond sharpness your Cartesian turn of phrase." "Elijah, nothing in the universe is worthy of my delirium tonight, except your eyes." "The man who lives free from folly is not so wise as he thinks." "People can do whatever they want whenever they want, as long as it doesn't frighten the horses." "Steph, I know that! That's from G. B. Shaw's essay on Ibsen!" "Where did you rip that off, honey bun?"

They go to bed and watch the late show, the late late show.

At 2 A.M. Stephanie decides to do her meditation on the terrace. Her mind is clear. She has not had any Demerol that day. She sits in the lotus position overlooking the man-made Biblical desert, the still Arizona night. The moonlight is like everything else at Lake Powell, larger and brighter than anywhere else, heartlessly large, heartlessly cold. The desert is what she wants at this time of her life, as against the lushness of forests and lakes, the plenitude of seashores. She starts counting her breath. Whenever Elijah sees her taking the lotus he turns the television off, becomes quiet, stares at her from the bed. That particular night the breath counting is not channeling her attention, not emptying her mind enough. She stares at the desert and attempts Gregory's exercises. Nothing. The key word is "nothing." She murmurs it softly to herself, identifies with it until she feels it to be the very texture of her breath. Nothing. Nothing. At times it comes to her as No Thing, a negative and double entity, at other times the beauty of the single full word swells up in her like a desert, like a tide of sand inside her consciousness. Reality the way it was before there was anything, before there was any matter or consciousness. Before there was even any time. Disintegration of matter. Anarchy. Peace. "I'm about to fall asleep," Elijah says, "I love you, Steph, L-O-V-E." "Are you afraid of dying in Venice anymore, Lijie, are you afraid?" "No sir, I can have a child of my own anytime now, I don't have to be alone anymore." Pride in his voice. She smiles. She continues to stare at the emptiness, the solitude of the desert.

"Billion-dollar baby," Elijah croons as they begin their way toward the Grand Canyon, "If I'm too rough tell me/ I'm so scared your little head/ will fall off in my hand . . ." He is at the wheel for a change. This landscape, Stephanie thinks, is like her future—cold, unstructured, necessary. Up to now everything has been prebuilt, architected for her, suddenly there is this—this Nihil, this huge person whose name is Nihil.

"Nihil," she says, reaching up to pat Elijah on the cheek. "Your name is Nihil, isn't that a cute name for you shnookums? Nini for short." He looks down at her, quizzical. Increasingly often now she is saying things to him which he doesn't understand, and she doesn't care whether he understands or not. When that happens he goes on singing more loudly, or starts a new song. . . . The sexlessness of this love, however, the nihil sex of it, is good, so good, it's part of the freedom, the playfulness, the second childhood she's seeking in this body-crazy world. How many times has she lain back, her eyes wide open, seeing a man's body heaving over hers, and unless she was discovering something new about his humanity she asked what is this about, what in hell is this moaning and groaning all about. "We must confront vague ideas with clear images," she announces gravely to Elijah. "An animal is loose in the night," he continues to sing, his foot violently stomping on the floor of the car, "some kind of animal is loose in the night." The Grand Canyon suddenly looms before them, in a sweep of purple haze. The inhumanity of its scale, the rape of the Indians, the violence of the West, the violence of the SDS. She must take notes about that, as soon as possible.

"Steph, tell me again about marriage," Elijah suddenly says, "about what it was like at first. I loved the way you told me that yesterday."

She feels comfortable with her head in his lap, she loves to be able to twist her head this way and that in his groin without being worried about a hard on. No tension, no confrontation, nothing.

"Steph, I asked you to tell me about that time."

"A beach in the Caribbean," she says slowly, "a cove, a tiny little bay of beach with no one else on it where we swam naked every day, surrounded by a whole grove of guava trees. Adam and Eve. We kept eating these fresh guavas. We'd been loaned the house of a screenwriter, I forget his name. There was this cook who came with the house who made these incredible tropical dishes for us—all breadfruit and coconut sauces and mangos and fresh fish brought to the house from the shore. . . ."

She stares up at Elijah. Suddenly, she feels certain there will be a good future for him. He could travel from man to woman, from woman to man, receiving food, vacations, money, flowered shirts, rare first editions, whatever he needed. Unless he turned fat from all his eating he might soon turn up with the Agnellis in Capri, diamonds on his fingers. That would be hysterical.

". . . We kept shuttling from the bed to the beach, from the dinner table back to bed to make love, from the beach to the guava grove."

"Sounds so great. Maybe someday I'll find Ms. Perfect."

"I'm sure you will. But you see . . . it's tricky. You're in this Eden, like in Eden before the Fall. Does anything have any value in Eden? Is there a beauty to that kind of innocence? I don't think so. It is not worthy, I mean it is not of any worth. It becomes boring too fast. I had this perception very, very early in life. I was seven or eight years old in catechism class and when the nuns asked us why Eve ate of the apple I said, 'Eden was so boring.' They were bored with perfection, perfection is untenable, perfection, in a sense, is death."

Clefts, great vaginal clefts of red rock, the upturned blue sky enters the rock's fissures like a great blue phallus. Goats palpitating two miles below at the bottom of the canyon. The hazy, blue-purple mountains beyond. "Wow," Elijah says, "a seven-thousand-foot drop to the bottom. What do you think, $F/125$ at one fiftieth, that should do the trick."

Elijah photographs the canyon. Stephanie sits in the car writing to Paul on a piece of motel paper. "My darling. Once more, I wish I could share this experience with you, however clear you've made it that it would bore you. It's just that the metaphysics of it are overwhelming, and I'm not used to being overwhelmed without you. Dear friend, old friend, what shall I say first? The scale is so immense that it goes way beyond that 'sublime' which is supposed to fill us with awe and a sense of the numinous—the sublime cancels itself here by the very inhumanity of the scale. I am staring right now at a sheer drop of three, four thousand feet, violets, madder violets, rose quartz, colors of gentle things ironically, a lot of pinks and baby blues, nursery colors. What I meant to say is that there is little left but an awesome and contradictory void which I think is at the very heart of the American experience—of American violence, American solitude, of the American need for communal ecstasy. Confronted with the gigantic spaces of this country, we must either huddle together or kill each other—a vastness which can be resolved only by mysticism or violence! I've hit here on a concept very relevant to all these analyses I've been making of the nature of American spirituality, of Americans' need for ecstatic communal experience. Perhaps such phenomena as our cycles of revivalism and ecstatic cults—which occurred in small doses in other cultures, but never on the scale that they did here—perhaps we needed them to survive the enormousness of the landscape. A simplistic thought. But one senses the fearful difficulty of creating any good civilization here. Well, you are the form and substance of my life, I couldn't help but share these thoughts with you. Even though I may complain about the difficulties of talking *with* you, when you just listen and stare at me with your anxious eyes I know you listen as few persons do, and we can rehash it all a few months later over a good bottle of wine. I'm so happy you are well, and that the boys aren't worried about me anymore. I've talked to them. Jeff seems to resent the 'pedantry' of his seminar in nineteenth-century Spanish literature. Which is normal, it's a bleak century. If you talk to him before I do, tell him how much happier he will be next semester with the twentieth-century South American novel, he should flip over Borges and Marquez. As for Tom, he seems ecstatic in his new environment, and what with his grades his future at Medical School is assured. That kid is so perpetually serene. I don't understand how two nervous racehorses such as you and I could have produced all that stalwartness. All through this illness of mine I've kept having extraordinarily vivid flashbacks to the past, particularly to my childhood and to our early marriage. I miss you darling. I love you very much. I may be back in a few weeks, a month. I've made peace with a lot of the anxieties that have swept through me since this stupid illness. I think, I hope, that I'll be in less pain when I come home, I can't stand exposing others to my pain, can't abide anyone's whining, you know that's my particular form of priggishness. I've been slowed up by Demerol, I hope to be able to cut down on it very soon. Ah, yes, another thought I wanted to share with you, not unfit for the Canyon. I couldn't have faced what I've faced without recalling the richness of the lives I've traveled, from the fineness of my conversations with Greg to the dregs of my Paris and Village days. I venture that those of us who are most serene when faced with the possibility of nothingness are the ones who've reached furthest to the downward and upward of their beings. Or, as Greg puts it, persons who hold a balance of the Dionysiac and Apollonian. . . ."

"Jesus Christ," Elijah is saying, "is there nothing to eat in this goddam desert but goat droppings? Is that all you can provide for me, Mother Earth? I'm going on strike. Osiris strikes at the Isis plant. Listen, Steph, when we get to Las Vegas tonight can't we check in at the Sands and go on to Caesar's Palace for a terrific champagne dinner?"

"Oh, come off it, stop the constant rip-off, will you—" She immediately checks herself, Do not suffer anger, Stephanie, when that happens breathe deeply and empty your mind for ten seconds, that's what it's all about. "I'm sorry, Elijah, we need gas. Could you kindly raise yourself into an erect position so I can get out?"

He looks at her with confusion in his eyes, holding out his palm to get cash for the soda machine.

"I'll go in with you," she says, "I'll go in for some tea."

She watches him walk about Howard Johnson's, pick up three Slim Jim sausages and a handful of pretzel packages from the counter when the attendant's back is turned. That's his bag, to keep reality a one-way traffic lane, all of it coming toward him, the little parasite. This is the generation that feels the world owes it everything. "Those great new tyrants, the kids," as Gregory calls them. The man at the cash register looks at Elijah slowly up and down, the theft unnoticed, and offers him a cigarette. Their hands brush lightly as Elijah holds out the cigarette for a light. "You're beautiful, I love you," Elijah says, and slips back into the car. "For Christ's sake, Elijah, can't you keep your hands off anybody's property? You don't feel satisfied, do you, if you don't rip something off someone every single day of your life." "Well well Isis is in a bad mood, can't fool Mother Nature, as the margarine ad says, or else crrrrrrrack goes the lightning. Listen, sweet pea, I'm an anarchist, I don't believe in property, so what's all this shit you're giving me? They're rich, I'm poor, I believe in equality, it's my form of civil disobedience. As long as there's inequality civil disobedience should be like breathing out and breathing in. Good old C. D., like in the sixties. Breathing in and breathing out, ahhhha, ahhhhha . . ." He closes his eyes, taking very deep, noisy breaths, ahhhhha, ahhhhha.

"You're a character," she says. "You're such a character that you might just inspire me to write my first novel."

"Far out, I'll be your Chopin."

They have stopped at the beginning of the Nevada desert. Elijah is giving a slow, thorough dusting to his lens.

"Listen, Steph, tell me that story again—about that walk you took in the mountains that time."

For the past three days he has been at her to hear some incident or other of her life with Paul. He has the insistence of a child who wants a set of stories repeated at bedtime.

"Well, I'll tell it to you one last time. . . . I've had similar experiences several times in my life, they have a different meaning each time. I think the point of this one is that we can only experience happiness in tiny strips or scraps, in the briefest illuminations. . . ."

"Dammit Steph, you always theorize so. Hey, catch this thing and wake up." He throws her a tin of used-up film. "Someday you're going to theorize the universe out of existence, just like that, poof. I only asked you to tell me that story again."

"Okay, chief, here it is. We're walking up a hill in the mountains, Paul and Tom and Jeff and I, the summer before I fell ill. It's a very brilliant afternoon, and suddenly I have this strong intimation of the fullness of life, I mean of its fullest, most bursting plenitude. I have the sense that right at that very moment I am surrounded by all that I have loved the most in life, that if I were able to choose a Something after death I would simply take the quintessence of this moment and keep it with me for all eternity. In other words, I am carried out of time and into a premonition of my future which is very terrifying but quite beautiful. I am climbing a high hill, there is a sea of umbrella pines before me, the tops of their domes are a blinding hue of viridian, so brilliant that they seem out of nature, neon-lit. . . ."

"Once out of nature I shall never take my shape from any natural thing," Elijah whispers, "Yeats, right?"

"Right, Elijah. . . . And the wind is singing the way it sings only through umbrella pines, with that swelling, rolling sound not unlike that of surf. The smell of thyme, sage, lavender is rampant, the ground is brilliant with dianthus, purple thistle, asphodel. The mountains are so very clear that suddenly they look as if they had just been sculpted out of violet clay a foot away, every one of their ridges become connected to me as if they were extensions of my own body. I'm holding on to each of my children—they're sixteen, seventeen, but we've brought them up without any of that Wasp shit about hiding emotions, we've kept on hugging and kissing them right into their manhood, the way Mediterranean families do—and that day I realize that they're as good and rich human beings as I've ever met, Jeff always so concerned with the state of the world, the shape of history, Tom with his bright optimistic nature and his incredible love for every animal and plant that thrives on this earth. Tom has just grabbed my hand to point to a bird in a bush of thyme, a hoopoe, and Paul is walking ahead of us and at that very moment he looks at us with that smile of his which can be cold, so patronizing at times, but which that day is like pure molten gold. And I'm overwhelmed with the sense that I'm surrounded with all that I have loved best in life—the white heat of that particular landscape, my children, the man I've loved the most in life, a difficult man yet after all my savior, the man who gave me all the tenderness to grow in I'd missed as a little child, the man who taught me to love, who exorcised me from my mother's world, who gave me the shelter that eventually enabled me to be a writer. You see, it was the same landscape which I'd crossed with him some ten years before on a day in which I'd felt only his dourness, his oppressiveness—that's the point, we've always got to be ready for the total transformation, the transfiguration of the other, perhaps the transfiguration of all reality. Oh God, Elijah, I think that may be one meaning of the word 'resurrection.' "

She lies in the back seat as he drives.

"Anyhow we come to a river bank and for a second I cannot see, I am struck as though blind, and at the same time a wind rushes through me as I know it will at the moment of my death. And I am filled with the most immense happiness, I know that if I can carry some distillation, some quintessence of that moment with me I . . . well, I can die any time, any time, without fear."

"That story spaces me out," Elijah says.

"Why in hell? You're such a skeptic."

"Because I have no such moment to carry with me, because

I've been so lonely, so miserable most of my life—an old man who beat me up much of my childhood, a sweet wishy-washy mom I can't begin to talk to, guys who last three months."

"Well, live on, Elijah."

They drive on, crossing the border from Utah to Nevada.

"The question is, *can* we?" Elijah says softly.

"Can we what?"

"Can we carry such a moment with us?"

"Perhaps that will be the great surprise, Elijah. Guess who said that."

For the past two days she has been calling him Elijah without shortening his name, no more Lija, Lijie. She has decided to be serious with him, talk about serious matters, stop babying him, the way we suddenly speak in a fiercer, more ponderous manner when a child turns fourteen or so. And he has faced up to it, he has stared at her with those great jewellike eyes and asked her serious questions, what's life, what's death, what's hope.

For two hours before reaching Las Vegas they cross the Nevada desert, it is the first time they are seeing it, they marvel at the grayness, the dourness, the somber and harsh splendor of it. It is as dark as the face of an unshaven man, smoky as the beard of a prophet, crossing it is like running one's hand across the body of an austere gray patriarch. It is the color of smoke, of age, of austerity. And out of this tenebrous male expanse there rises before them a city that is like the body of Marilyn Monroe, ripe and florid to the verge of decay, the decay of a torpid orchid. The city is all orifices, all fruit-colored nostrils, nipples, mouths, apertures, the orifices of florid flowers nestled on the dour expanse of patriarchal desert. Neons sweet-hued as soda pop are blinking, winking, sucking, reflecting, inhaling each other. Stephanie and Elijah check in at the Sands, they go to the bar to drink Black Marias. "Cripes!" Elijah yells. "Patti Page, Elvis Presley, Dean Martin! I was still in diapers when they were in their heyday!" All about them stand the omnivorous slot machines—the watermelons, oranges, lemons, strawberries twist and whirl like thousands of greedy, sucking little mouths. Tens of thousands of pouting greedy little Marilyn Monroe mouths sucking for more money, screaming, Fill me! Fill me! America's greed. America's starvation. America's satiety. All the people around the machines are feeding themselves, chewing on tacos, gum, peanuts, sucking on ice-cream cones, licking at frozen custards, lapping at banana splits. Yes, mature couples, husbands and wives in their fifties, snacking on banana splits with whipped cream and nuts at eleven at night, and many tease-coiffed blondes also stand about the machines, holding double-malted-frappé cardboard containers filled with the quarters that will feed the greedy, sucking little mouths.

"Genital America is hard to find," Stephanie says, swigging down her drink.

"I never know what they mean by 'genital,' Steph," Elijah says very patiently. "I have terrible difficulty with all psychiatric terms."

"I'll explain some other time," she snaps, impatiently. "From anal Utah to oral Las Vegas is what I mean. From anal sex to oral you."

"Really. Steph, could I have some quarters to play the machines?"

"Of course." She gives him a ten-dollar bill. "Make some money for us, sweet pea, and we'll go on."

Stephanie feels a pain returning, the first in several days. She takes a pill with her third Black Maria. At midnight Elijah is fed up with the machines and they go on to a gigantic all-night boite called Circus Circus. At Circus Circus the bar revolves slowly about its axis, at one revolution a minute, among hundreds of pinball machines that emulate hockey games, motorcycle races, car crashes, cowboy shootouts, tennis matches, battleship blowups, plane crashes. By the bar a wall-size computer tended by gum-chewing peroxided blondes offers hand-writing personality analysis. "Know Who You Are," the machine says, "Discover Yourself." "I want one," Elijah shouts, "I want a personality analysis! Immediately!" "Which one will it be, friend," the girl says, eying Elijah slowly from head to toe, chewing her wad of gum. "What do you mean, which one?" "We have two kinds: Your character today, or for life." "Hell Elijah," Stephanie says, "take today, it's a better buy." He writes two lines of Wordsworth on the computer paper in his large, exuberant hand:

> Though nothing can bring back the hour
> Of splendor in the grass, of glory in the flower

The blonde slips the paper into the metal wall. It comes out of the other side, saying, YOU ARE INTOLERANT INSOLENT IN-SOUCIANT INSTINCTIVE INTELLIGENT INTEMPERATE INTRACTABLE INTRANSIGENT INTRIGANT INVULNERABLE. "Oh shit, shit," Elijah says, "the fucker's gotten stuck." He goes to sit with the bartenders at the center of the bar, which revolves slowly around its axis, casting myriad reflections of smoky lights upon the room. Stephanie drinks alone at the bar's periphery. Aerial artists in phosphorescent costumes swarm through the upper reaches of the large vaulted space, swinging on trapezes, climbing ladders, diving into nets, bicycling on wires, rolling hoops on platforms, wheeling trained monkeys in baby carriages. Elijah is drinking his eighth, ninth Black Maria. "I love you, I love you," he yells at Stephanie each time his part of the bar travels back toward her. Stephanie smiles and waves back at Elijah once a minute, trying to control her pain by emptying her mind, by doing absolutely nothing but counting her breath. One, two, three, four, breath is life, life, there was once a dog named Life, back to breath, breath, breathing in, breathing out. After a few minutes she ceases to wave at Elijah and he forgets about her too, he raises his glass toward every point of the horizon from his slowly revolving perch, shouting I love you California, I love you Alaska, I love you Michigan, I love you Ohio, I love you New York, I love you D.C., I love you, Tennessee, I love you I love you I love you! An affectionate, drinking crowd has gathered about Elijah, toasting him, cheering him on.

To live, Stephanie thinks, is to be like a lonely skunk spraying his scent about the forest to offer clues to the world, and to himself. To live is to be like a horny dog peeing on twenty bushes a minute, telling the conscious mind, Follow me, follow me. And the writer is like a courtesan, dropping perfumed handkerchiefs about the floors of a great house so that the cavaliers can find her room. I have dropped all these clues to myself, and where am I now?

The magic word is the jailor's name. Identify the enemy, and then you may begin to love him.

Make an effort to remember to remember to remember the kingdom of your history. And if you can't recall it, invent it.

Stephanie looks up at the ceiling and stares at an acrobat walking above her on the high wire. He/she has long light-brown hair to below its shoulders, slender hairy legs, pointed, girlish buttocks. A pink ballet tutu struts out crisply below the stretch of purple jersey that molds its delicate torso. It has savagely painted its face with a chalk-white paint, its lipsticked mouth lies ruby red upon its tragic, clownlike cheeks. The lids sheltering its great amethyst eyes are glued with sequins of many confetti colors—green, violet, silver, gold. The acrobat swings one leg around into an arabesque of infinite grace, raising itself high on the wire upon the point of its pink satin slipper. He bends toward Stephanie and gives her a sweet, sad smile. His sequined eyes blaze at her like so many stars. She blows him a kiss. Metamorphosis. Transfiguration. No more Nihil. My son the aerial artist. The angel of the imagination. We can all be reborn. I am better off now, much better off, I am total, complete, like the great round ball of light before it was divided, I can be more, I can be two, I can be the Other. Children can also be cannibals, sons and lovers can be killers. In the next months I shall caress only images, bathe them, feed them, give them life. I shall live alone, or with others, for myself. I've done it again, kiddo, I've done it better than ever, this time I've exorcised myself of one hell of a bunch of oppressors. The stars are thickening. The night is ashine with splendor and with hope. Here, at last, is a beginning.